It was just a whispe
was bending his hea
softly, his mouth gra

Sophie's breathing hitched, her world stopped as his lips moved downward to suck the drips on her chin as her lips parted helplessly and a tidal wave of lust and longing was unleashed inside her. It washed away everything, so that her head was empty of questions, doubts, uncertainties, everything except the dark, swirling whirlpool of need. Her body did the thinking, the deciding for her as it arched toward him, her hands coming up of their own volition to grip his rock-hard shoulders and tangle in his hair.

This was what she knew. This meeting of mouths and bodies, this igniting of pheromones and stoking of fires—these were feelings she understood and could deal with expertly. Familiar territory.

Or, it had been.

Not now.

Not *this...*

A self-confessed romance junkie, **India Grey** was just thirteen years old when she first sent off for the Harlequin writers' guidelines. She subsequently whiled away many a dull school day staring out of the window and dreaming of the perfect hero. She kept these guidelines with her for the next ten years, tucking them carefully inside the cover of each new diary in January, and beginning every list of New Year's resolutions with the words *Start Novel*. In the meantime she gained a degree in English literature and language from Manchester University, and in a stroke of genius on the part of the gods of romance, met her gorgeous future husband on the very last night of their three years there. She has never really stopped daydreaming about romance. She's just profoundly grateful to have finally got an excuse to do it legitimately!

Books by India Grey

Harlequin Presents

The Secret She Can't Hide
Taken for Revenge, Bedded for Pleasure
At the Argentinean Billionaire's Bidding
The Italian's Defiant Mistress

Bride on Approval

The Society Wife

The Balfour Brides

Emily and the Notorious Prince

At His Service

Powerful Italian, Penniless Housekeeper

Visit the Author Profile page at Harlequin.com.

INDIA GREY

TEMPTED *by a* STRANGER

HARLEQUIN PRESENTS® EPICS

Recycling programs
for this product may
not exist in your area.

ISBN-13: 978-0-373-20837-1

Tempted by a Stranger

Copyright © 2017 by Harlequin Books S.A.

The publisher acknowledges the copyright holder
of the individual works as follows:

Craving the Forbidden
Copyright © 2011 by India Grey

In Bed with a Stranger
Copyright © 2011 by India Grey

This edition published by arrangement with Harlequin Books S.A.

For questions and comments about the quality of this book,
please contact us at CustomerService@Harlequin.com.

® and TM are trademarks of the publisher. Trademarks indicated with ® are registered in the United States Patent and Trademark Office, the Canadian Intellectual Property Office and in other countries.

www.Harlequin.com

Printed in U.S.A.

For my blog regulars,
with thanks for listening, sharing
and making me smile.

CONTENTS

TEMPTED BY A STRANGER

Part One

CHAPTER ONE

'LADIES AND GENTLEMEN, *welcome aboard the 16.22 East Coast Mainline service from King's Cross to Edinburgh. This train will be calling at Peterborough, Stevenage...*'

Heart hammering against her ribs from the mad, last-minute dash down the platform carrying a bag that was about to burst at the seams, Sophie Greenham leaned against the wall of the train and let out a long exhalation of relief.

She had made it.

Of course, the relief was maybe a little misplaced given that she'd come straight from the casting session for a vampire film and was still wearing a black satin corset dress that barely covered her bottom and high-heeled black boots that were rather more vamp than vampire. But the main thing was she had caught the train and wouldn't let Jasper down. She'd just have to keep her coat on to avoid getting arrested for indecent exposure.

Not that she'd want to take it off anyway, she thought grimly, wrapping it more tightly around her as the train gave a little lurch and began to move. For weeks now the snow had kept falling from a pewter-grey sky and the news headlines had been dominated by The Big Freeze. Paris had been just as bad, although there the snow *looked* cleaner, but when Sophie had left her little rented apartment two days ago there had been a thick layer of ice on the inside of the windows.

She seemed to have been cold for an awfully long time.

It was getting dark already. The plate-glass windows of the office blocks backing onto the railway line spilled light out onto the grimy snow. The train swayed beneath her, changing tracks and catching her off guard so that she tottered on the stupid high-heeled boots and almost fell into an alarmed-looking student on his way back from the buffet car. She really should go and find a loo to change into something more respectable, but now she'd finally stopped rushing she was overwhelmed with tiredness. Picking up her bag, she hoisted it awkwardly into the nearest carriage.

Her heart sank. It was instantly obvious that every seat was taken, and the aisle was cluttered with shopping bags and briefcases and heavy winter coats stuffed under seats. Muttering apologies as she staggered along, trying not to knock cardboard cartons of coffee out of the hands of commuters with her bag, she made her way into the next carriage.

It was just as bad as the last one. The feeling of triumph she'd had when she'd made it onto the train in time ebbed slowly away as she moved from one carriage to the next, apologising as she went, until finally she came to one that was far less crowded.

Sophie's aching shoulders dropped in relief. And tensed again as she took in the strip of plush carpet, the tiny lights on the tables, the superior upholstery with the little covers over the headrests saying 'First Class'.

Pants.

It was occupied almost entirely by businessmen who

didn't bother to look up from their laptops and newspapers as she passed. Until her mobile rang. Her ringtone—'Je Ne Regrette Rien'—had seemed wittily ironic in Paris, but in the hushed carriage it lost some of its charm. Holding the handles of her bag together in one hand while she scrabbled in the pocket of her coat with the other and tried to stop it falling open to reveal the wardrobe horror beneath, she was aware of heads turning, eyes looking up at her over the tops of glasses and from behind broadsheets. In desperation she hitched her bag onto the nearest table and pulled the phone from her pocket just in time to see Jean-Claude's name on the screen.

Pants again.

A couple of months ago she would have had a very different reaction, she thought, hastily pressing the button to reject the call. But then a couple of months ago her image of Jean-Claude as a free-spirited Parisian artist had been intact. He'd seemed so aloof when she'd first seen him, delivering paintings to the set of the film she was working on. Aloof and glamorous. Not someone you could ever imagine being suffocating or possessive or…

Nope. She wasn't going to think about the disaster that had been her latest romantic adventure.

She sat down in the nearest seat, suddenly too tired to go any further. You couldn't keep moving for ever, she told herself with a stab of bleak humour. In the seat opposite there was yet another businessman, hidden behind a large newspaper that he'd thoughtfully folded so that the horoscopes were facing her.

Actually, he wasn't *entirely* hidden; she could see his hands, holding the newspaper—tanned, long-fingered, strong-looking. Not the hands of a businessman, she thought abstractly, tearing her gaze away and looking for Libra. 'Be prepared to work hard to make a good impression,' she read. 'The full moon on the 20th is a perfect opportunity to let others see you for who you really are.'

Hell. It was the twentieth today. And while she was prepared to put on an Oscar-worthy performance to impress Jasper's family, the last thing she wanted was for them to see her for who she really was.

At that moment Edith Piaf burst into song again. She groaned—why couldn't Jean-Claude take a hint? Quickly she went to shut Edith up and turn her phone off but at that moment the train swayed again and her finger accidentally hit the 'answer' button instead. A second later Jean-Claude's Merlot-marinated voice was clearly audible, to her and about fifteen businessmen.

'Sophie? Sophie, where are you—?'

She thought quickly, cutting him off before he had a chance to get any further. 'Hello, you haf reached the voicemail service for Madame Sofia, astrologist and reader of cards,' she purred, shaking her hair back and narrowing her eyes at her own reflection in the darkening glass of the window. 'Eef you leaf your name, number and zodiac sign, I get back to you with information on what the fates haf in store for you—'

She stopped abruptly, losing her thread, a kick of electricity jolting through her as she realised she was staring straight into the reflected eyes of the man sitting opposite.

Or rather that, from behind the newspaper, *he* was staring straight into *her* eyes. His head was lowered, his face ghostly in the glass, but his dark eyes seemed to look straight into her.

For a second she was helpless to do anything but look back. Against the stark white of his shirt his skin was tanned, which seemed somehow at odds with his stern, ascetic face. It was the face of a medieval knight in a Pre-Raphaelite painting—beautiful, bloodless, remote.

In other words, absolutely not her type.

'Sophie—is zat you? I can 'ardly 'ear you. Are you on Eurostar? Tell me what time you get in and I meet you at Gare du Nord.'

Oops, she'd forgotten all about Jean-Claude. Gathering herself, she managed to drag her gaze away from the reflection in the window and her attention back to the problem quite literally in hand. She'd better just come clean, or he'd keep ringing for the whole weekend she was staying with Jasper's family and rather ruin her portrayal of the sweet, starry-eyed girlfriend.

'I'm not on the Eurostar, no,' she said carefully. 'I'm not coming back tonight.'

'*Alors*, when?' he demanded. 'The painting—I need you here. I need to see your skin—to feel it, to capture contrast with lily petals.'

'Nude with Lilies' was the vision Jean-Claude claimed had come to him the moment he'd first noticed her in a bar in the Marais, near where they'd been filming. Jasper had been over that weekend and thought it was hilarious. Sophie, hugely flattered to be singled out and by Jean-Claude's extravagant compliments about her 'skin like lily petals' and 'hair like flames', had thought being painted would be a highly erotic experience.

The reality had turned out to be both extremely cold and mind-numbingly boring. Although, if Jean-Claude's gaze had aroused a similar reaction to that provoked by the eyes of the man in the glass, it would have been a very different story...

'Oh, dear. Maybe you could just paint in a few more lilies to cover up the skin?' She bit back a breathless giggle and went on kindly, 'Look, I don't know when I'll be back, but what we had wasn't meant to be for ever, was it? Really, it was just sex—'

Rather fittingly, at that point the train whooshed into a tunnel and the signal was lost. Against the blackness beyond the window the reflected interior of the carriage was bright, and for the briefest moment Sophie caught the eye of the man opposite and knew he'd been looking at her again. The grey remains of the daylight made the reflection fade before she had time to read the expression on his face, but she was left in no doubt that it had been disapproving.

And in that second she was eight years old again, holding her mother's hand and aware that people were staring at them, judging them. The old humiliation flared inside her as she heard her mother's voice inside her head, strident with indignation. *Just ignore them, Summer. We have as much right to be here as anyone else...*

'Sophie?'

'Yes,' she said, suddenly subdued. 'Sorry, Jean-Claude. I can't talk about this now. I'm on the train and the signal isn't very good.'

'*D'accord.* I call you later.'

'No! You can't call me *at all* this weekend. I-I'm... working, and you know I can't take my phone on set. Look, I'll call you when I get back to London on Monday. We can talk properly then.'

That was a stupid thing to say, she thought wearily

as she turned her phone off. There was nothing to talk *about*. What she and Jean-Claude had shared had been fun, that was all. Fun. A romantic adventure in wintry Paris. Now it had reached its natural conclusion and it was time to move on.

Again.

Shoving her phone back into her pocket, she turned towards the window. Outside it was snowing again and, passing through some anonymous town, Sophie could see the flakes swirling fatly in the streetlamps and obliterating the footprints on the pavements, and rows of neat houses, their curtains shut against the winter evening. She imagined the people behind them; families slumped together in front of the TV, arguing cosily over the remote control, couples cuddled up on the sofa sharing a Friday evening bottle of wine, united against the cold world outside.

A blanket of depression settled on her at these mental images of comfortable domesticity. It was a bit of a sore point at the moment. Returning from Paris she'd discovered that, in her absence, her flatmate's boyfriend had moved in and the flat had been turned into the headquarters of the Blissful Couples Society. The atmosphere of companionable sluttishness in which she and Jess had existed, cluttering up the place with make-up and laundry and trashy magazines, had vanished. The flat was immaculate, and there were new cushions on the sofa and candles on the kitchen table.

Jasper's SOS phone call, summoning her up to his family home in Northumberland to play the part of his girlfriend for the weekend, had come as a huge relief. But this was the way it was going to be, she thought sadly as the town was left behind and the train plunged onwards into darkness again. Everyone pairing up, until she was the only single person left, the only one who actively didn't want a relationship or commitment. Even Jasper was showing worrying signs of swapping late nights and dancing for cosy evenings in as things got serious with Sergio.

But why have serious when you could have *fun*?

Getting abruptly to her feet, she picked up her bag and hoisted it onto the luggage rack above her head. It wasn't easy, and she was aware as she pushed and shoved that not only was the hateful dress riding up, but her coat had also fallen open, no doubt giving the man in the seat opposite an eyeful of straining black corset and an indecent amount of thigh. Prickling all over with embarrassment, she glanced at his reflection in the window.

He wasn't looking at her at all. His head was tipped back against the seat, his face completely blank and remote as he focused on the newspaper. Somehow his indifference felt even more hurtful than his disapproving scrutiny earlier. Pulling her coat closed, she sat down again, but as she did so her knee grazed his thigh beneath the table.

She froze, and a shower of glowing sparks shimmered through her.

'Sorry,' she muttered, yanking her legs away from his and tucking them underneath her on the seat.

Slowly the newspaper was lowered, and she found herself looking at him directly for the first time. The impact of meeting his eyes in glassy reflection had been powerful enough, but looking directly into them was like touching a live wire. They weren't brown, as she'd thought, but the grey of cold Northern seas, heavy-

lidded, fringed with thick, dark lashes, compelling
enough to distract her for a moment from the rest of
his face.

Until he smiled.

A faint ghost of a smile that utterly failed to melt
the ice in his eyes, but did draw her attention down to
his mouth…

'No problem. As this is First Class you'd think
there'd be enough legroom, wouldn't you?'

His voice was low and husky, and so sexy that her
spirits should have leapt at the prospect of spending the
next four hours in close confinement with him. However, the slightly scornful emphasis he placed on the
words 'first' and 'class' and the way he was looking at
her as if she were a caterpillar on the chef's salad in
some swanky restaurant cancelled out his physical at-
tractiveness.

She had issues with people who looked at her like
that.

'Absolutely,' she agreed, with that upper-class self-
assurance that gave the people who genuinely possessed
it automatic admittance to anywhere. 'Shocking, really.'
And then with what she hoped was utter insouciance
she turned up the big collar of her shabby military-style
coat, settled herself more comfortably in her seat and
closed her eyes.

KIT FITZROY PUT down the newspaper.

Usually when he was on leave he avoided reading
reports about the situation he'd left behind; somehow
the heat and the sand and the desperation never quite
came across in columns of sterile black and white. He'd
bought the newspaper to catch up on normal things like

rugby scores and racing news, but had ended up reading all of it in an attempt to obliterate the image of the girl sitting opposite him, which seemed to have branded itself onto his retinas.

It hadn't worked. Even the laughably inaccurate report of counter-terrorist operations in the Middle East hadn't stopped him being aware of her.

It was hardly surprising, he thought acidly. He'd spent the last four months marooned in the desert with a company made up entirely of men, and he was still human enough to respond to a girl wearing stiletto boots and the briefest bondage dress beneath a fake army coat. Especially one with a husky nightclub singer's voice who actually seemed to be complaining to the lovesick fool on the other end of the phone that all she'd wanted was casual sex.

After the terrible sombreness of the ceremony he'd just attended her appearance was like a swift shot of something extremely potent.

He suppressed a rueful smile.

Potent, if not particularly sophisticated.

He let his gaze move back to her. She had fallen asleep as quickly and neatly as a cat, her legs tucked up beneath her, a slight smile on her raspberry-pink lips, as if she was dreaming of something amusing. She had a sweep of black eyeliner on her upper lids, flicking up at the outside edges, which must be what gave her eyes their catlike impression.

He frowned. No—it wasn't just that. It was their striking green too. He could picture their exact shade— the clear, cool green of new leaves—even now, when she was fast asleep.

If she really was asleep. When it came to deception Kit Fitzroy's radar was pretty accurate, and this girl had set it off from the moment she'd appeared. But there was something about her now that convinced him that she wasn't faking this. It wasn't just how still she was, but that the energy that had crackled around her before had vanished. It was like a light going out. Like the sun going in, leaving shadows and a sudden chill.

Sleep—the reward of the innocent. Given the shamelessness with which she'd just lied to her boyfriend it didn't seem fair, especially when it eluded him so cruelly. But it had wrapped her in a cloak of complete serenity, so that just looking at her, just watching the lock of bright coppery hair that had fallen across her face stir with each soft, steady breath made him aware of the ache of exhaustion in his own shoulders.

'Tickets, please.'

The torpor that lay over the warm carriage was disturbed by the arrival of the guard. There was a ripple of activity as people roused themselves to open briefcases and fumble in suit pockets. On the opposite side of the table the girl's sooty lashes didn't even flutter.

She was older than he'd first thought, Kit saw now, older than the ridiculous teenage get-up would suggest—in her mid-twenties perhaps? Even so, there was something curiously childlike about her. If you ignored the creamy swell of her cleavage against the laced bodice of her dress, anyway.

And he was doing his best to ignore it.

The guard reached them, his bland expression changing to one of deep discomfort when he looked down and saw her. His tongue flicked nervously across his lips and he raised his hand, shifting from foot to foot as he reached uneasily down to wake her.

'*Don't.*'

The guard looked round, surprised. He wasn't the only one, Kit thought. Where had that come from? He smiled blandly.

'It's OK. She's with me.'

'Sorry, sir. I didn't realise. Do you have your tickets?'

'No.' Kit flipped open his wallet. 'I—*we*—had been planning to travel north by plane.'

'Ah, I see, sir. The weather has caused quite a disruption to flights, I understand. That's why the train is so busy this evening. Is it a single or a return you want?'

'Return.' Hopefully the airports would be open again by Sunday, but he wasn't taking any chances. The thought of being stuck indefinitely at Alnburgh with his family in residence was unbearable.

'Two returns—to Edinburgh?'

Kit nodded absently and as the guard busied himself with printing out the tickets he looked back at the sleeping girl again. He was damned certain she didn't have a first-class ticket and that, in spite of the almost-convincing posh-girl accent, she wouldn't be buying one if she was challenged. So why had he not just let the guard wake her up and move her on? It would have made the rest of the journey better for him. More legroom. More peace of mind.

Kit Fitzroy had an inherent belief in his duty to look out for people who didn't have the same privileges that he had. It was what had got him through officer training and what kept him going when he was dropping with exhaustion on patrol, or when he was walking along a deserted road to an unexploded bomb. It didn't usually compel him to buy first-class tickets for strangers on the train. And anyway, this girl looked as if she was more than capable of looking after herself.

But with her outrageous clothes and her fiery hair and her slight air of mischief she had brightened up his journey. She'd jolted him out of the pall of gloom that hung over him after the service he'd just attended, as well as providing a distraction from thinking about the grim weekend ahead.

That had to be worth the price of a first-class ticket from London to Edinburgh. Even without the glimpse of cleavage and the brush of her leg against his, which had reminded him that, while several of the men he'd served with weren't so lucky, he at least was still alive...

That was just a bonus.

CHAPTER TWO

SOPHIE CAME TO with a start, and a horrible sense that something was wrong.

She sat up, blinking beneath the bright lights as she tried to get her bearings. The seat opposite was empty. The man with the silver eyes must have got off while she was sleeping, and she was just asking herself why on earth she should feel disappointed about that when she saw him.

He was standing up, his back towards her as he lifted an expensive-looking leather bag down from the luggage rack, giving her an excellent view of his extremely broad shoulders and narrow hips encased in beautifully tailored black trousers.

Mmm… *That* was why, she thought drowsily. Because physical perfection like that wasn't something you came across every day. And although it might come in a package with industrial-strength arrogance, it certainly was nice to look at.

'I'm sorry—could you tell me where we are, please?'

Damn—she'd forgotten about the posh accent, and after being asleep for so long she sounded more like a barmaid with a sixty-a-day habit than a wholesome society girl. Not that it really mattered now, since she'd never see him again.

He shrugged on the kind of expensive reefer jacket

men wore in moody black-and-white adverts in glossy magazines. 'Alnburgh.'

The word delivered a jolt of shock to Sophie's sleepy brain. With an abrupt curse she leapt to her feet, groping frantically for her things, but at that moment the train juddered to an abrupt halt. She lost her balance, falling straight into his arms.

At least that was how it would have happened in any one of the romantic films she'd ever worked on. In reality she didn't so much fall into his waiting, welcoming arms as against the unyielding, rock-hard wall of his chest. He caught hold of her in the second before she ricocheted off him, one arm circling her waist like a band of steel. Rushing to steady herself, Sophie automatically put the flat of her hand against his chest.

Sexual recognition leapt into life inside her, like an alarm going off in her pelvis. He might look lean, but there was no mistaking the hard, sculpted muscle beneath the Savile Row shirt.

Wide-eyed with shock, she looked up at him, opening her mouth in an attempt to form some sort of apology. But somehow there were blank spaces in her head where the words should be and the only coherent thought in her head was how astonishing his eyes were, close up; the silvery luminescence of the irises ringed with a darker grey...

'I have to get off—now,' she croaked.

It wasn't exactly a line from the romantic epics. He let her go abruptly, turning his head away.

'It's OK. We're not in the station yet.'

As he spoke the train began to move forwards with another jolt that threatened to unbalance her again. As if she weren't unbalanced enough already, she thought shakily, trying to pull down her bulging bag from where it was wedged in the luggage rack. Glancing anxiously out of the window, she saw the lights of cars waiting at a level crossing slide past the window, a little square signal box, cosily lit inside, with a sign saying 'Alnburgh' half covered in snow. She gave another futile tug and heard an impatient sound from behind her.

'Here, let me.'

In one lithe movement he leaned over her and grasped the handle of her bag.

'No, wait—the zip—' Sophie yelped, but it was too late. There was a ripping sound as the cheap zip, already under too much pressure from the sheer volume of stuff bundled up inside, gave way and Sophie watched in frozen horror as a tangle of dresses and tights and shoes tumbled out.

And underwear, of course.

It was terrible. Awful. Like the moment in a nightmare just before you wake up. But it was also pretty funny. Clamping a hand over her open mouth, Sophie couldn't stop a bubble of hysterical laughter escaping her.

'You might want to take that back to the shop,' the man remarked sardonically, reaching up to unhook an emerald-green satin balcony bra that had got stuck on the edge of the luggage rack. 'I believe Gucci luggage carries a lifetime guarantee?'

Sophie dropped to her knees to retrieve the rest of her things. Possibly it did, but cheap designer fakes certainly didn't, as he no doubt knew very well. Getting up again, she couldn't help but be aware of the length of his legs, and had to stop herself from reaching out and grabbing hold of them to steady herself as the train finally came to a shuddering halt in the station.

'Thanks for your help,' she said with as much haughtiness as she could muster when her arms were full of knickers and tights. 'Please, don't let me hold you up any more.'

'I wouldn't, except you're blocking the way to the door.'

Sophie felt her face turn fiery. Pressing herself as hard as she could against the table, she tried to make enough space for him to pass. But he didn't. Instead he took hold of the broken bag and lifted it easily, raising one sardonic eyebrow.

'After you—if you've got everything?'

Alnburgh station consisted of a single Victorian building that had once been rather beautiful but which now had its boarded up windows covered with posters advertising family days out at the seaside. It was snowing again as she stepped off the train, and the air felt as if it had swept straight in from Siberia. Oh, dear, she really should have got changed. Not only was her current ensemble hideously unsuitable for meeting Jasper's family, it was also likely to lead to hypothermia.

'There.'

Sophie had no choice but to turn and face him. Pulling her collar up around her neck, she aimed for a sort of Julie-Christie-in-Doctor-Zhivago look—determination mixed with dignity.

'You'll be OK from here?'

'Y-yes. Thank you.' Standing there with the snow settling on his shoulders and in his dark hair he looked more brooding and sexy than Omar Shariff had ever done in the film. 'And thank you for...'

Jeepers, what was the matter with her? Julie Christie would never have let her lines dry up like that.

'For what?'

'Oh, you know, carrying my bag, picking up my... things.'

'My pleasure.'

His eyes met hers and for a second their gazes held. In spite of the cold stinging her cheeks, Sophie felt a tide of heat rise up inside her.

And then the moment was over and he was turning away, his feet crunching on the gritted paving stones, sliding his hands into the pockets of his coat just as the guard blew the whistle for the train to move out of the station again.

That was what reminded her, like a bolt of lightning in her brain. Clamping her hand to her mouth, she felt horror tingle down her spine at the realisation that she hadn't bought a ticket. Letting out a yelp of horror, followed by the kind of word Julie Christie would never use, Sophie dashed forwards towards the guard, whose head was sticking out of the window of his van.

'No—wait. Please! I didn't—'

But it was too late. The train was gathering pace and her voice was lost beneath the rumble of the engine and the squealing of the metal wheels on the track. As she watched the lights of the train melt back into the winter darkness Sophie's heart was beating hard, anguish knotting inside her at what she'd inadvertently done.

Stolen something. That was what it amounted to, didn't it? Travelling on the train without buying a ticket was, in effect, committing a criminal act, as well as a dishonest one.

An act of theft.

And that was one thing she would never, *ever* do.

The clatter of the train died in the distance and Sophie was aware of the silence folding all around her. Slowly she turned to walk back to pick up her forlorn-looking bag.

'Is there a problem?'

Her stomach flipped, and then sank like a stone. Great. Captain Disapproval must have heard her shout and come back, thinking she was talking to him. The station light cast dark shadows beneath his cheekbones and made him look more remote than ever. Which was quite something.

'No, no, not at all,' she said stiffly. 'Although before you go perhaps you could tell me where I could find a taxi.'

Kit couldn't quite stop himself from letting out a bark of laughter. It wasn't kind, but the idea of a taxi waiting at Alnburgh station was amusingly preposterous.

'You're not in London now.' He glanced down the platform to where the Bentley waited, Jensen sitting impassively behind the wheel. For some reason he felt responsible—touched almost—by this girl in her outrageous clothing with the snowflakes catching in her bright hair. 'Look, you'd better come with me.'

Her chin shot up half an inch. Her eyes flashed in the station light—the dark green of the stained glass in the Fitzroy family chapel, with the light shining through it.

'No, thanks,' she said with brittle courtesy. 'I think I'd rather walk.'

That really *was* funny. 'In those boots?'

'Yes,' she said haughtily, setting off quickly, if a little

unsteadily, along the icy platform. She looked around, pulling her long army overcoat more tightly across her body.

Catching up with her, Kit arched an eyebrow. 'Don't tell me,' he drawled. 'You're going to join your regiment.'

'No,' she snapped. 'I'm going to stay with my boyfriend, who lives at Alnburgh Castle. So if you could just point me in the right direction…'

Kit stopped. The laughter of a moment ago evaporated in the arctic air, like the plumes of their breaths. In the distance a sheep bleated mournfully.

'And what is the name of your…*boyfriend*?'

Something in the tone of his voice made her stop too, the metallic echo of her stiletto heels fading into silence. When she turned to face him her eyes were wide and black-centred.

'Jasper.' Her voice was shaky but defiant. 'Jasper Fitzroy, although I don't know what it has to do with you.'

Kit smiled again, but this time it had nothing to do with amusement.

'Well, since Jasper Fitzroy is my brother, I'd say quite a lot,' he said with sinister softness. 'You'd better get in the car.'

CHAPTER THREE

INSIDE THE CHAUFFEUR-DRIVEN Bentley Sophie blew her cheeks out in a long, silent whistle.

What was it that horoscope said?

The car was very warm and very comfortable, but no amount of climate control and expensive upholstery could quite thaw the glacial atmosphere. Apart from a respectfully murmured 'Good evening, Miss,' the chauffeur kept his attention very firmly focused on the road. Sophie didn't blame him. You could cut the tension in the back of the car with a knife.

Sophie sat very upright, leaving as much seat as possible between her fishnetted thigh and his long, hard flannel-covered one. She didn't dare look at Jasper's brother, but was aware of him staring, tense-jawed, out of the window. The village of Alnburgh looked like a scene from a Christmas card as they drove up the main street, past a row of stone houses with low, gabled roofs covered in a crisp meringue-topping of snow, but he didn't look very pleased to be home.

Her mind raced as crazily as the white flakes swirling past the car window, the snatches of information Jasper had imparted about his brother over the years whirling through it. Kit Fitzroy was in the army, she knew that much, and he served abroad a lot, which would account for the unseasonal tan. Oh, and Jasper had once described him as having a 'complete emotion-bypass'. She recalled the closed expression Jasper's face wore on the rare occasions he mentioned him, the bitter edge his habitual mocking sarcasm took on when he said the words 'my brother'.

She was beginning to understand why. She had only known him for a little over three hours—and most of that time she'd been asleep—but it was enough to find it impossible to believe that this man could be related to Jasper. Sweet, warm, funny Jasper, who was her best friend in the world and the closest thing she had to family.

But the man beside her was his *real* flesh and blood, so surely that meant he couldn't be all bad? It also meant that she should make some kind of effort to get on with him, for Jasper's sake. And her own, since she had to get through an entire weekend in his company.

'So, you must be Kit, then?' she offered. 'I'm Sophie. Sophie Greenham.' She laughed—a habit she had when she was nervous. 'Bizarre, isn't it? Whoever would have guessed we were going to the same place?'

Kit Fitzroy didn't bother to look at her. 'Not you, obviously. Have you known my brother long?'

OK. So she was wrong. He was every bit as bad as she'd first thought. Thinking of the horoscope, she bit back the urge to snap, *Yes, as a matter of fact. I've known your brother for the last seven years, as you would have been very well aware if you took the slightest interest in him*, and kept her voice saccharine sweet as she recited the story she and Jasper had hastily come up with last night on the phone when he'd asked her to do this.

'Just since last summer. We met on a film.'

The last bit at least was true. Jasper was an assistant director and they had met on a dismal film about the Black Death that mercifully had never seen the light of day. Sophie had spent hours in make-up having sores applied to her face and had had one line to say, but had caught Jasper's eye just as she'd been about to deliver it and noticed that he was shaking with laughter. It had set her off too, and made the next four hours and twenty-two takes extremely challenging, but it had also sealed their friendship, and set its tone. It had been the two of them, united and giggling against the world, ever since.

He turned his head slightly. 'You're an actress?'

'Yes.'

Damn, why did that come out sounding so defensive? Possibly because he said the word 'actress' in the same faintly disdainful tone as other people might say 'lap dancer' or 'shoplifter'. What would he make of the fact that even 'actress' was stretching it for the bit parts she did in films and TV series? Clamping her teeth together, she looked away—and gasped.

Up ahead, lit up in the darkness, cloaked in swirling white like a fairy castle in a child's snow globe, was Alnburgh Castle.

She'd seen pictures, obviously. But nothing had prepared her for the scale of the place, or the impact it made on the surrounding landscape. It stood on top of the cliffs, its grey stone walls seeming to rise directly out of them. This was a side of Jasper's life she knew next to nothing about, and Sophie felt her mouth fall open as she stared in amazement.

'Bloody hell,' she breathed.

It was the first genuine reaction he'd seen her display,

Kit thought sardonically, watching her. And it spoke volumes.

Sympathy wasn't an emotion he was used to experiencing in relation to Jasper, but at that moment he certainly felt something like it now. His brother must be pretty keen on this girl to invite her up here for Ralph Fitzroy's seventieth birthday party, but from what Kit had seen on the train it was obvious the feeling wasn't remotely mutual.

No prizes for guessing what the attraction was for Sophie Greenham.

'Impressive, isn't it?' he remarked acidly.

In the dimly lit interior of the car her eyes gleamed darkly like moonlit pools as she turned to face him. Her voice was breathless, so that she sounded almost intimidated.

'It's incredible. I had no idea…'

'What, that your boyfriend just happened to be the son of the Earl of Hawksworth?' Kit murmured sardonically. 'Of course. You were probably too busy discussing your mutual love of art-house cinema to get round to such mundane subjects as family background.'

'Don't be ridiculous,' she snapped. 'Of course I knew about Jasper's background—*and* his family.'

She said that last bit with a kind of defiant venom that was clearly meant to let him know that Jasper hadn't given him a good press. He wondered if she thought for a moment that he'd care. It was hardly a well-kept secret that there was no love lost between him and his brother—the spoiled, pampered golden boy. Ralph's second and favourite son.

The noise of the Bentley's engine echoed off the walls of the clock tower as they passed through the arch beneath it. The headlights illuminated the stone walls, dripping with damp, the iron-studded door that led down to the former dungeon that now housed Ralph's wine cellar. Kit felt the invisible iron-hard bands of tension around his chest and his forehead tighten a couple of notches.

It was funny, he spent much of his time in the most dangerous conflict zones on the globe, but in none of them did he ever feel a fraction as isolated or exposed as he did here. When he was working he had his team behind him. Men he could trust.

Trust wasn't something he'd ever associated with home life at Alnburgh, where people told lies and kept secrets and made promises they didn't keep.

He glanced across at the woman sitting beside him, and felt his lip curl. Jasper's new girlfriend was going to fit in very well.

SOPHIE DIDN'T WAIT until the chauffeur came round to open the door for her. The moment the car came to a standstill she reached for the handle and threw the door open, desperate to be out of the confined space with Kit Fitzroy.

A gust of salt-scented, ice-edged wind cleared her head but nearly knocked her sideways, whipping her hair across her face. Impatiently she brushed it away again. Alnburgh Castle loomed ahead of her. And above her and around her too, she thought weakly, turning to look at the fortress-thick walls that stretched into the darkness all around her, rising into huge, imposing buildings and jagged towers.

There was nothing remotely welcoming or inviting

about it. Everything about the place was designed to scare people off and keep them out.

Sophie could see that Jasper's brother would be right at home here.

'Thanks, Jensen. I can manage the bags from here.'

'If you're sure, sir…'

Sophie turned in time to see Kit take her bag from the open boot of the Bentley and turn to walk in the direction of the castle's vast, imposing doorway. One strap of the green satin bra he had picked up on the train was hanging out of the top of it.

Hastily she hurried after him, her high heels ringing off the frozen flagstones and echoing around the walls of the castle courtyard.

'Please,' Sophie persisted, not wanting him to put himself out on her account any more than he had—so unwillingly—done already. 'I'd rather take it myself.'

He stopped halfway up the steps. For a split second he paused, as if he was gathering his patience, then turned back to her. His jaw was set but his face was carefully blank.

'If you insist.'

He held it out to her. He was standing two steps higher than she was, and Sophie had to tilt her head back to look up at him. Thrown for a second by the expression in his hooded eyes, she reached out to take the bag from him but, instead of the strap, found herself grasping his hand. She snatched hers away quickly, at exactly the same time he did, and the bag fell, tumbling down the steps, scattering all her clothes into the snow.

'Oh, knickers,' she muttered, dropping to her knees as yet another giggle of horrified, slightly hysterical amusement rose up inside her. Her heart was thumping madly from the accidental contact with him. His hand had felt warm, she thought irrationally. She'd expected it to be as cold as his personality.

'Hardly,' he remarked acidly, stooping to pick up a pink thong and tossing it back into the bag. 'But clearly what passes for them in your wardrobe. You seem to have a lot of underwear and not many clothes.'

The way he said it suggested he didn't think this was a good thing.

'Yes, well,' she said loftily, 'what's the point of spending money on clothes that I'm going to get bored of after I've worn them once? Underwear is a good investment. Because it's practical,' she added defensively, seeing the faint look of scorn on his face. 'God,' she muttered crossly, grabbing a handful of clothes back from him. 'This journey's turning into one of those awful drawing-room farces.'

Straightening up, he raised an eyebrow. 'The entire weekend is a bit of a farce, wouldn't you say?'

He went up the remainder of the steps to the door. Shoving the escaped clothes back into her bag with unnecessary force, Sophie followed him and was about to apologise for having the wrong underwear and the wrong clothes and the wrong accent and occupation and attitude when she found herself inside the castle and her defiance crumbled into dust.

The stone walls rose to a vaulted ceiling what seemed like miles above her head, and every inch was covered with muskets, swords, pikes and other items of barbaric medieval weaponry that Sophie recognised from men-in-tights-with-swords films she'd worked on, but couldn't begin to name. They were arranged into intricate patterns around helmets and pieces of armour, and the light from a huge wrought-iron lantern that hung on a chain in the centre of the room glinted dully on their silvery surfaces.

'What a cosy and welcoming entrance,' she said faintly, walking over to a silver breastplate hanging in front of a pair of crossed swords. 'I bet you're not troubled by persistent double-glazing salesmen.'

He didn't smile. His eyes, she noticed, held the same dull metallic gleam as the armour. 'They're seventeenth century. Intended for invading enemies rather than double-glazing salesmen.'

'Gosh.' Sophie looked away, trailing a finger down the hammered silver of the breastplate, noticing the shining path it left through the dust. 'You Fitzroys must have a lot of enemies.'

She was aware of his eyes upon her. Who would have thought that such a cool stare could make her skin feel as if it were burning? Somewhere a clock was ticking loudly, marking out the seconds before he replied, 'Let's just say we protect our interests.'

His voice was dangerously soft. Sophie's heart gave a kick, as if the armour had given her an electric shock. Withdrawing her hand sharply, she jerked her head up to look at him. A faint, sardonic smile touched the corner of his mouth. 'And it's not just invading armies that threaten those.'

His meaning was clear, and so was the thinly veiled warning behind the words. Sophie opened her mouth to protest, but no words came—none that would be any use in defending herself against the accusation he was making anyway, and certainly none that would be acceptable to use to a man with whose family she was going to be a guest for the weekend.

'I-I'd better find Jasper,' she stammered. 'He'll be wondering where I am.'

He turned on his heel and she followed him through another huge hallway panelled in oak, her footsteps making a deafening racket on the stone-flagged floor. There were vast fireplaces at each end of the room, but both were empty, and Sophie noticed her breath made faint plumes in the icy air. This time, instead of weapons, the walls were hung with the glassy-eyed heads of various large and hapless animals. They seemed to stare balefully at Sophie as she passed, as if in warning.

This is what happens if you cross the Fitzroys.

Sophie straightened her shoulders and quickened her pace. She mustn't let Kit Fitzroy get to her. He had got entirely the wrong end of the stick. She was Jasper's friend and she'd come as a favour to him precisely *because* his family were too bigoted to accept him as he really was.

She would have loved to confront Kit Superior Fitzroy with that, but of course it was impossible. For Jasper's sake, and also because there was something about Kit that made her lose the ability to think logically and speak articulately, damn him.

A set of double doors opened at the far end of the hallway and Jasper appeared.

'*Soph!* You're *here!*'

At least she thought it was Jasper. Gone were the layers of eccentric vintage clothing, the tattered silk-faced dinner jackets he habitually wore over T-shirts and torn drainpipe jeans. The man who came towards her, his arms outstretched, was wearing well-ironed chinos and a V-necked jumper over a button-down shirt and—Sophie's incredulous gaze moved downwards—what looked suspiciously like brogues.

Reaching her, this new Jasper took her face between his hands and kissed her far more tenderly than normal. Caught off guard by the bewildering change in him, Sophie was just about to push him away and ask what he was playing at when she remembered what she was there for. Dropping her poor, battered bag again, she wrapped her arms around his neck.

Over Jasper's shoulder, through the curtain of her hair, she was aware of Kit Fitzroy standing like some dark sentinel, watching her. The knowledge stole down inside her, making her feel hot, tingling, restless, and before she knew it she was arching her body into Jasper's, sliding her fingers into his hair.

Sophie had done enough screen and stage kisses to have mastered the art of making something completely chaste look a whole lot more X-rated than it really was. When Jasper pulled back a little a few seconds later she caught the gleam of laughter in his eyes as he leaned his forehead briefly against hers, then, stepping away, he spoke in a tone of rather forced warmth.

'You've met my big brother, Kit. I hope he's been looking after you.'

That was rather an unfortunate way of putting it, Sophie thought, an image of Kit Fitzroy, his strong hands full of her silliest knickers and bras flashing up inside her head. Oh, hell, why did she always smirk when she was embarrassed? Biting her lip, she stared down at the stone floor.

'Oh, absolutely,' she said, nodding furiously. 'And I'm afraid I needed quite a lot of looking after. If it wasn't for Kit I'd be halfway to Edinburgh now. Or at least, my underwear would.'

It might be only a few degrees warmer than the arctic, but beneath her coat Sophie could feel the heat creeping up her cleavage and into her cheeks. The nervous smile she'd been struggling to suppress broke through as she said the word 'underwear', but one glance at Kit's glacial expression killed it instantly.

'It was a lucky coincidence that we were sitting in the same carriage. It gave us a chance to…get to know each other a little before we got here.'

Ouch.

Only Sophie could have understood the meaning behind the polite words or picked up the faint note of menace beneath the blandness of his tone.

He's really got it in for me, she realised with a shiver. Suddenly she felt very tired, very alone, and even Jasper's hand around hers couldn't dispel the chilly unease that had settled in the pit of her stomach.

'Great.' Oblivious to the tension that crackled like static in the air, Jasper pulled her impatiently forwards. 'Come and meet Ma and Pa. I haven't stopped talking about you since I got here yesterday, so they're dying to see what all the fuss is about.'

And suddenly panic swelled inside her—churning, black and horribly familiar. The fear of being looked at. Scrutinised. Judged. That people would see through the layers of her disguise, the veils of evasion, to the real girl beneath. As Jasper led her towards the doors at the far end of the hall she was shaking, assailed by the same doubts and insecurities that had paralysed her the only time she'd done live theatre, in the seconds before she went onstage. What if she couldn't do it? What if the lines wouldn't come and she was left just being herself? Acting had been a way of life long before it became a way of making a living, and playing a part was second nature to her. But now...*here*...

'Jasper,' she croaked, pulling back. 'Please—wait.'

'Sophie? What's the matter?'

His kind face was a picture of concern. The animal heads glared down at her, as well as a puffy-eyed Fitzroy ancestor with a froth of white lace around his neck.

And that was the problem. Jasper was her closest friend and she would do anything for him, but when she'd offered to help him out she hadn't reckoned on all this. Alnburgh Castle, with its history and its million symbols of wealth and status and *belonging*, was exactly the kind of place that unnerved her most.

'I can't go in there. Not dressed like this, I mean. I—I came straight from the casting for the vampire thing and I meant to get changed on the train, but I...'

She opened her coat and Jasper gave a low whistle.

'Don't worry,' he soothed. 'Here, let me take your coat and you can put this on, otherwise you'll freeze.' Quickly he peeled off the black cashmere jumper and handed it to her, then tossed her coat over the horns of a nearby stuffed stag. 'They're going to love you whatever you're wearing. Particularly Pa—you're the perfect birthday present. Come on, they're waiting in the drawing room. At least it's warm in there.'

With Kit's eyes boring into her back Sophie had no choice but to let Jasper lead her towards the huge double doors at the far end of the hall.

Vampire thing, Kit thought scornfully. Since when had the legend of the undead mentioned dressing like an escort in some private men's club? He wondered if it was going to be the kind of film the boys in his unit sometimes brought back from leave to enjoy with a lot of beer in rest periods in camp.

The thought was oddly unsettling.

Tiredness pulled at him like lead weights. He couldn't face seeing his father and stepmother just yet. Going through the hallway in the direction of the stairs, he passed the place where the portrait of his mother used to hang, before Ralph had replaced it, appropriately, with a seven-foot-high oil of Tatiana in plunging blue satin and the Cartier diamonds he had given her on their wedding day.

Jasper was right, Kit mused. If there was anyone who would appreciate Sophie Greenham's get-up it was Ralph Fitzroy. Like vampires, his father's enthusiasm for obvious women was legendary.

Jasper's, however, was not. And that was what worried him. Even if he hadn't overheard her conversation on the phone, even if he hadn't felt himself the white-hot sexuality she exuded, you only had to look at the two of them together to know that, vampire or not, the girl was going to break the poor bastard's heart and eat it for breakfast.

THE ROOM JASPER led her into was as big as the last, but stuffed with furniture and blazing with light from silk-shaded lamps on every table, a chandelier the size of a spaceship hovering above a pair of gargantuan sofas and a fire roaring in the fireplace.

It was Ralph Fitzroy who stepped forwards first. Sophie was surprised by how old he was, which she realised was ridiculous considering the reason she had come up this weekend was to attend his seventieth birthday party. His grey hair was brushed back from a florid, fleshy face and as he took Sophie's hand his eyes almost disappeared in a fan of laughter lines as they travelled down her body. And up again, but only as far as her chest.

'Sophie. Marvellous to meet you,' he said, in the kind of upper-class accent that Sophie had thought had become extinct after the war.

'And you, sir.'

Oh, for God's sake—*sir*? Where had that come from? She'd be bobbing curtsies next. She was supposed to be playing the part of Jasper's girlfriend, not the parlour-maid in some nineteen-thirties below-stairs drama. Not that Ralph seemed to mind. He was still clasping her hand, looking at her with a kind of speculative interest, as if she were a piece of art he was thinking of buying.

Suddenly she remembered Jean-Claude's 'Nude with Lilies' and felt pins and needles of embarrassment prickle her whole body. Luckily distraction came in the form of a woman unfolding herself from one of the overstuffed sofas and coming forwards. She was dressed immaculately in a clinging off-white angora dress that was cleverly designed to showcase her blonde hair and peachy skin, as well as her enviable figure and the triple string of pearls around her neck. Taking hold of Sophie's shoulders, she leaned forwards in a waft of expensive perfume and, in a silent and elaborate pantomime, kissed the air beside first one cheek and then the other.

'Sophie, how good of you to come all this way to join us. Did you have a dreadful journey?'

Her voice still bore the unmistakable traces of a Russian accent, but her English was so precise that Sophie felt more than ever that they were onstage and reciting lines from a script. Tatiana Fitzroy was playing the part of the gracious hostess, thrilled to be meeting her adored son's girlfriend for the first time. The problem was she wasn't that great at acting.

'No, not at all.'

'But you came by train?' Tatiana shuddered slightly. 'Trains are always so overcrowded these days. They make one feel slightly grubby, don't you think?'

No, Sophie wanted to say. Trains didn't make her feel remotely grubby. However, the blatant disapproval in Kit Fitzroy's cool glare—now that had definitely left her feeling in need of a scrub down in a hot shower.

'Come on, darling,' Ralph joked. 'When was the last time you went on a train?'

'First Class isn't *too* bad,' Sophie said, attempting to sound as if she would never consider venturing into standard.

'Not really enough legroom,' said a grave voice behind her. Sophie whipped her head round. Kit was standing in the doorway, holding a bundle of envelopes, which he was scanning through as he spoke.

The fire crackled merrily away, but Sophie was aware that the temperature seemed to have fallen a couple of degrees. For a split second no one moved, but then Tatiana was moving forwards, as if the offstage prompt had just reminded her of her cue.

'Kit. Welcome back to Alnburgh.'

So, she wasn't the only one who found him impossible, Sophie thought, noticing the distinct coolness in Tatiana's tone. As she reached up to kiss his cheek Kit didn't incline his head even a fraction to make it easier for her to reach, and his inscrutable expression didn't alter at all.

'Tatiana. You're looking well,' Kit drawled, barely glancing at her as he continued to look through the sheaf of letters in his hand. He seemed to have been built on a different scale from Jasper and Ralph, Sophie thought, taking in his height and the breadth of his chest. The sleeves of his white shirt were rolled back to reveal tanned forearms, corded with muscle.

She looked resolutely away.

Ralph went over to a tray crowded with cut-glass decanters on a nearby table and sloshed some more whisky into a glass that wasn't quite empty. Sophie heard the rattle of glass against glass, but when he turned round to face his eldest son his bland smile was perfectly in place.

'Kit.'

'Father.'

Kit's voice was perfectly neutral, but Ralph seemed to flinch slightly. He covered it by taking a large slug of whisky. 'Good of you to come, what with flights being cancelled and so on. The invitation was…' he hesitated '…a courtesy. I know how busy you are. Hope you didn't feel obliged to accept.'

'Not at all.' Kit's eyes glittered, as cold as moonlight on frost. 'I've been away too long. And there are things we need to discuss.'

Ralph laughed, but Sophie could see the colour rising in his florid cheeks. It was fascinating—like being at a particularly tense tennis match.

'For God's sake, Kit, you're not still persisting with that—'

As he spoke the double doors opened and a thin,

elderly man appeared between them and nodded, almost imperceptibly, at Tatiana. Swiftly she crossed the Turkish silk rug in a waft of Chanel No 5 and slipped a hand through her husband's arm, cutting him off mid-sentence.

'Thank you, Thomas. Dinner is ready. Now that everyone's here, shall we go through?'

CHAPTER FOUR

DINNER WAS ABOUT as enjoyable and relaxing as being stripped naked and whipped with birch twigs.

When she was little, Sophie had dreamed wistfully about being part of the kind of family who gathered around a big table to eat together every evening. If she'd known this was what it was like she would have stuck to the fantasies about having a pony or being picked to star in a new film version of *The Little House on the Prairie*.

The dining room was huge and gloomy, its high, green damask-covered walls hung with yet more Fitzroy ancestors. They were an unattractive bunch, Sophie thought with a shiver. The handsomeness so generously bestowed on Jasper and Kit must be a relatively recent addition to the gene pool. Only one—a woman in blush-pink silk with roses woven into her extravagantly piled up hair and a secretive smile on her lips—held any indication of the good looks that were the Fitzroy hallmark now.

Thomas, the butler who had announced dinner, dished up watery consommé, followed by tiny rectangles of grey fish on something that looked like spinach and smelled like boiled socks. No wonder Tatiana was so thin.

'This looks delicious,' Sophie lied brightly.

'Thank you,' Tatiana cooed, in a way that suggested

she'd cooked it herself. 'It has taken years to get Mrs Daniels to cook things other than steak and kidney pudding and roast beef, but finally she seems to understand the meaning of low-fat.'

'Unfortunately,' Kit murmured.

Ignoring him, Ralph reached for the dusty bottle of Chateau Marbuzet and splashed a liberal amount into his glass before turning to fill up Sophie's.

'So, Jasper said you've been in Paris? Acting in some film or other?'

Sophie, who had just taken a mouthful of fish, could only nod.

'Fascinating,' said Tatiana doubtfully. 'What was it about?'

Sophie covered her mouth with her hand to hide the grimace as she swallowed the fish. 'It's about British Special Agents and the French Resistance in the Second World War,' she said, wondering if she could hide the rest of the fish under the spinach as she used to do at boarding school. 'It's set in Montmartre, against a community of painters and poets.'

'And what part did you play?'

Sophie groaned inwardly. It would have to be Kit who asked that. Ever since she sat down she'd been aware of his eyes on her. More than aware of it—it felt as if there were a laser trained on her skin.

She cleared her throat. 'Just a tiny role, really,' she said with an air of finality.

'As?'

He didn't give up, did he? Why didn't he just go the whole hog and whip out a megawatt torch to shine in her face while he interrogated her? Not that those silvery eyes weren't hard enough to look into already.

'A prostitute called Claudine who inadvertently betrays her Resistance lover to the SS.'

Kit's smile was as faint as it was fleeting. He had a way of making her feel like a third year who'd been caught showing her knickers behind the bike sheds and hauled into the headmaster's office. She took a swig of wine.

'You must meet such fascinating people,' Tatiana said.

'Oh, yes. Well, I mean, sometimes. Actors can be a pretty self-obsessed bunch. They're not always a laugh a minute to be around.'

'Not as bad as artists,' Jasper chipped in absently as he concentrated on extracting a bone from his fish. 'They hired a few painters to produce the pictures that featured in the film, and they turned out to be such prima donnas they made the actors look very down-to-earth, didn't they, Soph?'

Somewhere in the back of Sophie's mind an alarm bell had started drilling. She looked up, desperately trying to telegraph warning signals across the table to Jasper, but he was still absorbed in exhuming the skeleton of the poor fish. Sophie's lips parted in wordless panic as she desperately tried to think of something to say to steer the subject onto safer ground...

Too late.

'One of them became completely obsessed with painting Sophie,' Jasper continued. 'He came over to her in the bar one evening when I was there and spent about two hours gazing at her with his eyes narrowed as he muttered about lilies.'

Sophie felt as if she'd been struck by lightning, a terrible rictus smile still fixed to her face. She didn't dare look at Kit. She didn't need to—she could feel the disapproval and hostility radiating from him like a force field. Through her despair she was aware of the woman with the roses in her hair staring down at her from the portrait. Now the smile didn't look secretive so much as if she was trying not to laugh.

'If I thought the result would have been as lovely as that I would have accepted like a shot,' she said in a strangled voice, gesturing up at the portrait. 'Who is she?'

Ralph followed her gaze. 'Ah—that's Lady Caroline, wife of the fourth Earl and one of the more flamboyant Fitzroys. She was a girl of somewhat uncertain provenance who had been a music hall singer—definitely not countess material. Christopher Fitzroy was twenty years younger than her, but from the moment he met her he was quite besotted and, much to the horror of polite society, married her.'

'That was pretty brave of him,' Sophie said, relief at having successfully moved the conversation on clearly audible in her voice.

The sound Kit made was unmistakably derisive. 'Brave, or stupid?'

Their eyes met. Suddenly the room seemed very quiet. The arctic air was charged with electricity, so that the candle flames flickered for a second.

'Brave,' she retorted, raising her chin a little. 'It can't have been easy, going against his family and society, but if he loved her it would have been worth the sacrifice.'

'Not if *she* wasn't worth the sacrifice.'

The candle flames danced in a halo of red mist before Sophie's eyes, and before she could stop herself she heard herself give a taut, brittle laugh and say, 'Why? Because she was too *common*?'

'Not at all.' Kit looked at her steadily, his haughty

face impassive. 'She wasn't worth it because she didn't love him back.'

'How do you know she didn't?'

Oh, jeez, what was she doing? She was supposed to be here to impress Jasper's family, not pick fights with them. No matter how insufferable they were.

'Well…' Kit said thoughtfully. 'The fact that she slept with countless other men during their marriage is a bit of a clue, wouldn't you say? Her lovers included several footmen and stable lads and even the French artist who painted that portrait.'

He was still looking at her. His voice held that now-familiar note of scorn, but was so soft that for a moment Sophie was hypnotised. The candlelight cast shadows under his angular cheekbones and brought warmth to his skin, but nothing could melt the ice chips in his eyes.

Sophie jumped slightly as Ralph cut in.

'French? Thought the chap was Italian?'

Kit looked away. 'Ah, yes,' he said blandly. 'I must be getting my facts mixed up.'

Bastard, thought Sophie. He knew that all along, and he was just trying to wind her up. Raising her chin and summoning a smile to show she wouldn't be wound, she said, 'So—what happened to her?'

'She came to a sticky end, I'm afraid. Not nice,' Ralph answered, topping up his glass again and emptying the remains of the bottle into Sophie's. Despite the cold his cheeks were flushed a deep, mottled purple.

'How?' Her mind flashed back to the swords and muskets in the entrance hall, the animal heads on the wall. You messed with a Fitzroy—or his brother—and a sticky end was pretty inevitable.

'She got pregnant,' Kit said matter-of-factly, picking up the knife on his side-plate and examining the tarnished silver blade for a second before polishing it with his damask napkin. 'The Earl, poor bastard, was delighted. At last, a long-awaited heir for Alnburgh.'

Sophie took another mouthful of velvety wine, watching his mouth as he spoke. And then found that she couldn't stop watching it. And wondering what it would look like if he smiled—really smiled. Or laughed. What it would feel like if he kissed her—

No. *Stop.* She shouldn't have let Ralph give her the rest of that wine. Hastily she put her glass down and tucked her hands under her thighs.

'But of course, she knew that it was extremely unlikely the kid was his,' Kit was saying in his low, slightly scornful voice. 'And though he was too besotted to see what was going on, the rest of his family certainly weren't. She must have realised that she'd reached a dead end, and also that the child was likely to be born with the rampant syphilis that was already devouring her.'

Sophie swallowed. 'What did she do?'

Kit laid the knife down and looked straight at her. 'In the last few weeks of her pregnancy, she threw herself off the battlements in the East Tower.'

She wouldn't let him see that he'd shocked her. Wouldn't let the sickening feeling she had in the pit of her stomach show on her face. Luckily at that moment Jasper spoke, his cheerful voice breaking the tension that seemed to shiver in the icy air.

'Poor old Caroline, eh? What a price to pay for all that fun.' He leaned forwards, dropping his voice theatrically. 'It's said that on cold winter nights her ghost walks the walls, half mad with guilt. Or maybe it's the syphilis—that's supposed to make you go mad, isn't it?'

'Really, Jasper. I think we've heard enough about Fitzroys.' Tatiana laid down her napkin with a little pout as Thomas reappeared to collect up the plates. 'So, Sophie—tell us about *your* family. Where do your people come from?'

People? Her *people*? She made it sound as if everyone had estates and villages and hordes of peasants at their command. From behind Tatiana's head Caroline the feckless countess looked at Sophie with amused pity. *Get yourself out of this one*, she seemed to say.

'Oh. Um, down in the south of England,' Sophie muttered vaguely, glancing at Jasper for help. 'We travelled around a lot, actually.'

'And your parents—what do they do?'

'My mother is an astronomer.'

It was hardly a lie, more a slip of the tongue. Astronomy/astrology…people got them mixed up all the time anyway.

'And your—'

Jasper came swiftly to the rescue.

'Talking of stars, how did your big charity auction go last week, Ma? I keep meaning to ask you who won the premiere tickets I donated.'

It wasn't the most subtle of conversational diversions, but it did the trick so Sophie was too relieved to care. As the discussion moved on and Thomas reappeared to clear the table she slumped back in her chair and breathed out slowly, waiting for her heartbeat to steady and her fight-or-flight response to subside. With any luck that was the subject of her family dealt with and now she could relax for the rest of the weekend.

If it were possible to relax with Kit Fitzroy around.

Before she was aware it was happening or could stop

it her gaze had slid back to where he sat, leaning back
in his chair, his broad shoulders and long body making
the antique rosewood look as fussy and flimsy as doll's-
house furniture. His face was shuttered, his hooded eyes
downcast, so that for the first time since the train she
was able to look at him properly.

A shiver of sexual awareness shimmered down her
spine and spread heat into her pelvis.

Sophie had an unfortunate attraction to men who
were bad news. Men who didn't roll over and beg to
be patted. But even she had to draw a line somewhere,
and 'emotion-bypass' was probably a good place. And
after the carnage of her so-called casual fling with Jean-
Claude, this was probably a good time.

'...really fabulous turnout. People were so generous,'
Tatiana was saying in her guttural purr, the diamonds
in her rings glittering in the candlelight as she folded
her hands together and rested her chin on them. 'And
so good to catch up with all the people I don't see, stuck
out here. As a matter of fact, Kit—your name came up
over dinner. A girlfriend of mine said you have broken
the heart of a friend of her daughter's.'

Kit looked up.

'Without the name of the friend, her daughter or her
daughter's friend I can't really confirm or deny that.'

'Oh, come on,' Tatiana said with a brittle, tinkling
laugh. 'How many hearts have you broken recently?
I'm talking about Alexia. According to Sally Rothwell-
Hyde, the poor girl is terribly upset.'

'I'm sure Sally Rothwell-Hyde is exaggerating,' Kit
said in a bored voice. 'Alexia was well aware from the
start it was nothing serious. It seems that Jasper will
be providing Alnburgh heirs a lot sooner than I will.'

He looked across at Sophie, wondering what smart response she would think up to that, but she said nothing. She was sitting very straight, very still. Against the vivid red of her hair, her face was the same colour as the wax that had dripped onto the table in front of her.

'Something wrong?' he challenged quietly.

She looked at him, and for a second the expression in her eyes was one of blank horror. But then she blinked, and seemed to rouse herself.

'I'm sorry. What was that?' With an unsteady hand she stroked her hair back from her face. It was still as pale as milk, apart from a blossoming of red on each cheekbone.

'Soph?' Jasper got to his feet. 'Are you OK?'

'Yes. Yes, of course. I'm absolutely fine.' She made an attempt at a laugh, but Kit could hear the raw edge in it. 'Just tired, that's all. It's been a long day.'

'Then you must get to bed,' Tatiana spoke with an air of finality, as if she was dismissing her. 'Jasper, show Sophie to her room. I'm sure she'll feel much better after a good night's sleep.'

Kit watched Jasper put his arm round her and lead her to the door, remembering the two hours of catatonic sleep she'd had on the train. Picking up his wine glass, he drained it thoughtfully.

It certainly wasn't tiredness that had drained her face of colour like that, which meant it must have been the idea of producing heirs.

It looked as if she was beginning to get an idea of what she'd got herself into. And she was even flakier than he'd first thought.

CHAPTER FIVE

ROTHWELL-HYDE.

Wordlessly Sophie let Jasper lead her up the widest staircase she'd ever seen. It was probably a really common surname, she thought numbly. The phone book must contain millions of Rothwell-Hydes. Or several anyway, in smart places all over the country. Because surely no one who lived up here would send their daughter to school down in Kent?

It was a second before she realised Jasper had stopped at the foot of another small flight of stairs leading to a gloomy wood-panelled corridor with a single door at the end.

'Your room's at the end there, but let's go to mine. The fire's lit, and I've got a bottle of Smirnoff that Sergio gave me somewhere.' He took hold of her shoulders, bending his knees slightly to peer into her face. 'You look like you could do with something to revive you, angel. Are you OK?'

With some effort she gathered herself and made a stab at sounding casual and reassuring. 'I'm fine now, really. I'm so sorry, Jasper—I'm supposed to be taking the pressure off you by posing as your girlfriend, but instead your parents must be wondering why you ended up going out with such a nutter.'

'Don't be daft. You're totally charming them—or you

were until you nearly fainted face down on your plate. I know the fish was revolting, but really…'

She laughed. 'It wasn't that bad.'

'What then?'

Jasper was her best friend. Over the years she'd told him lots of funny stories about her childhood, and when you'd grown up living in a converted bus painted with flowers and peace slogans, with a mother who had inch-long purple hair, had changed her name to Rainbow and given up wearing a bra, there were lots of those.

There were also lots of bits that weren't funny at all, but she kept those to herself. The years when she'd been taken in by Aunt Janet and had been sent to an exclusive girls' boarding school in the hope of 'civilising' her. Years when she'd been at the mercy of Olympia Rothwell-Hyde and her friends…

She shook her head and smiled. 'Just tired. Honest.'

'Come on, then.' He set off again along the corridor, rubbing his arms vigorously. 'God, if you stand still for a second in this place you run the risk of turning into a pillar of ice. I hope you brought your thermal underwear.'

'Please, can you not mention underwear,' Sophie said with a bleak laugh. 'The contents of my knicker drawer have played far too much of a starring role in this weekend already and I've only been here a couple of hours.' Her heart lurched as she remembered again the phone conversation Kit had overheard on the train. 'I'm afraid I got off on completely the wrong foot with your brother.'

'Half-brother,' Jasper corrected, bitterly. 'And don't worry about Kit. He doesn't approve of anyone. He just sits in judgment on the rest of us.'

'That's why I'm here, isn't it?' said Sophie. 'It's Kit's opinion you're worried about, not your parents'.'

'Are you kidding?' Jasper said ironically. 'You've met my father. He's from the generation and background that call gay men "nancy boys" and assume they all wear pink scarves and carry handbags.'

'And what's Kit's excuse?'

Pausing in front of a closed door, Jasper bowed his head. Without the hair gel and eyeliner he always wore in London his fine-boned face looked younger and oddly vulnerable.

'Kit's never liked me. I've always known that, growing up. He never said anything unkind or did anything horrible to me, but he didn't have to. I always felt this… *coldness* from him, which was almost worse.'

Sophie could identify with that.

'I don't know,' he went on, 'now I'm older I can understand that it must have been difficult for him, growing up without his mother when I still had mine.' He cast her a rueful look. 'As you'll have noticed, my mother isn't exactly cosy—I don't think she particularly went out of her way to make sure he was OK, but because I was her only child I did get rather spoiled, I guess…'

Sophie widened her eyes. 'You? Surely not!'

Jasper grinned. 'This is the part of the castle that's supposed to be haunted by the mad countess's ghost, you know, so you'd better watch it, or I'll run away and leave you here…'

'Don't you dare!'

Laughing, he opened the door. 'This is my room. Damn, the fire's gone out. Come in and shut the door to keep any lingering traces of warmth in.'

Sophie did as she was told. The room was huge,

and filled with the kind of dark, heavy furniture that looked as if it had come from a giant's house. A sleigh bed roughly the size of the bus that had formed Sophie's childhood home stood in the centre of the room, piled high with several duvets. Jasper's personal stamp was evident in the tatty posters on the walls, a polystyrene reproduction of Michelangelo's *David*, which was rakishly draped in an old school tie, a silk dressing gown and a battered trilby. As he poked at the ashes in the grate Sophie picked her way through the clothes on the floor and went over to the window.

'So what happened to Kit's mother?'

Jasper piled coal into the grate. 'She left. When he was about six, I think. It's a bit of a taboo subject around here, but I gather there was no warning, no explanation, no goodbye. Of course there was a divorce eventually, and apparently Juliet's adultery was cited, but as far as I know Kit never had any contact with her again.'

Outside it had stopped snowing and the clouds had parted to show the flat disc of the full moon. From what Sophie could see, Jasper's room looked down over some kind of inner courtyard. The castle walls rose up on all sides—battlements like jagged teeth, stone walls gleaming like pewter in the cold, bluish light. She shivered, her throat constricting with reluctant compassion for the little boy whose mother had left him here in this bleak fortress of a home.

'So she abandoned him to go off with another man?'

Sophie's own upbringing had been unconventional enough for her not to be easily shocked. But a mother leaving her child…

'Pretty much. So I guess you can understand why he ended up being like he is. Ah, look—that's better.'

He stood back, hands on hips, his face bathed in orange as the flames took hold. 'Right—let's find that bottle and get under the duvet. You can tell me all about Paris and how you managed to escape the clutches of that lunatic painter, and in turn I'm going to bore you senseless talking about Sergio. Do you know,' he sighed happily, 'he's having a tally of the days we're apart tattooed on his chest?'

THE ANCIENT STONES on top of the parapet were worn smooth by salt wind and wild weather, and the moonlight turned them to beaten silver. Kit exhaled a cloud of frozen air, propping his elbows on the stone and looking out across the battlements to the empty beach beyond.

There was no point in even trying to get to sleep tonight, he knew that. His insomnia was always at its worst when he'd just come back from a period of active duty and his body hadn't learned to switch off from its state of high alert. The fact that he was also back at Alnburgh made sleep doubly unlikely.

He straightened up, shoving his frozen fingers into his pockets. The tide was out and pools of water on the sand gleamed like mercury. In the distance the moon was reflected without a ripple in the dark surface of the sea.

It was bitterly cold.

Long months in the desert halfway across the world had made him forget the aching cold here. Sometimes, working in temperatures of fifty degrees wearing eighty pounds of explosive-proof kit, he would try to recapture the sensation, but out there cold became an abstract concept. Something you knew about in theory, but couldn't imagine actually *feeling*.

But it was real enough now, as was the complicated mix of emotions he always experienced when he returned. He did one of the most dangerous jobs on the planet without feeling anything, and yet when he came back to the place he'd grown up in it was as if he'd had a layer of skin removed. Here it was impossible to forget the mother who had left him, or forgive the studied indifference of the father who had been left to bring him up. Here everything was magnified: bitterness, anger, frustration…

Desire.

The thought crept up on him and he shoved it away. Sophie Greenham was hardly his type, although he had to admit that doing battle with her at dinner had livened up what would otherwise have been a dismal evening. And at least her presence had meant that he didn't feel like the only outsider.

It had also provided a distraction from the tension between him and his father. But only temporarily. Ralph was right—Kit hadn't come up here because the party invitation was too thrilling to refuse, but Ralph's seventieth birthday seemed like a good time to remind his father that if he didn't transfer the ownership of Alnburgh into Kit's name soon, it would be too late. The estate couldn't possibly survive the inheritance tax that would be liable on it after Ralph's death, and would no doubt have to be sold.

Kit felt fresh anger bloom inside him. He wasn't sure why he cared—his house in Chelsea was conveniently placed for some excellent restaurants, was within easy taxi-hailing range for women he didn't want to wake up with, and came without ghosts. And yet he did care. Because of the waste and the irresponsibility and the sheer bloody shortsightedness, perhaps? Or because he could still hear his mother's voice, whispering to him down the years?

Alnburgh is yours, Kit. Don't ever forget that. Don't ever let anyone tell you it's not.

It must have been just before she left that she'd said that. When she knew she was going and wanted to assuage her guilt; to feel that she wasn't leaving him with nothing.

As if a building could make up for a mother. Particularly a building like Alnburgh. It was an anachronism. As a home it was uncomfortable, impractical and unsustainable. It was also the place where he had been unhappiest. And yet he knew, deep down, that it mattered to him. He felt responsible for it, and he would do all he could to look after it.

And much as it surprised him to discover, that went for his brother too. Only Jasper wasn't at risk from dry rot or damp, but the attentions of a particularly brazen redhead.

Kit wondered if she'd be as difficult to get rid of.

SOPHIE OPENED HER EYES.

It was cold and for a moment her sleep-slow brain groped to work out where she was. It was a familiar feeling—one she'd experienced often as a child when her mother had been in one of her restless phases, but for some reason now it was accompanied by a sinking sensation.

Putting a hand to her head, she struggled upright. In the corner of the room the television was playing quietly to itself, and Jasper's body was warm beside her, a T-shirt of Sergio's clasped in one hand, the half-empty bottle of vodka in the other. He had fallen asleep sprawled diagonally across the bed with his head thrown back, and something about the way the lamplight fell on his face—or maybe the shuttered blankness sleep had lent it—reminded her of Kit.

Fragments of the evening reassembled themselves in her aching head. She got up, rubbing a hand across her eyes, and carefully removed the bottle from Jasper's hand. Much as she loved him, right now all she wanted was a bed to herself and a few hours of peaceful oblivion.

Tiptoeing to the door, she opened it quietly. Out in the corridor the temperature was arctic and the only light came from the moon, lying in bleached slabs on the smooth oak floorboards. Shivering, Sophie hesitated, wondering whether to go back into Jasper's room after all, but the throbbing in her head was more intense now and she thought longingly of the paracetamol in her washbag.

There was nothing for it but to brave the cold and the dark.

Her heart began to pound as she slipped quickly between the squares of silver moonlight, along the corridor and down a spiralling flight of stone stairs. Shadows engulfed her. It was very quiet. Too quiet. To Sophie, used to thin-walled apartments, bed and breakfasts, buses and camper vans on makeshift sites where someone was always strumming a guitar or playing indie-acid-trance, the silence was unnatural. Oppressive. It buzzed in her ears, filling her head with whistling, like interference on a badly tuned radio.

She stopped, her chest rising and falling rapidly as she looked around.

Passageways stretched away from her in three directions, but each looked as unfamiliar as the other. Oh, hell. She'd been so traumatised earlier that she hadn't paid attention to Jasper when he pointed out her room…

But that could be it, she thought with relief, walking quickly to a door at the end of the short landing to her left. Gingerly she turned the handle and, heart bursting, pushed open the door.

Moonlight flooded in from behind her, illuminating the ghostly outlines of shrouded furniture. The air was stale with age. The room clearly hadn't been opened in years.

This is the part of the castle that's supposed to be haunted by the mad countess's ghost, you know…

Retreating quickly, she slammed the door and forced herself to exhale slowly. It was fine. No need to panic. Just a question of retracing her steps, thinking about it logically. A veil of cloud slipped over the moon's pale face and the darkness deepened. Icy drafts eddied around Sophie's ankles, and the edge of a curtain at one of the stone windows lifted slightly, as if brushed by invisible fingers. The whistling sound was louder now and more distinctive—a sort of keening that was almost human. She couldn't be sure it was just in her head any more and she broke into a run, glancing back over her shoulder as if she expected to see a swish of pink silk skirt disappearing around the corner.

'I'm being stupid,' she whispered desperately, fumbling at the buttons of her mobile phone to make the screen light up and act as a torch. 'There's no such thing as ghosts.' But even as the words formed themselves on her stiff lips horror prickled at the back of her neck.

Footsteps.

She clamped a hand to her mouth to stifle her moan of terror and stood perfectly still. Probably she'd imagined it—or possibly it was just the mad drumming of her heart echoing off the stone walls...

Nope. Definitely footsteps.

Definitely getting nearer.

It was impossible to tell from which direction they were coming. Or maybe if they were ghostly footsteps they weren't coming from any particular direction, except beyond the grave? It hardly mattered—the main thing was to get away from here and back to Jasper. Back to light and warmth and TV and company. Shaking with fear, she darted back along the corridor, heading for the stairs that she had come down a few moments ago.

And then she gave a whimper of horror, icy adrenaline sluicing through her veins. A dark figure loomed in front of her, only a foot or so away, too close even for her to be aware of anything beyond its height and the frightening breadth of its shoulders. She shrank backwards, bringing her hands up to her face, her mouth opening to let out the scream that was rising in her throat.

'Oh, no, you don't...'

Instantly she was pulled against the rock-hard chest and a huge hand was put across her mouth. Fury replaced fear as she realised that this was not the phantom figure of some seventeenth-century suitor looking for the countess, but the all-too-human flesh of Kit Fitzroy.

All of a sudden the idea of being assaulted by a ghost seemed relatively appealing.

'Get *off* me!' she snapped. Or tried to. The sound she actually made was a muffled, undignified squawk, but he must have understood her meaning because he let her go immediately, thrusting her away from his body as if she were contaminated. Shaking back her hair, Sophie glared at him, trying to gather some shreds of dignity. Not easy when she'd just been caught behaving like a histrionic schoolgirl because she thought he was a ghost.

'What do you think you're *doing*?' she demanded.

His arched brows rose a fraction, but other than that his stony expression didn't change. 'I'd have thought it was obvious. Stopping you from screaming and waking up the entire castle,' he drawled. 'Is Jasper aware that you're roaming around the corridors in the middle of the night?'

'Jasper's asleep.'

'Ah. Of course.' His hooded gaze didn't leave hers, but she jumped as she felt his fingers close around her wrist, like bands of iron, and he lifted the hand in which her mobile phone was clasped. His touch was as cold and hard as his tone. 'Don't tell me, you got lost on the way to the bathroom and you were using the GPS to find it?'

'No.' Sophie spoke through clenched teeth. 'I got lost on the way to my bedroom. Now, if you'd just point me in the right—'

'*Your* bedroom?' He dropped her wrist and stepped away. 'Well, it definitely won't be here. The rooms in this part of the castle haven't been used for years. But why the hell aren't you sharing with Jasper? Or perhaps you prefer to have your own...*privacy*?'

He was so tall that she had to tilt her head back to look at his face. The place where they were standing was dark and it was half in shadow, but, even so, she didn't miss the faint sneer that accompanied the word.

'I just thought it wouldn't be appropriate to sleep with Jasper in his parents' house, that's all,' she retorted haughtily. 'It didn't feel right.'

'You do a passable impression of indignant respectability,' he said in a bored voice, turning round and beginning to walk away from her down the corridor. 'But unfortunately it's rather wasted on me. I know exactly why you want your own bedroom, and it has nothing to do with propriety and everything to do with the fact that you're far from in love with my brother.'

It was those words that did it. *My brother.* Until then she had been determined to remain calm in the face of Kit Fitzroy's towering arrogance; his misguided certainty and his infuriating, undeniable sexual magnetism. Now something snapped inside her.

'No. You're *wrong*,' she spat.

'Really?' he drawled, turning to go back along the passageway down which she'd just come.

'Yes!'

Who the hell was he to judge? If it wasn't for him Jasper wouldn't have had to ask her here in the first place, to make himself look 'acceptable' in the contemptuous eyes of his brother.

Well, she couldn't explain anything without giving Jasper away, but she didn't have to take it either. Following him she could feel the pulse jumping in her wrist, in the place where his fingers had touched her, as fresh adrenaline scorched through her veins.

'I know you think the worst of me and I can understand why, but I just want to say that it wasn't—*isn't*—

what you think. I would *never* hurt Jasper, or mess him around. He's the person I care most about in the world.'

He went up a short flight of steps into the corridor Sophie now remembered, and stopped in front of the door at the end.

'You have a funny way of showing it,' he said, very softly. 'By sleeping with another man.'

He opened the door and stood back for her to pass. She didn't move. 'It's not like that,' she said in a low voice. 'You don't know the whole story.'

Kit shook his head. 'I don't need to.'

Because what was there to know? He'd seen it all countless times before—men returning back to base from leave, white-lipped and silent as they pulled down pictures of smiling wives or girlfriends from their lockers. Wives they thought they could trust while they were away. Girlfriends they thought would wait for them. Behind every betrayal there was a story, but in the end it was still a betrayal.

Folding her arms tightly across her body, she walked past him into the small room and stood by the bed with her back to him. Her hair was tangled, reminding him that she'd just left his brother's bed. In the thin, cold moonlight it gleamed like hot embers beneath the ashes of a dying fire.

'Is it common practice in the army to condemn without trial and without knowing the facts?' she asked, turning round to face him. 'You barely even *know* Jasper. You did your best to deny his existence when he was growing up, and you're not exactly going out of your way to make up for it now, so please don't lecture me about not loving him.'

'That's *enough*.'

The words were raw, razor-sharp, spoken in the split second before his automatic defences kicked in and the shutters came down on his emotions. Deliberately Kit unfurled his fists and kept his breathing steady.

'If you think finding your way around the castle is confusing I wouldn't even try to unravel the relationships within this family if I were you,' he said quietly. 'Don't get involved in things you don't need to understand.'

'Why? Because I won't be around long enough?' she demanded, coming closer to him again.

Kit stiffened as he caught the scent of her again— warm, spicy, delicious. He turned away, reaching for the door handle. 'Goodnight. I hope you have everything you need.'

He shut the door and stood back from it, waiting for the adrenaline rush to subside a little. Funny how he could work a field strewn with hidden mines, approach a car loaded with explosives and not feel anything, and yet five feet five of lying redhead had almost made him lose control.

He hated deception—too much of his childhood had been spent not knowing what to believe or who to trust— and as an actress, he supposed, Sophie Greenham was quite literally a professional in the art.

But unluckily for her he was a professional too, and there was more than one way of making safe an incendiary device. Sometimes you had to approach the problem laterally. If she wouldn't admit that her feelings for Jasper were a sham, he'd just have to prove it another way.

CHAPTER SIX

SOPHIE FELT AS if she'd only just fallen asleep when a
knock at the door jolted her awake again. Jasper appeared, grinning sheepishly and carrying a plate of
toast in one hand and two mugs of coffee in the other,
some of which slopped onto the carpet as he elbowed
the door shut again.

'What time is it?' she moaned, dropping back onto
the pillows.

Jasper put the mugs down on the bedside table and
perched on the bed beside her. 'Nearly ten. Kit said he'd
bumped into you in the middle of the night trying to
find your room, so I thought I'd better not wake you.
You've slept for Britain.'

Sophie didn't have the heart to tell him she'd been
awake most of the night, partly because she'd been frozen, partly because she'd been so hyped up with indignation and fury and the after-effects of what felt like
an explosion in the sexual-chemistry lab that sleep had
been a very long time coming.

He picked up a mug and looked at her through the
wreaths of steam that were curling through the frigid
air. 'Sorry for leaving you to wander like that. Just as
well you bumped into Kit.'

Sophie grunted crossly. 'Do you think so? I thought

he was the ghost of the nymphomaniac countess. No such luck.'

Jasper winced. 'He didn't give you a hard time, did he?'

'He thought it was extremely odd that we weren't sharing a room.' Sophie reached for a coffee, more to warm her hands on than anything. 'I'm not exactly convincing him in my role as your girlfriend, you know. The thing is, he overheard me talking to Jean-Claude on the train and now he thinks I'm a two-timing trollop.'

'Oops.' Jasper took another sip of coffee while he digested this information. 'OK, well, that is a bit unfortunate, but don't worry—we still have time to turn it around at the party tonight. You'll be every man's idea of the perfect girlfriend.'

Sophie raised an eyebrow. 'In public? In front of your parents? From my experience of what men consider the perfect girlfriend, that wouldn't be wise.'

'Wicked girl,' Jasper scolded. 'I meant demure, devoted, hanging on my every word—that sort of thing. What did you bring to wear?'

'My Chinese silk dress.'

With a firm shake of his head Jasper put down his mug. 'Absolutely *not*. Far too sexy. No, what we need is something a little more…understated. A little more *modest*.'

Sophie narrowed her eyes. 'You mean frumpy, don't you? Do you have something in mind?'

Getting up, Jasper went over to the window and drew back the curtains with a theatrical flourish. 'Not something, some*where*. Get up, Cinderella, and let's hit the shops of Hawksworth.'

JASPER DROVE RALPH'S four-by-four along roads that had been turned into ice rinks. It was a deceptively beautiful day. The sun shone in a sky of bright, hard blue and made the fields and hedgerows glitter as if each twig and blade of grass was encrusted with Swarovski crystals. He had pinched a navy-blue quilted jacket of Tatiana's to lend to Sophie, instead of the military-style overcoat of which Kit had been so scathing. Squinting at her barefaced reflection in the drop-down mirror on the sun visor, she remarked that all that was missing was a silk headscarf and her new posh-girl image would be complete. Jasper leaned over and pulled one out of the glove compartment. She tied it under her chin and they roared with laughter.

They parked in the market square in the centre of a town that looked as if it hadn't altered much in the last seventy years. Crunching over gritted cobblestones, Jasper led her past greengrocers, butchers and shops selling gate hinges and sheep dip, to an ornately fronted department store. Mannequins wearing bad blonde wigs modelled twinsets and patterned shirtwaister dresses in the windows.

'Braithwaite's—the fashion centre of the North since 1908' read the painted sign above the door. Sophie wondered if it was meant to be ironic.

'After you, madam,' said Jasper with a completely straight face, holding the door open for her. 'Evening wear. First floor.'

Sophie stifled a giggle. 'I love vintage clothing, as you know, but—'

'No buts,' said Jasper airily, striding past racks of raincoats towards a sweeping staircase in the centre of the store. 'Just think of it as dressing for a part. Tonight,

Ms Greenham, you are *not* going to be your gorgeous, individual but—let's face it—slightly eccentric self. You are going to be perfect Fitzroy-fiancée material. And that means Dull.'

At the top of the creaking staircase Sophie caught sight of herself in a full-length mirror. In jeans and Tatiana's jacket, the silk scarf still knotted around her neck a lurid splash of colour against her un-made-up face, dull was exactly the word. Still, if dull was what was required to slip beneath Kit Fitzroy's radar that had to be a good thing.

Didn't it?

She hesitated for a second, staring into her own wide eyes, thinking of last night and the shower of shooting stars that had exploded inside her when he'd touched her wrist; the static that had seemed to make the air between them vibrate as they'd stood in the dark corridor. The blankness of his expression, but the way it managed to convey more vividly than a thousand well-chosen words his utter contempt…

'What do you think?'

Yes. Dull was good. The duller the better.

'Hello-*o*?'

Pasting on a smile, she turned to Jasper, who had picked out the most hideous concoction of ruffles and ruches in the kind of royal blue frequently used for school uniforms. Sophie waved her hand dismissively.

'Strictly Come Drag Queen. I thought we were going for dull—that's attention-grabbing for all the wrong reasons. No—we have to find something *really* boring…' She began rifling through rails of pastel polyester. 'We have to find the closest thing The Fashion Capital of the North has to a shroud… Here. How about this?'

Triumphantly she pulled out something in stiff black fabric—long, straight and completely unadorned. The neck was cut straight across in a way that she could imagine would make her breasts look like a sort of solid, matronly shelf, and the price tag was testament to the garment's extreme lack of appeal. It had been marked down three times already and was now almost being given away.

'Looks good to me.' Jasper flipped the hanger around, scrutinising the dress with narrowed eyes. 'Would madam like to try it on?'

'Nope. It's my size, it's horrible and it's far too cold to get undressed. Let's just buy it and go to the pub. As your fiancée I think I deserve an enormous and extremely calorific lunch.'

Jasper grinned and kissed her swiftly on the cheek. 'You're on.'

THE BULL IN Hawksworth was the quintessential English pub: the walls were yellow with pre-smoking-ban nicotine, a scarred dartboard hung on the wall beside an age-spotted etching of Alnburgh Castle and horse brasses were nailed to the blackened beams. Sophie slid behind a table in the corner by the fire while Jasper went to the bar. He came back with a pint of lager and a glass of red wine, and a newspaper folded under his arm.

'Food won't be a minute,' he said, taking a sip of lager, which left a froth of white on his upper lip. 'Would you mind if I gave Sergio a quick call? I brought you this to read.' He threw down the newspaper and gave her an apologetic look as he took out his phone. 'It's just it's almost impossible to get a bloody signal at Alnburgh, and I'm always terrified of being overheard anyway.'

Sophie shrugged. 'No problem. Go ahead.'

'Is there a "but" there?'

Taking a sip of her wine, she shook her head. 'No, of course not.' She put her glass down, turning the stem between her fingers. In the warmth of the fire and Jasper's familiar company she felt herself relaxing more than she had done in the last twenty-four hours. 'Except,' she went on thoughtfully, 'perhaps that I wonder if it wouldn't be easier if you came clean about all this.'

'Came out, you mean?' Jasper said with sudden weariness. 'Well, it wouldn't. It's easier just to live my own life, far away from here, without having to deal with the fallout of knowing I've let my whole family down. My father might be seventy, but he still prides himself on the reputation as a ladies' man he's spent his entire adult life building. He sees flirting with anything in a skirt as a mark of sophisticated social interaction—as you may have noticed last night. Homosexuality is utterly alien to him, so he thinks it's unnatural full stop.' With an agitated movement of his hand he knocked his pint glass so that beer splashed onto the table. 'Honestly, it would finish him off. And as for Kit—'

'Yes, well, I don't know what gives Kit the right to go around passing judgment on everyone else, like he's something special,' Sophie snapped, unfolding the paper as she moved it away from the puddle of lager on the table. 'It's not as if he's better than you because he's straight, or me because he's posh—'

'Holy cow,' spluttered Jasper, grasping her arm.

Breaking off, she followed his astonished gaze and felt the rest of the rant dissolve on her tongue. For there, on the front of the newspaper—in grainy black-and-white, but no less arresting for it—was Kit. Beneath the headline *Heroes Honoured* a photograph showed him in half profile, his expression characteristically blank above his dress uniform with its impressive line of medals.

Quickly, incredulously, Jasper began to read out the accompanying article.

'Major Kit Fitzroy, known as "the heart-throb hero", was awarded the George Medal for his "dedication to duty and calm, unflinching bravery in the face of extreme personal risk". Major Fitzroy has been responsible for making safe over 100 improvised explosive devices, potentially saving the lives of numerous troops and civilians, a feat which he describes as "nothing remarkable".'

For long moments neither of them spoke. Sophie felt as if she'd swallowed a firework, which was now fizzing inside her. The barmaid brought over plates of lasagne and chips and retreated again. Sophie's appetite seemed to have mysteriously deserted her.

'I suppose that does give him the right to act like he's a *bit* special, and *slightly* better than you and me,' she admitted shakily. 'Did you know anything about this?'

'Not a thing.'

'But wouldn't your father want to know? Wouldn't he be pleased?'

Jasper shrugged. 'He's always been rather sneery about Kit's army career, maybe because he's of the opinion people of our class don't work, apart from in pointless, arty jobs like mine.' Picking up his pint, he frowned. 'It might also have something to do with the fact his older brother was killed in the Falklands, but I don't know. That's one of those Things We definitely Do Not Mention.'

There seemed to be quite a lot of those in the Fitz-roy family, Sophie thought. She couldn't stop looking at the photograph of Kit, even though she wanted to. Or help thinking how attractive he was, even though she didn't want to.

It had been easy to write him off as an obnoxious, arrogant control-freak but what Jasper had said about his mother last night, and now this, made her see him, reluctantly, in a different light.

What was worse, it made her see herself in a differ-ent light too. Having been on the receiving end of ig-norant prejudice, Sophie liked to think she would never rush to make ill-informed snap judgments about people, but she had to admit that maybe, just maybe, in this in-stance she had.

But so had he, she reminded herself defiantly. He had dismissed her as a shallow, tarty gold-digger when that most definitely wasn't true. The gold-digger part, anyway. Hopefully tonight, with the aid of the nunlike dress and a few pithy comments on current affairs and international politics, she'd make him see he'd been wrong about the rest too.

For Jasper's sake, obviously.

As they left she picked up the newspaper. 'Do you think they'd mind if I took this?'

'What for?' Jasper asked in surprise. 'D'you want to sleep with the heart-throb hero under your pillow?'

'No!' Annoyingly Sophie felt herself blush. 'I want to swot up on the headlines so I can make intelligent conversation tonight.'

Jasper laughed all the way back to the car.

RALPH ADJUSTED HIS bow tie in the mirror above the drawing room fireplace and smoothed a hand over his brushed-back hair.

'I must say, Kit, I find your insistence on bringing up the subject of my death in rather poor taste,' he said in an aggrieved tone. 'Tonight of all nights. A milestone birthday like this is depressing enough without you reminding me constantly that the clock is ticking.'

'It's not personal,' Kit drawled, mentally noting that he'd do well to remember that himself. 'And it is boring, but the fact remains that Alnburgh won't survive the inheritance tax it'll owe on your death unless you've transferred the ownership of the estate to someone else. Seven years is the—'

Ralph cut him off with a bitter, blustering laugh. 'By someone else, I suppose you mean you? What about Jasper?'

Alnburgh is yours, Kit. Don't let anyone tell you it's not.

In the pockets of his dinner-suit trousers Kit's hands were bunched into fists. Experience had taught him that when Ralph was in this kind of punchy, belligerent mood the best way to respond was with total detachment. He wondered fleetingly if that was where he first picked up the habit.

'Jasper isn't the logical heir,' he said, very evenly.

'Oh, I don't know about that,' Ralph replied with unpleasant, mock joviality. 'Let's look at it this way— Jasper is probably going to live another sixty or seventy years, and, believe me, I have every intention of lasting a lot more than seven years. Given your job I'd say you're the one who's pushing your luck in that department, don't you think? Remember what happened to my dear brother Leo. Never came back from the Falklands. Very nasty business.'

Ralph's eyes met Kit's in the mirror and slid away. He was already well on the way to being drunk, Kit realised wearily, and that meant that any further attempt at persuasion on his part would only be counterproductive.

'Transfer it to Jasper if you want.' He shrugged, picking up the newspaper that lay folded on a coffee table. 'That would certainly be better than doing nothing, though I'm not sure he'd thank you for it since he hates being here as much as Tatiana does. It might also put him at further risk from ruthless gold-diggers like the one he's brought up this weekend.'

The medals ceremony he'd attended yesterday was front-page news. Idly he wondered whether Ralph had seen it and chosen not to say anything.

'Sophie?' Ralph turned round, putting his hands into his pockets and rocking back on the heels of his patent shoes. 'I thought she was quite charming. Gorgeous little thing, too. Good old Jasper, eh? He's got a cracker there.'

'Except for the fact that she couldn't give a toss about him,' Kit commented dryly, putting down the paper.

'Jealous, Kit?' Ralph said, and there was real malice in his tone. His eyes were narrowed, his face suddenly flushed. 'You think you're the one who should get all the good-looking girls, don't you? I'd say you want her for yourself, just like—'

At that moment the strange outburst was interrupted by Jasper coming in. Ralph broke off and turned abruptly away.

'Just like what?' Kit said softly.

'Nothing.' Ralph pulled a handkerchief from his

pocket and mopped his brow. As he turned to Jasper his face lost all its hostility. 'We were just talking about you—and Sophie.'

Heading to the drinks tray, Jasper grinned. 'Gorgeous, isn't she? And really clever and talented too. Great actress.'

In his dinner suit and with his hair wet from the shower Jasper looked about fifteen, Kit thought, his heart darkening against Sophie Greenham.

'So I noticed,' he said blandly, going to the door. He turned to Ralph. 'Think about what I said about the estate transfer. Oh, and I promised Thomas I'd see to the port tonight. Any preference?'

Ralph seemed to have recovered his composure. 'There's an excellent '29. Though, on second thoughts, open some '71.' His smile held a hint of challenge. 'Let's keep the really good stuff for my hundredth, since I fully intend to be around to celebrate it.'

Crossing the portrait hall in rapid, furious strides, Kit swore with such viciousness a passing waiter shot behind a large display of flowers. So he'd failed to make Ralph see sense about the estate. He'd just have to make sure he was more successful when it came to Sophie Greenham.

IT WAS JUST as well she hadn't eaten all that lasagne at lunchtime, Sophie reflected grimly, tugging at the zip on the side of the black dress. Obviously, with hindsight, trying it on in the shop would have been wise—all the croissants and baguettes in Paris must have taken more of a toll than she'd realised. Oh, well—if it didn't fit she'd just have to wear the Chinese silk that Jasper had decreed was too sexy…

Hope flared inside her. Instantly she stamped it out.

No. Tonight was not about being sexy, or having fun, she told herself sternly. Tonight was about supporting Jasper and showing Kit that she wasn't the wanton trollop he had her down as.

She thought again of the photo in the paper—unsmiling, remote, heroic—and her insides quivered a little. Because, she realised with a pang of surprise, she actually didn't want him to think that about her.

With renewed effort she gave the zip another furious tug. It shot up and she let out the lungful of air she'd been holding, looking down at the dress with a sinking heart. Her cell-like bedroom didn't boast anything as luxurious as a full-length mirror, but she didn't need to see her whole reflection to know how awful she looked. It really was the most severely unflattering garment imaginable, falling in a plain, narrow, sleeveless tube from her collarbones to her ankles. A slit up one side at least meant that she could walk without affecting tiny geishalike steps, but she felt as if she were wrapped in a roll of wartime blackout fabric.

'That's *good*,' she said out loud, giving herself a severe look in the little mirror above the sink. Her reflection stared back at her, face pale against the bright mass of her hair. She'd washed it and, gleaming under the overhead light, the colour now seemed more garish than ever. Grabbing a few pins, she stuck them in her mouth, then pulled her hair back and twisted it tightly at the back of her neck.

Standing back again, she pulled a face.

There. Disfiguring dress and headmistress hair. Jasper's dull girlfriend was ready for her public, although at least Sophie had the private satisfaction of knowing that she was also wearing very naughty underwear and what Jasper fondly called her 'shag-me' shoes. Twisting round, she tried to check the back view of the dress, and gave a snort of laughter as she noticed the price ticket hanging down between her shoulder blades.

Classy and expensive was always going to be a hard look for the girl who used to live on a bus to pull off, as Olympia Rothwell-Hyde and her cronies had never stopped reminding her. Attempting to do it with a label on her back announcing just how little she'd paid for the blackout dress would make it damned impossible.

She gave it a yank and winced as the plastic cut into her fingers. Another try confirmed that it was definitely a job for scissors. Which she didn't have.

She bit her lip. Jasper had already gone down, telling her to join them in the drawing room as soon as she was ready, but there was no way she could face Tatiana, who would no doubt be decked out in designer finery and dripping with diamonds, with her knock-down price ticket on display. She'd just have to slip down to the kitchens and see if the terrifying Mrs Daniels—or Mrs Danvers as she'd privately named her when Jasper had introduced her this morning—had some.

The layout of the castle was more familiar now and Sophie headed for the main stairs as quickly as the narrow dress would allow. The castle felt very different this evening from the cavernous, shadowy place at which she'd arrived last night. Now the stone walls seemed to resonate with a hum of activity as teams of caterers and waiting-on staff made final preparations in the staterooms below.

It was still freezing, though. In the portrait hall the smell of woodsmoke drifted through the air, carried on

icy gusts of wind that the huge fires banked in every
grate couldn't seem to thaw. It mingled with the scent
of hothouse flowers, which stood on every table and
window ledge.

Sophie hitched up the narrow skirt of her dress and
went more carefully down the narrow back stairs to
the kitchens. It was noticeably warmer down here, the
vaulted ceilings holding the heat from the ovens. A central stone-flagged passageway stretched beyond a row of
Victorian windows in the kitchen wall, into the dimly lit
distance. To the dungeons, Jasper had teased her earlier.

The dungeons, where Kit probably locked up two-
timing girlfriends, she thought grimly, shivering in spite
of the relative warmth. The noise of her heels echoed
loudly off the stone walls. The glass between the corridor and the kitchen was clouded with steam, but through
it Sophie could see that Mrs Daniels' domain had been
taken over by legions of uniformed chefs.

Of course. Jasper had mentioned that both she and
Thomas the butler had been given the night off. Well,
there was no way she was going in there. Turning on
her high heel, she hitched up her skirt and was hurrying back in the direction she'd just come when a voice
behind her stopped her in her tracks.

'Are you looking for something?'

Her heart leapt into her throat and she spun round.
Kit had emerged from one of the many small rooms
that led off the passageway, his shoulders, in a perfectly
cut black dinner suit, seeming almost to fill the narrow space. Their eyes met, and in the harsh overhead
bulk light Sophie saw him recoil slightly as a flicker
of some emotion—shock, or was it distaste?—passed
across his face.

'I was l-looking for M-Mrs Daniels,' she said in a strangled voice, feeling inexplicably as if he'd caught her doing something wrong again. God, no wonder he had risen so far up the ranks in the army. She'd bet he could reduce insubordinate squaddies to snivelling babies with a single glacial glare. She coughed, and continued more determinedly. 'I wanted to borrow some scissors.'

'That's a relief.' His smile was almost imperceptible. 'I assume it means I don't have to tell you that you have a price ticket hanging down your back.'

Heat prickled through her, rising up her neck in a tide of uncharacteristic shyness.

Quickly she cleared her throat again. 'No.'

'Perhaps I could help? Follow me.'

Sophie was glad of the ringing echo of her shoes on the stone floor as it masked the frantic thud of her heart. He had to duck his head to get through the low doorway and she followed him into a vaulted cellar, the brick walls of which were lined with racks of bottles that gleamed dully in the low light. There was a table on which more bottles stood, alongside a knife and stained cloth like a consumptive's handkerchief. Kit picked up the knife.

'Wh-what are you doing?'

Hypnotised, she watched him wipe the blade of the knife on the cloth.

'Decanting port.'

'What for?' she rasped, desperately trying to make some attempt at sensible conversation. Snatches of the article in the newspaper kept coming back to her, making it impossible to think clearly. *Heart-throb hero. Unflinching bravery. Extreme personal risk.* It was as if someone had taken her jigsaw puzzle image of him and broken it to bits, so the pieces made quite a different picture now.

His lips twitched into the faint half-smile she'd come to recognise, but his hooded eyes held her gravely. The coolness was still there, but they'd lost their sharp contempt.

'To get rid of the sediment. The bottle I've just opened last saw daylight over eighty years ago.'

Sophie gave a little laugh, squirming slightly under his scrutiny. 'Isn't it a bit past its sell-by date?'

'Like lots of things, it improves with age,' he said dryly, taking hold of her shoulders with surprising gentleness and turning her round. 'Would you like to try some?'

'Isn't it very expensive?'

What was it about an absence of hostility that actually made it feel like kindness? Sophie felt the hair rise on the back of her neck as his fingers brushed her bare skin. She held herself very rigid for a second, determined not to give in to the helpless shudder of desire that threatened to shake her whole body as he bent over her. Her breasts tingled, and beneath the severe lines of the dress her nipples pressed against the tight fabric.

'Put it this way, you could get several dresses like that for the price of a bottle,' he murmured, and Sophie could feel the warm whisper of his breath on her neck as he spoke. She closed her eyes, wanting the moment to stretch for ever, but then she heard the snap of plastic as he cut through the tag and he was pulling back, leaving her feeling shaky and on edge.

'To be honest, that doesn't say much about your port,' she joked weakly.

'No.' He went back over to the table and picked up

a bottle, holding it up to the light for a second before pouring a little of the dark red liquid into a slender, tear-drop-shaped decanter. 'It's a great dress. It suits you.'

His voice was offhand. So why did it make goose-bumps rise on her skin?

'It's a very *cheap* dress.' She laughed again, awkwardly, crossing her arms across her chest to hide the obvious outline of her nipples, which had to be glaringly obvious against the plainness of the dress. 'Or is that what you meant by it suiting me?'

'No.'

He turned to face her, holding the slim neck of the decanter. She couldn't take her eyes off his hands. Against the white cuffs of his evening shirt they looked very tanned and she felt her heart twist in her chest, catching her off guard as she thought of what he had done with those hands. And what he had seen with those eyes. And now he was looking at her with that cool, dispassionate stare and she almost couldn't breathe.

'I haven't got a glass, I'm afraid.' He swirled the port around in the decanter so it gleamed like liquid rubies, and then offered it up to her lips. 'Take it slowly. Breathe it in first.'

Oh, God.

At that moment she wasn't sure she was capable of breathing at all, but it was as if he had some kind of hypnotist's hold over her and somehow she did as he said, her gaze fixed unblinkingly on his as she inhaled.

It was the scent of age and incense and reverence, and instantly she was transported back to the chapel at school, kneeling on scratchy woollen hassocks to sip communion wine and trying to ignore the whispers of Olympia Rothwell-Hyde and her friends, saying that she'd go to hell because everyone knew she hadn't even been baptised, never mind confirmed. What vicar would christen a child with a name like Summer Greenham?

She pulled away sharply just as the port touched her lips, so that it missed her mouth and dripped down her chin. Kit's reactions were like lightning—in almost the same second his hand came up to cup her face, catching the drips of priceless liquor on the palm of his hand.

'I'm sorry,' she gasped. 'I didn't mean to waste it—'

'Then let's not.'

It was just a whisper, and then he was bending his head so that, slowly, softly, his mouth grazed hers. Sophie's breathing hitched, her world stopped as his lips moved downwards to suck the drips on her chin as her lips parted helplessly and a tidal wave of lust and longing was unleashed inside her. It washed away everything, so that her head was empty of questions, doubts, uncertainties: everything except the dark, swirling whirlpool of need. Her body did the thinking, the deciding for her as it arched towards him, her hands coming up of their own volition to grip his rock-hard shoulders and tangle in his hair.

This was what she knew. This meeting of mouths and bodies, this igniting of pheromones and stoking of fires—these were feelings she understood and could deal with expertly. Familiar territory.

Or, it had been.

Not now.

Not *this*…

His touch was gentle, languid, but it seared her like a blowtorch, reducing the memory of every man who'd gone before to ashes and dust. One hand rested on her hip, the other cupped her cheek as he kissed her with a

skill and a kind of brooding focus that made her trem-
ble and melt.

And want *more*.

The stiff fabric of the hateful dress felt like armour
plating. She pressed herself against him, longing to be
free of it, feeling the contours of the hard muscles of
his chest through the layers of clothes that separated
them. Her want flared, a fire doused with petrol, and
as she kissed him back her fingers found the silk bow
tie at his throat, tugging at the knot, working the shirt
button beneath it free.

And suddenly there was nothing gentle in the way
he pulled her against him, nothing languid about the
pressure of his mouth or the erotic thrust and dart of his
tongue. Sophie's hands were shaking as she slid them
beneath his jacket. She could feel the warmth of his
body, the rapid beating of his heart as he gripped her
shoulders, pushing her backwards against the ancient
oak barrels behind her.

Roughly she pushed his jacket off his shoulders. His
hands were at her waist and she yanked at her skirt,
pulling it upwards so that he could hitch her onto a barrel. She straddled its curved surface, her hips rising to
press against his, her fingers twisting in his shirt front
as she struggled to pull it free of his trousers.

She was disorientated with desire. Trembling, shaking, unhinged with an urgency that went beyond anything she'd known before. The need to have him against
her and in her.

'Now…please…'

She gasped as he stepped backwards, tearing his
mouth from hers, turning away. A physical sensation of
loss swept through her as her hands, still outstretched

towards him, reached to pull him back into her. Her breath was coming in ragged, thirsty gasps; she was unable to think of anything beyond satisfying the itch and burn that pulsed through her veins like heroin.

Until he turned back to face her again and her blood froze.

His shirt was open to the third button, his silk tie hanging loose around his neck in the classic, clichéd image from every red-blooded woman's slickest fantasy. But that was where the dream ended, because his face was like chiselled marble and his hooded eyes were as cold as ice.

And in that second, in a rush of horror and pain, Sophie understood what had just happened. What she had just done. He didn't need to say anything because his expression—completely deadpan apart from the slight curl of his lip as he looked at her across the space that separated them—said it all.

She didn't hesitate. Didn't think. It was pure instinct that propelled her across that space and made her raise her hand to slap his face.

But her instinct was no match for his reflexes. With no apparent effort at all he caught hold of her wrist and held it absolutely still for a heartbeat before letting go.

'You unutterable bastard,' she breathed.

She didn't wait for a response. Somehow she made her trembling legs carry her out of the wine cellar and along the corridor, while her horrified mind struggled to take in the enormity of what had just happened. She had betrayed Jasper and given herself away. She had proved Kit Fitzroy right. She had played straight into his hands and revealed herself as the faithless, worthless gold-digger he'd taken her for all along.

CHAPTER SEVEN

So in the end it hadn't even been as hard as he'd thought it would be.

With one quick, angry movement Kit speared the cork in another dusty bottle and twisted it out with far less care and respect than the vintage deserved.

He hadn't exactly anticipated she would be a challenge to seduce, but somehow he'd imagined a little more in the way of token resistance; some evidence of a battle with her conscience at least.

But she had responded instantly.

With a passion that matched his own.

His hand shook, and the port he was pouring through the muslin cloth into the decanter dripped like blood over the backs of his fingers. Giving a muttered curse, he put the bottle down and put his hand to his mouth to suck off the drops.

What the hell was the matter with him? His hands were usually steady as a rock—he and his entire team would have been blown to bits long ago if they weren't. And if he hesitated, or questioned himself as he was doing now…

He had done what he set out to do, and her reaction was exactly what he'd predicted.

But his wasn't. His wasn't at all.

WIPING HER DAMP palms down the skirt of the horrible dress, Sophie stood in the middle of the portrait hall, halfway between the staircase and the closed doors to the drawing room. She was still shaking with horror and adrenaline and vile, unwelcome arousal and the urge to run back up to her bedroom, throw her things into her bag and slip quietly out of the servants' entrance was almost overwhelming. Wasn't that the way she'd always dealt with things—the way her mother had shown her? When the going got tough you walked away. You told yourself it didn't matter and you weren't bothered, and just to show you meant it you packed up and moved on.

The catering staff were putting the finishing touches to the buffet in the dining room, footsteps ringing on the flagstones as they brought up more champagne in ice buckets with which to greet the guests who would start arriving any minute. Sophie hesitated, biting down on her throbbing lip as for a moment she let herself imagine getting on a train and speeding through the darkness back to London, where she'd never have to see Kit Fitzroy again…

She felt a stab of pain beneath her ribs, but at that moment one of the enormous doors to the drawing room opened and Jasper appeared.

'Ah, there you are, angel! I thought you might have got lost again so I was just coming to see if I could find you.'

He started to come towards her, and Sophie saw his eyes sweep over her, widening along with his smile as he came closer.

'Saints Alive, Sophie Greenham, that *dress*…'

'I know,' Sophie croaked. 'Don't say it. It's dire.'

'It's not.' Slowly Jasper circled around her, looking her up and down as an incredulous expression spread across his face. 'How *could* we have got it so wrong? It might have been cheap as chips and looked like a shroud on the hanger, but on you it's bloody dynamite.' He gave a low whistle. 'Have you seen yourself? No red-blooded, straight male will be able to keep his hands off you.'

She gave a slightly hysterical laugh. 'Darling, don't you believe it.'

'Soph?' Jasper looked at her in concern. 'You OK?'

Oh, hell, what was she doing? She'd come here to shield him from the prejudices of his family, and so far she'd only succeeded in making things more awkward for him. The fact that his brother was the kind of cold-blooded, ruthless bastard who would stop at nothing to preserve the purity of the Fitzroy name and reputation was all the more reason she should give this her all.

'I'm fine.' Digging her nails into the palms of her hands, she raised her chin and smiled brightly. 'And you look gorgeous. There's something about a man in black tie that I find impossible to resist.'

Wasn't that the truth?

'Good.' Jasper pressed a fleeting kiss to her cheek and, taking hold of her hand, pulled her forwards. 'In that case, let's get this party started. Personally, I intend to get stuck into the champagne right now, before guests arrive and we have to share it.'

HEAD DOWN, KIT walked quickly in the direction of the King's Hall—not because he was in any hurry to get there, but because he knew from long experience that looking purposeful was the best way to avoid getting trapped into conversation.

The last thing he felt like doing was talking to anyone.

As he went up the stairs the music got louder. Obviously keen to recapture his youthful prowess on the dance floor Ralph had hired a swing band, who were energetically working their way through the back catalogue of The Beatles. The strident tones of trumpet and saxophone swelled beneath the vaulted ceiling and reverberated off the walls.

Kit paused at the top of the flight of shallow steps into the huge space. The dance floor was a mass of swirling silks and velvets but even so his gaze was instantly drawn to the girl in the plain, narrow black dress in the midst of the throng. She was dancing with Ralph, Kit noticed, feeling himself tense inexplicably as he saw his father's large, practised hand splayed across the small of Sophie's back.

They suited each other very well, he thought with an inward sneer, watching the way the slit in Sophie's dress opened up as she danced to reveal a seductive glimpse of smooth, pale thigh. Ralph was a lifelong womaniser and philanderer, and Sophie Greenham seemed to be pretty indiscriminate in her favours, so there was no reason why she shouldn't make it a Fitzroy hat-trick. He turned away in disgust.

'Kit, darling! I thought it must be you—not many people fill a dinner jacket that perfectly, though I must say I'm rather disappointed you're not in dress uniform tonight.'

Kit's heart sank as Sally Rothwell-Hyde grasped his shoulders and enveloped him in a cloud of asphyxiating perfume as she stretched up to kiss him on both cheeks. 'I saw the picture on the front of the paper, you dark horse,' she went on, giving him a girlish look from beneath spidery eyelashes. 'You looked utterly mouth-watering, and the medal did rather add to the heroic effect. I was hoping to see it on you.'

'Medals are only worn on uniform,' Kit remarked, trying to muster the energy to keep the impatience from his voice. 'And being in military dress uniform amongst this crowd would have had a slight fancy-dress air about it, don't you think?'

'Very dashing fancy dress, though, darling.' Leaning in close to make herself heard above the noise of the band, Sally fluttered her eyelashes, which were far too thick and lustrous to be anything but fake. 'Couldn't you have indulged us ladies?'

Kit's jaw clenched as he suppressed the urge to swear. To Sally Rothwell-Hyde and her circle of ladies who lunched, his uniform was just a prop from some clichéd fantasy, his medals were nothing more than covetable accessories. He doubted that it had crossed her mind for a moment what he had gone through to get them. The lost lives they represented.

His gaze moved over her sunbed-tanned shoulder as he looked for an escape route, but she wasn't finished with him yet. 'Such a shame about you and Alexia,' she pouted. 'Olympia said she was absolutely heartbroken, poor thing. She's taken Lexia skiing this weekend, to cheer her up. Perhaps she'll meet some hunky instructor and be swept off her skis…'

Kit understood that this comment was intended to make him wild with jealousy, but since it didn't he could think of nothing to say. Sophie was still dancing with Ralph, but more slowly now, both of his hands gripping her narrow waist while the band, ironically, played 'Can't Buy Me Love'. She had her back to Kit, so as she inclined her head to catch something his father said Kit could see the creamy skin at the nape of her neck and suddenly remembered the silky, sexy underwear that had spilled out of her broken bag yesterday. He wondered what she was wearing under that sober black dress.

'Is that her replacement?'

Sally's slightly acerbic voice cut into his thoughts, which was probably just as well. Standing beside him, she had followed the direction of his stare, and now took a swig of champagne and looked at him pointedly over the rim of her glass.

'No,' Kit replied shortly. 'That's Jasper's girlfriend.'

'Oh! *Really*?' Her ruthlessly plucked eyebrows shot up and she turned to look at Sophie again, murmuring, 'I must say I never really thought there was anything in those rumours.' Before Kit could ask her what the hell she meant her eyes had narrowed shrewdly. 'Who is she? She looks vaguely familiar from somewhere.'

'She's an actress. Maybe you've seen her in something.' His voice was perfectly steady, though his throat suddenly felt as if he'd swallowed gravel.

'An actress,' Sally repeated thoughtfully. 'Typical Jasper. So, what's she like?'

Lord, all that champagne and he didn't have a drink himself. Where the hell were the bloody waiters? Kit looked around as his mind raced, thinking of a suitable answer. *She's an unscrupulous liar and as shallow as a puddle, but on the upside she's the most alive person I've ever met and she kisses like an angel...*

'I'll get Jasper to introduce you,' he said blandly, moving away. 'You can see for yourself.'

JUST AS SOPHIE was beginning to suspect that the band were playing the Extended-Groundhog-Club-Remix version of 'Can't Buy Me Love' and that she would be locked for ever in Ralph Fitzroy's damp and rather-too-intimate clutches, the song came to a merciful end.

She'd been relieved when he'd asked her to dance as it had offered a welcome diversion from the task of avoiding Kit, which had been the sole focus of her evening until then.

'Gosh—these shoes are murder to dance in!' she exclaimed brightly, stepping backwards and forcing Ralph to loosen his death-grip on her waist.

Ralph took a silk handkerchief from the top pocket of his dinner jacket and mopped his brow. Sophie felt a jolt of unease at the veins standing out in his forehead, the dark red flush in his cheeks, and suddenly wondered if it was lechery that had made him cling to her so tightly, or necessity. 'Darling girl, thank you for the dance,' he wheezed. 'You've made an old man very happy on his birthday. Look—here's Jasper to reclaim you.'

Slipping through the people on the dance floor, Jasper raised his hand in greeting. 'Sorry to break you two up, but I have people demanding to meet you, Soph. Pa, you don't mind if I snatch her away, do you?'

'Be my guest. I need a—' he broke off, swaying slightly, looking around '—need to—'

Sophie watched him weave slightly unsteadily through the crowd as Jasper grabbed her hand and started to pull her forwards. 'Jasper—your father,' she hissed, casting a worried glance over her shoulder. 'Is he OK? Maybe you should go with him?'

'He's fine,' Jasper said airily. 'This is the standard Hawksworth routine. He knocks back the booze, goes and sleeps it off for half an hour, then comes back stronger than ever and out-parties everyone else. Don't worry. A friend of my mother's is dying to meet you.'

He ran lightly up the steps and stopped in front of a petite woman in a strapless dress of aquamarine chiffon that showed off both her tan and the impressive diamonds around her crêpey throat. Her eyes were the colour of Bombay Sapphire gin and they swept over Sophie in swift appraisal as Jasper introduced her.

'Sophie, this is Sally Rothwell-Hyde, bridge partner-in-crime of my mother and all round bad influence. Sally—the girl of my dreams, Sophie—'

An icy wash of panic sluiced through her.

Great. Just *perfect*. She'd thought that there was no way that an evening that had started so disastrously could get any worse, but it seemed that fate had singled her out to be the victim of not one but several humiliating practical jokes. Just as Olympia Rothwell-Hyde used to do at school.

'Pleased to meet you,' Sophie cut in quickly before Jasper said her surname.

'Sophie…'

Sally Rothwell-Hyde's face bore a look of slight puzzlement as her eyes—so horribly reminiscent of the cold, china-doll blue of her daughter's—bored into Sophie. 'I'm trying to place you. Perhaps I know your parents?'

'I don't think so.'

Damn, she'd said that far too quickly. Sweat was

prickling between her shoulder blades and gathering in the small of her back, and she felt slightly sick. She moistened her lips. Think of it as being onstage, she told herself desperately as the puzzled look was replaced by one of surprise and Sally Rothwell-Hyde gave a tinkling laugh.

'Gosh—well, if it isn't that I can't think what it could be.' Her eyes narrowed. 'You must be about the same age as my daughter. You're not a friend of Olympia's, are you?'

Breathe, Sophie told herself. She just had to imagine she was in the audience, watching herself playing the part, delivering the lines. It was a fail-safe way of coping with stage fright. Distance. Calm. Step outside yourself. Inhabit the character. And above all resist the urge to shriek, *'A friend of that poisonous cow? Are you insane?'*

She arranged her face into a thoughtful expression. 'Olympia Rothwell-Hyde?' She said the loathed name hesitantly, as if hearing it for the first time, then shook her head, with just a hint of apology. 'It doesn't ring any bells. Sorry. Gosh, isn't it warm in here now? I'm absolutely dying of thirst after all that dancing, so if you'll excuse me I must just go and find a drink. Isn't it ironic to be surrounded by champagne when all you want is water?'

She began to move away before she finished speaking, glancing quickly at Jasper in a silent plea for him to rein back his inbred chivalry and keep quiet. He missed it entirely.

'I'll get—'

'No, darling, please. You stay and chat. I'll be back in a moment.'

She went down the steps again and wove her way quickly through the knots of people at the edge of the dance floor. Along the length of the hall there were sets of double doors out onto the castle walls and someone had opened one of them, letting in a sharp draft of night air. Sophie's footsteps stalled and she drank it in gratefully. It was silly—she'd spent the twenty-four hours since she'd arrived at Alnburgh freezing half to death and would have found it impossible to imagine being glad of the cold.

But then she'd have found it impossible to imagine a lot of the things that had happened in the last twenty-four hours.

A waiter carrying a tray laden with full glasses was making his way gingerly along the edge of the dance floor. He glanced apologetically at Sophie as she approached. 'Sorry, madam, I'm afraid this is sparkling water. If you'd like champagne I can—'

'Nope. Water's perfect. Thank you.' She took a glass, downed it in one and took another, hoping it might ease the throbbing in her head. At the top of the steps at the other end of the hall she could see Jasper still talking to Olympia Rothwell-Hyde's mother, so she turned and kept walking in the opposite direction.

She would explain to Jasper later. Right now the only thing on her mind was escape.

Stepping outside was like slipping into still, clear, icy water. The world was blue and white, lit by a paper-lantern moon hanging high over the beach. The quiet rushed in on her, as sudden and striking an assault on her senses as the breathtaking cold.

Going forwards to lean on the wall, she took in a gulp of air. It was so cold it flayed the inside of her lungs, and she let it go again in a cloud of white as she looked down. Far, far beneath her the rocks were sharp-edged and silvered by moonlight, and she found herself remembering Kit's voice as he told her about the desperate countess, throwing herself off the walls to her death. Down there? Sophie leaned further over, trying to imagine how things could have possibly been bleak enough for her to resort to such a brutal solution.

'It's a long way down.'

Sophie jumped so violently that the glass slipped from her hand and spiralled downwards in a shower of sparkling droplets. Her hand flew to her mouth, but not before she'd sworn, savagely and succinctly. In the small silence that followed she heard the sound of the glass shattering on the rocks below.

Kit Fitzroy came forwards slowly, so she could see the sardonic arch of his dark brows. 'Sorry. I didn't mean to startle you.'

Sophie gave a slightly wild laugh. 'Really? After what happened earlier, forgive me if I don't believe that for a second and just assume that's exactly what you meant to do, probably in the hope that it might result in another "accident" like the one that befell the last unsuitable woman to be brought home by a Fitzroy.'

She was talking too fast, and her heart was still banging against her ribs like a hammer on an anvil. She couldn't be sure it was still from the fright he'd just given her, though. Kit Fitzroy just seemed to have that effect on her.

'What a creative imagination you have.'

'Somehow it doesn't take too much creativity to imagine that you'd want to get rid of me.' She turned round, looking out across the beach again, to avoid having to look at him. 'You went to quite a lot of trouble to set me up and manipulate me earlier, after all.'

He came to stand beside her, resting his forearms on the top of the wall.

'It was no trouble. You were depressingly easy to manipulate.'

His voice was soft, almost intimate, and entirely at odds with the harshness of the words. But he was right, she acknowledged despairingly. She had been a pushover.

'You put me in an impossible position.'

'It wasn't impossible at all,' he said gravely. 'It would have been extremely workable, *if* I'd ever intended to let it get that far, which I didn't. Anyway, you're right. I do want to get rid of you, but since I'd have to draw the line at murder I'm hoping you'll leave quietly.'

'Leave?' Sophie echoed stupidly. A drumbeat of alarm had started up inside her head, in tandem with the dull throb from earlier. She hadn't seen this coming, and suddenly she didn't know what to say any more, how to play it. What had started off as being a bit of a game, a secret joke between her and Jasper, had spun out of control somewhere along the line.

'Yes. Leave Alnburgh.'

In contrast with the chaotic thoughts that were rushing through her brain, his voice was perfectly emotionless as he straightened up and turned to face her.

'I gather from Tatiana that Jasper's planning to stay on for a few days, but I think it would be best if you went back to London as soon as possible. The rail service on Sundays is minimal, but there's a train to Newcastle at about eleven in the morning and you can get a connection from there. I'll arrange for Jensen to give you a lift to the station.'

Sophie was glad she had the wall to lean on because she wasn't sure her legs would hold her up otherwise. She didn't turn to look at him, but was still aware of his height and the power contained in his lean body. It made her quail inside but it also sent a gush of hot, treacherous longing through her. She laughed awkwardly.

'Well, Major Fitzroy, you've got it all worked out, haven't you? And what about Jasper? Or have you forgotten him?'

'It's Jasper I'm thinking of.'

'Ah.' Sophie smacked herself comically on the forehead. 'Silly me, because I thought all this was for your benefit. I thought you wanted me gone because my face and my clothes and my accent don't fit and because I'm not scared of you like everyone else is. Oh, yes, and also because, no matter how much you'd like to pretend otherwise, you weren't entirely faking what happened earlier.'

For a second she wondered if she'd gone too far as some emotion she couldn't quite read flared in the icy fathoms of his eyes, but it was quickly extinguished.

'No.' His voice was ominously soft. 'I want you gone because you're dangerous.'

The anger that had fuelled her last outburst seemed suddenly to have run out. Now she felt tired and defeated, as the stags on the walls must have felt when the Fitzroy guns had appeared on the horizon.

'And what am I supposed to tell him?'

Kit shrugged. 'You'll think of something, I'm sure. Your remarkable talent for deception should make it easy for you to find a way to let him down gently. Then he can find someone who'll treat him with the respect he deserves.'

'Someone who also fits your narrow definition of suitable.' Sophie gave a painful smile, thinking of Sergio. The irony would have been funny if it hadn't all got so serious, and so horribly humiliating. 'Gosh,' she went on, 'who would have guessed that under that controlling, joyless exterior beat such a romantic heart?'

'I'm not romantic.' Kit turned towards her again, leaning one hip against the wall as he fixed her with his lazy, speculative gaze. 'I just have this peculiar aversion to unscrupulous social climbers. As things stand at the moment I'm prepared to accept that you're just a pretty girl with issues around commitment and the word "no", but if you stay I'll be forced to take a less charitable view.'

From inside came a sudden chorus of 'Happy Birthday to You.' Automatically Sophie looked through the window to where everyone had assembled to watch Ralph cut his birthday cake. The light from the huge chandeliers fell on the perma-tanned backs of the women in their evening dresses and made the diamonds at their throats glitter, while amongst them the dinner-suited men could have been the rich and the privileged from any era in the last hundred years.

I really, really do not belong here, Sophie thought.

Part of her wanted to stand up to Kit Fitzroy and challenge his casual, cruel assumptions about her, as her mother would have done, but she knew from bitter experience that there was no point. Inside, through the press of people, she could see Sally Rothwell-Hyde, all gleaming hair and expensive white teeth, as she sang, and suddenly Sophie was sixteen again, standing in the corridor at school with her packed trunk and her hockey stick beside her, watching through the glass doors of the hall as the other girls sang the school hymn and she waited for Aunt Janet to arrive.

She clenched her teeth together to stop them chattering, suddenly realising that she was frozen to the bone. Inside the rousing chorus of 'Happy Birthday' was coming to an end. If she went in now she could probably slip past unnoticed and reach the staircase while all eyes were focused on the cake.

Lifting her chin, she met Kit Fitzroy's eyes. They were as cold and silvery as the surface of the moonlit sea.

'OK. You win. I'll go.' She faked a smile. 'But do me a favour—spend some time with Jasper when I'm gone, would you? You'll like him when you get to know him.'

She didn't wait for his reply. Turning on her heel, holding herself very upright, she walked back to the door and pulled it open, stepping into the warmth just as the party-goers finished singing and burst into a noisy round of cheering and applause. Sophie paused as her eyes adjusted to the brightness in the hall. At the top of the steps at the far end an elaborate cake made to look like Alnburgh Castle stood on a damask-covered table, the light from the candles glowing in its battlements briefly illuminating Ralph's face as he leaned forwards to blow them out.

He seemed to hesitate for a moment, his mouth opening in an O of surprise. And then he was pitching sideways, grasping the tablecloth and pulling it, and the cake, with him as he fell to the floor.

CHAPTER EIGHT

'SOMEBODY *DO* SOMETHING!'

Tatiana's voice, shrill with panic, echoed through the sudden silence. Before Sophie had time to process what had happened Kit was pushing past her, shrugging his jacket off as he ran across the hall towards the figure on the floor. The stunned onlookers parted to let him through, recognising by some mutual instinct that he was the person to deal with this shocking turn of events. As the crowd shifted and fell back Sophie caught a glimpse of Ralph's face. It was the colour of old parchment.

Kit dropped to his knees beside his father, undoing his silk bow tie with swift, deft fingers and working loose the button at his throat.

'Does anyone know how to do mouth-to-mouth or CPR?' he shouted.

The tense silence was broken only by the shuffling of feet as people looked around hopefully, but no one spoke. Before she could think through the wisdom of what she was doing Sophie found herself moving forwards.

'I do.'

Kit didn't speak or look up as she knelt down opposite him. Bunching up his dinner jacket, he put it beneath Ralph's feet.

'Is he breathing?' she asked in a low voice.

'No.'

Tatiana, supported now on each side by male guests, let out a wail of distress.

'Jasper,' Kit barked icily, 'take her to the drawing room. You can phone for an ambulance from there. Tell them the roads are bad and they'll need to send a helicopter. Do it *now*.'

Bastard, thought Sophie in anguish, glancing round to where Jasper was standing, his face ashen against his black dinner jacket, his eyes wide and glassy with shock. How dared Kit talk to him like that at a time like this? But his voice seemed to snap Jasper out of his trance of shock and he gathered himself, doing as he was told.

'Breathing or heart?'

He was talking to her, Sophie realised. 'Breathing,' she said quickly, and regretted it almost straight away. At the moment she could barely breathe for herself, never mind for Ralph too, but there was no time for second thoughts.

Kit had already pulled his father's shirt open and started chest compressions, his lips moving silently as he counted. Sophie's hand shook as she tilted Ralph's head back and held his jaw. His skin had a clammy chill to it that filled her with dread, but also banished any lingering uncertainty.

OK, so she'd only done this on fellow actors in a TV hospital drama, but she'd been taught the technique by the show's qualified medical advisor and right now that looked like Ralph's best hope. She had to do it. And fast.

Kit's hands stilled. 'Ready?'

For the briefest second their eyes met, and she felt

an electrical current crackle through her, giving her strength. She took in a breath and bent her head, placing her mouth over Ralph's and exhaling slowly.

The seconds ticked by, measured only by the steady tide of her breath, the rhythmic movement of Kit's hands. They took it in turns, each acutely aware of the movements of the other. It was like a dance in which she let Kit lead her, watching him for cues, her eyes fixed unwaveringly on his as she waited for his signal. Fifteen rapid compressions. Two long, slow breaths.

And then wait.

Sophie lost track of time. She lost track of everything except Kit's eyes, his strong, tanned hands locked together on Ralph's grey chest…the stillness of that chest. Sometimes she thought there were signs of life—too tenuous for her to feel relief, too strong for her to give up, so again and again she bent her head and breathed for Ralph, willing the life and heat and adrenaline of her own body into the inert figure on the floor.

And then at last as she lifted her head she saw Ralph's chest convulse in a sharp, gasping breath of his own. Her gaze flew to Kit's face as he looked down at his father, pressing his fingers to Ralph's neck, waiting to see if a pulse had returned. Except for the small frown of concentration between his brows it was expressionless, but a muscle twitched in his jaw.

And then Ralph breathed again and Kit looked at her.

'Good girl.'

The sound of running feet echoed through the hall, breaking the spell. Sophie's head jerked round and she was surprised to see that the guests had all vanished and the huge room was empty now—except for the he-

licopter paramedics coming towards them, like orange-
suited angels from some sci-fi film.

Kit got to his feet in one lithe movement and dragged
a hand through his hair. For the first time Sophie saw
that he was grey with exhaustion beneath his tan.

'He's been unconscious for about seventeen minutes. He's breathing again. Pulse is weak but present.'

A female paramedic carrying a defibrillator kit
glanced at him, then did a classic double take. 'Well
done,' she said in a tone that bordered on awestruck.
'That makes our job so much easier.'

'Come on, sweetheart. We can take over now.'

Sophie jumped. One of the other paramedics was
kneeling beside her, gently edging her out of the way
as he fitted an oxygen mask over Ralph's face.

'Oh, I'm so sorry,' she muttered, attempting to get to
her feet. 'I was miles away… I mean, I wasn't thinking…'

Her dress was too tight and her legs were numb from
kneeling, making it difficult to stand. Somehow Kit was
beside her, his hand gripping her elbow as she swayed
on her high heels.

'OK?'

She nodded, suddenly unable to speak for the lump
of emotion that had lodged in her throat. Relief, perhaps. Delayed shock. Powerful things that made her
want to collapse into his arms and sob like a little girl.

She had no idea why. Even when she was a little girl
she couldn't ever remember sobbing so now was hardly
the time to start. And Kit Fitzroy, who not half an hour
ago had coldly ordered her to leave his family home,
was definitely not the person to start on.

Raising her chin and swallowing hard, she stepped
away from him, just as Jasper appeared.

'Soph—what's h—?'

He stopped, his reddened eyes widening in horror as the paramedics strapped his father's body onto the stretcher. Quickly Sophie went to his side, putting her arms around his trembling body.

'It's OK,' she soothed, suddenly poleaxed with exhaustion. 'He's alive, he's breathing and he's in the very best hands now.'

Briefly he leaned against her and she smelled the booze on his breath and felt his shoulders shake as he sobbed. 'Sophie, thank God you were here.' He pulled away, hastily wiping his eyes. 'I should go. To the hospital, to be with Mum.'

Sophie nodded.

'I'm afraid there's only room for one person in the helicopter,' the pretty blonde paramedic apologised as they lifted the stretcher. 'The rest of the family will have to follow by car.'

Momentary panic flashed across Jasper's face as he made a mental calculation of alcohol units.

'I can't—'

'I can.' Kit stepped forwards. 'Tatiana can go in the helicopter and I'll take Jasper.' His eyes met Sophie's. 'Are you coming?'

For a long moment they looked at each other. Blood beat in Sophie's ears and her heart seemed to swell up, squeezing the air from her lungs. She shook her head.

'No. No, I'll stay and make sure everything's OK here.'

For a few minutes—seventeen apparently, who knew?—they had shared something. A connection. But it was gone again now. She might just have helped to save his father's life, but that didn't alter the fact that

Kit Fitzroy had made it very clear he wanted her out of Jasper's. And his. The sooner the better.

HOURS LATER, STANDING in the softly lit corridor of the private hospital, Kit rubbed a hand over his stinging eyes.

He could defuse a landmine and dismantle the most complex and dangerous IED in extreme heat and under enemy fire, but he couldn't for the life of him work out how to get a cup of instant coffee from the machine in front of him.

Stabilised by drugs and hooked up to bags of fluid, Ralph was sleeping peacefully now. The hospital staff, hearing that Lord Hawksworth was on his way, had telephoned Ralph's private physician at home. He had arranged for Ralph to be admitted to the excellently equipped private hospital in Newcastle, which looked like a hotel and had facilities for relatives to stay too. Once she was reassured that her husband wasn't in any immediate danger Tatiana, claiming exhaustion, had accepted the sleeping pill the nurse offered and retired to the room adjoining Ralph's. Jasper, who had obviously knocked back enough champagne to float half the British Navy, didn't need medication to help him sleep and was now snoring softly in the chair beside Ralph's bed.

Which just left Kit.

He was used to being awake when everyone else was asleep. The silence and stillness of the small hours of the morning were tediously familiar to him, but he had found that the only way of coping with insomnia was to accept it. To relax, even if sleep itself was elusive.

He groaned inwardly. Tonight even that was out of the question.

Back in Ralph's room a small light was on over the bed, by which Kit could see his father's skin had lost its bluish tinge. An image floated in front of his eyes of Sophie, lowering her head, her mouth opening to fill Ralph's lungs with oxygen, again and again.

He closed his eyes momentarily. Details he'd been too focused to take in at the time rising to the surface of his mind. The bumps of her spine standing out beneath the pale skin at the base of her neck. Her green gaze fixing on his in a way that shut out the rest of the world. In a way that showed that she trusted him.

He winced. In view of everything that had taken place between them that evening, that was something of a surprise.

But then there was quite a lot about Sophie Greenham that surprised him, such as her ability to make a cheap dress look like something from a Bond Street boutique. The way she'd stood up to him. Fought back. The fact that she could give the kiss of life well enough to make a dead man breathe again.

And another one feel again.

Rotating his aching shoulders, he paced restlessly over to the window, willing away the throb of arousal that had instantly started up inside him again.

The incident in the wine cellar seemed like days rather than hours ago, and thinking about it now he felt a wave of self-disgust. He had told himself he was acting in Jasper's best interests, that somehow he was deliberately seducing his brother's girlfriend *for his benefit.*

Locking his fingers behind his neck, Kit exhaled deeply and made himself confront the unwelcome truth Sophie had flung at him earlier. He had done it to prove himself right, to get some small, petty revenge on his father and score a private victory over the girl who had so unsettled him from the moment he'd first laid eyes on her. He had barely thought of Jasper at all.

But he forced himself to look at him now. Slumped in the chair, Jasper slept on, his cheek resting on one hand, his closed eyelids red and puffy from crying. He looked very young and absurdly fragile.

A pickaxe of guilt smashed through Kit's head.

Always look out for your weakest man—his army training overruled the natural inclination forged by his family circumstances. *Never exploit that weakness, or take risks with it.* Even when it had irritated the hell out of you for as long as you could remember.

Jasper might lack the steel Kit was used to in the men he served with, but that didn't give Kit the right to kiss his girlfriend, just to show that he could. And to enjoy kissing her, so much that he had spent the evening thinking of nothing else but kissing her again. Right up until the moment he'd ordered her to leave.

Horrified realisation jolted through him. He swore sharply.

'Are you OK there?'

Kit spun round.

A plump, homely-looking nurse had appeared on silent feet and was checking the bag of fluid that was dripping into Ralph's arm. She glanced at Kit.

'Can I get you anything—coffee perhaps?'

'No, thanks.' Picking up his car keys, he headed for the door, his need for caffeine paling into insignificance in the light of this new imperative. To get back to Alnburgh and make sure that Sophie Greenham was still there. And that she would stay. For as long as Jasper needed her.

THE RED TAIL lights of the last catering van had disappeared under the archway and the sound of the engines faded into a thick silence that was broken only by the distant hiss of the sea. Shivering with cold and fear, Sophie turned and went back inside, shutting the massive oak door with a creaking sound that came straight from *The Crypt* and sliding the bolts across with clumsy, frozen fingers.

She still felt weak with shock and there was a part of her that wished she were in one of those vans, sweeping down the drive to civilisation and a warm bed in a centrally heated home. Going through the hallway beneath the rows of glassy eyes, she hummed the opening lines of 'My Favourite Things', but if anything the eerie echo of her voice through the empty rooms made her feel more freaked out than ever. She shut up again.

Her mind would insist on replaying events from the moment she'd seen Ralph fall, like one of those annoying TV adverts that seemed to be on twice in every break. She found herself hanging on to the memory of Kit's strength and assurance, his control of the situation. And the way, when her resolve was faltering, he'd wrapped her in his gaze and said 'good girl'.

Good girl.

He'd also said an awful lot of other things to her tonight, she reminded herself with a sniff, so it was completely illogical that those two should have made such an impression. But he was the kind of stern, upright person from whom you couldn't help but crave approval, that was why it was such a big deal. And that was the biggest irony of all. Because he was also the kind of person who would never in a million years approve of someone like her.

Miserably she switched the lights out and went into the portrait hall.

Not just the person he thought she was—Jasper's two-timing girlfriend—but the real Sophie Greenham, the girl who had been haphazardly brought up on a bus, surrounded by an assortment of hippies and dropouts. The girl who had no qualifications, and who'd blown her chance to get any by being expelled from school. The girl whose family tree didn't even stretch back as far as her own father, and whose surname came—not from William the Conqueror—but from the peace camp where her mother had discovered feminism, cannabis and self-empowerment.

In her gilded frame opposite the staircase the superior expression on Tatiana's painted face said it all.

Sophie flicked off the light above the portrait and trailed disconsolately into the King's Hall. The chandeliers still blazed extravagantly, but it was like looking at an empty stage after the play had finished and the actors had gone home. She had to steel herself to look at the place where Ralph had collapsed, but the caterers had cleaned up so that no evidence remained of the drama that had taken place there only a few hours earlier. She was just switching the lights off when she noticed something lying on the steps. Her pulse quickened a little as she went over to pick it up.

Kit's jacket.

She stood for a second, biting her lip as she held it. It *was* very cold, and there was absolutely no way she was going to go upstairs along all those dark passageways where the countess's ghost walked to get a jumper. Quickly she closed her eyes and slid it across her shoul-

ders. Pulling it close around her, she breathed in the
scent of him and revelled in the memory of his kiss…

A kiss that should never have happened, she told herself crossly, opening her eyes. A kiss that in the entire
history of disastrous, mistaken, ill-advised kisses would
undoubtedly make the top ten. She had to stop this sudden, stupid crush in its tracks; it was doomed from the
outset, which of course was why it felt so powerful.
Didn't she always want what she knew would never
be hers?

In the drawing room the fire had burned down to
ashes. There was no way she was going to brave the
ice-breathed darkness upstairs, so she piled logs on,
hoping there was enough heat left for them to catch.

In the meantime she would keep the jacket on,
though…

It was going to be a long, cold night.

PERCHED ON ITS platform of rock above the sea, Alnburgh
Castle was visible for ten miles away on the coast road,
so by the time Kit pulled into the courtyard he already
knew that it was entirely in darkness.

Lowering his head against the sabre-toothed wind,
he let himself in through the kitchen door, remembering how he'd often done the same thing when he came
home from boarding school for the holidays and found
the place deserted because Ralph and Tatiana were at
a party, or had gone away. He'd never been particularly
bothered to find the castle empty back then, but now…

Lord, she'd better still be here.

His footsteps sounded as loud as gunshots as he
walked through the silent rooms. Passing the foot of the
stairs, he glanced at the grandfather clock and felt a sud-

den beat of hope. It was half past three in the morning—
of course—she'd be in bed, wouldn't she?

He took the stairs two at a time, aware that his heart
was beating hard and unevenly. Outside the door to
her room he tipped his head back and inhaled deeply,
clenching his hand into a fist and holding it there for a
second before knocking very softly. There was no answer, so, hardly breathing, he opened the door.

It was immediately obvious the room was empty.
The curtains were undrawn, the moonlight falling on
a neatly made bed, an uncluttered chest of drawers.

She might be in bed, he thought savagely. The question was, whose?

Adrenaline was circulating like neat alcohol through
his bloodstream as he went back down the stairs. How
the hell was he going to break the news to Jasper that
she'd gone?

And that it was all his fault?

He headed for the drawing room, suddenly in desperate need of a drink. Pushing open the door, he was
surprised to see that the fire was hissing softly in the
grate, spilling out a halo of rosy light into the empty
room. He strode over to the table where the drinks tray
was and was just about to turn on the light beside it
when he stopped dead.

Sophie was lying on the rug in front of the fire, hidden from view by the sofa when he'd first come into the
room. Her head was resting on one outstretched arm,
and she'd pulled the pins from her hair so that it fell,
gleaming, over the white skin of her wrist like a pool of
warm, spilled syrup. She was lying on her side, wearing a man's dinner jacket, but even though it was miles

too big for her it couldn't quite disguise the swooping contours of her hip and waist.

He let out a long, slow breath, unaware until that moment that he'd been holding it in. Tearing his gaze away from her with physical effort, he reached for a glass and splashed a couple of inches of brandy into it, then walked slowly around the sofa to stand over her.

If the impact of seeing her from behind had made him forget to breathe, the front view was even more disturbing. Her face was flushed from the warmth, and the firelight made exaggerated shadows beneath the dark lashes fanning over her cheeks and the hollow above the cupid's bow of her top lip. Tilting his head, he let his eyes move over her, inch by inch, adjusting his jaded perception of her to fit the firelit vision before him.

She looked...

He took a swallow of brandy, hoping it might wash away some of the less noble adjectives that arrived in his head, courtesy of six months spent in the company of a regiment of sex-starved men. *Vulnerable*, that was it, he thought with a pang. He remembered watching her sleep on the train and being struck by her self-containment. He frowned. Looking at her now, it appeared to him more like self-protection, as if she had retreated into some private space where she was safe and untouchable.

He felt a sudden jolt pass through him, like a tiny electric shock, and realised that her eyes had opened and she was looking up at him. Like a cat she raised herself into a sitting position, flexing the arm she'd been sleeping on, arching her spine.

'You're back,' she said in a voice that was breathy with sleep.

He took another mouthful of brandy, registering for the first time the sheer relief he'd felt when he saw her, which had got rather subsumed by other, more urgent sensations.

'I thought you'd gone.'

It was as if he'd dropped an ice cube down her back. Getting to her feet, she turned away from him, smoothing the wrinkled dress down over her hips. He could see now that jacket she was wearing was his, and a fresh pulse of desire went through him.

'Sorry. Obviously I would have, but I didn't think there would be any trains in the middle of the night.' There was a slight hint of sarcasm in her voice, but it was a pale echo of her earlier bravado. 'And I didn't want to leave until I knew how Ralph was. Is he—?'

'He's the same. Stable.'

'Oh.' She turned to him then, her face full of tentative hope in the firelight. 'That's good, isn't it?'

Kit exhaled heavily, remembering the quiet determination with which she'd kept fighting to keep Ralph alive, reluctant to take the hope away. 'I don't know. It might be.'

'Oh.' She nodded once, quickly, and he knew she understood. 'How's Tatiana? And Jasper?'

'Both asleep when I left. They gave Tatiana a sleeping pill.' He couldn't keep the cynicism from his tone. 'Unsurprisingly Jasper didn't need one.'

Sophie's laugh had a break in it. 'Oh, God. He'll be unconscious until mid-morning. I hope the nurses have a megaphone and a bucket of iced water.'

Kit didn't smile. He came towards the sofa and leaned against the arm, swilling the last mouthful of brandy around his glass so that it glinted like molten sunlight. Warily, Sophie watched him, hardly able to breathe. The fire held both of them in an intimate circle, sealed together against the darkness of the room, the castle, the frozen world beyond.

'He was very emotional. I know he's had a lot to drink, but even so...'

Sophie sat down on the edge of a velvet armchair. 'That's Jasper. He can't help it. He wears his heart on his sleeve. It's one of the things I love most about him.'

'It's one of the things that irritate me most about him,' Kit said tersely. 'He was in bits all the way to the hospital—sobbing like a baby and saying over and over again that there was so much he still needed to say.'

Bloody hell, Jasper, Sophie thought desperately. Coming out to his family was one thing. Getting drunk and dropping heavy hints so they guessed enough to ask her was quite another. 'He was upset, that's all,' she said quickly, unable to keep the defensiveness from her tone. 'There's nothing wrong with showing emotion— some people might regard it as being normal, in fact. He'd just seen his father collapse in front of him and stop breathing—'

'Even so. This is just the beginning. If he can't cope now—'

'What do you mean, this is just the beginning?'

Kit got up and went to stand in front of the fire, looking into the flames. 'Who knows how long this will go on for? The doctors are saying he's stable, which Tatiana and Jasper seem to think is just a stage on the way back to complete recovery.'

'And you think differently,' Sophie croaked. Oh, dear. Something about the sight of his wide shoulders silhouetted against the firelight had made it hard to speak. She tucked her legs up beneath her, her whole body tightening around the fizz of arousal at its core.

'He was without oxygen for a long time,' Kit said flatly.

'Oh.' Sophie felt the air rush from her lungs and felt powerless to take in any more to replace it. She had tried. She had tried so hard, but it hadn't been enough.

'So what are you saying?'

'I'm saying it's highly likely he won't come out of this. That at some point in the next few days Jasper's going to have to deal with Ralph's death.'

'Oh. I see,' she said faintly. 'That soon?' Something about the way he was talking set alarm bells off in some distant part of her brain. He's going to tell me he wants me to leave now, she thought in panic. Tonight, before Jasper gets back…

'I think so.' His voice was low and emotionless. 'And if I'm right, I think it would be better if he didn't also have to deal with the girl he's crazy about running out on him.'

Steeling herself as if against a blow, Sophie blinked in confusion. 'But… I don't understand. You asked me to go…'

Kit turned around to look at her. The firelight gilded his cheekbones and brought an artificial warmth to his cold silver eyes. 'Things have changed,' he drawled softly, giving her an ironic smile. 'And now I'm asking you to stay. You've played the part of Jasper's doting girlfriend for two days. I'm afraid you'll just have to play it a bit longer.'

CHAPTER NINE

KIT WAS USED to action. He was used to giving an order and having it obeyed, working out what needed to be done and doing it, and in the days that followed trying to penetrate the dense forest of bureaucracy that choked the Alnburgh estate tested his patience to the limit.

He spent most of his time in the library, which was one of the few staterooms at Alnburgh to have escaped the attention of Tatiana's interior designer. A huge oriel window overlooked the beach, and on a day like today, when sea, sky and sand were a Rothko study of greys, the bleakness of the view made the inside seem warm by comparison.

Putting the phone down after yet another frustrating conversation with the Inland Revenue, Kit glanced along the beach, subconsciously looking for the slender figure, bright hair whipped by the wind, who had made it so bloody difficult to concentrate yesterday. But apart from a couple of dog walkers the long crescent of sand was deserted.

He turned away, irritation mixing with relief.

It had been three days since Ralph's heart attack, three days since he'd asked Sophie to stay on at Alnburgh, and things had settled into a routine of sorts. Every morning he drove a pale, shaken Jasper and a tight-lipped Tatiana to the hospital in Newcastle to sit at Ralph's bedside, though Ralph remained unconscious and unaware of their vigil. He stayed long enough to have a brief consultation with one of the team of medical staff and then returned to Alnburgh to avoid Sophie and begin to work his way through the landslide of overdue bills, complaints from estate tenants and unfollowed-up quotes from builders and surveyors about the urgent work the castle required.

It was a futile task, of that he was certain. Often, as he came across yet another invoice from Ralph's wine merchant or Tatiana's interior designer, he remembered Ralph saying, *I have every intention of lasting a lot more than seven years.*

Now it looked as if he wouldn't make it to seven days, and his inexplicable refusal to acknowledge the existence of British inheritance tax probably meant that the Alnburgh estate was doomed. It would be sold off in lots and the castle would be turned into a hotel, or one of those awful conference centres where businessmen came for team-building weekends and bonding exercises.

Ironically, because in thirty-four years there Kit hadn't formed any kind of bond with the rest of his family.

He walked back to the desk, leaning on it for a moment with his arms braced and his head lowered, refusing to yield to the avalanche of anger and bitterness and sheer bloody frustration that threatened to bury him.

There's nothing wrong with showing emotion—some people might regard it as being normal.

Sophie's voice drifted through his head, and he straightened up, letting out a long, ragged breath. It was something that had happened with ridiculous regularity these last few days, when time and time again he'd found himself replaying conversations he'd had with her, thinking about things she'd said, and wondering what she'd say about other stuff.

It made him uncomfortable to suspect that a lot of the time she'd talked a lot of sense. He'd wanted to write her off as a lightweight. An airhead actress who was easy on the eye, and in other respects too, but who wasn't big on insight.

But if that was the case, why did he find himself wanting to talk to her so badly now?

Because Jasper was either drunk or hungover and Tatiana was—well, Tatiana, he thought wearily. Sophie was the only other person who hadn't lost the plot.

An outsider, just like him.

SOPHIE DREAMED THAT she was being pulled apart by rough hands. She curled up tightly into a ball, hugging her knees to her chest, trying to stop shivering, trying to stop the hurting deep inside and calling out to Kit because he was the only one who could help her. She needed his strong, big hands to press down and stop the blood from coming.

She awoke to see a thin light breaking through the gap in the curtains. Her body was stiff with cold, and from the cramped position that she'd slept in, but as she unfurled her legs she felt a familiar spasm of pain in her stomach and let out a groan of dismay.

Her mind spooled backwards. Had it really been a month since that December night in Paris? Jean-Claude had called at the apartment in the early hours, reeking of wine and sweat and cigarettes, almost combusting with lust after an evening working on 'Nude with Lilies'. Bent

double with period pain, Sophie had only gone down
to let him in because she'd known he'd wake the whole
street if she didn't. That might have been preferable to the
unpleasant little scene that had followed. Jean-Claude had
been unwilling to take no for an answer, and it was only
thanks to the amount of booze he'd sunk that Sophie had
been able to fend him off. He'd fallen asleep, snoring at
ear-splitting volume, sprawled across the bed, and Sophie
had spent the rest of the night sitting on a hard kitchen
chair, curled around a hot-water bottle, deliberately not
thinking of anything but the pain blossoming inside her.

Tentatively she sat up now, wincing as the fist in
her belly tightened and twisted. Since she was thirteen
she'd suffered seven kinds of hell every month with her
period. The cramps always came first, but it wouldn't
be long before the bleeding started. Which meant she'd
better get herself to a chemist pretty quickly, since she
hadn't come prepared and neither Tatiana nor Mrs Daniels were the kind of cosy, down-to-earth women she
could ask for help. Just the thought of saying the words
'sanitary protection' to either of them brought her out
in a cold sweat.

She got out of bed, stooping slightly with the pain,
and reached for her clothes.

It was the coldest winter in forty years. The temperature in the castle hardly seemed to struggle above freezing, and Sophie was forced to abandon all ambitions
of style in favour of the more immediate need to ward
off death by hypothermia. This had meant plundering
Jasper's wardrobe to supplement her own, and she'd
taken to sleeping in his old school rugby shirt, which
was made to keep out the chill of a games field in the
depths of winter and was therefore just about suitable

for the bedrooms at Alnburgh. She couldn't bear the thought of exposing any flesh to the icy air so pulled her jeans on with it, zipping them up with difficulty over her tender, swollen stomach, and grabbed her purse.

Going down the stairs, clutching the banister for support, she glanced at the grandfather clock in the hall below. Knickers, she'd slept late—Jasper would have gone to the hospital ages ago.

She felt a twist of anguish as she wondered if he'd been hungover again this morning. Sergio had been putting pressure on Jasper to let him come up and be with him through all this, and Jasper was finding it increasingly hard to deal with his divided loyalties. Sophie didn't blame him for trying, though. Kit had given her a hard enough time—what would he do to flamboyant, eccentric drama-queen Sergio?

Not kiss him, presumably…

'Morning. Just about.'

Talk of the devil. His sardonic, mocking voice startled her. That was why her mouth was suddenly dry and her heart had sped up ridiculously.

'Morning.'

She attempted to sound aloof and distracted, but as she hadn't spoken a word since she'd woken up she just sounded bad-tempered. He was wearing a dark blue cashmere sweater and in the defeated grey light of the bitter morning he looked tanned and incongruously handsome, like some modern-day heart-throb superimposed on a black-and-white background. Maybe that accounted for the bad-tempered tone slightly as well.

His deadpan gaze swept over her, one arched brow rising. 'Off to rugby training?'

She was confused for a second, until she remembered she was wearing Jasper's rugby shirt.

She faked an airy smile. 'I thought I'd give it a miss today and have a cigarette behind the bike sheds instead. To be honest, I'm not sure it's really my game.'

'Oh, I don't know,' he drawled quietly with the faintest smile. 'I think you'd make a pretty good hooker.'

'Very funny.' She kept going, forcing herself to hold herself more upright in spite of the feeling of having been kicked in the stomach by a horse. 'I'm going to the village shop. I need to pick up a few things.'

'Things?'

Bloody hell, why did she always feel the need to explain herself to him? If she hadn't said anything she wouldn't have put herself in the position of having to lie. Again.

'I'm coming down with a cold. Tissues, aspirin—that sort of thing.'

'I'm sure Mrs Daniels would be able to help you out with all that,' he said blandly. 'Would you like me to ask her?'

'No, thank you,' she snapped. The kicked-by-a-horse feeling was getting harder to ignore. She paused on the bottom step, clinging to the newel post as nausea rose inside her. The pain used to make her sick when she was younger and, though it hadn't happened for a few years, her body seemed to have developed a keen sense of comedy timing whenever Kit Fitzroy was around. 'I'll go myself, if that's OK? I wasn't aware I was under house arrest?'

From where she was standing his hooded eyes were on a level with hers. 'You're not.'

Sophie gave a brittle little laugh. 'Then why are you treating me like a criminal?'

He waited a moment before replying, looking at her steadily with those cold, opaque eyes. A muscle was flickering slightly in his taut, tanned cheek. 'I suppose,' he said with sinister softness, 'because I find it hard to believe that you've suddenly been struck with an urgent desire to go shopping when it's minus five outside and you're only half dressed.'

'I don't have time for this,' she muttered, going to move past him, desperate to escape the scrutiny of his gaze. Desperate for fresh air, even if it was of the Siberian variety. 'I'm dressed perfectly adequately.'

'I suppose it depends what for,' he said gravely as she passed him. 'Since you're clearly not wearing a bra.'

With a little gasp of outrage, Sophie looked down and saw that the neck of the rugby shirt was open wide enough to reveal a deep ravine of cleavage. Jasper's fourteen-year-old chest was obviously considerably smaller than hers. She snatched the collar and wrenched it together.

'Because I've just got out of bed.'

'And you're just about to rush into someone else's while Jasper's not here?' Kit suggested acidly.

That did it. The contempt in his voice, combined with another wringing cramp, made her lose her temper. 'No,' she cried, hands clenched into fists at her sides, cheeks flaming. 'I really *am* rushing to the village shop. In minus five temperatures and with stomach cramps that possibly register on the Richter scale, not because I *want* to, but because I'm about to start the period from hell and I am completely unprepared for it. So now perhaps you'll just let me go before it all gets messy.'

For a moment there was silence. Complete. Total. Kit took a step backwards, out of the orbit of her anger, and Sophie saw the spark of surprise in his eyes. And then the shutters went down and he was back in control.

'In that case you're not going anywhere,' he said with a faint, ironic smile. 'Or only as far as the library anyway—at least you won't freeze to death in there. Leave it to me. I'll be back as soon as I can.'

SITTING IN THE car and waiting for the fan to thaw the ice on the windscreen, Kit dropped his head into his hands.

He had always thought of himself as level-headed. Rational. Fair. A man who was ruled by sense rather than feeling. So in that encounter how come he'd emerged as some kind of bullying jailer?

Because there was something about this girl that made him lose reason. Something about her smile and her eyes and the way she tried to look haughty but could never quite pull it off that made him *feel* far too much. And still want to feel more.

Her body, for a start. All of it. Without clothes.

He started the engine with an unnecessary roar and shot forwards in a screech of tyres. Lord, no matter how incredible he found it, she was his younger brother's girlfriend and the only reason she was still here was because he'd ordered her to stay. That made two good reasons why he should be civil to her, so he'd better start by behaving less like a fascist dictator and more like a decent human being.

After that he could have a look through his address book and find someone who would be happy to supply him with the sexual release he so obviously needed before going back to his unit and channelling his energy into the blessedly absorbing task of staying alive.

Sophie managed to wait until Kit had left the library and shut the door before putting her hands over her burning cheeks and letting out a low moan of mortification.

Saints in heaven, why had she blurted all that out? She was supposed to be an *actress*. Why couldn't she ever manage to act mysterious, or poised, or *elegant*?

Especially around Kit Fitzroy, who must be used to silken officer's-wife types, with perfect hair and manners to match. Women who would never do anything as vulgar as swear or menstruate. Or lose their temper. Or kiss someone without realising they were being set up, or put themselves in a position where someone would want to set them up in the first place…

Women with class, in other words.

She let her hands drop again and looked up, noticing the room properly for the first time. Even seen through a fog of humiliation she could see straight away that it was different from the other rooms she'd been in at Alnburgh. There was none of the blowsy ostentation of the drawing room with its raw-silk swagged curtains and designer wallpaper, nor the comfortless, neglected air of upstairs. In here everything was faded, used and cherished, from the desk piled with papers in the window to the enormous velvet Knole sofa in front of the fire.

But it was the books that jolted her out of her self-pity. Thousands of them, in shelves stretching up to the high ceiling, with a narrow galleried walkway halfway up. Where she had grown up the only books were the few tattered self-help manuals that the women at the peace camp had circulated between themselves, with titles like *Freeing the Warrior Woman Within* and *The Harmonious Vegan*, and even when Sophie had managed to get hold of a book of her own from a second hand shop or jumble sale there had never been anywhere quiet to read it. She had always dreamed of a room like this.

Almost reverentially she walked along the bookcases, trailing her finger along the spines of the books. They were mostly old, faded to a uniform brown, the gold titles almost unreadable, but in the last section, by the window, there were some more modern paperbacks—Dick Francis, Agatha Christie and—joy—a handful of Georgette Heyer. Moving the faded curtain aside, Sophie gave a little squeak of delight as she spotted *Devil's Cub*, and felt a new respect for Tatiana. Maybe they did have something in common after all.

In her embarrassment she'd temporarily forgotten about the pain in her tummy, but the dragging feeling was back again now so she took Georgette over to the sofa and sank down gratefully. At the age of fourteen she'd fallen spectacularly in love with Vidal, and known with fervent adolescent certainty that she would never find a man who could match him in real life.

Her mouth twisted into an ironic smile. At fourteen everything seemed so black and white. At twenty-five, it was all infinitely more complicated. Her teenage self had never considered the possibility that she might meet her Vidal, only for him to dismiss her as…

Her thoughts stalled as a piece of paper slid out of the book onto her knee.

Unfolding it, she saw straight away that it was a letter and felt a frisson of excitement. The date at the top was thirty years ago, the writing untidy, masculine and difficult to read, but she had no trouble making out the first line.

My Darling—

Technically Sophie was well aware that it was wrong to read other people's letters, but surely there was some kind of time limit on that rule? And anyway, any letter that began so romantically and was found in a Georgette Heyer novel was begging to be read. With a sense of delicious guilt she tucked her knees up tighter and scanned the lines.

It's late and the heat is just about bearable now the sun has gone down. I'm sitting on the roof terrace with the remains of the bottle of gin I brought back from England—I'd rather like to finish it all right now, but I couldn't bear the thought of Marie throwing the bottle away in the morning. It was the one we bought in London, that you held underneath your coat when we ran back to the hotel in the rain. How can I throw anything away that's been so close to your body?

Oh, how gorgeous! Sophie thought delightedly, trying to imagine Ralph writing something so intimate. Or doing anything as romantic as dashing through the rain to ravish the woman he loved in a hotel room.

Thank you, my love, for sending the photograph of K in your last letter. He's growing up so quickly—what happened to the plump baby I held

in my arms on my last visit to Alnburgh? He is a
boy now—a person in his own right, with a real
character emerging—such fearless determination!
Saying goodbye to him was so much harder this
time. I never thought that anything would come
close to the pain of leaving you, but at least your
letters keep me going, and the memories of our
time together. Leaving my son felt like cutting
out a piece of myself.

Sophie's heart lurched and the written lines jumped
before her eyes. Was K referring to Kit? Thirty years
ago he must have been a small boy of three or four.
Breathlessly she read on.

I suppose I've learned to accept sharing you with
Ralph because I know you don't belong to him in
any real sense, but the fact that K will grow up
thinking of R as his father makes me rage against
the injustice of everything.
    Why couldn't I have found you first?

Her mouth had fallen open. Incredulously she read
the lines again. After thirty years the sense of despair
in them was still raw enough to make her throat close,
but her brain couldn't quite accept the enormity of what
she was reading.
    Ralph Fitzroy wasn't Kit's father?
    The sound of the door opening behind her made her
jump about a mile in the air. Hastily, with trembling,
nerveless fingers, she slid the letter back between the
pages of Georgette Heyer and opened it randomly, pre-
tending to read.

'Th-that was quick,' she stammered, turning round to see Kit come into the room carrying a bulging carrier bag. He was wearing the dark blue reefer jacket she remembered from the train and above the upturned collar his olive tan glowed with the cold. As he moved around the sofa he brought with him a sharp breath of outside—of frost and pine and ozone.

'I sensed that there was a certain amount of urgency involved.'

He put the bag down on the other end of the sofa and pulled out a huge box of tampons, which he tossed gently to her. Catching it, she couldn't meet his eye. The embarrassment of having him buy her sanitary products had paled into near-insignificance by the enormity of the discovery she'd just made.

'Thanks,' she muttered, looking round for her purse.

Taking off his jacket, he looked at her, slightly guarded. 'You're welcome. It's the least I could do for being so—' a frown appeared between his dark brows '—controlling. I'm sorry.'

'Oh, please—don't be,' Sophie said quickly. She meant it. The last thing she needed now was him standing here looking like the beautiful hero from an arthouse film and being *nice*, wrenching open the huge crack that had appeared in her Kit-Fitzroy-proof armour after reading the letter.

He glanced at her in obvious surprise. 'I anticipated you'd be harder to make up to,' he said, delving back into the bag, pulling out the most enormous bar of chocolate. 'I thought this might be needed, at least. And possibly even this.' He held up a bottle.

'Gin?' Sophie laughed, though her heart gave another flip as she thought of the letter, and Kit's mother and her unknown lover drinking gin in bed while it poured down outside.

Oh, dear. Best not to think of bed.

Kit took the bottle over to a curved-fronted cupboard in the corner of the room behind the desk. 'Mrs Watts in the village shop, who under different circumstances would have had a brilliant career in the CID, looked at the other things I was buying and suggested that gin was very good for period pains.'

'Oh, God—I'm so sorry—how embarrassing for you.'

'Not at all, though I can't comment on the reliability of Mrs Watts's information.'

'Well, gin is a new one on me, but to be honest if someone suggested drinking bat's blood or performing naked yoga on the fourth plinth, I'd try it.'

'Is it that bad?' he said tonelessly, opening the cupboard and taking down a can of tonic water. Sophie watched the movements of his long fingers as he pulled the ring and unscrewed the gin bottle.

'N-not too bad this time. But sometimes it's horrendous. I mean, not compared to lots of things,' she added hastily, suddenly remembering that he was used to working in war zones, dealing with the aftermath of bombings. 'On a bad month it just makes it, you know…difficult.'

'There's some ibuprofen in the bag.' He sloshed gin into a glass. 'What does the doctor say?'

'I haven't seen one.' She wasn't even registered with one. She'd never really been in the same place for long enough, and Rainbow had always been a firm believer in remedies involving nettles and class B drugs. 'I looked it up on the Internet and I think it might be something called endometriosis. Either that, or one of twenty-five different kinds of terminal cancer—unlikely since I've had it for the last twelve years—appendicitis—ditto—or arsenic poisoning. I decided to stop looking after that.'

Kit came towards her, holding out a large glass, frosted with cold and clinking with ice cubes. 'You should see a doctor. But in the meantime try a bit of self-medicating.'

There was something about the sternness of his voice when combined with the faintest of smiles that made her feel as if she'd had a couple of strong gins already. Reaching up to take it from him, she felt herself blushing all over again.

'I don't have many unbreakable rules, but drinking hard spirits, on my own, in the middle of the morning is actually one I try to stick to. Aren't you having one too?' she said, then, realising that now he'd fulfilled his obligation he might be wanting to escape, added quickly, 'Unless you have something else you need to do, of course.'

'Not really. Nothing that won't keep anyway.' He turned away, picking up another log from the huge basket by the fireplace and dropping it into the glowing grate before going to pour another gin and tonic. 'I'm trying to go through some of the paperwork for the estate. It's in a hell of a mess. My father isn't exactly one for organisation. The whole place has been run on the ostrich principle for decades.'

'So Jasper gets his tendency to bury his head in the sand from Ralph?'

'I'm afraid so.' He sat down at the other end of the massive sofa, angling his body so he was facing her. 'And his tendency to drink too much and rely on charm to get him out of the more unpleasant aspects of life.'

He broke off to take a large swig of his drink and shook his head. 'Sorry, I shouldn't be talking about him like that to you. To be fair, the womanising gene seems to have passed him by.'

'Yes.' Sophie's laugh went on a little too long. If only Kit knew the truth behind that statement. 'You're right, though. He and Ralph are astonishingly alike in lots of ways.'

She took a quick sip of her drink, aware that she was straying into dangerous territory. Part of her wanted desperately to ask him about the letter, or more specifically the shattering information it contained, but the rest of her knew she would never dare make such a personal assault on Kit Fitzroy's defences.

Silver eyes narrowed, he looked at her over the rim of his glass.

'Whereas I'm not like him at all.'

It was as if he had read her thoughts. For a moment she didn't know what to say, so she took another mouthful of gin and, nearly choking on it, managed to croak, 'Sorry. It's none of my business. I didn't—'

'It's fine.' Leaning back on the huge sofa, he tipped his head back wearily for a moment. 'It's no secret that my father and I don't get on. That's why I don't feel the need to spend every minute at his bedside.'

The room was very quiet. The only sounds were the hissing of the logs in the grate and the clink of ice in Sophie's glass as the hand that held it shook. Largely with the effort of stopping it reaching out and touching him

'Why?' she asked in a slightly strangled voice. 'Why don't you get on with him?'

He shrugged. 'It's always been like that. I don't remember having much to do with him before my mother left, and after she went you'd have thought we would have been closer.'

'Weren't you?'

'Exactly the opposite. Maybe he blamed me.' Kit held up his glass, looking through it dispassionately. The fire turned the gin the colour of brandy. 'Maybe he didn't, and just took it out on me, but what had previously been indifference became outright hostility. He sent me to boarding school at the soonest possible opportunity.'

'Oh, God, you poor thing.' Just thinking of her own brief boarding school experience made Sophie's scalp prickle with horror.

'God, no. I loved it. I was the only kid in the dorm who used to dread holidays.' He took a mouthful of gin, his face deadpan as he went on, 'He used to call me into the drawing room on my first evening home and go through my report, seizing on anything he could—a mark dropped here, a team captaincy missed there—and commenting on it in this strange, sarcastic way. Unsurprisingly it made me more determined to try harder and do better.' He smiled wryly. 'So then he'd mock me for being too clever and on too many teams.'

Sophie's heart turned over. She could feel it beating against her ribs with a rapid, jerky rhythm. The book, with its outrageous secret folded between the pages, stuck up slightly from the sofa cushions just inches from her right hip.

'Why would he do that?'

'I have no idea,' Kit drawled softly. 'It would be nice to think that he just wasn't someone who liked children, or could relate to them, but his unbridled joy when Jasper came along kind of disproves that. Anyway, it hasn't scarred me for life or anything, and I gave up trying to work it out a long time ago.'

'But you keep coming back here,' Sophie murmured. 'I'm not sure I would.' She looked down at the crescent of lemon stranded on the ice cubes in the bottom of her glass, letting her hair fall over her face in case it gave away how much of a howling understatement that was.

'I come back because of Alnburgh,' he said simply. 'It might sound mad but the place itself is part of my family as much as the people who live in it. And Ralph's approach to looking after the castle has been similar to the way he looked after his sons.'

She lifted her head. 'What do you mean?'

'All or nothing—five thousand pounds for new curtains in the drawing room, while the roof goes unmaintained.'

Their eyes met. He gave her that familiar brief, cool smile, but his eyes, she noticed, were bleak. Compassion beat through her, mixing uneasily with the longing churning in her tender stomach. *I know why it is,* she wanted to blurt out. *I know why he was always vile to you, and it isn't your fault.*

The moment stretched. Their gazes stayed locked together. Sophie felt helpless with yearning. The heat from the fire seemed to be concentrated in her cheeks, her lips…

She jumped out of her skin as the phone rang.

Kit moved quickly. He got to his feet to answer it so he didn't have to lean across her.

'Alnburgh.' His voice was like ground glass.

Sophie's hands flew to her face, pressing against her burning cheeks with fingers splayed. Her heart was galloping. From miles away, his voice reduced to a tinny echo, she could just make out that it was Jasper on the phone.

'That's good,' said Kit tonelessly. Then, after a pause, 'Ask her yourself.'

He held out the phone. Sophie couldn't look at him as she took it.

'Soph, it's good news.' Jasper's voice was jubilant. 'Dad's regained consciousness. He's groggy and a bit breathless but he's talking, and even managed a smile at the pretty blonde nurse.'

'Jasper, that's wonderful!' Sophie spoke with as much warmth as possible, given what she'd just found out about Ralph Fitzroy. 'Darling, I'm so pleased.'

'Yes. Look, the thing is, neither Ma nor I want to leave him while he's like this, so I was wondering if you'd mind very much if we didn't come back for dinner? Will you be OK on your own?'

'Of course.' Unconsciously she found her gaze moving back to Kit. He was standing in front of the fire, head bent, shoulders tensed. 'Don't worry. I'll be fine.'

'The other thing is,' Jasper said apologetically, 'Ma gave Mrs Daniels the day off...'

Sophie laughed. 'Believe it or not, some of us have evolved to the stage where we can survive without staff. Now, go and give Ralph...my regards.'

Her smile faded quickly as she put the phone down. The room was quiet again, as if it were waiting.

'They're not coming back,' she said, trying to sound casual. 'He just wanted to check we'd be OK, since it's Mrs Daniels' day off and I'm not known for my culinary skills.' She gave a nervous laugh. 'Where's the nearest Indian takeaway?'

'Hawksworth.' Kit turned round. His face was blank. 'But forget takeaway. I don't know about you but I need to get away from here. Let's go out.'

CHAPTER TEN

IT'S NOT A DATE, it's not a date, it's not a date.

Sophie looked at herself sternly in the mirror as she yanked a comb roughly through her wet hair. After a walk on the beach this afternoon it had needed washing anyway. She wasn't making any special effort because she was going out for dinner with Kit.

Her stomach dipped. *Period pain*, she told herself.

It would be rude not to make a little bit of effort, and, after being shut up at Alnburgh for days without seeing a soul apart from the odd dog walker on the beach, it was actually pretty good to have an excuse to liven up her corpselike pallor with blusher and put on something that wasn't chosen solely for its insulating properties.

But what?

She stopped combing, and stood still, her mind running over the possibilities. She was sick and tired of jeans, but discounting them only left the black shroud, the vampire corset thing or the Chinese silk dress Jasper had ruled out for Ralph's party on the grounds that it was too sexy. Tapping a finger against her lip, she considered.

It's not a date...

Absolutely not. But she wasn't wearing the shroud. And the corset would look as if a she were meeting a client and charging for it. The Chinese silk it would have to be.

A wave of undeniable nervousness rolled through her and she had to sit down on the edge of the bed. She was being ridiculous, getting dressed up and wound up about a dinner arrangement that was based purely on practical and logical reasons. Jasper wasn't coming back, Mrs Daniels was away, neither of them could cook and they were both going stir-crazy from being cooped up in the castle for too long. Unlike every other dinner invitation she'd ever had, this one very definitely wasn't the opening move in a game that would finish up in bed.

No matter how fantastic she sensed going to bed with Kit Fitzroy would be.

Stop it, she told herself crossly, getting up and slapping foundation onto her flushed cheeks. This was nothing to do with sex. That look that had passed between them in the library earlier had *not* been the precursor to a kiss…a kiss that would have led to who-knew-what if the phone hadn't rung. *No.* It was about finally, miraculously putting their differences behind them. Talking. About her being there at a rare moment when he had needed to offload.

She sighed. The trouble was, in a lot of ways that felt a whole lot more special and intimate than sex.

Her hands were shaking so much it took three goes to get her trademark eyeliner flick right. Then there was nothing else to do but put on the Chinese silk dress. She shivered as the thick crimson silk slid over her body, pulling tight as she did up the zip.

'*It's not a date*,' she muttered one more time, pulling a severe face at her reflection in the little mirror above the sink. But her eyes still glittered with excitement.

IN THE LIBRARY Kit put down the folder of Inland Revenue correspondence he'd been going through and looked at his watch. Seven o'clock—his lip curled slightly—about three minutes later than the last time he'd checked.

He got up, stretching his aching back and feeling fleetingly glad that he didn't have a desk job. He felt stiff and tired and restless; frustrated from being inside all day and surrounded by papers. That was all it was. Nothing to do with the persistent throb of desire that had made concentrating on tax impossible, or the fact that his mind kept going back to that moment on the sofa just before the phone rang.

The moment when he had been about to kiss her. Again. Only this time it wouldn't have been because he was trying to prove anything or score points or catch her out, but because he wanted to. *Needed* to.

Letting out a ragged sigh, he ran his hands through his hair and down over his face.

What the hell was he doing asking her out to dinner?

He was looking after her for Jasper, that was all. Trying to make up a little for the unrelenting misery of her visit, and for boring her with his life story earlier.

Especially for that.

It wasn't a *date* or anything.

Grimly he turned the lights out in the library and strode through into the hall, rubbing a hand across his chin and feeling the rasp of stubble. As he went into the portrait hall he heard footsteps echoing on the stone stairs and looked up.

His throat closed and his heart sank. He had to clench his teeth together to stop himself from swearing.

Because she was beautiful. Undeniably, obviously,

hit-you-between-the-eyes beautiful, and it was going to be impossible to sit across a table from her all evening and not be aware of that for every minute. She was wearing a dress of Chinese silk that hugged her body like a second skin, but was high-necked and low-hemmed enough to look oddly demure.

Her footsteps slowed. She was looking at him, her expression uncertain, and it struck him that she was waiting for his reaction.

Swiftly he cleared his throat, rubbing his jaw again to unclench it. 'You look…great,' he said gruffly. He'd been about to say beautiful, but stopped himself at the last minute. It seemed too intimate.

'I'm way overdressed.' She'd come to a standstill halfway down the stairs and turned around, preparing to bolt back up again. 'I didn't really have anything else, but I can put on jeans—'

'No.'

The word came out more forcefully than he'd meant and echoed off the stone walls. Her eyes widened with shock, but she didn't move.

'You're fine as you are, and I'm starving. Let's just go, shall we?'

HE TOOK HER to a restaurant in Hawksworth. Tucked away in a small courtyard off the market square, it had a low-beamed ceiling, a stone-flagged floor and fires burning in each of its two rooms. Candles stuck into old wine bottles flickered on every table, throwing uneven shadows on the rough stone walls. Thanks to these it was mercifully dark and Sophie felt able to relax a little bit in her too-smart dress.

'You were right,' she said brightly, studying the menu

without taking in a single thing on it. 'It is good to be away from the castle. And it's good to be warm, too.'

The maître d', recognising Kit, had shown them to the best table in a quiet corner of the far room, next to the fire. Its warmth stole into Sophie's body, but somehow she couldn't stop herself from shivering.

'Alnburgh hasn't quite lived up to your expectations, then?' Kit asked dryly as he studied the wine list, and Sophie remembered that journey from the station in the back of the Bentley when she'd seen the castle for the first time.

'Let's just say I'm a big fan of central heating. When I was little I used to think that I wouldn't mind where I lived as long as it was warm.'

Oh, dear, that was a stupid thing to say. She looked down, picking bits of fossilised wax off the wine bottle candle-holder with a fingernail and hoping he wouldn't pick up the subject of when she was little. The last thing she wanted to talk about was her childhood.

Actually, come to think of it, there were quite a lot of things she didn't want to talk about. Or couldn't. She'd better not drink too much or she'd be letting skeletons, and Jasper, out of the closet by dessert time.

'So where *do* you live?' he asked, putting the menu down and looking at her directly.

'Crouch End.' Beneath his gaze she felt ridiculously shy. 'I share a flat with a girl called Jess. Or I did, but then I went to Paris for two months for the Resistance film and when I got back her boyfriend had moved in. I guess it might be time to look for somewhere else.'

'Would you move in with Jasper?'

She shook her head, suppressing a rueful smile as

she imagined Sergio's reaction if she did. 'I love Jasper, but it's not—'

She stopped as the waitress appeared; a slim, dark-skinned girl who slid a pencil out of her casually piled up hair to take their order. Sophie, who couldn't remember a single thing from the menu, spotted linguine on the specials board behind Kit and ordered that, cursing herself almost instantly for choosing something so inelegant to eat.

No sooner had the waitress sauntered off with cat-walk grace than the maître d' brought a dish of olives and the wine, pouring it into glasses the size of goldfish bowls with a great deal of theatre. Sophie's pulse went into overdrive as the incident in the wine cellar came rushing back to her. Looking away, she felt her cheeks flame and wondered if Kit was remembering the same thing.

When they were alone again he raised his glass and said, 'Go on.'

She made a dismissive gesture, deliberately choosing to misremember where she'd got up to. Jasper was probably one of the subjects best placed on the 'Avoid' list.

'So anyway, I'll probably be flat-hunting when I get back to London, unless I stick it out at Love Central until I find out if I've got the vampire film role, because that'll involve about four weeks' filming in Romania...' She picked up her glass and took a huge mouthful, just to shut herself up. The glass was even bigger than she thought and some of the wine dripped down her chin, reminding her even more painfully of the port.

'Is it a big part?'

Kit's voice was low. In contrast to her he was utterly relaxed, his face impassive in the firelight. But why wouldn't he be relaxed? she thought despairingly. He didn't have a thumping great crush to hide, as well as most of the truth about himself.

'No. Lots of scenes but not many lines, which is perfect—' She looked up at him from under her lashes with a grimace of embarrassment. 'The only downside is the costume. My agent is always sending me scripts for bigger parts, but I don't want to go down that route. I'm quite neurotic enough as it is.'

Aware that she was babbling again, she picked up an olive, putting it in her mouth and sucking the salty oil off her fingers while she steadied herself to continue. 'I love what I do now,' she said more slowly. 'It's fun and there's no pressure. I'm not trained or anything and I just fell into it by chance, but it means I get to travel and do interesting things, and pick up the odd useful skill too.'

The waitress arrived and set plates down between them before sauntering off again.

'Such as?'

Kit's eyes were heavy-lidded, dark-lashed, gleaming.

Sophie looked down, knowing for certain there was no way she was going to be able to eat linguine when her stomach was already in knots. She picked up her fork anyway.

'Let me see… Archery. You never know when you might have to face an invading army with only a bow and arrow—especially at Alnburgh. Milking a cow. Pole dancing. Artificial respiration.'

Kit looked up at her in surprise. 'You learned that through acting?'

'I did a season in a TV hospital drama series.' She wound ribbons of pasta around her fork, assuming a lofty tone. 'I'm surprised you don't remember it actually—it was the highlight of my career, until the scriptwriters decided to kill me off in a clifftop rescue scene in the Christmas episode instead of letting me go on to marry the consultant and do another series.'

His smile was sudden and devastating. The firelight had softened his face, smoothing away the lines of tension and disapproval, making him look less intimidating and simply very, very sexy.

'Were you disappointed?'

She shook her head. 'Not really. It was good money but too much like commitment.'

'What, marrying the consultant or doing another series?'

The low, husky pitch of his voice seemed to resonate somewhere inside her, down in the region of her pelvis.

'Both.'

THE PLACE HAD emptied and the waitress was looking bored and sulky by the time Kit eventually stood up, stooping slightly to avoid the low beams as he went to sort out the bill.

Sophie watched him, her mouth dry, her trembling hands tucked beneath her thighs on the wooden bench. The gaps in the conversation had got longer and more loaded, the undercurrents of meaning stronger. Or so it had felt to her. Maybe he had just run out of things to say to her?

They drove back in silence. The sky was moonless, and veils of mist swathed the castle like chiffon scarves, making it look oddly romantic. Sophie's hands were folded in her lap and she held herself very stiffly, as if she were physically braced against the waves of longing that were battering at her. In the light of the dashboard Kit's face was tense and unsmiling. She gave an inward moan of despair as she wondered if he'd been totally bored by the whole evening.

He pulled into the courtyard and got out of the car immediately, as if he was at pains to avoid drawing the evening out a moment longer than he had to. Sophie followed, misery and disappointment hitting her more forcefully than the cold. For all her self-lecturing earlier, she had secretly longed to break through the barriers of Kit's reserve and rekindle the spark of intimacy that had glowed so briefly between them.

She caught up with him at the top of the steps as he keyed in the number.

'Thank you for a lovely evening,' she said in an oddly subdued voice. 'It seems awful to have had such a good time when Jasper and Tatiana are at the hospital. I hope Ralph is OK.'

'Given the mess Alnburgh's finances are going to be in if he dies, I do too,' Kit said sardonically as he opened the door. Standing back to let her through, he rubbed a hand across his forehead. 'Sorry. I didn't mean it to sound like that.'

'I know.'

She stopped in front of him, instinctively reaching up to touch the side of his face.

He stiffened, and for a moment she felt a jolt of horror at the thought that she'd got it badly wrong *again*. But then he dropped his hand and looked at her, and in the split second before their mouths met she saw desire and despair there that matched her own. She let out a moan of relief as his lips touched hers, angling her head back and parting her lips as he took her face between his hands and kissed her.

It was as though he was doing something that hurt him. The kiss was hard but gentle at the same time, and the expression on his face as he pulled away was resigned—almost defeated. Arrows of anguish pierced Sophie's heart and she slid her hand round his neck, tangling her fingers in his hair as she pulled his head down again.

The door swung shut behind them, giving a bang that echoed through the empty halls. They fell back against it, Sophie pressing her shoulders against the ancient wood as her hips rose up to meet his. Her hands slid over the sinews of his back, feeling them move as their bodies pressed together and their mouths devoured each other in short, staccato bursts of longing.

'Soph? Soph, darling, is that you?'

'Jasper,' she whimpered.

Kit pulled away, jerking his head back as if he'd been struck. They could hear footsteps approaching across the stone flags of the hall. Beneath the light of the vast lantern high above, Kit's face looked as if it had been carved from ice.

Helplessly Sophie watched him turn away, then, smoothing her skirt down, she went forwards, willing her voice not to give her away.

'Yes, it's me. We didn't expect you back so...'

Her words trailed off as Jasper appeared in the doorway. His face was swollen and blotched from crying, and tears still slid from his reddened eyes.

'Oh, my darling—' she gasped.

Jasper raised his hands in a gesture of hopelessness. 'He died.'

And in an instant Sophie was beside him, taking him into her arms, stroking his hair as he laid his head on her shoulder and sobbed, murmuring to him in a voice that ached with love.

Over his shoulder she watched Kit walk away. She willed him to turn round, to look back and catch her eye and understand.

He didn't.

CHAPTER ELEVEN

AND SO, NOT quite a week after Ralph's lavish birthday party, preparations were made at Alnburgh for his funeral.

Kit returned to London the morning following Ralph's death. Sophie didn't see him before he left and though Thomas murmured something about appointments with the bank, Sophie, rigid with misery she couldn't express, wondered if he'd gone deliberately early to avoid her.

She was on edge the whole time. It felt as if her heart had been replaced with an alarm clock, like the crocodile in *Peter Pan*, making her painfully aware of every passing second. The smallest thing seemed to set her alarm bells jangling.

The bitter weather continued. The snow kept falling; brief, frequent flurries of tiny flakes that were almost invisible against the dead sky. Pipes in an unused bathroom burst, making water cascade through the ceiling in a corner of the armoury hall and giving the pewter breastplates their first clean in half a century. Thomas, who since Ralph's death seemed to have aged ten years, shuffled around helplessly, replacing buckets.

After that time in the hall Sophie didn't see Jasper cry again, but his grief seemed to turn in on itself and, without the daily focus of sitting at Ralph's bedside and the hope of his recovery to cling to, he quietly went to pieces. He was haunted by regret that he hadn't had the courage to come out about his sexuality to his father, driven to despair by the knowledge that now it was too late.

Sophie's nerves were not improved by a lonely, insecure Sergio ringing the castle at odd hours of the day and night and demanding to speak to Jasper. She fielded as many of the calls as possible. Now was not the time for the truth, but the charade had come to seem pointless and the main difficulty in Jasper and Sergio's relationship was not that it was homosexual but that Sergio was such an almighty, selfish prima donna.

On the occasions when Jasper did speak to Sergio he came off the phone with hollow eyes and a clenched jaw, and proceeded to get drunk. That was something else Sophie was worried about. It was becoming harder to ignore the fact that as the days wore on he was waking up later and making his first visit to the drinks tray in the library earlier.

But there was no one she could talk to about it. Tatiana barely emerged from her room, and Sophie sensed that speaking to Mrs Daniels or Thomas, as staff, would break some important social taboo. Of course, it was Kit that she really longed to talk to, but even if he had been there what could she say? Unless she was prepared to break Jasper's confidence, any concerns she expressed about his welfare would only serve to make Kit think more badly of her. Who could blame Jasper for drinking too much when his girlfriend had been about to leap into bed with his brother, while he was with his dying father?

As the week dragged on she missed him more and

more. She even found herself counting the days to the funeral, where she knew she would see him again.

Looking forwards to a funeral, she told herself bleakly, was a mark of a truly bad person.

THE DAY BEFORE the funeral Sophie was perched on top of a stepladder in the armoury hall. Taking down the antique pistols that had got soaked in the burst-pipe deluge, she dried them, one by one, as Thomas was anxious that, left alone, the mechanisms would rust. Sophie was very glad to have something to occupy her while Jasper huddled on the drawing room sofa, mindlessly watching horseracing.

Her roots were beginning to come through, and what she would really have liked to do was disappear into the bathroom with a packet of hair dye, but there was a line of shallowness that even she couldn't bring herself to cross. Anyway, the pistol-cleaning was curiously therapeutic. Close up, many of them were very beautiful, with delicate filigree patterns engraved into their silver barrels. She held one up to the light of the wrought-iron lantern, feeling the weight of it in her hand and wondering under what circumstances it had last been fired. A duel, perhaps, between two Fitzroy brothers, fighting over some ravishing aristocratic virgin.

The despair that was never far away descended on her again, faster than the winter twilight. If she was ravishing, or aristocratic—or a virgin for that matter— would Kit feel enough for her to want to fight for her?

Theatrically she pressed the barrel of the gun to her ribs, just below her breasts. Closing her eyes, she imagined him standing in front of her, in tight breeches and a ruffled white muslin shirt, his face tormented with silent anguish as he begged…

'Don't do it.'

Her eyes flew open. Kit was standing in the doorway, his face not tormented so much as exhausted. Longing hit her first—the forked lightning before the rumble of scarlet embarrassment that followed.

'Tell me,' he drawled coolly, picking up the stack of letters that had come in the last few days, 'had you considered suicide before, or is it being here that's driven you to make two attempts in the last week?'

Sophie made an attempt at a laugh, but it dried up in her throat and came out as a sort of bitter rasp. 'It must be. I was perfectly well adjusted before. How was your trip?'

'Frustrating.'

He didn't look up from the envelopes he was sifting through. Sophie averted her eyes in an attempt not to notice how sexy he looked, especially from her vantage point where she could see the breadth of his shoulders and the way his hair curled into the back of his neck, however, her nipples tingled in treacherous recognition. She stared at the pistol in her hand, polishing the barrel with brisk strokes of the cloth.

'I expect you'll be going back to London yourself when the funeral's over,' he said absently, as if it were of no consequence to him.

'Oh.' The idea had come out of the blue and she felt suddenly disorientated, and a little dizzy up there on the ladder. She took a quick breath, polishing harder. 'Yes. I expect so. I hadn't really thought. Are you going to be staying here for a while?'

He took one letter from the pile and threw the rest down again. 'No. I'm going back.'

'To London?'

To give her an excuse not to look at him she put the gun back on its hooks on the wall, but her hands were shaking and it slipped from her fingers. She gave a cry of horror, but with lightning reactions Kit had stepped forwards and caught it.

'Careful. There's a possibility that some of these guns might still be loaded,' he said blandly, handing it back to her. 'No. Not London. Back to my unit.'

For a moment the pain in Sophie's chest felt as if the gun *had* gone off.

'Oh. So soon?'

'There's not much I can do here.' For the first time their eyes met and he gave a brief, bitter smile. 'And at least it's a hell of a lot warmer out there.'

Sophie's heart was thumping hard enough to shake the stepladder. She could tell from his offhand tone and his abstracted expression that he was about to walk away, and she didn't know when she would see him alone again, or get the chance to say any of the millions of things that flooded her restless head at night when sleep wouldn't come and she lay awake burning for him.

'I only came back to pick this up.' He held up the letter. 'I have an appointment with Ralph's solicitor in Hawksworth, so—'

'Kit—wait.' She jumped down from the stepladder, which was a bit higher than she thought, and landed unsteadily in front of him so he had to reach out a hand to grab her arm. He withdrew it again immediately.

Sophie's cheeks flamed. 'The other night—' she began miserably, unable to raise her head. 'I just wanted you to know that it wasn't a mistake. I knew what I was doing, and I—'

His eyes held a sinister glitter, like the frost outside. Beautiful but treacherous. 'Is that supposed to make it better?'

She shook her head, aware that it was coming out wrong. 'I'm trying to explain,' she said desperately. 'I don't want you to think that Jasper and I— It's not— we're not—'

Kit's mouth twisted into a smile of weary contempt. 'I'm not blaming *you* for what happened—it was just as much my fault. But I don't think either of us can really pretend it wasn't wrong.' Moving past her, he went to the huge arched door and put his hand on the iron latch. 'Like you, I don't have that many unbreakable rules but I wasn't aware until recently that one of them is that you don't touch your brother's woman. Under any circumstances.'

'But—'

'Particularly not just because you're both bored and available.'

The cruelty of his words made her incapable of reply. The door gave its graveyard creak as he opened it and went out, leaving nothing but an icy blast of winter in his wake.

THE WINDSCREEN WIPERS beat in time to the throbbing in Kit's head, swiping the snow from in front of his eyes. But only for a minute. No sooner was the glass clear than more snow fell, obscuring everything again.

It seemed hideously symbolic of everything else in his life right now.

In London, trying to make some sense of Alnburgh's nightmarishly complicated legal and financial position, he had come up against nothing but locked doors and dead ends. But at least there he had had some perspective on the situation with Sophie.

Being back within touching distance of her had blown it all out of the water again.

Was it her acting ability or the way she looked up at him from under her eyelashes, or the fact that watching her rub the barrel of that gun had almost made him pull her down off the ladder and take her right there, against the door, that made him want to believe her? Wanted to make him accept it without question when she said that a little thing *like being Jasper's girlfriend* was no obstacle to them sleeping together?

He pulled up in the market square and switched the car engine off. For a moment he just sat there, staring straight ahead without seeing the lit-up shops, the few pedestrians, bundled up against the weather as they picked their way carefully over the snowy pavements.

Since his mother had left when he was six years old, Kit had lived without love. He didn't trust it. He had come to realise that he certainly didn't need it. Instead he had built his life on principles. Values. Moral codes. They were what informed his choices, not *feelings*.

And they were what he had to hold on to.

He got out of the car and slammed the door with unnecessary force and headed for the offices of Baines and Stanton.

THE BULL WAS beginning to fill up with after-work drinkers when Kit came out of his meeting with the solicitor. He knocked back his first whisky in a single mouthful standing at the bar, and ordered another, which he took to a table in the corner.

He intended to be there for a while; he might as well make himself comfortable. And inconspicuous. On the wall opposite he noticed the Victorian etching of Alnburgh Castle. It looked exactly the same now as it had done a hundred years ago, he thought dully. Nothing had changed at all.

Apart from the fact it was no longer anything to do with him because *Ralph Fitzroy wasn't his father.*

It was funny, he thought, frowning down into the amber depths of his glass, several whiskies later. He was a bomb-disposal expert, for God's sake. He was trained to locate explosives and disarm them before they did any damage, and all the time he'd been completely oblivious to the great big unexploded bombshell in the centre of his own life.

It explained everything, he mused as the whisky gave a sort of warm clarity to his thoughts. It explained why Ralph had been such a spiteful *bastard* when he was growing up. And why he had always refused to discuss the future of the estate. It explained…

He scowled, struggling to fit in the fact that his mother had left him with a man who wasn't his father, and failing.

Oh, well, it explained some things. But it changed everything.

Everything.

He stood up, his chest suddenly tight, his breath clogging in his throat. Then, draining his whisky in one mouthful, left the bar.

WRAPPED IN A TOWEL, still damp from the bath, Sophie put her bag on the bed and surveyed the contents in growing dismay.

Out of long habit she hadn't ever bothered to unpack, so she couldn't, even for a moment, enjoy a glimmer of hope that there might be something she'd temporarily forgotten about hanging in the wardrobe. Something smart. And black. And suitable for a funeral.

Black she could do, she thought, rifling through the contents of her case, which was like a Goth's dressing up box. It was smart and suitable where she fell down.

Knickers.

How could she have been so stupid as to spend most of the day looking for displacement activities and polishing pistols when she could have nipped out to The Fashion Capital of the North, which must surely do an extensive range of funeral attire? But it was way too late now. And she was pretty much left with one option.

She'd balled her last unlucky purchase from Braithwaite's in the bottom of the bag, from whence she'd planned to take it straight to the nearest charity shop when she got back to London, but she pulled it out again now and regarded it balefully. It was too long obviously, but if she cut it off at the knee and wore it with her black blazer, it might just do…

Rubbing herself dry, she hastily slipped on an oversized grey jumper of Jasper's and some thick hiking socks and set off downstairs. It was late. Tatiana had retired to her room ages ago and had supper on a tray, Thomas had long since gone back to his flat in the gatehouse and Sophie had helped a staggering, slightly incoherent Jasper to bed a good hour ago, after he had fallen asleep on the sofa watching *The Wizard of Oz*. However, the fact that all the lights were still on downstairs suggested Kit hadn't come back yet.

Her heart gave an uneven thud of alarm. Passing

through the portrait hall, she looked at the grandfather clock. It was almost midnight. Kit had said something about him going to see the solicitor—surely he should have been back hours ago?

Visions of icy roads, twisted metal, blue lights zigzagged through her head, filling her with anguish. How ridiculous, she told herself grimly, switching the light on to go down the kitchen steps. It was far more likely that he'd met some old flame and had gone back to her place.

The anguish of that more realistic possibility was almost worse.

She switched the kitchen light on. On the long table in the centre of the room a roast ham and roast joint of beef stood under net domes, waiting to be sliced up for the buffet at the funeral tomorrow. After that she'd be going back to London, and Kit would be leaving for some dusty camp somewhere in the Middle East.

Sophie felt her throat constrict painfully.

She'd probably never see him again. After all, she'd been friends with Jasper all these years without meeting him. She remembered the photo in the paper and wondered if she'd catch glimpses of him on the news from time to time. A horrible thought struck her: please, God, not in one of those reports about casualties—

She jumped as she heard a noise from the corridor behind her. It was a sort of rusty grating; metal against metal: the noise made by an old-fashioned key being turned in a lock—yet another piece from Alnburgh's archive of horror-film sound effects. Sophie turned around, pressing herself back against the worktop, the scissors held aloft in her hand—as if that would help.

In the dark corridor the basement door burst open.

Kit stood there, silhouetted against the blue ice-light outside. He was swaying slightly.

'Kit.' Dropping the scissors, Sophie went towards him, concern quickening inside her. 'Kit, what happened? Are you OK?'

'I'm fine.'

His voice was harsh; as bleak and cold and empty as the frozen sky behind him.

'Where's the car?' Her heart was pumping adrenaline through her, making her movements abrupt and shaky as she stepped past him and slammed the door. In the light from the kitchen his face was ashen, his lips white, but his eyes were glittering pools of darkness.

'In town. Parked in the square outside the solicitor's office. I walked back.'

'Why?'

'Because I was well over the limit to drive.'

He didn't feel it. No gentle, welcome oblivion for him. The six-mile walk home had just served to sharpen his senses and give a steel-edged sharpness to every thought in his head.

And every step of the way he'd been aware of the castle, black and hulking against the skyline, and he'd known how every potential intruder, every would-be enemy invader, every outsider, for God's sake, for the last thousand years had felt when confronted with that fortified mass of rock.

One thought had kept him going forwards. The knowledge that the six-foot-thick walls and turrets and battlements contained Sophie. Her bright hair. Her quick smile. Her irreverence and her humour. Her sweet, willing body...

'What happened?'

She was standing in front of him now, trembling slightly. Or maybe shivering with the cold. She was always cold. He frowned down at her. She appeared to be wearing a large sweater and nothing else. Except thick woollen socks, which only seemed to make her long, slender legs look even more delicious. They were bare from mid-thigh downwards, which made it hard to think clearly about the question she'd just asked, or want to take the trouble to reply.

'Kit? Was it something the solicitor said?'

She touched his hand. Her skin was actually warm for once. He longed to feel it against his.

'Ralph wasn't my father.'

He heard his own voice say the words. It was hard and maybe, just maybe a tiny bit bitter. Damn. He didn't want to be bitter.

'Oh, Kit—'

'None of this is mine,' he said, more matter-of-factly now, walking away from her into the kitchen. He turned slowly, looking around him as if seeing it all for the first time.

'It all belongs to Jasper, I suppose. The castle, the estate, the title...'

She had come to stand in the doorway, her arms folded tightly across her chest. She was looking up at him, and her eyes were liquid with compassion and understanding and...

'I don't.'

Her voice low and breathless and vibrating with emotion as she came towards him. 'I want you to know that I don't belong to Jasper. I don't belong to *anyone*.'

'And I don't have a brother any more.'

For a moment they stared at each other wordlessly.

And then he caught her warm hand in his and pulled her forwards, giving way to the onslaught of want that had battered at his defences since she'd sat down opposite him on the train.

Together they ran up the stairs, pausing halfway up at the turn of the staircase to find each other's mouths. Kit's face was frozen beneath Sophie's palms and she kissed him as if the heat of her longing could bring the warmth back into his body. His jaw was rough with stubble, his mouth tasted of whisky and as he slid his hands up beneath the sweater she gasped at the chill of his hands on her bare breasts while almost boiling over with need.

'God, Sophie...'

'Come on.'

Seizing his hand, she ran onwards, up the rest of the stairs. Desire made her disorientated, and at the top she turned right instead of left, just as she had that first night. Realising her mistake, she stopped, but before she could say anything he had taken her face in his hands and was pushing her up against the panelled wall, kissing her until she didn't care where they were, just so long as she could have him soon.

Her hips ground helplessly against him, so she could feel the hardness of his erection beneath his clothes.

'My room,' she moaned. 'It's the other way—'

'Plenty more.' He growled against her mouth and, without taking his lips from hers, felt along the panelling for the handle of the door a few feet away. As it opened he levered himself away from the wall and stooped to hoist her up against him. She wrapped her legs tightly around his waist as he carried her forwards.

Sophie wasn't sure if this was the same room she'd

stumbled into on her first night, or another one where the air was damp and the furniture draped in dust sheets. The window was tall, arched, uncurtained, and the blue light coming through it gleamed dully on the carved oak posts of an enormous bed.

As he headed towards it her insides turned liquid with lust. The room was freezing, but his breath was warm against her breasts, making her nipples harden and fizz. He was still dressed, the wool of his jacket rough and damp against her thighs. As she slid out of his arms and onto the hard, high bed she pulled it off his shoulders.

She was on her knees on the slippery damask bedspread and he stood in front of her. His face was bleached of colour, its hard contours thrown into sharp relief, his heavy-lidded eyes black and fathomless.

He was so beautiful.

Her breath caught. Her hands were shaking as she reached out to undo the buttons of his shirt. He closed his eyes, tipping his head back, and Sophie could see the muscles quilt in his jaw as he fought to keep control.

It was one battle he wasn't going to win.

Gently now, she slid her hands beneath his open shirt, feeling him flinch with his own raw need. His skin still felt chilled. Tenderness bloomed and ached inside her, giving her desire a poignancy that scared her. She felt as if she were dancing, barefoot, free, but right on the edge of a precipice.

His shirt fell away and quickly she peeled off her jumper. Slowly, tightly, she wrapped her arms around him, pressing her warm, naked body against his cold one, cradling his head, kissing his mouth, his cheekbones, his eyes, his jaw as he lowered her onto the bed.

His heartbeat was strong against her breasts. Their
ribs ground together as he undid his jeans with one hand
and kicked them off. Sophie reached up and yanked
at the damask cover so she could pull it over them, to
warm him again. She was distantly aware of its musty
smell, but she couldn't have cared less because he was
cupping her cheek, trailing the backs of his fingers with
exquisite, maddening lightness over her breast until her
nerves screamed with desperation.

Reality blurred into a dreamlike haze where she was
aware of nothing but his skin against hers, his breath
in her ear, his lips on her neck. She kept her eyes fixed
on his, swimming in their gleaming depths as beneath
the sheets his hands discovered her body.

And with each stroke of his palm, each well-placed
brush of his fingers she was discovering herself. Sex
was something she was relaxed about, comfortable with.
She knew what she was doing, and she enjoyed it. It
was *fun*.

And this was as far removed from anything she'd
ever felt before as silk was from sackcloth. This wasn't
fun, it was essential. As he entered her, gently, deeply,
she wasn't sure if it was more like dying or being born
again.

Her cry of need hung in the frigid air.

She had never known anything more perfect. For a
moment they were both still, adjusting to the new bliss
of being joined together, and, looking into his eyes, she
wanted to make it last for ever.

But it was impossible. Her body was already crying out for more, her hips beginning to move of their
own accord, picking up their rhythm from him. His
thumb brushed over her lips, and she caught it between

her teeth as with the other hand he found her clitoris, moving his fingertip over it with every slow, powerful thrust.

The thick, ages-old silence of the room pooled around them again. The massive bed was too strong to creak as their bodies moved. Sophie wanted to look at him for ever. She wanted to hold for a lifetime the image of his perfect face, close to hers, as she spiralled helplessly into the most profound chasm of sensation. Their legs were entwined, his muscles hard against hers, and she didn't know where he ended and she began.

She didn't know anything any more. As a second cry—her high, broken sob of release—shattered the stillness she could only feel that everything she'd ever thought she believed was ashes and dust.

KIT SLEPT.

Whether it was the whisky or the six-mile walk or the shattering, deathlike orgasm he didn't know, but for the first time in years he slept like the angels.

He woke as the sun was coming up, streaking the sky with rose-pink ribbons and filling the room with the melting light of dawn. In his arms Sophie slept on, her back pressed against his chest, her bottom warm and deliciously soft against his thighs.

Or, more specifically, against his erection.

Gritting his teeth, he willed it away as remorse began to ebb through him, dissolving the haze of repletion and leaving him staring reality in the face. He closed his eyes again, not wanting to look at reality, or at Sophie, whose vibrant beauty had an ethereal quality in the pink half-light. As a way of blotting out the anger and the hurt and the shock of his discovery, last night had been perfect—more than he could have hoped for, and certainly more than he deserved. But it was a one-off. It couldn't happen again.

Sophie stirred in his arms, moving her hips a fraction, pressing herself harder against the ache of his erection. He bit back a moan, dragging his mind back from the memories of her unbuttoning his shirt, wrapping her arms around him and holding him when he most needed to be held, folding herself around him as he entered her...

The whisky might have blunted the pain and temporarily short-circuited his sense of honour, but it hadn't dulled his memory. Every detail was there, stored and ready for instant replay in the back of his head. A fact that he suspected was going to prove extremely inconvenient in the nights ahead when he was alone in a narrow bunk, separated from the rest of his men by the thinnest of makeshift walls.

Rolling out of bed, he picked his jeans up from the floor and pulled them on. The pink light carried an illusion of warmth, but the room was like a fridge and he had to clench his teeth together to stop them chattering as he reached into the sleep-warm depths of the bed and slid his arms under her.

She sighed as he gathered her up as gently as possible, but she didn't wake. Kit found himself fighting the urge to smile as he recalled the swiftness with which she'd fallen asleep on the train the first time he'd seen her, and the way it had both intrigued and irritated him. But, looking down into her face as he carried her down the shadowy corridor to her own room, the smile faded again. She was like no woman he'd ever known before. She'd appeared from nowhere, defiant, elusive, contradictory, and somehow managed to slip beneath his defences when he'd wanted only to push her away.

How had she done that?

With one shoulder he nudged open the door to her room. The window faced north, so no dawn sunlight penetrated here, and it was even colder, if that were possible, than the room they'd just left. It was also incredibly neat, he noticed with a flash of surprise, as if she was ready to leave at any moment. Her hair was fragrant and silken against his bare chest as he laid her gently down on the bed, rolling her sideways a little so he could pull back the covers and ease them over her.

Her eyes half opened as he tucked her in and she gazed up at him for a moment, her lips curving into a sleepy smile as she reached out and stroked the back of her hand down his midriff.

'It's cold without you,' she murmured. 'Come back.'

'I can't.' His voice was like sandpaper and he grasped her hand before it went any lower, his fingers tightening around hers for a moment as he laid it back on the bed. 'It's morning.'

She rolled onto her back and gave a little sighing laugh. 'It's over, you mean.'

'It has to be.' He pushed the heels of his hands into his eyes, physically stopping himself from looking at her as he spoke so his resolve wouldn't weaken. 'We can't change what we did last night, but we can't repeat it either. We just need to get through today without giving Jasper any reason to suspect.'

Against the pillow her face was still and composed, her hair spilling around it and emphasising its pallor. She closed her eyes.

'OK.'

The small, resigned word wasn't what he had expected and it pushed knives of guilt into his gut. Why was she making him feel as if this were his fault? Last night they had both been reckless but the result was just the logical conclusion to everything that had happened between them since the moment they'd met. It had felt inevitable somehow, but nonetheless forbidden.

Kit turned away and walked to the door, bracing his arm against the frame before he opened it and saying with great weariness, 'Sophie, what did you expect?'

Her eyes opened slowly, and the smile she gave him was infinitely sad.

'Nothing,' she said softly. 'Nothing.'

After he'd gone Sophie rolled over and let the tears spill down her cheeks.

He had slept with her because he'd finally found a get-out clause in his moral rule book. He no longer had a duty to Jasper, and that made it OK for him. But what about her?

Last night she thought he understood, without making her spell it out, that she wasn't betraying Jasper by sleeping with him.

It seemed he didn't.

She hadn't expected for ever. She hadn't expected declarations of undying love. Only for him to trust her.

CHAPTER TWELVE

'THE CARS are here, madam.'

Thomas appeared in the hallway, his face rigidly blank as he made his announcement. But Sophie heard the slight break in his voice and felt the lump of emotion in her throat swell a little.

She mustn't cry. Not when Tatiana was holding herself together with such dignity. Getting into the gleaming black Bentley, she was the picture of sober elegance in a narrow-fitting black skirt and jacket, her eyes hidden by a hat with a tiny black net veil. Jasper got in beside her. He was grey-faced, hollow-cheeked, a ghost of the languid, laughing boy she knew in London. She noticed his throat working as he glanced at the hearse in front, where Ralph's polished coffin lay decked in white flowers, and as he settled himself in the back of the car he had to twist his hands together to stop them shaking.

Poor Jasper. She had to stay strong for him. Today was going to be such an ordeal, and his grief was so much more profound than anything she'd ever experienced. She dug her nails into her palm. And anyway, what did she have to cry about? She'd hardly known Ralph. And it was stupid, *stupid* to be upset over a one-night stand with a man she wasn't going to see again after today.

'After you.'

She looked up and felt her knees buckle a little. Kit was standing behind her on the steps to the castle, his perfectly tailored black suit and tie cruelly highlighting his austere beauty. His face was completely expressionless, and his silver eyes barely flickered over her as he spoke.

His indifference was like knives in her flesh. It was as if last night had never happened.

'Oh. I'm not sure I should go in the official car,' she stammered, looking down at her shoes. 'I'm not family or anything.'

'That makes two of us,' he murmured acidly. 'You're Jasper's girlfriend, that's close enough. Just get in—unless you're planning to walk in those heels.'

She did as she was told, but without any of the grace with which Tatiana had performed the manoeuvre, and was aware that Kit would have got a very unflattering view of her bottom in the tight black dress. She wondered if he'd seen that the hem was stuck up with Sellotape where she'd hurriedly cut it off at the knee this morning and hadn't had time to sew it.

Further evidence of her lack of class. Another reason for him to put her in the category of 'Women to Sleep With' (subsection: Once) rather than 'Women to Date'.

He got in beside her and an undertaker with a permanent expression of compassionate respect shut the door. Sophie found herself huddling close to Jasper so she could leave an inch of cream leather seat between her leg and Kit's. As the car moved silently beneath the arched gateway she bit her lip and kept her head turned away from him, her gaze fixed out of the window. But she could still catch the faint dry, delicious scent of his skin and that was enough to make the memories of last night come flooding back. She wished she could switch them off, as Thomas had switched off the water supply when the pipe had burst. But even if she could, she thought sadly, her body would still remember and still throb with longing for him.

THE ROSE-PINK SUNRISE had delivered a beautiful winter's day for Ralph's send-off—crisp, cold and glittering, just like the day of his party. The leaden clouds of the last grim week had lifted to reveal a sky of clean, clear blue.

Outside the church of St John the Baptist people stood in groups, stamping their feet to keep warm as they talked. Some were smartly dressed in black, but most of them wore everyday outdoor gear, and Sophie realised they must be local people, drawn by the social spectacle rather than grief. They fell silent and turned sombre, curious faces towards them as the cars turned into the churchyard.

'I forgot to bring the monkey nuts,' muttered Jasper with uncharacteristic bitchiness.

'People are curious,' said Tatiana in a flat, cold voice. 'They want to see if we feel things differently from them. We don't, of course. The difference is we don't show our feelings.'

Sophie bit her lip. She was one of those people, with her cheap dress and her Sellotaped hem. She wasn't part of the 'we' that Tatiana talked about. She wasn't even Jasper's girlfriend, for pity's sake. As they got out of the car and Jasper took his mother's arm to escort her into the church, Sophie tried to slip to the back, looking for Thomas and Mrs Daniels to sit with. A firm hand gripped her arm.

'Oh, no, you don't,' said Kit grimly.

He kept hold of her arm as they progressed slowly down the aisle of the packed church, behind Tatiana and Jasper and the coffin. Torn between heaven and hell at his closeness, Sophie was aware of people's heads turning, curious eyes sweeping over her beneath the brims of countless black hats, no doubt wondering who she was and what right she had to be there. She felt a barb of anguish as she realised people must think she was with Kit.

If only.

'I am the resurrection and the life...'

Beside her Kit's hands were perfectly steady as he held his service sheet without looking at it. Sophie didn't allow herself to glance at him, but even so she knew that his gaze was fixed straight ahead and that his silver eyes would be hard and dry, because it was as if she had developed some supernatural power that made her absolutely instinctively aware of everything about him.

Was that what loving someone did to you?

She lifted her head and looked up at the stained-glass window above the altar. The winter sunlight was shining through it, illuminating the jewel-bright colours and making the saints' faces positively glow with righteousness. She smiled weakly to herself. It's divine retribution, isn't it? she thought. My punishment for playing fast and loose with the affections of Jean-Claude and countless others. For thinking I was above it all and being scornful about love...

There was a shuffling of feet as the organ started and the congregation stood up. Sophie hastily followed suit, turning over her service sheet and trying to work out where the words to the hymn were. She was aware of Kit, towering above her like some dark angel, as he handed her an open hymn book, tapping the right page with a finger.

'I vow to thee my country...'

It was a hymn about sacrifice. Numbly Kit registered the familiar lines about laying down your life for your nation and wondered what the hell Ralph knew about any of that. As far as Kit knew, Ralph had never put his own needs, his own desires anything but first. He had lived for pleasure. He had died, the centre of attention at his own lavish party, not alone and thousands of miles from home on some hot, dusty roadside.

He would never have sacrificed his happiness for the sake of his brother.

Was that yet another item on his list of character flaws, or evidence that he was a hell of a lot cleverer than Kit after all?

Kit let the hymn book in his hands drop and closed his eyes as the hymn reached its stirring climax. Everyone sat down again, and as Sophie moved beside him he caught a breath of her perfume and the warmth of her body on the arctic air.

Want whiplashed through him, so that he had to grip the back of the pew in front to steady himself. Kit had attended too many funerals, carried too many flag-draped coffins onto bleak airfields to be unaware that life was short. Rules and principles didn't help when you were dead.

Joy should be seized. Nights like the one he'd just spent with Sophie should be celebrated.

Shouldn't they?

In the elaborately carved pulpit supplied by another long-gone Fitzroy, the vicar cleared his throat and pre-

pared to start his address. Kit forced himself to drag his
attention away from Sophie's hands, resting in her lap.
The skin was translucent pale against her black dress.
They looked cold. He wanted to warm them, as she'd
warmed him last night.

'We come together today to celebrate the life of
Ralph Fitzroy, who to those gathered here was not just
the Earl of Hawksworth, but a husband, father and
friend.'

It was just sex. That was what she'd said on the phone
the first time he'd seen her, wasn't it? Just sex. He had
to forget it. Especially now, in the middle of a funeral…

'Let's just take a few moments of silent reflection,'
the vicar encouraged, 'to enjoy some personal memories of Lord Fitzroy, and reflect on the many ways in
which he touched our lives…'

Ye Gods, thought Kit despairingly, rubbing at the
tense muscles across his forehead. In his case, remembering the ways in which Ralph had touched his life
really wasn't such a good idea. All around him he
was aware of people reaching for tissues, sliding arms
around each other in mutual support while he sat locked
in the private dungeon of his own bitterness. Alone.

And then, very gently Sophie put her hand over his,
lacing her cold fingers through his, caressing the back
of his hand with her thumb with a touch that had nothing to do with sex, but was about comfort and understanding.

And he wasn't alone any more.

'LOVELY SERVICE,' PEOPLE MURMURED, dabbing their eyes
as they filed out into the sharp sunlight to the strains

of The Beatles singing 'In My Life'. That had been Jasper's idea.

'You OK?' Sophie asked him, slipping her arm through his as Tatiana was swept up in a subdued round of air-kissing and clashing hat brims.

'Bearing up.' He gave her a bleak smile. 'I need a drink.'

'What happens now?'

'We go back for the interment.' He shuddered. 'There's a Fitzroy family vault at Alnburgh, below the old chapel in the North Gate. It's tiny, and just like the location for a low-budget horror film, so I'll spare you that grisly little scene. Mum and I, and the vicar—and Kit too, I suppose—will do the honours, by which time everyone should have made their way back up to the castle for the drinks. Would you mind staying here and sort of shepherding them in the right direction?'

In spite of the sunshine the wind sweeping the exposed clifftop was like sharpened razor blades. Jasper was rigid with cold and spoke through clenched teeth to stop them chattering. Weight had dropped off him in the last week, Sophie noticed, but whether it was from pining for his father or for Sergio she wasn't sure. Reaching up, she pressed a kiss on his frozen cheek.

'Of course I will. Go and say your goodbyes.'

He got into the car beside Tatiana. 'Save a drink for me,' he said dismally. 'Don't let the hordes drink us dry.'

Sophie bent to look at him through the open door. 'Of course I will.'

She turned round. Kit was standing behind her, obviously waiting to get into the car, his eyes fixed on some point in the far distance rather than at her rear.

'Sorry.' Hastily Sophie stepped out of the way. 'Are

you going to the interment too?' she added in a low voice.

A muscle twitched in his cheek. 'Yes. For appearance's sake. At some point Jasper and I need to have a proper talk, but today isn't the right time.' He looked at her, almost reluctantly, with eyes that were as bleak as the snow-covered Cheviots stretching away behind him. 'At some point you and I should probably talk too.'

An icy gust of wind whipped a strand of hair across Sophie's face. Moving her head to flick it out of the way again, a movement in the distance caught her eye. Someone was vaulting over the low wall that separated the graveyard from the road, loping towards them between the frosty headstones.

Oh, no... Oh, please, no... Not now...

Sophie felt the blood drain from her head. It was a familiar enough figure, although incongruous in this setting. A bottle of vodka swung from one hand.

'Today might not be the best time for that either,' she said, folding her arms across her chest to steady herself. 'You should go—I think they're waiting.'

It was an answer of sorts, Kit thought blackly as he lowered himself into the Bentley and slammed the door. Just not the one he'd hoped for.

As the car began to move slowly away in the wake of the hearse Kit watched her take a few steps backwards, and then turn and slip into the cluster of people left behind outside the church. He lost sight of her for a few seconds, but then caught a glimpse of her hair, fiery against the monochrome landscape. She was hurrying in the direction of someone walking through the churchyard.

'Such a lot of people,' said Tatiana vaguely, pulling her black gloves off. 'Your father had so many friends.'

Jasper put an arm around her. 'It was a great service. Even Dad, who hated church, would have enjoyed it.'

Kit turned his face to the window.

The man's clothes marked him out as being separate from the funeral-goers. He was dressed neither as a mourner nor in the waterproofs and walking boots of the locals, but in skintight jeans, some kind of on-trend, tailored jacket with his shirt tails hanging down beneath it. Urban clothes. There was a kind of defiant swagger to the man's posture and movements, as if he was doing something reckless but didn't care, and as the car waited to pull out onto the main road Kit watched in the wing mirror as Sophie approached him, shaking her head. It looked as if she was pleading with him.

The car moved again, and for a few seconds the view in the wing mirror was a blur of hedge and empty sky. Kit stared straight ahead. His hands were clenched into fists, his heart beating heavily in his chest.

He waited, counting the beats. And then, just before the bend in the road when the church would be out of sight, he turned and looked back in time to see her put her arms around him.

When she'd taken his hand in church like that, it had changed something. Or maybe that was wrong—maybe it hadn't changed, so much as shown him what was there before that he hadn't wanted to admit.

That possibly what he wanted from her—with her—wasn't just sex. And the hope that, at some point, when she had settled things with Jasper, she might want that too.

It looked as if he'd been wrong.

'PLEASE, SERGIO. IT WON'T be for long. A couple of hours—maybe three, just until the funeral is over.'

Sergio twitched impatiently out of her embrace. 'Three hours,' he sneered. 'You make it sound like nothing, but every hour is like a month. I've waited over a week already and I've just spent all day on a stupid train. I *need* him, Sophie. And he needs me.'

'I know, I know,' Sophie soothed, glancing back at the church with its dwindling crowd of mourners, and sending up a silent prayer for patience. Or, failing that, forgiveness for putting her hands round Sergio's elegant, self-absorbed neck and killing him.

What had Kit meant, they needed to talk? And why did bloody Sergio have to choose the very moment when she could have asked him to stage his ridiculous, melodramatic appearance?

'You don't,' Sergio moaned theatrically. 'Nobody knows.'

'I know that Jasper's in despair without you,' Sophie said with exaggerated patience. 'I know he misses you every second, but I also know that his mother needs him right now. And he needs to get closure on this before he can be with you properly.'

It was the right thing to say. 'Closure' was the kind of psychological pseudoscience that Sergio lapped up.

'Do you think so?'

'Uh-huh.' Sensing victory, Sophie took the bottle out of his hand and began to lead him through the gravestones back in the direction from which he'd just come. 'And I also think that you're tired. You've had a horrible week and an exhausting journey. The pub in the village has rooms—why don't we see if they have anything available and I'll tell Jasper to join you there as soon as he can? It would be better than staying at the castle, just for now.'

Sergio cast a wistful glance up at Alnburgh Castle, its turrets and battlements gilded by the low winter sun. Sophie sensed rebellion brewing and increased her pace, which wasn't easy with her heels snagging into the frosty grass. 'Here—I'll come with you and make sure you're settled,' she said firmly. 'And then I'll go to Jasper and tell him where you are.'

Sergio took her arm and gave it a brief, hard squeeze, in the manner of a doomed character in a war film. His blue eyes were soulful. 'Thank you, Sophie, I do as you say. I *trust* you.'

THE HALLWAY WAS filled with the sound of voices and a throng of black-clad people, many of whom had been here only a week earlier for Ralph's party. After the surreal awfulness of the little scene in the Alnburgh vault Kit felt in desperate need of a stiff drink, but he couldn't go more than a couple of paces without someone else waylaying him to offer condolences, usually followed by congratulations on the medal.

His replies were bland and automatic, and all the time he was aware of his heart beating slightly too fast and his body vibrating with tension as he surreptitiously looked around for Sophie.

'Your father must have been immensely proud of you,' said an elderly cousin of Ralph's in an even more elderly fur coat. The statement was wrong in so many ways that for a moment Kit couldn't think what could have prompted her to make it. 'For the George Medal,' she prompted, taking a sip of sherry and looking at him expectantly.

It was far too much trouble to explain that such was
his father's indifference that he hadn't told him. Oh,
and that he wasn't actually his father either. Instead he
gave a neutral smile and made a polite reply before ex-
cusing himself and moving away.

Conversation was impossible when there was so
much that he couldn't say. To anyone except Sophie.

He had to find her.

'Kit.'

The voice was familiar, but unexpected. Feeling a
hand on his arm, Kit looked around to see a large black
hat and, beneath it, looking tanned, beautiful but dis-
tinctly uneasy, was Alexia.

'Darling, I'm so sorry,' she murmured, holding on
to her hat with one hand as she reached to kiss each of
his cheeks. 'Such a shock. You must all be devastated.'

'Something like that. I wasn't expecting to see you
here.'

Kit knew that his voice suggested that the surprise
wasn't entirely a pleasant one, and mentally berated
himself. It wasn't Alexia's fault he'd seen Sophie falling
into the arms of some tosser in a girl's jacket amongst
the headstones, or that she'd subsequently disappeared.

'Olympia and I were in St Moritz last weekend, but
when her mother told us what happened I just wanted to
be here. For you, really. I know I wasn't lucky enough
to know your father well, but…' Beneath her skiing tan
her cheeks were pink. 'I wanted to make sure you're
OK. I still care about you, you know…'

'Thanks.'

She bent her head slightly, so the brim of her hat hid
her face, and said quietly, 'Kit—it must be a horrible
time. Don't be alone.'

Kit felt a great wave of despair wash over him. What was this, International Irony Day? For just about the first time in his life he didn't *want* to be alone, but the only person he wanted to be with didn't seem to share the feeling.

'I'll bear that in mind,' he said wearily, preparing to make his escape. And no doubt he would, but not in the way she meant.

'Hello, Kit—so sorry about your father.'

If they were standing in the armoury hall, Kit reflected, at this point he would have had difficulty stopping himself grabbing one of the pistols so thoroughly polished by Sophie and putting it against his head. As it was he was left with no choice but to submit to Olympia Rothwell-Hyde's over-scented embrace and muster a death-row smile.

'Olympia.'

'Ma said you were an absolute *god* at the party, when it happened,' she said, blue eyes wide with what possibly passed for sincerity in the circles she moved in. 'Real heroic stuff.'

'Obviously not,' Kit said coolly, glancing round, 'since we find ourselves here…'

Olympia, obviously unaware that it was International Irony Day, wasn't thrown off her stride for a second. Leaning forwards, sheltering beneath the brim of Alexia's hat like a spy in an Inspector Clousseau film, she lowered her voice to an excited whisper.

'Darling, I have to ask… That redhead you sat next to in church. She looks terribly like a girl we used to know at school called Summer Greenham, but it *can't* be—'

Electricity snapped through him, jolting him out of his apathy.

'Sophie. She's called *Sophie* Greenham.'

'Then it *is* her!' Olympia's upper-crust voice held a mixture of incredulity and triumph as she looked at Alexia. 'Who can blame her for ditching that embarrassing drippy hippy name? She should have changed her surname too—apparently it came from the lesbian peace camp place. Anyway, darling, none of that explains what she's *doing* here. Does she work here, because if so I would *so* keep an eye on the family silver—'

'She's Jasper's girlfriend.' Maybe if he said it often enough he'd accept it.

'No way. No. *Way!* Seriously? Ohmigod!'

Kit stood completely still while this pantomime of disbelief was going on, but beneath his implacable exterior icy bursts of adrenaline were pumping through his veins.

'Meaning?'

Beside Olympia, Alexia shifted uneasily on her designer heels. Olympia ploughed on, too caught up in the thrill of gossip to notice the tension that suddenly seemed to crackle in the air.

'She came to our school from some filthy traveller camp—an aunt took pity on her and wanted to civilise her before it was too late, or something. Whatevs.' She waved a dismissive hand. 'Total waste of money as she was expelled in the end, for stealing.' She took a sip of champagne before continuing in her confident, bitchy drawl. 'It was just before the school prom and a friend of ours had been sent some money by her mother to buy a dress. Well, the cash disappeared from the dorm and suddenly—by astonishing coincidence—Miss Greenham-Extremely-Common, who had previously rocked the jumble-sale-reject look, appears with a *very* nice new dress.'

A pulse was throbbing in Kit's temple. 'And you put two and two together,' he said icily.

Olympia looked surprised and slightly indignant. 'And reached a very obvious four. Her aunt admitted she hadn't given her any money—I think the fees were quite enough of a stretch for her—and the only explanation Summer could give was that her mother had bought it for her. Her mother who lived on a *bus*, and hadn't been seen for, like, a *year* or something and so was conveniently unavailable for comment, having nothing as modern as a *telephone*...'

Looking down at the floor, Kit shook his head and gave a soft, humourless laugh. 'And therefore unavailable to back her up either.'

'Oh, come on, Kit,' said Olympia, in the kind of jolly, dismissive tone that suggested they were having a huge joke and he was spoiling it. 'Sometimes you don't need *evidence* because the truth is so obvious that everyone can see it. And anyway—' she gave him a sly smirk from beneath her blonde flicky fringe '—if she's Jasper's girlfriend, why would she have just been checking into a room in the pub in the village with some bloke? Alexia and I went for a quick drinkie to warm ourselves up after the service and saw her.' The smirk hardened into a look of grim triumph. 'Room three, if you don't believe me.'

IF SOPHIE HAD known she was going to walk back from the village to the castle in the snow, she would have left the shag-me shoes at home and worn something more sensible.

It was just as well her toes were frozen, since she suspected they'd be even more painful if they weren't. Unfortunately even the cold couldn't anaesthetise the raw blisters on her heels and it was only the thought of finding Kit, hearing what it was he had to say that kept her going.

She also had to find Jasper and break the news to him that Sergio had turned up. Having ordered an enormous breakfast for him to mop up some of the vodka and waited to make sure he ate it, she had finally left him crashed out on the bed. He shouldn't be any trouble for the next hour or so, but now the formal part of the funeral was over she knew that Jasper wouldn't want to wait to go and see him. And also she was guiltily keen to pass over the responsibility for him to Jasper as soon as possible. Sitting and listening to him endlessly talking about his emotions, analysing every thought that had flickered across his butterfly brain in the last week had made her want to start on the vodka herself. She had found herself thinking wistfully of Kit's reserve. His understatement. His emotional integrity.

Gritting her teeth against the pain, she quickened her steps.

The drive up to the castle was choked with cars. People had obviously decided they were staying for a while, and parked in solid rows, making it impossible for anyone to leave. Weaving through them, Sophie could hear the sound of voices spilling out through the open door and carrying on the frosty air.

Her heart was beating rapidly as she went up the steps, and it was nothing to do with the brisk walk. She paused in the armoury hall, tugging down her jacket and smoothing her skirt with trembling hands, noticing abstractedly that the Sellotaped hem was coming down.

'Is everything all right, Miss Greenham?'

Thomas was standing in the archway, holding a tray of champagne, looking at her with some concern. Sophie realised what a sight she must look in her sawn-off dress with her face scarlet from cold and exertion, clashing madly with her hair.

'Oh, yes, thank you. I just walked up from the village, that's all. Do you know where Jasper is?'

'Master Jasper went up to his room when he got back from the interment,' said Thomas, lowering his voice respectfully. 'I don't think he's come down yet.'

'OK. Thanks. I'll go up and see if he's all right.' She hesitated, feeling a warm blush gather in her already fiery cheeks. 'Oh, and I don't suppose you know where I could find Kit, do you?'

'I believe he's here somewhere,' Thomas said, turning round creakily, putting the champagne glasses in peril as he surveyed the packed room behind him. 'I saw him come in a little while ago. Ah, yes—there he is, talking to the young lady in the large hat.'

Of course, he was so much taller than everyone else so it wasn't too hard to spot him. He was standing with his back half to her, so she couldn't see his face properly, only the scimitar curve of one hard cheekbone. A cloud of butterflies rose in her stomach.

And then she saw who he was talking to. And they turned into a writhing mass of snakes.

CHAPTER THIRTEEN

A CHILDHOOD SPENT moving around, living in cramped spaces with barely any room for personal possessions, being ready to move on at a moment's notice, had left its mark on Sophie in many ways. One of them was that she travelled light and rarely unpacked.

Once she'd seen Jasper it didn't take her long to get her few things together. It took a little longer to get herself together, but after a while she felt strong enough to say goodbye to her little room and slip along the corridor to the back staircase.

It came out in the armoury hall. As she went down the sound of voices rose up to meet her—less subdued and funereal now as champagne was consumed, interspersed with laughter. She found herself listening out for Kit's voice amongst the others, and realised with a tearing sensation in her side that she'd never heard him laugh. Not really laugh, without irony or bitterness or cynicism.

But maybe he would be laughing now, with Olympia.

She came down the last step. The door was ahead of her, half-open and letting in arctic air and winter sunshine. Determined not to look round in case she lost her nerve, Sophie kept her head down and walked quickly towards it.

The cold air hit her as she stepped outside, making

her gasp and bringing a rush of tears to her eyes. She sniffed hard, and brushed them impatiently away with the sleeve of her faithful old coat.

'So you're leaving.'

She whirled round. Kit was standing at the top of the steps, in the open doorway. His hands were in his pockets, his top button undone and his tie pulled loose, but despite all that there was still something sinister in his stillness, the rigid blankness of his face.

The last glowing embers of hope in Sophie's heart went out.

'Yes.' She nodded, and even managed a brief smile although meeting his eye was too much to attempt. 'I saw you talking to Olympia. It's a small world. I suppose she told you everything.'

'Yes. Not that it makes any difference. So now you're going—just like that. Were you going to say goodbye?'

Sophie kept her eyes fixed on the ivy growing up the wall by the steps, twining itself around an old cast-iron downpipe. Of course it didn't make any difference, she told herself numbly. He already knew she was nothing. Her voice seemed to come from very far away. 'I'll write to Tatiana. She's surrounded by friends at the moment—I don't want to barge in.'

'It was Jasper I was thinking of. What about him?'

Sophie moved her bag from one hand to the other. She was conscious of holding herself very upright, placing her feet carefully together, almost as if if she didn't take care to do this she might just collapse. She still couldn't bring herself to look at him.

'He'll be OK now. He doesn't need me.'

At the top of the steps Kit made some sudden movement. For a moment she thought he had turned and was going to go inside, but instead he dragged a hand through his hair and swung back to face her again. This time there was no disguising the blistering anger on his face.

'So, who is he? I mean, he's obviously pretty special that he's come all this way to claim you and you can't even wait until the funeral is over before you go and fall into bed with him. Is it the same one I heard you talking to on the train, or someone else?'

After a moment of confusion it dawned on Sophie that he must have seen her with Sergio. And jumped, instantly, to the wrong conclusion.

Except there wasn't really such a thing as a wrong conclusion. In her experience 'wrong conclusion' tended to mean the same thing as 'confirmation of existing prejudice', and she had learned long ago that no amount of logical explanations could alter people's prejudices. That had to come from within themselves.

'Someone else.'

'Do you love him?' Suddenly the anger that had gripped him seemed to vanish and he just sounded very tired. Defeated almost.

Sophie shook her head. Her knees were shaking, her chest burning with the effort of holding back the sobs that threatened to tear her apart.

'No.'

'Then why? Why are you going to him?'

'Because he'd fight for me.' She took a deep breath and lifted her head. In a voice that was completely calm, completely steady she said, 'Because he trusts me.'

And then she turned and began to walk away.

BLINDLY KIT SHOULDERED his way through the people standing in the hall. Seeing his ashen face and the

stricken expression on it, some of them exchanged
loaded glances and murmured about grief striking even
the strongest.

Reaching the library, he shut the door and leaned
against it, breathing hard and fast.

Trust. That was the last thing he'd expected her to
say.

He brought his hands up to his head, sliding his fingers into his hair as his mind raced. He had learned
very early on in life that few people could be trusted,
and since then he had almost prided himself on his
cynicism. It meant he was one step ahead of the game
and gave him immunity from the emotional disasters
that felled others.

It also meant he had just had to watch the only
woman he wanted to be with walk away from him, right
into the arms of someone else. Someone who wore designer clothes and left his shirt tails trailing and *trusted*
her. Someone who would fight for her.

Well, trust might not be his strong suit, but fighting
was something he could do.

He threw open the door, and almost ran straight into
the person who was standing right on the other side of it.

'Alexia, what the—?'

'I wanted to talk.' She recovered from her obvious
fright pretty quickly, following him as he kept on walking towards the noise of the party. 'There's something
I need to tell you.'

'Now isn't a good time,' he said, moving through
the groups of people still standing in the portrait hall,
gritting his teeth against the need to be far more bru-
tally honest.

'I know. I'm sorry, but it's bothered me all these

years.' She caught up with him as he went through the archway into the armoury hall and moved in front of him as he reached the door. 'That thing that happened at school. It wasn't Summer, it was Olympia. She set it all up. I mean, Summer—Sophie—did have the dress and I don't know how she got the money to pay for it, but it certainly wasn't by stealing it from the dorm. Olympia just said it was.'

'I know,' Kit said wearily. 'I never doubted that bit.'

'Oh.' Alexia had taken her hat off now, and without it she looked oddly exposed and slightly crestfallen. 'I know it's ages ago and it was just some silly school-girl prank, but hearing Olympia say it again like that, I didn't like it. We're adults now. I just wanted to make sure you knew the truth.'

'The truth is slightly irrelevant really. It's what we're prepared to believe that matters.' He hesitated, his throat suddenly feeling as if he'd swallowed arsenic. 'The other thing—about her checking into the hotel with a man. Was that one of Olympia's fabrications too?'

'No, that was true.' Alexia was looking at him almost imploringly. 'Kit—are you really OK? Can I help?'

From a great distance he recognised her pain as being similar to his own. It made him speak gently to her.

'No, I'm not. But you have already.'

He wove his way through the parked cars jamming the courtyard and broke into a run as he reached the tower gate. At the sides of the driveway the snow was still crisp and unmarked, but as he ran down he noticed the prints Sophie's high-heeled shoes had made and they made her feel closer—as if she hadn't really gone. When he reached the road through the village they were lost amongst everyone else's.

The King's Arms was in the mid-afternoon lull between lunchtime and evening drinkers. The landlord sat behind the bar reading the *Racing Times*, but he got to his feet as Kit appeared.

'Major Fitzroy. I mean Lord Fitzr—'

Kit cut straight through the etiquette confusion. 'I'm looking for someone,' he said harshly. 'Someone staying here. Room three, I believe? I'll see myself up.'

Without giving the flustered landlord time to respond he headed for the stairs, taking them two at a time. Room three was at the end of the short corridor. An empty vodka bottle stood outside it. Kit hammered on the door.

'Sophie!'

Kit listened hard, but the only sounds were muted voices from a television somewhere and the ragged rasp of his own breathing. His tortured mind conjured an image of the man he'd seen earlier pausing as he unzipped Sophie's dress and her whispering, *Don't worry—he'll go away...*

But he wouldn't. Not until he'd seen her.

'Sophie!'

Clenching his hand into a fist, he was just about to beat on the door again when it opened an inch. A face—puffy-eyed, swarthy, unshaven—peered out at him.

'She's not here.'

With a curse of pure rage, Kit put his shoulder to the door. Whoever it was on the other side didn't put up much resistance and the door opened easily. Glancing at him only long enough to register that he was naked except for a small white towel slung around his hips, Kit pushed past and strode into the room.

In a heartbeat he took in the clothes scattered over

the floor—black clothes, like puddles of tar on the cream carpet—the wide bed with its passion-tumbled covers and the room darkened, and he thought he might black out.

'Kit—' Jasper leapt out of the bed, dragging the rumpled sheet and pulling it around himself. Blinking, Kit shook his head, trying to reconcile what he was actually seeing with what he had expected.

'Jasper?'

'Look, I didn't want you to find out like this.' Jasper paused and ducked his head for a moment, but then gathered himself and raised his head again, looking Kit squarely in the eye while the man in the white towel went to his side. 'But it's probably time you knew anyway. I can't go on hiding who I really am just because it doesn't fit the Fitzroy mould. I love Sergio. And I know what you're going to say but—'

Kit gave a short, incredulous laugh as relief burst through him. 'It's the best news I've had for a long time. Really. I can't tell you how pleased I am.' He turned and shook hands with the bewildered man in the white towel, and then went over to Jasper and embraced him briefly, hard. 'Now please—if Sophie's not here, where the hell is she?'

The smile faded from Jasper's face. 'She's gone. She's getting the train back to London. Kit, did something happen between you, because—?'

Kit turned away, putting his hands to his head as despair sucked him down. He swore savagely. Twice. And then strode to the door.

'Yes, something happened between us,' he said, turning back to Jasper with a suicidal smile. 'I was just too stupid to understand exactly what it was.'

THE GOOD NEWS was that Sophie didn't have to wait long for a train to come. The bad news was that there was only one straight-through express service to London every day, and that was long gone. The one she boarded was a small, clanking local train that stopped at every miniature village station all along the line and terminated at Newcastle.

The train was warm and virtually empty. Sophie slunk to a seat in the corner and sat with her eyes closed so she didn't have to look at Alnburgh, transformed by the sinking sun into a golden fairy tale castle from an old-fashioned storybook, get swallowed up by the blue haze.

She was used to this, she told herself over and over. Moving on was what she did best. Hadn't she always felt panicked by the thought of permanence? She was good at new starts. Reinventing herself.

But until now she hadn't really known who 'herself' was. Sophie Greenham was a construction; a sort of patchwork of bits borrowed from films and books and other people, fragments of fact layered up with wistful half-truths and shameless lies, all carried off with enough chutzpah to make them seem credible.

Beneath Kit's cool, incisive gaze all the joins had dissolved and the pieces had fallen away. She was left just being herself. A person she didn't really know, who felt things she didn't usually feel and needed things she didn't understand.

As she got further away from Alnburgh her phone came back into signal range and texts began to come in with teeth-grating regularity. Biting her cheeks against each sledgehammer blow of disappointment, Sophie couldn't stop herself checking every time to see if any were from Kit.

They weren't.

There were several from her agent. The vampire film people wanted to see her again. The outfit had impressed *them*, at least.

'Tickets from Alnburgh.'

She opened her eyes. The guard was making his way along the swaying carriage towards her. She sat up, fumbling in her broken bag for her purse as she blinked away the stinging in her eyes.

'A single to London, please.'

The guard punched numbers into his ticket machine with pudgy fingers. 'Change at Newcastle,' he said without looking at her. 'The London train goes from platform two. It's a bit of a distance so you'll need to hurry.'

'Thank you,' Sophie muttered, trying to fix those details in her head. Until then she'd only thought as far as getting on this train. Arriving at Newcastle, getting off and taking herself forwards from there felt like stepping into a void.

She dug her nails into her palms and looked unseeingly out of the window as a wave of panic washed over her. Out of nowhere a thought occurred to her.

'Actually—can you make that two tickets?'

'Are you with someone?'

For the first time the guard looked at her properly; a glare delivered over the top of his glasses that suggested she was doing something underhand. The reality was she was just trying to put something right.

'No.' Sophie heard the break in her voice. 'No, I'm alone. But let's just say I had a debt to pay.'

THE STATION AT Alnburgh was, unsurprisingly, empty. Kit stood for a moment on the bleak platform, breathing hard from running and looking desperately around, as if in some part of his mind he still thought there was a chance she would be there.

She wasn't. Of course she wasn't. She had left, with infinite dignity, and for good.

He tipped his head back and breathed in, feeling the throb of blood in his temples, waiting until the urge to punch something had passed.

'Missed your train?'

Kit looked round. A man wearing overalls and a yellow high-vis jacket had appeared, carrying a spade.

'Something like that. When's the next one to London?'

The man went over to the grit bin at the end of the platform and thrust the spade into it.

'London? The only straight-through London train from here is the 11.07 in the morning. If you need to get one before that you'll have to get to Newcastle.' He threw the spadeful of grit across the compacted snow.

Hopelessness engulfed Kit. Numbly he started walking away. If he caught a train from Newcastle, by the time he'd got to London she'd be long gone and he'd have no way of finding her. Unless…

Unless…

He spun round. 'Wait a minute. Did you say the only straight-through train was this morning? So the one that just left…'

'Was the local service to Newcastle. That's right.'

'Thanks.'

Kit broke into a run. He didn't stop until he reached the tower gate, and remembered the cars. The party was evidently still going on, and the courtyard was still rammed with vehicles. Kit stopped. Bracing his arms against the shiny black bonnet of the one nearest to him, letting his head drop as ragged breaths were torn from his heaving chest, almost like sobs.

She had gone. And he couldn't even go after her.

'Sir?'

Dimly he was aware of the car door opening and a figure getting out. Until that point he hadn't registered which car he was leaning against, or that there was anyone in it, but now he saw that it was the funeral car and the grey-haired man who had just got out was the undertaker.

'I was going to ask if you were all right, but clearly that would be a daft question,' he said, abandoning the stiff formality of his role. 'A better question would be, is there anything I can do to help?'

'Yes,' Kit rasped. 'Yes, there is.'

SOPHIE STOOD ON the platform and looked around in confusion.

Newcastle Central Station was a magnificent example of Victorian design and engineering. With its iron-boned canopy arching above her, Sophie felt as if she were standing in the belly of a vast whale.

Apart from the noise, and the crowds, maybe. Being inside a whale would probably be a blissfully quiet experience compared to this. People pushed past her, shouting into mobile phones to make themselves heard above the echoing announcement system and the noise of diesel engines.

Amongst them, Sophie felt tiny. Invisible.

It had been just a week and a half since she'd dashed

onto the 16.22 from King's Cross but now the girl with the stiletto boots and a corset dress and the who-cares attitude could barely bring herself to walk away from the little train that had brought her from Alnburgh. After the space and silence of the last ten days it felt as if the crowds were pressing in on her and that she might simply be swept away, or trampled underfoot. And that no one would notice.

But the guard had said she needed to hurry if she was going to catch the London connection. Adjusting her grip on her broken bag, holding it awkwardly to make sure it didn't spill its contents, she forced herself to move forwards.

Platform two. Where was platform two? Her eyes scanned the bewildering array of signs, but somehow none of the words made sense to her. Except one, high up on the lit-up board of train departures.

Alnburgh.

Sophie had never been homesick in her life, probably because she'd never really had a home to be sick for, but she thought the feeling might be something like the anguish that hollowed out her insides and filled her lungs with cement as she stared at the word.

She looked away. She didn't belong there—hadn't she told herself that countless times during the last ten days? The girl from nowhere with the made-up name and the made-up past didn't belong in a castle, or in a family with a thousand years of history.

So where did she belong?

Panic was rising inside her. Standing in the middle of the swarming station concourse, she suddenly felt as if she were falling, or disappearing, and there was nothing there to anchor her. She turned round, desperately searching for something familiar…

And then she saw him.

Pushing his way through the crowds of commuters, head and shoulders above everyone else, his face tense and ashen but so beautiful that for a moment Sophie couldn't breathe. She stood, not wanting to take her eyes off him in case he disappeared again, unable to speak.

'Kit.'

It was a whisper. A whimper. So quiet she barely heard it herself. But at that moment he turned his head and looked straight at her.

His footsteps slowed, and for a second the expression on his face was one she hadn't seen before. Uncertainty. Fear. The same things she was feeling—or had been until she saw him. And then it was gone—replaced by a sort of scowling ferocity as he crossed the distance between them with long, rapid strides. Gathering her into his arms, he kissed her, hungrily and hard.

There were tears running down Sophie's face when she finally pulled away. She felt tender and torn with emotions she couldn't begin to unravel—gratitude and joy and relief, undercut with the terrible anguish she was beginning to realise went with loving someone.

'My train…' she croaked, steeling herself for the possibility that he'd just come to say goodbye.

Slowly he shook his head. His eyes didn't leave hers. 'Don't get on it.'

'Why not?'

He took her face between his hands, drawing her close to him so that in the middle of the crowd they were in their own private universe. Under his silver gaze Sophie felt as if she were bathed in moonlight.

'Because then I would have to get on it too,' he murmured gravely, 'and I'd have to sit opposite you for the next two and a half hours, looking at you, breathing in your scent and wanting to take your clothes off and make love to you on the table.' He gave her a rueful smile that made her heart turn over. 'I've done that once before, so I know how hard it is. And because I hijacked a hearse and committed several civil and traffic offences to find you, and now I have I don't want to let you go again. Not until I've said what I have to say. Starting with sorry.'

Tears were still spilling down her cheeks. 'Kit, you don't have to—'

'I've been rehearsing this all the way from Alnburgh,' he said, brushing the tears away with his thumbs, 'so if you could listen without interrupting that would be good. I saw Jasper.'

'Oh! And—'

He frowned. 'I'm horrified...'

Sophie's mouth opened in protest, but before she could say anything he kissed her into silence and continued softly, '...that he ever thought I wouldn't *approve*. Lord, am I such a judgmental bastard?'

Sophie gave a hiccuping laugh that was half sob. 'I think you're asking the wrong person.'

He let her go then, dropping his hands to his sides and looking down at her with an expression of abject desolation. 'God, Sophie, I'm so sorry. I've spent my whole miserable life not trusting anyone so it had become something of a habit. Until Olympia told me what she did to you at school and I wanted to wring her neck, and it made me realise that I trusted you absolutely.'

'But what about with Sergio—you thought—'

Out of his arms, without his touch Sophie felt as if she were breaking up again. The crowed swelled and jostled around them. A commuter banged her leg with his briefcase.

'No.' It was a groan of surrender. An admission of defeat. He pulled her back into his arms and held her against him so that she could feel the beat of his heart. 'I was too bloody deranged with jealousy to think at all. I just wanted to tear him limb from limb. I know it's not big or clever, but I can't help it. I just want you for myself.'

Tentatively she lifted her head to look up at him, her vision blurred by wonder and tears.

'Really?'

In reply he kissed her again, this time so tenderly that she felt as if he were caressing her soul.

'It'll never work,' she murmured against his mouth. 'I'm not good enough for you.'

'I think…' he kissed the corner of her mouth, her jaw '…we've already established that you're far too good for me.'

She closed her eyes as rapture spiralled through her. 'Socially I mean. I'm nobody.'

His lips brushed her ear lobe. 'So am I, remember?'

It was getting harder to concentrate. Harder to think of reasons why she shouldn't just give in to the rising tide of longing inside her. Harder to keep her knees from buckling. 'I'd be disastrous for your career,' she breathed. 'Amongst all those officers' wives—'

He lifted his head and gazed at her with eyes that were lit by some inner light. 'You'll outshine them all,' he said softly, simply. 'They'll want to hate you for being so beautiful but they won't be able to. Now, have you any more objections?'

'No.'

He seized her hand. 'Then for God's sake, let's go and find the nearest hotel.'

Still Sophie held back. 'But I thought you had to report back for duty…'

'I called in some favours.' Gently he took her face between his hands and kissed her again. 'I have three weeks' compassionate leave following my father's death. But since Ralph wasn't actually my father I think we can just call it passionate leave. I intend to make the most of every second.'

EPILOGUE

IT WAS JUST a tiny piece in the property section of one of the Sunday papers. Eating brioche spread thickly with raspberry jam in the crumpled ruins of the bed that had become their world for the last three weeks, Sophie gave a little squeal.

'Listen to this!

'Unexpected Twist to Fitzroy Inheritance.
'Following the recent death of Ralph Fitzroy, eighth Earl of Hawksworth and owner of the Alnburgh estate, it has come to light that the expected heir is not, in fact, set to inherit. Sources close to the family have confirmed that the estate, which includes Alnburgh Castle and five hundred acres of land in Northumberland as well as a sizeable slice of premium real estate in Chelsea, will pass to Jasper Fitzroy, the Earl's younger son from his second marriage, rather than his older brother, Major Kit Fitzroy.'

Putting the last bit of brioche in her mouth, she continued,

'Major Fitzroy, a serving member of the armed forces, was recently awarded the George Medal for bravery. However, it's possible that his courage failed him when it came to taking on Alnburgh. According to locals, maintenance of the estate has been severely neglected in recent years, leaving the next owner with a heavy financial burden to bear. While Kit Fitzroy is rumoured to have considerable personal wealth, perhaps this is one rescue mission he just doesn't want to take on…'

She tossed the newspaper aside and, licking jam off her fingers, cast Kit a sideways glance from under her lashes.

'"Considerable personal wealth"?' She wriggled down beneath the covers, smiling as she kissed his shoulder. 'I like the sound of that.'

Kit, still surfacing from the depths of the sleep he'd been blessed with since he'd had Sophie in his bed, arched an eyebrow.

'I thought as much,' he sighed, turning over and looking straight into her sparkling, beautiful eyes. 'You're nothing but a shallow, cynical gold-digger.'

'You're right.' Sophie nodded seriously, pressing her lips together to stop herself from smiling. 'To be honest, I'm really only interested in your money, and your exceptionally gorgeous Chelsea house.' The sweeping gesture she made with her arm took in the bedroom with its view of the garden square outside. 'It's why I've decided to put up with your boring personality and frankly quite average looks. Not to mention your disappointing performance in bed—'

She broke off with a squeal as, beneath the sheets, he slid a languid hand between her thighs.

'Sorry, what was that?' he murmured gravely.

'I said…' she gasped '…that I was only interested in your…money.' He watched her eyes darken as he moved his hand higher. 'I've always wanted to be a rich man's plaything.'

He propped himself up on one elbow, so he could see her better. Her hair was spilling over the pillow—a gentler red than when he'd first seen her that day on the train—the colour of horse chestnuts rather than holly berries—and her face was bare of make-up. She had never looked more beautiful.

'Not a rich man's wife?' he asked idly, leaning down to kiss the hollow above her collarbone.

'Oh, no. If we're talking marriage I'd be looking for a title as well as a fortune.' Her voice turned husky as his lips moved to the base of her throat. 'And a sizeable estate to go with it…'

He smiled, taking his time, breathing in the scent of her skin. 'OK, that's good to know. Since I'm fresh out of titles and estates there's probably no point in asking.'

He felt her stiffen, heard her little gasp of shock and excitement. 'Well, there might be some room for negotiation,' she said breathlessly. 'And I'd say that right now you're in a pretty good bargaining position…'

'Sophie Greenham,' he said gravely, 'I love you because you are beautiful and clever and honest and loyal…'

'Flattery will get you a very long way,' she sighed, closing her eyes as his fingertips trailed rapture over the quivering skin on the inside of her thighs. 'And *that* will probably do the rest…'

His chest tightened as he looked down at her. 'I love you because you think underwear is a better investment than clothes, and because you're brave and funny and sexy, and I was wondering if you'd possibly consider marrying me?'

Her eyes opened and met his. The smile that spread slowly across her face was one of pure, incredulous happiness. It felt like watching the sun rise.

'Yes,' she whispered, gazing up at him with dazed, brilliant eyes. 'Yes, please.'

'I feel it's only fair to warn you that I've been disowned by my family…'

Serene, she took his face in her hands. 'We can make our own family.'

He frowned, smoothing a strand of hair from her cheek, suddenly finding it difficult to speak for the lump of emotion in his throat. 'And I have no title, no castle and no lands to offer you.'

She laughed, pulling him down into her arms. 'Believe me, I absolutely wouldn't have it any other way…'

* * * * *

TEMPTED BY A STRANGER

Part Two

PROLOGUE

London. March.

IT WAS JUST a tiny piece in the property section of one of the Sunday papers. Eating brioche spread thickly with raspberry jam in the crumpled ruins of the bed that had become their world for the last three weeks, Sophie gave a little squeal.

'Listen to this!'

> *'Unexpected Twist to Fitzroy Inheritance Following the recent death of Ralph Fitzroy, eighth Earl of Hawksworth and owner of the Alnburgh estate, it has come to light that the expected heir is not, in fact, set to inherit. Sources close to the family have confirmed that the estate, which includes Alnburgh Castle and five hundred acres of land in Northumberland as well as a sizeable slice of premium real estate in Chelsea, will pass to Jasper Fitzroy, the earl's younger son from his second marriage, rather than his older brother, Major Kit Fitzroy.'*

Putting the last bit of brioche in her mouth, she continued.

*'Major Fitzroy, a serving member of the armed
forces, was recently awarded the George Cross
for bravery. However, it's possible that his courage failed him when it came to taking on Alnburgh. According to locals, maintenance of the
estate has been severely neglected in recent years,
leaving the next owner with a heavy financial burden to bear. While Kit Fitzroy is rumoured to have
considerable personal wealth, perhaps this is one
rescue mission he just doesn't want to take on...'*

She tossed the newspaper aside and, licking jam off
her fingers, cast Kit a sideways glance from under her
lashes.

'"Considerable personal wealth"?' She wriggled
down beneath the covers, smiling as she kissed his
shoulder. 'I like the sound of that.'

Kit, still surfacing from the depths of the sleep he'd
been blessed with since he'd had Sophie in his bed,
arched an eyebrow.

'I thought as much.' He sighed, turning over and
looking straight into her sparkling, beautiful eyes.
'You're nothing but a shallow, cynical gold-digger.'

'You're right.' Sophie nodded seriously, pressing her
lips together to stop herself from smiling. 'To be honest, I'm really only interested in your money, and your
exceptionally gorgeous Chelsea house.' The sweeping
gesture she made with her arm took in the bedroom
with its view of the garden square outside where daf-
fodils nodded their heads along the iron railings. 'It's
why I've decided to put up with your boring personality
and frankly quite average looks. Not to mention your
disappointing performance in bed—'

She broke off with a squeal as, beneath the sheets, he slid a languid hand between her thighs.

'Sorry, what was that?' he murmured gravely.

'I said…' she gasped '…that I was only interested in your…money.' He watched her eyes darken as he moved his hand higher. 'I've always wanted to be a rich man's plaything.'

He propped himself up on one elbow, so he could see her better. Her hair was spilling over the pillow—a gentler red than when he'd first seen her that day on the train; the colour of horse chestnuts rather than holly berries—and her face was bare of make-up. She had never looked more beautiful.

'Not a rich man's wife?' he asked idly, leaning down to kiss the hollow above her collarbone.

'Oh, no. If we're talking marriage I'd be looking for a title as well as a fortune.' Her voice turned husky as his lips moved to the base of her throat. 'And a sizeable estate to go with it…'

He smiled, taking his time, breathing in the scent of her skin. 'OK, that's good to know. Since I'm fresh out of titles and estates there's probably no point in asking.'

He felt her stiffen, heard her little gasp of shock and excitement. 'Well, there might be some room for negotiation,' she said breathlessly. 'And I'd say that right now you're in a pretty good bargaining position…'

'Sophie Greenham,' he said gravely, 'I love you because you are beautiful and clever and honest and loyal…'

'Flattery will get you a very long way.' She sighed, closing her eyes as his fingertips trailed rapture over the quivering skin on the inside of her thighs. 'And *that* will probably do the rest…'

His chest tightened as he looked down at her. 'I love you because you think underwear is a better investment than clothes, and because you're brave and funny and sexy, and I was wondering if you'd possibly consider marrying me?'

Her eyes opened and met his. The smile that spread slowly across her face was one of pure, incredulous happiness. It felt like watching the sun rise.

'Yes,' she whispered, gazing up at him with dazed, brilliant eyes. 'Yes, please.'

'I feel it's only fair to warn you that I've been disowned by my family...'

Serene, she took his face in her hands. 'We can make our own family.'

He frowned, smoothing a strand of hair from her cheek, suddenly finding it difficult to speak for the lump of emotion in his throat. 'And I have no title, no castle and no lands to offer you.'

She laughed, pulling him down into her arms. 'Believe me, I absolutely wouldn't have it any other way...'

CHAPTER ONE

Five months later.
British Military Base, Theatre of Operations.
Thursday, 6.15 a.m.

THE SUN WAS RISING, turning the sky pink and the sand to gold. Rubbing his hand over eyes that were gritty with sand and exhaustion, Kit looked out across the desert and idly wondered if he'd be alive to watch it set again.

He'd slept for perhaps an hour, maybe two, and dreamed of Sophie. Waking in the dark, his body was taut with thwarted desire, his mind racing, and the scent of her skin was still in his nostrils.

He almost preferred the insomnia.

Five months. Twenty-two weeks. One hundred and fifty-four days. By now the craving for her should have faded, but if anything it had got more intense, more impossible to ignore. He hadn't phoned her, even though at times the longing to hear her voice burned like a laser inside him, knowing that if he did it would only add fuel to the fire. And knowing that there was nothing that could be said across six thousand miles that would possibly be enough.

Just one more day.

In twenty-four hours he would be flying out of here. Flying home. There was a sense of suppressed excitement amongst the men in his unit, a mixture of relief and exhilaration that had been building over the last week as the days dwindled.

It was a feeling Kit didn't share.

He'd been in bomb disposal for a long time. He'd never thought of it as anything other than a job; a dirty, awkward, challenging, exhausting, addictive, necessary job. But that was in the days when he thought rather than felt. When his emotions had been comfortably locked away in some part of him that was buried so deep he didn't even know it was there.

Everything was different now. He wasn't who he'd thought he was—quite literally thanks to the lies the man he'd called his father had told him all his life. But also, loving Sophie had blown him wide open, revealing parts of him he hadn't known existed, and now the job seemed dirtier, the stakes higher, the odds shorter. So much shorter.

One more day. Would his luck last?

'Major Fitzroy—coffee, sir. We're almost ready to move out.'

Kit turned. Sapper Lewis had emerged from the mess hut and was walking towards him, spilling most of the coffee. An earnest kid of nineteen, he had the gawky enthusiasm of a Great Dane puppy. It made Kit feel about a thousand years old. He took the enamel mug and grimaced as he swallowed.

'Thank you, Lewis,' Kit drawled. 'Other men I know have curvaceous secretaries to bring them coffee in the morning. I have you to bring me something that tastes like freshly brewed dirt.'

Lewis grinned. 'You'll miss me when you get home.'

'I sincerely doubt it.' Kit took another mouthful of

coffee and chucked the rest into the dust as he began to walk away. Not before he'd seen Lewis's face fall though.

'Fortunately you make a far better infantryman than a barista,' he called back over his shoulder. 'Bear that in mind when you get home, won't you?'

'Yes, sir!' Lewis hurried after him. 'And can I just say how great it's been working with you, sir? I've learned loads. Before this tour I wasn't sure I wanted to stay in the army, but watching you has made me decide to go into EOD.'

Kit stopped. Rubbing a hand across his jaw, he turned round.

'Do you have a girlfriend, Sapper?'

Lewis shifted from foot to foot, his face a mixture of pride and embarrassment. His Adam's apple bobbed. 'Yeah. Kelly. She's expecting a baby in two months' time. I'm going to ask her to marry me this leave.'

Narrowing his eyes as he looked out to the flat horizon, Kit nodded.

'You love her?'

'Yes, sir.' He scuffed the dust with the toe of his boot. 'We haven't been together long, but…yeah. I really love her.'

'Then take my advice. Learn to make a decent coffee and get yourself a job in Starbucks after all, because love and bomb disposal don't mix.' With a cool smile Kit handed the enamel mug back to him. 'Now, let's get out there and get this done so we can all go home.'

'SORRY I'M LATE.'

Smiling broadly in a way that didn't remotely suggest contrition and trying not to knock over anyone's designer beer with her shopping bags, Sophie slid into the chair opposite Jasper at the little metal table.

He eyed the bags archly. 'I take it you were unavoidably detained in…' His brows shot up another inch as he saw the discreet logo of Covent Garden's 'erotic boutique' on the corner of the biggest bag. 'Kit's in for a treat when he gets home.'

Shoving the bags under the table, Sophie tucked the great big bunch of vibrantly coloured flowers she'd just bought into the empty chair beside her and tried to stop herself from grinning like a love-struck loon.

'I've just spent an indecent amount of money,' she admitted, snatching up a menu and sliding her sunglasses onto the top of her head to read it. The table Jasper had chosen was in the shade of a red awning, which gave a healthy glow to his poetic pallor. He was so different from Kit it was incredible that they'd believed they were brothers for so long.

'On some pretty indecent stuff, if I know that shop.' Jasper peered into a corner of the bag.

'It's just a nightdress thing,' Sophie said hastily, hoping he wouldn't take out the wicked little slip of silvery-grey silk and display it in front of the lunch crowd outside Covent Garden's busiest restaurant. 'I was passing, and as I just got paid for the vampire movie, and Kit is coming home tomorrow, I thought, What the hell? But really, it was way too expensive.'

'Don't be daft. Your days of buying clothes from charity shops and bread from the reduced shelf in the supermarket are over now, darling.' Jasper looked around to catch the eye of the waiter, then turned back to her and rubbed his hands together as if in anticipation. 'Just a few hours left of single-girldom before Kits gets home and you become a full-time fiancée. Planning any wild parties?'

'I'm saving that for when he gets back, in about...' Sophie checked the time on her phone '...twenty-eight hours. Let's see...they're five hours ahead of us, so he should be just finishing his last shift about now.'

Jasper must have caught the note of anxiety in her voice because he covered her hand with his. 'Don't think about it,' he said firmly. 'You've done brilliantly—I'd have gone out of my mind with worry if it had been Sergio out there, dicing with death every day. You're very brave.'

'Hardly, compared to Kit.' Her throat dried and she looked down at the menu as the waiter made his way towards them. She tried to picture Kit now—hot, dirty, exhausted. For five months he had been looking after a battalion of men, putting their needs above his own. She wanted him home so she could look after him.

Amongst other things.

'Soph?'

'What? Oh, sorry.' Realising the waiter's pen was poised for her to give her order, Sophie asked for a Salade Niçoise, which was the first thing that caught her eye. Scribbling it down, the waiter moved away, his slim hips swaying as he wove through the tables.

'Kit's used to it,' Jasper said absently, watching him go. 'He's been doing it for years. How is he, anyway?'

'Oh...you know...he sounds OK,' she lied vaguely. 'But I want to hear about you. Are you and Sergio all packed and ready to hit tinseltown?'

Jasper leaned back in his chair and rubbed his hands over his face. 'The packing's ongoing, but, believe me, I have never been more ready for anything in my life. After everything that's happened in the last six months—Dad dying, the whole coming-out thing, Alnburgh turning out to be mine and not Kit's—I can't wait to get on that plane and just leave it all behind. I intend to spend the next three months lying by the pool drinking cocktails while Sergio's at work.'

'If I didn't know you better I'd say you were ruthlessly attempting to make me wild with envy.'

'Rumbled.' Jasper grinned as the waiter arrived, his tray held high. 'Is it working?'

'Nope.' The waiter placed a large gin and tonic clinking with ice in front of her. 'The pool and the cocktails sound lovely, but honestly for the first time in my life I have no desire to be anywhere other than here. Well, not *here*, obviously,' she said, nodding towards one of Covent Garden's famous street performers, 'since there's only so long I could watch a poncey out-of-work actor juggle with knives. But at home. With Kit.'

Jasper eyed her narrowly, tapping his pursed lips thoughtfully with a finger.

'I'm thinking alien abduction. I know there should be a more logical explanation for this complete character transformation from the girl who still has a phone on pay-as-you-go because a contract is too much commitment, to the woman whose idea of excitement is…' he waved a dismissive hand '…pegging out washing or something, but I just can't think what it could be…'

'Love,' Sophie said simply, taking a mouthful of gin. 'And maybe, having been on the move constantly all my life, I'm just ready to stay still now.' She glanced at him guiltily. 'I keep sneaking into furniture shops to look at sofas and I've developed a terrible obsession with paint colour charts. I suppose I just want a home.'

'Well, Kit's pad in one of Chelsea's most desirable garden squares isn't a bad start on the property ladder,' Jasper said, scooping up crab pâté on a piece of rye bread. 'Better than Alnburgh, anyway. You had a narrow escape there.'

'You can say that again. So, are you planning to move in when you get back from LA, then?'

Jasper grimaced. 'God, no. The windswept Northumberland coast is hardly the hub of the film industry and I can't exactly see Sergio walking down to the village shop and asking Mrs Watts for foie gras and the latest copy of *Empire* magazine.'

Taking another mouthful of gin, Sophie hid a smile. He was right; Sergio had shown up in Alnburgh for Ralph's funeral and it had been like seeing a parrot at the North Pole.

'So what will happen to it?' She speared an olive from her salad. Curiously, she cared much more about the future of Alnburgh Castle now there was no question of it involving Kit or her. She'd been so miserable there when she'd gone up to stay with Jasper last winter that the thought of actually living within its cold stone walls was enough to bring her out in goosebumps. But now that possibility had been removed, and sitting in the sunshine in the middle of Covent Garden, she could feel a sort of abstract affection for the place.

'I don't know.' Jasper sighed again. 'The legal situation is utterly incomprehensible and the finances are worse. It's such a bloody mess—I still can't forgive Dad for dropping a bombshell like that in his will. The fact that Kit isn't his natural son is just a technicality—he was brought up at Alnburgh and he's taken responsibility for the place almost single-handed for the last fif-

teen years. I guess that if I'm gutted by the way things
have turned out, it must be even worse for him. Has he
mentioned it in his letters or anything?'

Not meeting his eye, Sophie shook her head.

'No, he hasn't mentioned it.'

The fact was he hadn't mentioned anything much.
Before he went he'd warned her that phone calls were
frustrating and best avoided so she hadn't expected him
to ring, but she couldn't help being a bit disappointed
that he hadn't. She had written to him several times a
week—long letters, full of news and silly anecdotes and
how much she was missing him. His replies had been
infrequent, short and impersonal, and had left her feeling more lonely than if he hadn't written at all.

'I just hope he doesn't hate me too much, that's all,'
Jasper said unhappily. 'Alnburgh meant everything to
him.'

'Don't be silly. It's not your fault that Kit's mother
disappeared with another man when he was just a little
boy, is it? And anyway, it's all in the past now, and, as
my barking-mad mother would say, everything happens
for a reason. If Kit was the heir there'd be absolutely no
chance I'd be marrying him. He'd need a horsey wife
who came complete with her own heirloom tiara and
a three-year guarantee to produce a son. I'd fail on all
counts.'

Her tone was flippant, but her smile stiffened slightly
as she said the bit about the son. Jasper didn't seem to
notice.

'You come closer than Sergio. You'd both look good
in a tiara, but you certainly have the edge when it comes
to bearing heirs.'

'I wouldn't bet on it.'

It was no good. To her shame both her voice and her smile cracked and she had to press her hand to her mouth. Across the table Jasper looked horrified.

'Soph? What's wrong?'

She grabbed her drink and took a gulp. The gin was cold, bitter, good. It felt as if it was clearing her head, although that was probably an ironic illusion.

'I'm fine. I finally saw a doctor about the monthly hell that is my period, that's all.'

Jasper's eyes widened. 'God, Soph—it's nothing—?'

She waved a hand. 'No, no, nothing serious. It's as I thought—endometriosis. The good news is it's not life-threatening, but the bad news is that there's not much they can do about it and it could make getting pregnant a problem.'

'Oh, honey. I had no idea having children was so important to you.'

'Neither did I, until I met Kit.' Sophie slid her sunglasses back down, feeling in need of something to hide behind. Having spent years listening to her mother and the women in the haphazard commune in which she'd grown up analyse everything in minute, head-wrecking detail, she usually went out of her way to avoid any kind of serious discussion, but there was part of her that wanted to share this bittersweet new feeling. 'Finding out it might be difficult has made me realise how important it is—how's that for irony?' She sighed. 'Anyway, the doctor didn't say it was impossible, just that it could take a long time and it was best not to leave it too long.'

He reached across the table and took her hand.

'So when are you going to start trying?'

Sophie looked at her phone again and looked up at him with a determined smile. 'In about twenty-seven and a half hours.'

THE SECOND HAND quivered slightly as it edged wearily around the clock face. Sitting on a plastic chair in Intensive Care, watching it with wide-eyed fatigue, Kit kept thinking that it wouldn't make it through the next minute.

He knew the feeling.

He had been here since late afternoon, English time, when the emergency medical helicopter had finally landed, bringing Sapper Kyle Lewis home. Sedated into unconsciousness, with bullets in his head and chest, it wasn't quite the homecoming Lewis had looked forward to.

Kit sank his head into his hands. The now familiar, tingling numbness was back, stealing up through his fingertips until he felt as if he were dissolving.

'Coffee, Major Fitzroy?'

He jerked upright again. The nurse in front of him wore a blue plastic disposable apron and was smiling kindly, unaware of the stab of anguish her question caused. He looked away, his teeth gritted.

'No, thanks.'

'Can I get you anything for the pain?'

He turned, eyes narrowed. Did she know that *he* was the reason Lewis was in the room behind him, hooked up to machines that were breathing for him as his mother held his hand and wept softly, and the girl-friend he had spoken of so proudly kept her terrified eyes averted?

'Your face,' the nurse said gently. 'I know you were

seen to in the field hospital, but the medication they gave you will have worn off now.' She tilted her head, looking at him with great compassion. 'They might only be superficial, but these shrapnel wounds can be very painful as they heal.'

'It looks worse than it is.' He'd seen his face in the washroom mirror and felt dull surprise at the torn flesh and bruising around his eyes. 'Nothing that a large whisky wouldn't fix.'

The nurse smiled. 'I'm afraid I can't give you one of those here. But you could go home now, you know.' The plastic apron crackled as she moved past him to the door of Lewis's room, pausing with her hand on the doorplate. 'His family's here now. You've looked after these boys for five months, Major,' she said gently. 'It's time you looked after yourself.'

Kit got a brief glimpse of the inert figure in the bed before the door swung shut again. He exhaled heavily, guilt squeezing the air from his lungs.

Home.

Sophie.

The thought of her almost severed the last shreds of his self-control. He looked at the clock again, realising that although he'd been staring at it for hours he had no idea what time it was.

Almost six o'clock in the evening, and he was almost three hundred miles away. He stumbled to his feet, his mind racing, his heart suddenly beating hard with the need to get to her. To feel her in his arms and lose himself in her sweetness and forget…

Behind him a door opened, pulling him back into the present. Turning he saw Lewis's girlfriend come out of the room, her thin shoulders hunched, her pregnant stomach incongruously out of proportion with the rest of her. Slumping against the wall, she looked appallingly young.

'They won't say anything. I just want to know if he's going to be OK.' She spoke with a kind of sulky defiance, but Kit could see the fear in her face when she looked at him. 'Is he?'

'Wing Commander Randall's the army medic here. According to him, he's over the worst now,' Kit said tersely. 'If soldiers survive the airlift to the camp hospital their chances of survival are already ninety-seven percent. He's made it all the way home.'

Her scowl deepened. 'I don't mean is he going to survive. I mean is he going to be OK? I mean, back to normal. Because I don't think I could stand it if he wasn't…' She broke off, turning her face away. Kit could see her throat working frantically as she swallowed back tears. 'We don't even know each other that well,' she went on, after a moment. 'We'd not been going out long when *this* happened.' A sharp gesture of her head told him she was referring to the pregnancy. 'It wasn't exactly planned but, as my mum says, it was my own fault. Just got to get on with it now.' She looked at Kit with dead eyes then; inky tears were running down her face. 'And what about this? If he's… I dunno…*injured*, I'm stuck with it, aren't I? But whose fault is that?'

Mine, Kit wanted to say. *All mine.*

What right did he have to forget that?

SOPHIE'S EYES SNAPPED OPEN.

She lay very still, staring into the soft summer darkness, all her senses on high alert as she listened out for a repeat of the sound that had woken her.

Or maybe it hadn't even been a sound. Maybe it was just a feeling. A dream perhaps? Or an instinct…

She sat up, struggling from sleep, the hairs rising on the back of her neck. The blood was swishing in her ears, but outside she could hear the usual sounds of the city at night—traffic on the King's Road, a distant siren, a car moving through the square below.

And then something else, closer, inside the house. A muffled thud, like something being dropped, followed by the soft, heavy tread of someone coming slowly up the stairs.

Sophie froze.

Then, with a muttered curse, she kicked off the covers and scrambled to her feet on the bed, looking frantically around for a weapon and finding herself fervently wishing she'd taken up cricket or baseball. Her heart was galloping. It was no good—there was nothing remotely suited to fending off an intruder within reach, and she realised that she should simply have rolled off the bed and hidden underneath it…

A shape appeared in the doorway, filling it, just as Sophie's pounding heart seemed to have filled her throat. It was too late to move now, too late to do anything but brazen it out.

'Don't move,' she croaked. 'I have a weapon.'

With what sounded like a sigh the intruder took a step forwards.

'Where I've just come from we don't call that a weapon. We call that a TV remote.'

His voice was hoarse with fatigue, sexy as hell and instantly familiar.

'*Kit!*'

It was a cross between a shout of jubilation and a sob. In a split second Sophie had bounded across the bed and he caught her as she hurtled into his arms, wrapping her legs tightly around his waist as their mouths met. Questions half formed themselves in her brain, bubbling up then dissolving again in the more urgent need to feel him and touch him and keep on kissing him…

He lowered her onto the bed without breaking the kiss, and his mouth on hers was hard and hungry. Sliding her hands into his hair, she felt grit. He smelled of earth and antiseptic, but beneath that she caught the scent that made her senses reel—the dry cedar-scent that was all his own, that she had craved like a drug.

'I thought…' she gasped '…you weren't home…until tomorrow.'

His lips found hers again.

'I'm here now,' he rasped against her.

Now that they were both together on the bed, that was all that mattered.

Desire gushed through her, slippery and quick. Laying her down on the bed, he straightened up, towering over her for a second. Shadows obscured his face, but in spite of the darkness she caught the silvery glitter of his eyes and it sent another wave of urgent need crashing through her. Rising up onto her knees, she pulled off her T-shirt, stopping with her mouth the low moan he uttered as her naked body moved against him.

'Are you all right?' she murmured moments later, fumbling for the buttons on his shirt with shaking fingers.

'Yes.'

It was a primitive growl that came from low in his

chest. He pulled away, half turning as he yanked his shirt from his trousers and wrenched it over his head. In that moment the light from the street filtering through a gap in the curtains caught his face and Sophie gasped.

'No—you're hurt. Kit, your face—'

She got to her feet, reaching for him, taking his face between her hands and stroking her thumbs with great tenderness over the lacerations on his cheekbones until she felt him flinch away.

'It's nothing.'

His hands slid around her waist as his mouth came down on hers again, and the feel of his bare chest, hard against her breasts, was enough to banish the anxiety that had leapt in her, along with every other thought in her head that wasn't concerned with the immediate need to wrap herself around him. To feel him against her and inside her until there were no joins left and the distance of the last one hundred and fifty-four days was forgotten.

His hands were warm on her back, moving across her quivering skin with a certainty and steadiness of touch she couldn't possibly match as she struggled to undo his belt, impatient to get rid of the last barriers that stood between them. She gave a gasp of triumph as she managed to work the buttons free. Swiftly he kicked off his desert combats and they fell back onto the bed.

None of it was as she'd planned. There was no champagne, no sexy silk nightdress, no sense of seduction, no conversation, just skin and hands and a need so huge she felt as if it might break her wide open.

There would be a time for talking. Later. Tomorrow.

This was the best way she knew of bridging the spaces between them, of telling him what she wanted him to know, of reaching him. Just like the first time they'd made love, on the night he'd found out that Ralph Fitzroy wasn't his father. There had been nothing she could say then because it was too big, too raw, too complex, but for a while it had been flamed into insignificance in the heat of their passion.

His body was rigid with tension, his shoulders like concrete beneath her fingers. They were both shaking, but as he entered her she felt some of the tightness leave his body as if he too felt the wild, exhilarating rightness that surged through her. Her arms were locked around his neck, their foreheads touching, and the feel of his breath on her cheek, his skin, was almost enough to make her come. Her body shivered and burned, but fiercely she held back, tightening her muscles around him, holding on like a woman in danger of drowning.

With a moan he slid his arms beneath her back, gathering her up and pulling her hard against his chest as he sat up. Sophie wrapped her legs around his waist, and the increase in pressure was enough to tip her over the edge. She let go, arching backwards and gasping as her orgasm ripped through her.

He held her, waiting until it had subsided before pulling her back into his arms and burying his face in her neck. She could feel him inside her still, and slowly she rotated her pelvis, stroking his hair, holding him tightly until he stiffened and cried out her name.

Together they collapsed back onto the bed. Cradling his head against her breasts, Sophie stared up into the darkness and smiled.

CHAPTER TWO

KIT WOKE SUDDENLY, his body convulsing with panic.

It took a few seconds for reality to reassert itself. It was light—the cool, bluish light of an English morning, and the sheets were clean and smooth against his skin. Sophie was lying on her side, tucked into his body, one hand flat on his chest, over his frantically thudding heart.

The fact that he wasn't actually walking along a dust track towards a bridge with a bomb beneath it told him he must have slept. After a hundred and fifty-four largely sleepless nights it felt like a small miracle.

He shifted position slightly so he could look into Sophie's sleeping face, stretching limbs that had stiffened from being still for so long. His heart squeezed. God, she was so lovely. The summer had brought out a faint sprinkling of freckles over the bridge of her nose, and put a bloom into her creamy cheeks. Or maybe that was last night. The erection he'd woken up with intensified as he remembered, and he looked at her mouth. Her top lip with its steep upwards sweep and pronounced Cupid's bow was slightly swollen from his kisses.

It was also curved into the faintest and most secretive of smiles.

Deeply asleep, she looked serene and self-contained, as if she was travelling through wonderful places where he could never hope to follow, full of people he didn't know. No godforsaken, mine-strewn desert roads for her, he thought bleakly.

The light filtering through the narrow gap in the curtains gleamed on her smooth bare shoulder and cast a halo around her hair. Picking up a silken strand, he wound it lazily around his finger, thinking back to one of the last times he had lain here beside her and asked her to marry him.

What a fool. What a selfish, stupid fool.

Anything could have happened. He thought of Lewis's girlfriend; her terrified eyes and her swollen stomach. *We don't even know each other that well... If he's... injured, I'm stuck with it, aren't I?* What if it had been him instead of Lewis? They'd only had three weeks together. *Three weeks.* How could he have expected Sophie to stand by him for a lifetime when he barely knew her?

The gleaming lock of hair fell back onto her creamy shoulder, but he left his hand there, holding it in front of his face and stretching his fingers. They shook slightly, prickling with pins and needles, and he curled them into a fist, squeezing hard.

Harder.

The bones showed white beneath his sun-darkened skin and pain flared through the stretched tendons, but it didn't quite manage to drive away the numbness, or stop the slideshow that was replaying itself in his head again. The heat shimmering over the road, the hard sun glinting off windows in the buildings above. That eerie silence. The way everything had seemed to slip into slow motion, as if it were happening underwater. His hands trembling uncontrollably; the wire cutters slipping through his nerveless fingers as the voice in his earpiece grew more urgent, telling him that a sniper had been spotted...

And then the gunshots.

He sat up, swearing under his breath. Dragging a hand over his face, he winced as he caught a scab that had begun to form on one of the cuts across his cheekbone.

He was home, and back with Sophie. So why did it feel as if he were still fighting, and further away from her than ever?

SOPHIE STOPPED IN the kitchen doorway.

Kit was sitting at the table with the pile of letters that had come while he'd been away, drinking coffee. He was wearing jeans but no shirt, and his skin was tanned to the colour of mahogany. Sophie's stomach flipped.

'Hi.'

Oh, dear. Having leapt out of bed almost as soon as she opened her eyes, brushed her teeth like a person on speeded-up film and even slapped a bit of tinted moisturiser onto her too-pale cheeks before running downstairs, it was ridiculous that that was all she could manage. *Hi*. And in a voice that was barely more than a strangled whisper.

He looked up. The morning light showed up the mess of cuts and bruising on his face, making him look battered and exhausted and beautiful.

'Hi.'

'So you *are* real,' she said ruefully, going across to fill the kettle. 'I thought I might have dreamed it. It wouldn't be the first time I'd done that while you've been gone—dreamed about you so vividly that waking up was like saying goodbye all over again.' She stopped, before she said any more and gave herself away as being a terrifying, crazy, obsessive fiancée. To make it sound as if she were joking she asked, 'Did they let you off a day early for good behaviour?'

'Unfortunately not.' He put down the letter he was reading and pushed a hand through his hair. It was still wet from the shower, but she could see that it had been lightened by the sun, giving the kind of tawny streaks only the most expensive hairdressers could produce. 'A man in my unit was badly injured yesterday. I flew home with him.'

'Oh, Kit, I'm so sorry.' Filled with contrition for thinking such shallow thoughts, Sophie went over to stand beside him. 'How is he?'

'Not good.'

His voice was flat, toneless, and he looked down at the letter again, as if the subject was closed. On the other side of the kitchen the kettle began its steam-train rattle. Sophie touched his cheekbone with her fingertips.

'What happened?' she said softly. 'Was it an explosion?'

For a moment he said nothing, but she saw his eyelids flicker, as if he was remembering something he didn't want to remember; reliving something he didn't want to relive.

'Yes…'

His forehead creased into a sudden frown of pain and for a second she thought he was going to say more. But then the shutters descended and he looked up at her with a cool smile that was more about masking emotion than conveying it.

Sophie pulled out the chair beside him and sat down, turning to face him. 'How badly hurt is he?'

'It's hard to tell at the moment,' he said neutrally. 'It looks like he'll live, but it's too early to say how bad his injuries will be.' His smile twisted. 'He's only nineteen.'

'Just a boy,' she murmured. The kettle boiled in a billow of steam and hissed into silence. Aching for him, Sophie took his hand between hers, feeling the hard skin on the undersides of his fingers, willing him to open up to her. 'It's good that you stayed with him. It must have made a huge difference to him, having you there, and to his family, knowing that someone was looking after him…'

She trailed off as he got abruptly to his feet, giving her no choice but to let go of his hand.

'Coffee?'

'Yes, please.' Hurt blossomed inside her but she didn't let it seep into her tone. 'Sorry—there's only instant. I was going to go shopping today to get things in for when you came back.'

She thought of all the plans she had made for his homecoming; the food she was going to buy that could be eaten in bed—olives, quails' eggs, tiny dim sum and Lebanese pastries from the deli around the corner— champagne and proper coffee, piles of croissants and brioche for breakfast. And the X-rated silk nightdress, of course. Now they all seemed to belong to a silly, frilly fantasy in which Kit took the part of the Disney Prince, doe-eyed with adoration.

The reality was turning out to be slightly different.

'What on earth have you been living on?' he said, his voice an acerbic drawl. 'I was going to make you breakfast, but the cupboard seems to be bare.'

'I usually eat on the go,' she said lightly, getting up and going over to the designer stainless-steel bread bin. 'But look, there's bread. And...' she opened a cupboard and pulled down a jar with a flourish '...chocolate spread.'

Splinters of guilt lodged themselves in Kit's throat. She was making a good attempt to hide it but behind the show of nonchalance he could tell she was hurt. She'd tried to reach out to him—to *talk* to him like a normal human being, and he'd behaved as if she'd done something indecent.

It must have made a huge difference to him, having you there, and to his family, knowing that someone was looking after him...

How she overestimated him. In so many ways.

He looked at her. She was putting bread into the toaster and her glossy hair was tousled, her legs long and bare beneath an old checked shirt she must have taken from his wardrobe. He felt his chest tighten with remorse and desire. He wasn't brave enough to shatter her illusions about him yet, but he could at least try to make up to her for being such a callous bastard.

Gently he took the jar from her and unscrewed the lid. He peered inside and then looked at her, raising an eyebrow.

'You actually *eat* this stuff?'

She shrugged, reaching for a knife from the cutlery drawer. 'What else would you do with it?'

'I'm surprised,' he said gravely, taking the knife from her too, 'that you need to ask that...'

Looking at her speculatively, keeping his face completely straight, he reached out and undid the buttons of her shirt. He felt her jump slightly at his touch and she let out a little sound of surprise. But as he took hold of her waist and lifted her onto the countertop her green eyes glittered with instant excitement.

Slowly, with great focus he dipped the tip of the blade into the jar, loading it with soft, velvety chocolate. The moment stretched as he turned the knife around in his hand, then turned his attention to her, moving the edge of her shirt aside to expose her bare breast.

It took considerable self-control to keep the lust that was rampaging through him from showing on his face, or in his movements. His hand shook slightly as he cupped her warm, perfect breast. Behind them, the toast sprang up in the toaster and she jumped, giving a little indrawn breath. In one smooth sweep, Kit spread the chocolate over her skin.

Abstractly, as he parted his lips to taste her, he thought how beautiful it looked—the chocolate against the vanilla cream of her skin. But then all thoughts were driven from his head as he took her chocolate-covered nipple into his mouth and felt her stiffen and arch against him.

His tongue teased her, licking her clean. The chocolate was impossibly sweet and cloying and it masked the taste of her skin, so without lifting his head he reached behind her and turned the tap on, running cold water into the cup of his hand. Straightening up, he let it trickle onto her, watching her eyes widen in shock as the cold water ran down her skin.

'Kit, you—!'

His mouth was on hers before she could finish. Sitting on the granite countertop, she was the same height as he was and he put his hands on her bottom, pulling her forwards so that her thighs were tight around his waist, her pelvis hard against his erection.

God, he loved her. He loved her straightforwardness, her generosity. He loved the way she seemed to understand him, and her willingness to give him what he needed. He didn't have to find words, not when he could show her how he felt this way.

Her arms were around his neck, her fingers tangling in his damp hair. He was just about to lift her up, hitch her around him and haul her over to the table where he could take her more easily when there was a loud knock at the front door.

He stopped, stepping backwards, cursing quietly and with more than a hint of irony, given his choice of word.

'Don't answer it.'

It was tempting, so tempting, given how utterly, outrageously sexy she looked sprawled on the kitchen countertop, her wet shirt open, her mouth bee-stung from his kisses. He dragged a hand over his face, summoning the shreds of his control.

'I have to,' he said ruefully, heading for the door. 'It's breakfast. I ordered it when you were sleeping, and since they only agreed to home delivery as a special favour…'

Left alone in the kitchen, Sophie pulled her shirt together and slid shakily down from the worktop, her trembling legs almost giving way beneath her as she tried to stand. Through the thick fog of desire she was dimly aware of voices in the hallway—one Kit's, the other vaguely familiar. Dreamily she picked up the chocolate spread and dipped her finger into it, closing her eyes and tipping her head back as she put it in her mouth.

'In here?'

The vaguely familiar voice was closer now and she jumped, opening her eyes in time to see an even more familiar face come into the kitchen; so familiar that for a moment she thought it was someone she must know from way back—a friend of Jasper's, perhaps?

'Hi. You must be Sophie.'

Grinning, the man put a wooden crate stacked with aluminium cartons on the table and held out his hand. Sophie shook it, feeling guilty that she couldn't quite place him and managing to say hello without making it obvious she couldn't remember his name.

Kit came in carrying a bottle of champagne.

'Thanks, I appreciate this.'

'No big deal—it's the least I can do considering you've spent the last five months being a hero. It's good to see you back in one piece—or nearly.'

He gestured to the shrapnel wounds on Kit's face. Sophie noticed the tiny shift in Kit's expression; the way it darkened, tightened.

'How's the restaurant?' he asked smoothly.

'Good, thanks, although I don't get to spend as much time there as I'd like, thanks to the TV stuff. I just got back from filming for a new series in the US.'

Horror congealed like cold porridge in Sophie's stomach as her eyes flew back to the man. She now realised why he was vaguely familiar. Suddenly she was aware that she was standing in the same kitchen as one of the country's top celebrity chefs wearing a wet shirt that barely skimmed her bottom and clung to her breasts, eating chocolate spread with her finger straight from the jar.

Surreptitiously she put the jar down and tried to shrink backwards behind the large vase of flowers she'd bought in Covent Garden. Luckily the Very Famous Chef was engrossed in a discussion about business with Kit as they headed back towards the door, but he did pause in the doorway and look back at her.

'Nice to meet you, Sophie. You must get Kit to bring you to the restaurant some time.'

Not on your life, thought Sophie, smiling and nodding; not now he'd seen her like this. As soon as he'd gone she picked up the jar of chocolate spread and was eating it with a spoon when Kit came back in.

'You could have warned me,' she moaned between spoonfuls.

'Sorry,' Kit drawled, 'but I was pretty distracted myself.'

'He's a friend of yours?'

'That depends on your definition of friend. I know him reasonably well because his restaurant is just around the corner from here and I've been there enough times over the years.'

Sophie took another spoonful of chocolate spread. People didn't go to restaurants on their own. She pictured the kind of women Mr Celeb-Chef must have seen with Kit in the past, and the contrast they must have made with her, now.

Kit was looking at the foil trays in the crate. 'Put down that revolting sweet stuff; we have smoked-salmon bagels, blueberry pancakes, almond croissants, proper coffee, oh—and this, of course.' He held up the bottle of champagne. 'So—do you want to eat here, or in bed?'

Sophie's resistance melted like butter in a microwave. She found that she was smiling.

'What do you think?'

SOPHIE WALKED SLOWLY back to Kit's house, trailing her fingers along the railings outside the smart houses, a bag filled with supplies from the uber-stylish organic supermarket on the King's Road bumping against her leg. She felt she had some ground to make up after the incriminating chocolate-spread incident this morning.

The thought of chocolate spread drew her attention to the pleasurable ache in her thighs as she walked, and she couldn't stop her mind from wandering ahead of her, to the house with the black front door at the far end of the square. From this distance it looked the same as all its expensive, exclusive neighbours, but Sophie felt a little quiver inside her at the thought that Kit was there.

She had left him going through yet more of the post that had arrived while he'd been away, and she reluctantly had to admit it had been almost a relief to have an excuse to get out of the house. They had eaten breakfast and made love, slowly and luxuriously, then lain drowsily together as the clouds moved across the clean blue sky beyond the window and the morning slid into afternoon. Then they had made love again.

It had been wonderful. More than wonderful—completely magical. So why did she have the uneasy feeling that it was a substitute for talking?

There was so much she wanted to say, and even more that she wanted him to tell her. She thought of the contraceptive pills she'd thrown in the bin and felt a hot tide of guilt that she hadn't actually got round to mentioning that. But how could she when it felt as if he had put up an emotion-proof fence around himself? There might as well be a sign above his head: 'Touch, but Don't Talk.'

She was being ridiculous, she told herself sternly, reaching into her pocket for her key. They'd spent whole days in bed before he'd gone away and gone for hours without speaking a word, lost in each other's bodies or just lying with their limbs entwined, reading. It wasn't a sign that something was wrong. If anything, surely it was the opposite?

She slid the key into the lock and opened the door.

The house was silent, but the atmosphere was different now Kit was home. There was a charge to it. An electricity, which both excited and unnerved her. Going into the sleek granite and steel kitchen, she remembered what she'd said to Jasper about wanting a home. The flowers she'd bought in such a surge of optimism and excitement stood in the centre of the black granite worktop, a splash of colour against the masculine monochrome.

She put the kettle on.

For the last five months this had been her home, around the time she'd spent in Romania filming the stupid vampire movie, but now Kit was back it suddenly seemed to be his house again, a place where she was the guest. Even her flowers looked wrong—as out of place as her low-rent white sliced bread in his designer bread bin and her instant coffee in his tasteful Conran Shop mugs.

Dispiritedly she spooned fragrant, freshly ground Fairtrade coffee into the coffee maker, hoping she'd got that right at least. Taking down a tray, she set it with mugs, and milk in a little grey jug, but then wondered if that was trying too hard? After a moment's indecision she took them off again. Pouring the coffee straight into the mugs, she picked them up and went to find Kit.

He was upstairs, in the room at the front of the house

that he used as a study. Outside the half-open door she hesitated, then knocked awkwardly.

'Yes?'

'I made you some coffee.'

'Thank you.' From inside the room his voice was an amused drawl. 'Do I have to come out to collect it, or are you going to bring it in?'

'I don't want to disturb you,' she muttered, pushing the door open and going in.

The surface of the desk in front of him was covered in piles of letters, and the waste-paper bin was full of envelopes. Sophie felt a fresh wave of lust and love and shyness as she looked at him. The cuts over his cheek-bones were still raw-looking, the bruising beneath his eyes still dark, making him look inexpressibly battered and weary.

'Hmm…that's a good point,' he murmured wryly, trailing his fingers up the back of her bare leg beneath the skirt of her little flowered dress as she bent to put the mug on the desk. 'You are *very* disturbing.'

Desire leapt inside her, inflaming flesh that already burned. She doused it down. Turning round, she leaned her bottom on the edge of the desk and looked at him over the rim of her mug, determined to attempt a form of communication that didn't end in orgasm for once.

'So, is there anything interesting in all that?'

Picking up his coffee, Kit shrugged, his expression closed. 'Not much. Bank statements and share reports. Some more information about the Alnburgh estate.' He stopped and took a mouthful of coffee. Then, after a moment's hesitation, picked up a letter from one of the piles and held it out to her. 'And this.'

Scanning down the first few formal lines, Sophie frowned in confusion.

'What is it?'

'A letter from Ralph's solicitors in Hawksworth. They received this letter to forward on to me.'

He slid a folded piece of paper out from the pile and tossed it onto the desk beside her. Something in the abruptness of his movements told her that it was significant, though his face was as inscrutable as ever, his eyes opaque.

Warily Sophie picked up the thick pale blue paper and unfolded it. The script on it was even and sloping—the hand of a person who was used to writing letters rather than sending texts or emails, Sophie thought vaguely as she began to read.

My Dear Kit—
I know this letter will come as a surprise, and after all this time am not foolish enough to believe it will be a pleasant one, however I must put aside my selfish trepidation and confront things I should have dealt with a long time ago.

Sophie's heart had started to beat very hard. She glanced up at Kit, her mouth open to say something, but his head was half turned away from her as he continued working his way through the pile of post, not inviting comment. She carried on reading.

I'm sorry—that's the first thing I want to say, although those words are too little, too late. There is so much more I need to add to them. There are things I'd like to explain for my own selfish rea-

*sons, in the hope you might understand and per-
haps even forgive, and other things I need to tell
you that are very much in your interest. Things
that will affect you now, and will go on affecting
your family far into the future.*

A pulse of adrenaline hit Sophie's bloodstream as
she read that bit. She carried on, skimming faster now,
impatient to find out what it all meant.

*The last thing I want to do is pressure you for any
kind of response, so on the basis that you have
my address at the top of this letter and the warm-
est and most sincere of invitations to come here
at any time to suit you, I will leave you to make
your own decision.*

   *Know, though, how much it would mean to me
to see you.*
Your hopeful mother
Juliet Fitzroy

Slowly Sophie put down the letter, her head spinning.
'So your mother wants you to go and see her?' she
said, admittedly rather stupidly.

Kit tossed another envelope into the bin. 'So it would
appear, Mr Holmes.'

'Will you go?' With shaking fingers Sophie scrabbled to unfold the paper again, to see where exactly Juliet Fitzroy lived. 'Imlil,' she said in a puzzled voice,
then read the line below on the address. 'Blimey—
Morocco?'

'Exactly.' Kit sounded offhand to the point of boredom as the contents of the envelope followed it into the

bin. 'It's not exactly a few stops on the District line, and I can't think what she could say that would make the trip worthwhile.'

Sophie tapped a finger against her closed lips, her thoughts racing ahead. Morocco. Heat and sand and… harem pants. Probably. In truth she didn't know an awful lot about Morocco beyond the fact that she'd always liked the sound of it and that, right now, it seemed like a very favourable alternative to Chelsea, and the oppressive atmosphere that seemed to be stifling them both in the quiet, immaculate house.

'I've always wanted to go to Morocco,' she said, with a hint of wistfulness. 'I wonder how she ended up living there? And why she's chosen to get in touch now, after all this time?'

'I assume because she knows her little secret will have been uncovered by Ralph's death.' Kit was writing something on the bottom of a letter from the bank. 'Perhaps she wants to introduce me to my real father— although that's assuming she knows who he is. There could be thousands of possible candidates for all I know.'

Oh, God. Sophie suddenly felt dizzy as she remembered a letter she had found tucked into a book in the library at Alnburgh. She'd known at the time it was wrong to read it, but one look at the first line and she'd been unable to resist. She wished now that she'd been stronger, so she wouldn't be in the position of knowing more about Kit's paternity than he did.

Getting up from the edge of the desk, she paced to the bookcase on the other side of the room, deliberately turning her back on him. 'There aren't.' She took a deep breath and closed her eyes, wincing. 'She knows.'

There was a pause. On the bookcase in front of her, between the volumes of military history and thick books on Middle Eastern politics, was a photograph. It showed a Kit she didn't know, standing in the centre of a group of men in camouflage jackets in front of an army truck.

'How do you know?'

He spoke with sinister softness. Light-headed with apprehension, Sophie turned round. 'Do you remember that day at Alnburgh, when I was…ill…?' She'd got her period and had been completely unprepared, and Kit had stepped in and taken control. She smiled faintly. 'You showed me into the library while you went to the village shop.'

'I remember.' His voice held an edge of steel that made the smile wither. 'And?'

'And I looked at the books while I was waiting.' She went over to lean against the desk beside him again, longing to touch him but not quite knowing how to. 'I found some old Georgette Heyer—she's my absolute favourite, so I took one down and opened it, and a letter fell out.' She looked down at her hands, picking at one of the ragged nails she'd meant to file before he came home. 'A love letter. It was addressed to "My Darling Juliet".'

Kit wasn't looking at her. He was staring straight ahead, out of the window, the slats of the blind casting bars of shadows on his damaged face so that he looked as if he were in a cage. When he said nothing, Sophie went on in a voice that was husky and hesitant.

'A-at first I assumed it was from Ralph and I was amazed. It was so beautifully romantic—so tender and passionate, and I just couldn't imagine him writing anything like that.'

'So who was it from?'

'I don't know. I didn't have a chance to finish it before you came back, and…' she couldn't stop herself from reaching out then, touching his cheek with the backs of her fingers as she recalled the tension that had vibrated between them '…then it kind of went out of my head for a while. I did look later, when I put the book back, but it wasn't signed with a name.'

He got to his feet, taking a few steps away from her.

'So how do you know it wasn't Ralph?'

'Because it talked about *you*,' Sophie said, very softly, standing up too. 'You must only have been tiny and he'd obviously just come back from visiting. He said how painful it was for him to leave you, knowing it was Ralph you thought of as your father.'

'Why didn't you tell me this before?' Kit demanded icily.

Sophie swallowed. 'It was none of my business at the time. I knew straight away that I shouldn't have read it, and, let's face it, we didn't exactly know each other well enough for me to drop that kind of information casually into the conversation. And then afterwards…there just wasn't the chance.' She paused, nervously moistening her lips as she gathered the courage to voice the misgivings that had been silently closing in on her since she'd woken that morning. 'I don't know, Kit, sometimes I think we hardly know each other any better now.'

Her stomach was in knots as she waited for him to reply. Standing with his back to her, his shoulders looking as if they'd been carved from granite. And then he sighed, and some of the tension went out of them.

'I'm sorry.' He turned round. 'I don't understand it, that's all. Why the hell didn't she just leave Ralph and go to be with him—whoever he was—and take me with her?'

The bitterness in his tone made her heart ache with compassion, but at the same time a part of it sang. Because anger was emotion, and because he was *talking* to her about it.

She shrugged, taking care to sound casual. 'Maybe that's what she wants to explain.' Going over to him, she stretched up to lightly kiss his lips. 'Let's go. Let's go to Morocco and find out.'

CHAPTER THREE

AND SO, WITH her characteristic clear-sightedness, Sophie made the decision that they should go to see Juliet. All that was left for Kit to do was make the arrangements.

If it hadn't been for her he would simply have put the letter into the waste-paper bin, along with all the rest of the junk mail. He had long ago closed his heart to the woman who had walked out on him when he was six years old, promising to return. That broken promise, perhaps more than her abandonment, had sown seeds of wariness and mistrust in him that grew over the years into a forest of thorns around his heart. Sophie alone had slipped through its branches.

And in the same way, when he'd shown her the letter she had cut through the anger and bitterness and made it all seem so simple. So obvious. About facts, not emotions.

Odd that he of all people should need reminding of that.

'First class?' Sophie murmured, looking up at him from under her lashes as he steered her in the direction of the passenger lounge at London City Airport. 'How sweet of you to remember I never travel any other way.'

Her eyes sparkled, and he knew she was thinking of the way they'd met, when she'd sat opposite him—without a ticket—in the first-class carriage on the train from London to Northumberland. He'd spent the entire four-hour journey trying not to look at her, and trying to stop thinking about touching her.

It was going to be the same story today, he thought dryly. They'd spent the morning in bed, but in spite of the fact she'd managed to pack and get ready in under an hour she looked utterly delectable in loose, wide-legged white linen trousers and a grey T-shirt that showed off the outline of her gorgeous breasts.

'Not this time, I'm afraid,' he said gravely as Air Hostess Barbie came towards them, her dazzling smile faltering a little as she saw the state of his face. 'Major Fitzroy? Your plane is waiting, if you'd like to follow me.'

As she stepped onto the tarmac Sophie's eyes widened and her mouth opened as she saw the small Citation jet.

'Holy cow…' she squeaked. He couldn't stop himself from bending his head and kissing her smiling mouth.

'Major Fitzroy.' Neither of them noticed the pilot approaching until he was almost beside them. Unhurriedly Kit raised his head, but kept a hand on the small of Sophie's back as he reached out and shook the one the pilot offered.

'Good to see you, Kit.' Beneath his dark glasses the man's face broke into a grin. 'I'd like to say you're looking well, but—'

Kit nodded, automatically raising a hand to touch the cuts on his face. 'Your natural charm is outweighed by your honesty, McAllister,' he said dryly.

The pilot's expression suddenly became more serious. 'You just back from a tour?'

'Two days ago.'

Kit's tone was deliberately bland. By contrast the pilot spoke with feeling.

'I don't envy you. It's absolute hell being out there, and then almost worse coming home.'

Smoothly Kit changed the subject by turning to Sophie. 'Nick, let me introduce you to Sophie Greenham. Sophie, Nick McAllister. He's an old friend.'

'He's flattering me.' Grinning again, Nick McAllister shook Sophie's hand firmly. 'I was far too low down the pecking order to be a friend of Major Fitzroy. We served alongside each other in some fairly joyless places, until I couldn't take any more and quit to get married and do a nice, safe job.'

'Do you miss it?' Sophie asked. It was impossible not to like him, and it was always a good idea to be nice to the person who was about to fly you across Europe.

'Not in the slightest, but then I'm not made of the same heroic stuff as Kit. Leaving it all behind was the best thing I ever did, especially as my wife only agreed to marry me if I gave up. She's expecting our second child in a few days.'

Sophie felt as if something sharp had just pierced her side. 'Congratulations,' she managed in an oddly high-pitched voice.

Luckily Kit was already beginning to move away. 'In that case we'd better get going or you'll be on the way to Marrakech while she's on her way to the delivery room,' he said.

THE CABIN OF the small plane was the most insanely luxurious thing Sophie had ever seen. Everything was in toning shades of pale caramel and crème, even the stewardess who appeared as soon as they were airborne with champagne and strawberries. It reminded Sophie of the villain's lair in a James Bond film.

'Kit Fitzroy, you big show-off,' she said, struggling to suppress a huge smile as the stewardess disappeared through the suede curtains again. 'You don't impress me with your fancy private plane, you know. Just think of your carbon footprint—how do you live with the guilt?'

'Years of practice.' He took a mouthful of champagne, and for a split second a shadow passed across his face. 'But I'd heard the recession has had an impact on business and I was selflessly prepared to put Nick's income before my carbon footprint.'

'Spoken like a true hero.' Sophie settled back in a huge cream leather seat and looked around. 'He seems happy enough that he made the right decision though,' she added casually, idly twirling a strawberry around by its stem. 'Would you ever consider...?'

'Giving up my career to get married?' Kit drawled in mock outrage. 'In *this* day and age?'

Taking a mouthful of champagne, Sophie almost snorted it out of her nose. 'Shut up,' she spluttered, laughing. 'You know what I mean.'

Suddenly his face was serious again, his silvery eyes luminous in the clear light above the clouds. 'Yes. And yes.' He gave her a twisted smile that made her stomach flip. 'I don't want to go back. The question is, do you still want to marry me?'

Below them the sea stretched in a glittering infinity. Sophie's heart soared. This was exactly the kind of conversation that had seemed so impossible in the big, empty house in Chelsea, but up here it was different. She could be herself.

'Of *course* I do,' she moaned, then added hastily, 'I mean, if that's what you want.'

He put his glass down on the gleaming wood ledge. His eyes were on hers.

'Come here,' he said softly.

She was about to mutter something about seat belts, but stopped herself just in time as she realised those kind of rules didn't apply to private planes. And anyway, she couldn't imagine anything safer than being held by Kit. She went over, settling herself sideways on his lap, her feet hanging over the arm of his seat.

'I don't need a piece of paper or anything, you know that,' she said quietly. 'I know that five months is a long time and a lot has happened since then. You've been away and… I don't know, I thought that maybe when you'd had time to think about it you might have decided it wasn't such a good idea.'

Taking a deep breath in, Kit closed his eyes and let his head fall back against the leather headrest. That was exactly what he'd decided yesterday morning, waking up beside her and realising that they were little more than strangers. Understanding that what had happened to Lewis could so easily have happened to him, and that his life wasn't the only one he was playing Russian roulette with any more.

But now, with her body folded into his, her hair soft against his jaw, the decision was abstract. Irrelevant. The rightness of his initial instinct to make her his and never let her go was indisputable.

'I haven't.' He picked up her hand, stroking his thumb over her empty third finger. 'And I need to get you a ring as soon as possible so you don't think that again.'

'A ring? Ooh—exciting! How soon can we do it?'

He couldn't stop a smile from spreading across his face as the uncertainty and darkness receded. 'Well, we can do it tomorrow if you don't mind having a ring that comes from a back alley in the souk and costs the same as a glass of Chardonnay in a pub in Chelsea, or as soon as we get home we can—'

She silenced him by kissing the corner of his mouth. 'I wouldn't mind that at all, but I didn't mean the ring. I meant how soon can we get married? Can we do it when we get home?'

He reached around her to pick up his champagne. 'I think there might be a few things you have to do first, like get a licence and book a place and a person to do it.'

She shifted her position so that she was sitting astride him. 'That can't take too long, surely?' She licked her lips and didn't quite meet his eye. 'I mean, we don't want one of those full-scale epics with a football team of bridesmaids, a cake the size of Everest and three hundred guests.'

'No? I thought that was what every bride wanted?'

He actually felt her shudder. 'Not me. Or not unless there are two hundred and ninety-nine people you want to invite, and I get to have Jasper on my side of the church.'

'You must have people you want there? Family?'

In spite of the clear light flooding the cabin her eyes had darkened to the colour of old green glass, but he only glimpsed them for a moment before her lashes swept down and hid them from view.

'I don't have family. And I certainly don't have a father to walk me down the aisle and make a touching speech recapping significant moments on my journey to being the woman in the meringue dress.'

Her tone was light enough but everything else resisted further questioning. He could feel the tension in her body, and see from the way she was avoiding his eye that they'd stumbled into a no-go area. Very gently he ran a fingertip down her cheek, tilting her face upwards when he reached her chin.

'You have a mother,' he said softly. 'And most mothers would probably say that getting to be Mother of the Bride is one of the highlights of the job.'

She slid off his knee, getting up and taking the champagne bottle from the ice bucket in which the stewardess had left it. Kit felt a moment of desolation as the contact with her body was lost.

'My mother is not most mothers,' she said in a tone of deep, self-deprecating irony as she poured champagne into her glass. Too fast—the froth surged upwards and spilled over. 'Oh, knickers—sorry,' she muttered, making a grab for it and trying to suck up the cascading fizz.

'It's fine—leave it.' Taking the glass and the bottle from her, he tilted the glass as he refilled it. 'So, why wasn't she like other mothers?'

'Well, for a start I wasn't even allowed to call her that.' She slid back into her own seat, took a mouthful of champagne before continuing, 'Not "Mother" or "Mum" or anything that would pin her into a narrow gender-stereotyped role that carried political and social associations of subservience and oppression.' She rolled her eyes elaborately and he could hear the inverted commas she put around the phrase.

'So what did you call her?'

Sophie shrugged. 'Rainbow, like everyone else.'

'Was that her name?'

'It was for as long as I can remember.' Absently she trailed her finger through the little puddle of champagne. Two lines were etched between her narrow

brows, and Kit found himself longing to reach over
and smooth them away. 'It was only when I went to
live with my Aunt Janet when I was fifteen that I discovered her real name was Susan.'

'So why did she call herself Rainbow?'

Sighing, Sophie slumped back in the seat, her glossy
maple-coloured hair bright and beautiful against the
pale upholstery. Nick ought to hire her as a promo
model, Kit thought wryly, then instantly dismissed the
thought. Over his dead body.

'For the same reason she called me Summer, I suppose. Because it fitted in with her barmy hippy friends,
and marked us out to be "alternative" and "different"
and "free". Which to her, was a good thing.'

'But not to you?'

She threw him a pitying glance. 'Please. You try
being the only person in the school assembly hall wearing a violently coloured stripey handknit jumper and
patchwork dungarees instead of a grey skirt and a navy
cardigan because your mother believes "every individual has a right to be an individual".'

She said this last bit in a tone of dreamy wistfulness
that gave Kit an instant snapshot of her mother; Rainbow, the feminist, peace-campaigning free spirit. None
of those were bad things to be, he reflected idly, and
behind Sophie's exasperation he sensed genuine love.

'At least your mother was there,' he said wryly.

'Yes. Even if I often wished she wasn't.' She gave a
swift smile that dimpled her cheeks and told him that
she'd had enough of serious stuff. Through the window
the sunlight had lost its dazzling golden glare and deepened to the colour of good cognac. Kit was no artist, or

photographer, but looking at Sophie as she leaned her chin on her cupped hand he wished he were.

'So when are we seeing her? Juliet, I mean.'

'Tomorrow evening.' He grimaced. 'She did invite us to stay with her, but I politely declined. I've booked us into a hotel in Marrakech, and we'll drive out there for dinner.'

'How was it—talking to her?'

Kit thought. Hearing her voice had been strange, but in an abstract way. It didn't affect him any more. Sophie had healed so much of the damage she had done to him.

'It was brief and to the point, as I hope seeing her will be. This isn't about her, or rebuilding a relationship. I just want answers.'

'About your father?'

'Yes.'

Reaching to pick up his glass, Kit was aware again of the burning numbness in his fingers. It came and went, but there was no doubt he'd felt it for the first time on this last tour, since he'd found out that Ralph Fitzroy wasn't his father. Maybe finding out who he was would stop the feeling that he was dissolving.

He was saved from having to say any more by the appearance of the colour-coordinated stewardess, bearing plates of canapés.

'Captain McAllister hopes you're enjoying the flight, and asked me to tell you that we'll be landing at Marrakech-Menara in just over an hour.'

In the seat opposite Sophie arched her back and unfolded the leg that she'd had tucked up beneath her on the seat. Her bare foot brushed his knee.

'Thanks,' Kit said blandly to the stewardess as lust lashed through him. 'Can you ask him if he can go any faster?'

CHAPTER FOUR

THEY STEPPED DOWN from the plane into a rose and indigo evening. Sophie almost hadn't wanted the flight to end, but it was impossible not to feel excited when she'd looked out of the window and seen Marrakech below. 'The Red City', they called it, and in the light of the dying sun it was easy to see why.

A porter went ahead of them into the terminal building with their luggage while Nick waited on the tarmac to say goodbye. He and Kit shook hands, agreeing that Kit would be in touch to arrange a return flight, then he turned to Sophie.

'Enjoy Morocco.' He grinned.

'I will.' She already was. The air was as warm and thick as soup, and as spicily fragrant. She breathed it in and impulsively reached up and gave him a quick hug. 'Thank you for bringing us.'

In the airport building Kit went to change money and she looked around, her pulse quickening as she listened to the unfamiliar languages filling the magnificent and curiously cathedral-like space. She loved travelling, and this was the feeling she always got in a new place—a sense of promise, of discoveries waiting to be made and adventures yet to be had.

'Ready?' he asked huskily.

Their eyes met and she nodded, torn between the

desire to rush to the nearest hotel with him, and the urge to get out and explore the city that lay tantalisingly just beyond the soaring criss-crossed pillars of the terminal building.

Kit walked ahead of her, stuffing the wad of dirhams he had just exchanged into the back pocket of his jeans. Sophie's throat dried with instant lust, and along with it the glib warning she was about to give him about the danger of pickpockets. No one would mess with Kit.

A car from their hotel was waiting for them, sleek and gleaming amongst the battered, dusty taxis. The driver got out, nodding respectfully at Kit as he came round to open the door for them. Smiling shyly, Sophie slid into the car while Kit spoke to the driver in rapid, fluent French and tipped the porter who had brought out their bags.

Another gush of desire crashed through Sophie, and she leaned back against the seat, inwardly outraged at her own weakness as Kit got in beside her. She was the girl who'd always prided herself on her independence, her ability to go anywhere and do anything on her own, and here she was being treated like some fragile princessy type, cosseted from the need to take control of anything.

God, it was sexy though. As the car moved through wide streets that, despite the lateness of the hour, were still choked with vehicles, freed from the need to be responsible she felt deliciously reckless. Maybe it was too much free champagne on the aeroplane. Or maybe it was just Kit—the intoxicating effect of his strength and assurance. His *masculinity*. Not to mention his knee-weakening gorgeousness and the memory of what he'd done to her earlier with the chocolate spread…

'Djamaa El Fna.' Kit's husky voice close to her ear half roused her out of her thoughts, half plunged her deeper into them. 'Marrakech's famous square.'

Suppressing a shiver of longing, she turned to look out of the window. The dusk was lit up with the strings of lights swinging beneath the canopies of stalls, and the flames from braziers. Wreaths of smoke blurred the lights into orbs of brightness, which highlighted the faces of the stallholders and gave the scene an atmosphere of theatre. Even from inside the car Sophie could smell roasting meat and spices and hear a rapid, frantic drumbeat. It seemed to reach down inside her, echoing the primitive, restless thud of her own heart.

She turned to Kit. His face was shadowed, but the lights from the square made his eyes gleam like beaten silver.

'Let's get out,' she said breathlessly. 'I want to see it.'

Kit said something to the driver and the car pulled to the side of the road. Sophie had reached for the door handle and was opening the door before the car had even stopped.

It was like nothing she'd ever seen or experienced before. The rhythm of the drums shimmered down her spine, making her hips move instinctively as she moved forwards. She could feel herself smiling as the heat of the night melted bones that felt as if they'd been frozen for a long, long time. From behind Kit hooked an arm around her neck, drawing her back against the hard wall of his body.

'Slow down, gypsy girl,' he murmured into her hair. 'I don't want to lose you.'

She twisted herself around so that she was facing

him. The lights shone in eyes that were dark with excitement. They looked like pools of reflected stars.

'I'm not going anywhere without you.' She smiled, moving her hands down to his hips and sliding her fingers into the pockets of his jeans, pulling him against her. He could feel her hips moving, snake-like, as if the music weren't just all around them, but was inside her too.

Dangerous thought.

'If you carry on doing that, the only place you'll be going is back to the hotel, as quickly as possible,' he growled, pulling away, capturing her hands and drawing her with him as he began to walk forwards.

She was like a chameleon, he thought. Wherever you put her she had a way of adapting, becoming part of the scene. For a second he thought of what the other women he'd dated, with their expensive shoes and glossy Knightsbridge hair, would make of this place. The idea brought a smile to his lips.

'Come on, I'm hungry,' she said, pulling on his hand. Her excitement was completely infectious. The smile widened.

'What do you want to eat?'

He had to bend down and speak close to her ear to make himself heard above the noise of the marketplace. The scent of her made his head spin and took him back to earlier, on the kitchen worktop. London seemed like another lifetime, but in that moment the two worlds collided and desire rushed through him, dilating his veins with heat.

'Do you think anywhere sells chocolate spread?' she asked innocently.

'Stop it,' he warned.

She laughed, turning and beginning to walk between
the crowded stalls again. Her hair hung loose down her
back, gleaming in the lights as she turned to look at
the displays of jewel-coloured fruit and golden, deep-
fried prawns and tiny pastries. Kit didn't really take in
the food on offer. He was too busy looking at her high,
rounded bottom beneath the thin linen trousers, which
was far lusher than any of the pomegranates and mel-
ons on display.

The music got louder as they approached a break
in the stalls where a group of musicians had gathered,
squatting on the ground around their framedrums and
reed-like pipes, a woman in silken robes undulating
in front of them. Sophie's pace slowed, and fragrant
smoke wreathed her as she turned to face him. The
bright lights beneath the canopies made her skin glow
gold and her eyes, as she looked up at him, were dark
and dilated.

'I don't know where to start. There's so much I want
to try.'

Food, Kit reminded himself sternly. She's talking
about *food*. Reaching out, he brushed his thumb over
her slightly parted lips.

'What do you feel like?'

Looking up into his eyes, she shrugged slowly. 'Anything that I haven't tried before. Something that'll blow
my mind.'

Kit dragged his gaze away from her. The smoke was
coming from a stall opposite that was laid out with
just about every kind of local delicacy, both tempting
and alarming, and a man standing behind it, impassively laying skeins of small sausages onto a searing
hot grill. Kit spoke to him, and he glanced at Sophie,

his dark eyes gleaming with approval as he took the money Kit offered.

'What did you ask for?'

'You'll just have to wait and see,' he said gruffly. 'Close your eyes.'

Hesitantly, Sophie did as she was told. The noise around her seemed to increase as darkness flooded her head, and the scent of cedar smoke and spices and meat and garlic and hot, salty bread intensified so that her mouth was instantly alive. And beneath it all, close and strong and most delicious of all, was the scent of Kit's skin as he raised his hand to her lips.

'Are you ready?'

She nodded. A great happiness was simmering inside her, threatening to bubble over. She was in love with the moment, the place, the man she was with and everything seemed sharply, almost painfully wonderful. Tentatively she opened her mouth, her senses on high alert, both afraid and excited.

She breathed in chilli-scented steam for a second, then tasted something strong, spicy, smoky-rich on her tongue and guessed it was one of the tiny local sausages she'd seen the man put on the grill.

'Mmm…gorgeous,' she murmured, swallowing and opening her eyes. 'More, please.'

Kit towered above her; inscrutable, beautiful. The cuts and bruising on his face seemed less noticeable here somehow; perhaps because everything was more real, more raw than in England. The painted sign that swung above the stall was chipped and rusting, the face of the woman at the next stall was creased like crumpled paper, her smile gap-toothed, joyful.

'Close your eyes. Keep them closed.'

Sophie pressed her lips together holding back her own smile. Kit's fingertips on her lips made a shiver of longing travel down her spine.

'Open your mouth.'

He dropped a fat olive onto her tongue and she held it between her teeth for a second, enjoying the feel of its skin on her tongue-tip before biting into it with an explosion of flavour. A dense, dry lamb kefteh followed, then a slice of tomato, slippery with olive oil and mint leaves. Gripping the metal pole of the canopy, she kept her eyes closed as he'd said, giving herself up to the succession of sensations and flavours, murmuring her appreciation as oil moistened her lips and dripped down her chin. The music and the drums and the warm, smoky air wrapped around them, so that it was easy to imagine it was just her and Kit, alone under the dark blue African sky...

Easy, but perhaps not wise. There was a throbbing at the apex of her thighs and her skin was so sensitive that the lightest touch of his fingers brought goosebumps up on her bare arms.

'Enough?'

Kit's voice was a husky whisper, but she could hear the amusement in it. Her senses sang. She shook her head.

'More.'

More quickly now he fed her bread, soft and airily dissolving beneath its hard crust, meltingly tender meat, battered prawns and crisp fried squid. She pulled a face as she chewed that, and next he gave her something spicy loaded onto bread that made her lips tingle.

'Mmm...better...' she murmured.

'What about this? Open wide...'

Juice, redolent of cumin and garlic, ran onto her tongue and a second later she felt something lightly touch her lips. With a low moan of greed she opened them, trying to capture it as it quivered just out of reach. She heard Kit laugh, a low throaty sound that made her longing crank up another notch. Sticking her tongue out, she caught whatever it was he was holding, his fingers with it, sucking them hard until he let it go.

It was like nothing she'd tasted before—soft, but at the same time oddly tough and with an earthy flavour that she couldn't name. She swallowed.

'What was it?'

He brought his head down so his lips grazed the lobe of her ear, and let them linger.

'Snail.'

Her eyes flew open. 'Really?'

'Well, when you didn't object to the sheep's head...'

'Kit! You—'

Laughing, he caught her wrist as she went to hit him, and it was then that she noticed the crowd of people—locals in djellabas, curious tourists, the musicians from opposite—standing around her in a circle, watching. They burst into a round of applause, and the man came round from behind the stall to shake her hand, clearly delighted to have such excellent free advertising.

Sophie looked up at Kit, smiling sweetly, speaking so softly only he could hear. 'You are in *such trouble* when we get to the hotel.'

Kit's teeth showed white as he flashed her a grin. 'I can't wait.'

Taking advantage of the assembled crowd, the musicians started up again. Sophie wondered when they'd stopped. The dancing girl came forward, holding her hands out. Her face was half veiled and above it her dark eyes warm and melting. Sophie took the hands she offered, casting a deliberately wicked look over her shoulder at Kit.

'You might have to...'

'Sophie—'

Already she had slipped her little jewelled ballet flats off and Kit felt his smile set like concrete as desire kicked him in the ribs. He stood back helplessly and watched her move to the centre of the circle of people, tying her shirt above her midriff then raising her arms above her head like the Berber girl, rotating her hips.

Of course, he knew she'd be good at it. But she wasn't just good. She was...hypnotic. She didn't have the technical precision of the other girl with her intricate moves, but there was a more earthy sensuality about the way she undulated. The circle of onlookers thickened, became two deep as the beat got faster, the musicians responding to the writhing bodies of the two women—one veiled and mysterious, the other fiery and sensual. Kit couldn't take his eyes off Sophie's midriff, the snake-like undulations of her flesh.

Where had she learned how to do that? And why hadn't she shown him before now? In the privacy of a bedroom where it wouldn't take every shred of his self-control to subdue his raging erection and withstand the urge to hoist her over his shoulder in a fireman's lift and bear her away.

Night had descended properly now and a full moon floated high up in the sky like a white balloon. The crowd was pressing in closer. In the glow of the lamps the musicians wore rapt, trance-like expressions on their faces. Sophie was half turned away from him now. Her

face was hidden by her hair, but he could see the rise
and fall of her chest as she breathed hard, see the gleam
of moisture on her skin.

Kit couldn't wait any longer. She had had her revenge. Going forwards, he slid his arm around her waist
and pulled her into his body, scooping her up in one
swift, decisive movement.

She didn't resist. Tipping her head back, she looked
at him with eyes that glittered like black diamonds.

'Time to find the hotel, I think,' he said grimly, turning and heading away from the little clapping, whoop-
ing crowd.

The music got fainter, swallowed up by the sounds
of the market. Stretching up, Sophie pressed her lips
to the column of his throat, where a pulse was beating
with the same insistence as the fading drum.

'I thought you'd never ask.'

THE CAR WAS cool and quiet after the sultry, throbbing
air outside. They carefully didn't touch, sitting at opposite ends of the wide seat, knowing that any physical contact would be dangerous—like putting a lighted
match into a box of fireworks.

Looking at each other was bad enough. But Sophie
couldn't take her eyes off him. The ten minutes it took
to get to the hotel seemed like a lot longer.

The car slid to a halt in front of an unassuming building—little more than a huge, arched wooden door,
flanked by lemon trees, set into a wall. The driver got
out and walked round to open the passenger doors.

'Leave this to me,' Kit growled.

Sophie was about to ask what he was talking about,
but he'd already got out of the car and come quickly

round to her side. Leaning in and sliding one arm around her shoulders, the other beneath her knees, he pulled her against his chest again.

'Kit, I can—'

'Shh.'

His face was set and there was a muscle flickering in his jaw. Sophie let herself go pliant in his arms, but had to clamp her teeth together to stop herself from moaning out loud as he carried her towards an imposing and ancient-looking set of wooden doors. She could feel his erection pressing against her hip.

'Are you by any chance using me as a human shield?' she murmured.

His lips twitched into a momentary smile, but then it was gone and his face resumed its deadpan expression as the driver who had brought them opened one of the giant-sized wooden doors.

Sophie had to admire Kit's cool. Aside from keeping her rampaging desire in check she also had to try to stop her jaw from dropping at the sheer magnificence of her surroundings. The door had opened into a courtyard, surrounded on all sides by cloisters of pure white stone that, in the blue dimness, looked like sugar-icing. A rectangular pool stretched the length of the courtyard, and beyond it light spilled through another arched doorway, spreading golden ripples onto the water. Candles in glass lanterns were placed at intervals along it, their flames dipping as Kit passed, as if they were bowing.

The contrast with the vibrant chaos of the night market couldn't have been greater.

A woman of quite extraordinary beauty appeared in the doorway.

'Welcome to Dar Roumana.'

Her long black hair was fastened back from her olive-skinned, heart-shaped face and she was dressed in some kind of simple white linen shift. Gosh, thought Sophie weakly. The whole thing really had taken on the aspect of an Arabian Nights–type fantasy. She wouldn't have been surprised if a genie had swept down on a flying carpet.

'It's Kit Fitzroy. I have a reservation, but my wife is feeling faint. If you could show us to our room I'll check in properly later.'

'Of course.'

Sophie bit her lip to stop herself smirking. Faint with lust, possibly. They followed her into the lamplit room, where she took down a large silver key from a row of hooks on the wall behind a desk, then up a curving staircase and into a high stone corridor that overlooked the courtyard below. Tiny candles in glass votives were placed along the tiled floor, throwing their flickering shadows onto the walls as they went.

How could shadows look so erotic?

'Here is your room.'

Turning the key, the dark-haired woman opened the door and stood back respectfully. 'My name is Malika. If there is anything I can do for you…'

'That's very kind,' Kit said curtly, 'but there's nothing for now.'

'Some mint tea, for your wife, if she is ill…?'

'Oh…th-thanks, but I'll be fine,' Sophie squeaked. 'I just need to lie down.'

Malika retreated, closing the door silently.

The second she'd gone Kit gave a low, animal-sounding moan and Sophie wriggled free from his arms, sliding to the floor as their mouths met and their bodies collided, limbs tangling as they struggled to free each other of their clothes.

'Just need…to…lie down,' Sophie gasped when their open mouths parted long enough for Kit to pull her top over her head. Wildly she looked around, too dazed with the immediacy of her need to be naked and horizontal to take in the spectacular suite.

'Through here,' Kit growled, heading towards a set of double doors inlaid with silver, through which it was just possible to see a low bed, made up in white linen and piled high with cushions. However, they'd only got halfway when she took off her bra and he had to pull her into his arms and kiss her again, splaying his hands over her warm bare back before dipping his head and tracing the tip of his tongue around one rosy nipple.

The sound she made was almost one of pain. He felt her body stiffen and arch beneath his hands and took her into his mouth as her fingers slid into his hair, twisting, pulling.

It had only been a matter of hours since they'd made love in bed at home, but his need to have her again was as sharp and all-consuming as if he'd been starved of sex for a year. Being in such close proximity to her on the plane, putting food in her mouth in the marketplace and seeing the sensual absorption with which she'd tasted it had cranked his desire up to an uncomfortable level. Watching her dance had tipped him over the edge of uncomfortable and into full-on pain.

A series of shudders rocked her and she cried out, wrenching herself away and hauling him up so she could reach the fastening of his trousers. Her hands were shaking and when one accidentally brushed against his erection he almost came.

'I have a feeling…' she breathed raggedly, taking hold of his pulsing length '…that this is going to be *quick.*'

'What gave you that idea?' he rasped through gritted teeth, yanking her trousers open so that buttons bounced over the tiled floor.

'Not sure…'

There was the sound of ripping fabric as she struggled to free herself of the thin linen trousers. A second later there was another as he didn't bother to struggle to free her of her knickers.

Both naked, they gazed at each other for a second, their breathing loud and rapid. And then he was taking hold of her shoulders, fastening his mouth to hers, hitching her up against him as he carried her to the low bed.

They fell on it together. With the same kind of sensual flick of her hips he had seen her do when she was dancing she moved so she was astride him.

The room had a single huge window, covered with a kind of wooden fretwork shutter that cast intricate shadows over her naked body. Eyes half closed, she gazed down at him, her face haughty and abstracted as she raised herself up onto her knees and took him inside her. Kit bit back a cry, clenching his teeth with the effort of not letting go.

'Don't fight it,' she breathed, moving her hips. 'Don't hold back—I want you—'

He took her waist in his hands, holding her as she rode him, not taking his eyes off her face. Then he let one hand slip down to the place where their bodies joined.

He only had to brush her clitoris with his thumb to precipitate the orgasm that had been building with each hard, neat flick of her hips. And as her mouth opened and her eyes closed in ecstasy he felt a moment of pure, clear joy and finally gave in to his own wild climax.

She sank down on top of him, their skin sticky with sweat, their hearts thudding against each other. And for the first time in a long time Kit slipped easily into sleep, completely at peace.

CHAPTER FIVE

THE CALL TO prayer echoed out from minarets across the city; a thin wail, crescendoing to a discordant chorus that floated through the limpid dawn.

Kit's eyes flew open, his body catapulting into a sitting position.

For a moment he didn't move. His heart was pounding, his skin covered with an icy sweat. The bedroom was bathed in the melting Turkish-delight pink of a perfect dawn, and beside him Sophie slept on. Half draped in a white linen sheet, she looked like a voluptuous goddess from some rococo-painted ceiling, and for a moment his panic ebbed as he watched the gentle rise and fall of her chest as she breathed.

Marrakech, he reminded himself. He was in *Marrakech*. Off duty.

He exhaled heavily, easing himself back onto the pillows. The pins-and-needles sensation in his hands was back again. The call to prayer continued, a plaintive refrain that took Kit back and made him remember all the things that last night had made him so comprehensively forget.

God.

His heart lurched and instantly he was out of bed, looking round for his phone. He had *wanted* to forget the heat and the sweat and the constant, low-key adrenaline.

He had wanted to forget walking along that road to the bridge where the bomb was half concealed in a tangle of scrubby weeds and rubbish. But Lewis…

What right did he have to forget about him?

'Kit?' From the bed Sophie's voice was as warm and thick as honey. He tensed against it.

'It's OK. Go back to sleep.' He found his phone from the pocket of his kicked-aside jeans and headed for the door to the terrace. 'I need to make a phone call, then I'll order breakfast.'

Sophie turned over onto her stomach, burying her face into pillows that were still warm and breathing in the scent of him. Him and sex. It was a delicious and intoxicating combination. Happiness seeped through her, a gentler echo of the wild bliss she'd felt last night, and the day stretched out ahead, ripe with promised pleasure. Beyond the walls of the hotel she could almost sense the city that had already so enthralled her waking up, drawing her out.

It would have to wait, she thought drowsily. Breakfast first, and then she had plans for Kit in the Olympic-swimming-pool-sized marble bath…

She drew her knees up to her chest, hugging her stomach. Last night had been the most rapturous sex of her life and she couldn't help wondering whether the joy she'd felt was simply from the earth-shattering orgasm Kit had given her, or something even more magical…

Talking to him about her childhood on the plane yesterday, she had finally understood just how much she had wanted the normal, settled family life that other people took for granted. She couldn't turn the clock back, but she felt now as if she'd been given another chance. A new start, to create a secure family unit of

her own. With Kit, in a beautiful sunny house somewhere, that they would fill with treasures from their
travels, and children. Lots of children…

At that moment anything seemed possible, and as
she drifted back into sleep she was smiling.

THE SUN WAS high overhead in a sky as hard and polished and blue as the little inlaid tiles that decorated
the walls of the buildings and little cafés that lined the
dusty streets.

The densely packed stalls of last night had been
cleared away from the city's main square, but the wide
expanse was still filled with performers, medicine men,
acrobats and orange juice sellers. Kit was aware of Sophie taking everything in with wide-eyed delight. She
was wearing a narrow, ankle-skimming dress in white
muslin, and with her hair tied in a loose knot at the back
of her head and brass bangles jangling on her wrist she
looked completely at home.

'It reminds me of the music festivals I used to go
to with Rainbow when I was a child,' she said, lacing
her fingers through his. 'Oh, look—there's even a tarot
reader! Rainbow would have been all over that.'

Kit said nothing. It reminded him of the place he'd
just left. The place where Lewis's blood had glistened
blackly as it soaked into the sand. There had been no
change, the nurse had told him over the phone earlier.
They were keeping Lewis sedated to give his body the
best chance of healing, so it was impossible to tell what
the long-term damage was yet. They'd have a better
idea tomorrow.

Kit pushed sweat-damp hair back from his forehead

with a hand that was completely numb, but steady. It was only inside that he was shaking.

He had woken from one nightmare and walked straight into another, and there was no escaping this one. It was the heat, the punishing sun, the dark eyes looking at him from beneath headscarves and veils. It was the man hauling a fresh sheep's carcass on his shoulder, the scent of blood filling the narrow alley as he passed. It was the groups of men standing in doorways, watching.

Watching. For a moment he thought he could hear that voice in his earpiece again.

Sophie slowed in front of a snake charmer playing a whiny-sounding instrument to a resolutely impassive cobra. Seeing her looking at him, the snake charmer nudged the basket with his foot. With visible reluctance the snake roused itself, desultorily swaying for a few bars before subsiding again. Sophie gave a shout of laughter.

'Oh, poor snake! She's about as enthusiastic as a bored nightclub hostess performing for a crowd of ageing businessmen.'

Kit smiled, pressing the palm of his hand onto the middle of her back.

'You're burning.'

'I can't be. You applied the cream very thoroughly...' She looked up at him with eyes that glittered with mischief.

'Twice, in fact.' The first time it had got rubbed off all over the sheets when, hopelessly aroused, they'd fallen back onto the bed.

'And how is it fair that I'm burning in factor fifty when you don't even have cream on?' she asked huskily.

He wound a tendril of flame-coloured hair that had escaped from the knot around his finger.

'You're more sensitive than I am. Come on.' He pulled her forwards, away from the snake charmer with his steady black stare. 'Let's get out of the sun. Preferably by going back to the hotel.'

Sophie laughed, quickening her pace to keep up with him. 'No way,' she said firmly. 'I want to see more. I love it here.'

She steered him into one of the souk's dim alleyways, out of the blowtorch heat of the sun. Adrenaline stung through Kit's veins as his gaze automatically scanned the street.

'Oh, look—'

Sophie's voice reached him as if from a long distance. He turned his head automatically to see what she was pointing out to him, but was aware only of shadowed doorways where a sniper could hide, flat roofs that would provide the perfect position for a gunman to take aim.

'These are beautiful...'

She had gone over to a stall that was hung with silk clothing and was running her fingers down an olive-green scarf threaded with gold, lifting one corner so that a shaft of sunlight shone through the gossamer fabric. Kit gritted his teeth and rubbed a hand over his eyes, forcing back the blackness.

What the hell was wrong with him? It was pathetic. He had to get a grip.

'Put it on.'

His voice was hoarse, his fingers fizzing as he took down the scarf and laid it over her hair. Winding it gently around her neck in the Eastern way, he focused on the shape of her lips and the scent of her skin to stop his mind from wandering back along those dark and twisting pathways. She was here and she was real, and with the scarf around her head she looked oddly demure and very beautiful. Desire kneed him in the groin and a wave of relief and passionate gratitude swept through him. He took her face in his hands and fastened his mouth on hers.

Kissing her anchored him. His hands, now they were holding her, felt normal again and the darkness in his head was benevolent once more, filled with images from last night, of her body, tattooed by shadows as she kneeled astride him. As always, her desire rose to meet his and he felt her move towards him so that her breasts were brushing his chest.

With a muffled curse he pulled away.

'Don't stop,' she murmured, her eyes still closed and her face tipped up to his.

'If I don't I'll be taking that dress off right here and making love to you on a pile of silk cushions,' he said gruffly, 'and they're pretty strict about that here.'

She looked down, biting her lip.

Gently he unwound the scarf and picked up a tunic in the same colour. The shopkeeper had emerged from the back of his cave-like stall and was looking at them expectantly. His face was seamed with age, his dark stare gimlet-sharp but friendly enough. There was no trace of the suspicion and mistrust Kit saw in people's eyes when he was in uniform. So why was his heart beating faster, his fingers buzzing and nerveless?

He suddenly felt inexpressibly weary. This morning he had been eaten up with guilt for putting it all behind him and forgetting. Now he knew that if he didn't, the remembering would drive him mad.

If he wasn't there already.

He handed the money over without bothering to haggle and went back to Sophie, draping the scarf around her shoulders.

'Now, Salome,' he said dryly, 'if I tell you that the hotel has a highly recommended hammam, can I tempt you to come back with me?'

LYING ON HER tummy in the dense, smoky heat of the Dar Roumana's hammam, Sophie closed her eyes and tried to empty her mind, focusing on nothing but the sensation of warm oiled hands moving across her back.

The trouble was her mind didn't want to be empty. It was too full of Kit, and if she let her guard down the hands of the masseuse would reawaken the rapture in which he had drenched her. When they'd got back from the souk, hot and dusty, he had stripped her off and carried her into the enormous walk-in rainshower. Turning the setting to 'mist', they had lain on the limestone tiles and wordlessly drunk each other in.

But he hadn't *talked* to her, hissed a nasty little voice in her head. From the moment they'd woken up this morning she'd sensed a kind of tension in him, which had become increasingly obvious in the souk earlier. When she tried to ask what was bothering him he brushed her off, so she still had no idea what demons crouched at his back or what had put them there.

She was so lost in thought that it was a moment before she realised that the masseuse had stopped rubbing her back. Sophie opened her eyes. Gracefully the girl unfurled a towel and held it out to her.

'Time for wash now.'

'Wash?' Thinking of the shower, Sophie was about to say that wouldn't be necessary.

'Is Moroccan hammam speciality. This way.'

Hastily doing up the clasp of her bikini top, Sophie followed her into a hexagonal room whose pale marble walls dripped with moisture. A huge marble slab stood, altar-like, in the centre of the space. Climbing onto it, Sophie felt like an offering.

The heat was intense. Rivulets of sweat dripped down her back. The girl scooped a bowl of water out of a wooden bucket and tipped it over her shoulders. Sophie tucked her knees up and rested her chin on them, submitting to her ministrations like an obedient child.

She had thought that getting away from London would make it easier. Perhaps he just needed time, she thought wistfully, allowing the masseuse to take hold of her arm and soap it from wrist to shoulder. Sophie had spent enough time on film sets to understand the bond created when people were thrown together in an intense environment. She knew the feeling of disorientation when returning to real life in the outside world, when for a while it felt impossible to connect with anyone who wasn't there.

For Kit, returning from a war zone rather than a film set, that feeling must be intensified a thousandfold. She knew how concerned he was about the boy who was hurt. Surely he would talk to her when he was ready?

Having soaped her upper body all over, the masseuse took up an innocuous-looking sponge. Sophie stiffened and gave a little cry of surprise and pain as the girl began to rub her shoulders with it and she realised it was made of something scratchy. Sandpaper perhaps. Or steel wool.

She bit her lip. It hurt, but at the same time it felt good. Like loving Kit.

Defiantly she gritted her teeth against the pain.

He loved her too—every touch, every kiss told her that. Words were unnecessary. Didn't their bodies say it all?

KIT REACHED THE end of the long swimming pool and surfaced for air before twisting beneath the water to begin another length.

In that brief second he got a glimpse of the faded sky and realised that he'd been in the water for a long time. Initially he had focused all his energy on not thinking—on forgetting about Lewis and what had happened in the medina that morning—and instead thought of nothing beyond blankly counting the number of lengths. After a while even that blurred into meaninglessness and he just swam.

And that was what you had to do, he told himself wearily, ploughing through the water. You just had to keep going, keep shutting it out and eventually it would go away. An image of Lewis's girlfriend hung in the greenish water in front of his eyes for a second before he pushed it away with a stroke of his arm.

He couldn't spill it all out to Sophie. She was so sweet and sure and easy-going; there was no way he was going to inflict on her the dark thoughts that kept him awake at nights and had now begun to seep into his waking hours too. He'd sort it out alone, in his own way.

Reaching the other end of the pool, he broke the surface of the water again, took a lungful of air and was just about to turn around again when a movement caught his eye.

Sophie was coming down the path from the hotel, the afternoon sun making her hair dance with auburn lights and turning her skin to warm honey. She was wearing the embroidered tunic they'd bought earlier, a thick leather belt slung around her hips, and as she walked the thin silk rippled against her, showing off every line and curve. Suddenly his body seemed to forget that it was sated from the most intense sex of his life and that he'd been swimming for heaven knew how long.

If only his head were as good at overlooking stuff.

As she got nearer she raised a hand to shield her eyes from the sun, and the hem of the tunic rose to reveal another inch of pale gold thigh.

'Aren't you forgetting something?'

'I've been trying to forget a lot of things,' he drawled, vaulting out of the pool and looking her over speculatively as he reached for a towel. 'It's a whole lot easier now you've appeared looking like that.'

'Like what?' she asked distractedly, looking down at the olive-green silk tunic and frowning. 'Oh—yes, I know, this is far too short to wear on its own, but I'm going to wait until the last minute to put on my white trousers or—'

He reached out a dripping hand and took hold of her chin, tipping her face up and stopping her from saying any more.

'Like you've been lit up from the inside.'

It was true. Maybe it was the low, syrupy sunlight or some clever kind of cosmetic he knew nothing about, or maybe it was just her smile and the sparkle of her eyes and the sheen on her hair, but she seemed to glow. To radiate beauty.

She rolled her eyes. 'Ah. That would be the industrial sander the masseuse used to remove the top five layers of my skin.'

Kit slid his hand up her arm, beneath the loose sleeve. 'So underneath this you're even more naked than before?' he asked, lazily caressing her skin as he smiled into her eyes.

'You could say that... But we don't have time. That's what I came to remind you—that it's nearly six o'clock. We need to go.'

Of course. To meet the mother he hadn't seen for almost thirty years. That was the other thing he'd been trying to forget.

You could only go on blocking things out for so long. It all caught up with you in the end.

CHAPTER SIX

THE ATLAS MOUNTAINS gleamed like icebergs in the distance, their snowy caps stained pink in the setting sun. Leaning back against the front seat of the huge Mercedes Kit had borrowed from the hotel, Sophie felt its last rays warm her face and kept her eyes fixed straight ahead.

Apart from the mountains, there wasn't much to see—just an endless stretch of dry red earth sparsely covered with even dryer khaki-coloured scrub—but she had to focus on something so that she didn't keep turning to look at Kit. His big hands, powerful on the steering wheel. His deep golden-brown forearms against the white linen shirt he wore with the sleeves rolled back. The way his thigh muscles rippled when he changed gear. His profile—stern, distant, perfect.

'You're staring at me,' he remarked with a faint smile, not taking his eyes from the road.

'Sorry.' Hastily Sophie looked away. 'I was trying not to.'

Kit ran a hand over his face, rubbing his fingertips tentatively over the worst of the gashes on his cheekbones. 'Let's hope she's not expecting some clean-cut merchant banker in chinos and an Oxford shirt,' he drawled with heavy irony, 'because if so she's going to be *very* disappointed.'

'You could never disappoint anyone. I, on the other hand…'

Flipping down the sun-visor, Sophie peered despondently at her own face in the little mirror. Why had she thought it was a good idea to be flayed with a pan scourer? Her skin wasn't so much lit up from the inside as on fire. She grabbed her make-up bag and took out a bottle of foundation to tone down her scarlet cheeks, but as she went to squirt some into her hand the car bounced over a pothole and a jet of ivory-rose skin-firming make-up, complete with SPF and AHAs and probably a PhD or two, gushed out onto her trousers.

Her *white* trousers.

She let out a wail of dismay, and began scrubbing at it with the ragged remains of a tissue, instantly making it about five times worse. 'What am I going to do now?'

Kit glanced across. 'Take them off. I told you you didn't need them anyway—it looks even better without.'

'To you, maybe, but that's because your judgment is clouded by testosterone. I don't think that wearing a knicker-skimming minidress is something most etiquette experts would advise when meeting one's prospective mother-in-law for the first time. She'll think I'm, I don't know…some kind of…tart.'

Running out of steam, she stopped scrubbing and looked at Kit. He was staring ahead, his face perfectly blank, but there was a muscle twitching in his jaw and on the steering wheel his knuckles showed white through the bronzed skin of his hands.

'This is the woman who cheated on her husband and let him bring up another man's child while she ran off with her lover, remember? I hardly think she's in a position to *judge* anyone.'

Sophie's heart skipped a beat at the ice that edged his words. She sensed a tiny crack had opened up in the dam that held back his emotion. She hesitated, moistening her lips, afraid of saying the wrong thing, of driving him into himself again.

'How well do you remember her?' She kept her voice as casual as possible, dabbing at the stain on her trousers again in the hope that it would look as if she were just making idle conversation.

'I don't remember much about her at all,' he said tersely. 'I was only six when she left.' There was a pause. Sophie put her head down, though she wanted so much to look at him, to touch him, but she knew there was a far greater chance of making him clam up again if she did.

'I remember her perfume,' he said with rusty reluctance. 'And I remember that I thought she was very beautiful. I also remember her saying goodbye.'

Sophie couldn't stop herself from lifting her head to look at him then.

'Oh, Kit—that must have been terrible.'

His face was still inscrutable, his heavy-lidded eyes narrowed as he kept them fixed on the empty slash of black tarmac in front of them.

'Not at the time. She promised she'd be back soon. She'd been away before...' his mouth twisted into a kind of smile '...living at Alnburgh you'd have to or else you'd go mad—so I had no reason not to believe her. She told me to look after the castle while she was away, because it was going to be mine one day. I'm not sure now if that was wishful thinking or deliberate deceit.'

Sophie turned to look out of the window. The empty scrubland had given way to softer terrain now—grassland where cows stood in languorous groups and horses grazed, their shadows long and spindly-legged in the sinking sun. Up ahead clusters of houses clung to the hillside: tiers of reddish brown interspersed by tall palm trees.

'She was probably trying to—I don't know, soften the blow a bit.'

Kit gave a hollow laugh. 'Believe me, if there's going to be a blow it's better to feel the pain and deal with it.'

He dragged a hand through his hair, making it stand up at the front, and showing the lighter streaks where the sun had bleached it. Sophie's stomach constricted with lust and she looked away quickly.

'Is that where she lives, up there?' she asked, gesturing to the village on the hill.

'Yes.'

He might be utterly unmoved, but she was suddenly nervous enough for both of them. The stain on her jeans seemed to have spread in diameter and intensified in colour. Impulsively, she kicked off her little gold sandals and frantically tried to wriggle out of her trousers without undoing the seat belt.

'What are you doing?'

'Taking these off. I think tarty is better than dirty, although—'

Assailed by doubt, she broke off and bit her lip. Kit sighed.

'Why are you so bothered by what she thinks? And so determined to make excuses for her?'

Sophie took a deep breath in, pressing down on her midriff to quell the cloud of butterflies that had risen there.

'I just want her to like me,' she said quietly. *To ap-*

prove, corrected a mocking voice inside her head. *To not see you as the grubby girl from the hippy camp.* She tugged down the green silk tunic and lifted her chin an inch. 'And I suppose it seems like I'm making excuses for her because I don't like jumping to conclusions about people, or thinking the worst of them without seeing for myself. People used to do that about us all the time when I was growing up.' She looked out of the window and added in an undertone, 'And because at least one of us has got to be on speaking terms with her when we get there or it's going to be a very, very awkward evening.'

VILLA LUANA WAS a little way out of the village, set into the hillside, surrounded by olive trees and cypresses and pines that perfumed the warm air with their dry, resinous scent. Like Alnburgh, there was something fortress-like about its high, narrow-windowed walls and towers, but if Alnburgh had come from some Gothic horror story, Villa Luana was straight out of Arabian Nights.

They drove through a gate and pulled up in a courtyard where the evening shadows gathered in pools of deep indigo. Ornate silver Moorish lanterns lit up walls that were the soft pink of tea roses. A man dressed in the traditional white djellaba appeared through an open doorway and gave a silent half-bow, indicating with a sweeping gesture of his arm that they should go into the house.

Sophie's nerves cranked up several notches, but Kit's stride was utterly nonchalant, vaguely predatory as she followed him into a huge, high-ceilinged room. Several long windows with delicately inlaid surrounds were set into each wall, giving a panoramic view across the hillside.

It was so beautiful that for a moment Sophie forgot to be nervous and walked across to one of the windows with a low gasp of astonishment. In the west the sun appeared through the branches of the trees like a fat, warm apricot, bathing the villa's garden in syrupy light and unfurling ribbons of shadow across velvety lawns and a mirror-still pool. Beyond that lay the mountains—ink-dark and majestic.

'Welcome to Villa Luana.'

The voice came from behind her and, though it was soft, it still made Sophie jump. Automatically she looked at Kit. In the golden evening sun his face looked curiously drained of colour, but his eyes glittered like frosted steel as he looked at his mother.

Slowly Sophie turned to follow his gaze.

The woman who came towards them was small, slender, dark-haired and still very beautiful. For some reason Sophie had expected her to have adopted the Moroccan style of dressing, or an English version of it, but she was dressed in an exquisite black linen shift dress that owed more to the couture houses of Paris than the souks of Marrakech. Her oval face wore an expression of perfect serenity, though as she came closer Sophie could see lines etched into her forehead and around her eyes.

Eyes that were exactly the same silver-grey as Kit's.

She stopped a few feet away from him.

'Kit. It's been such a long time.' Her voice was low, but it vibrated with suppressed emotion. She was gazing at him; hopefully, avidly, as if he held her future in his hands. As if she was afraid he would disappear again.

'Hasn't it?' Kit drawled quietly. 'Almost thirty years, in fact.'

'Yes.' The acid in his tone must have stung her because she turned away sharply, and noticed Sophie for the first time.

'And you're Kit's fiancée.'

'Yes, I'm Sophie. Sophie Greenham.' Perhaps it was nerves that made her go forward and give Juliet a hug instead of just shaking her hand. Or perhaps it was because, despite her incredible poise and elegance, there was something fragile about her, something vulnerable that made Sophie feel the need to compensate for Kit's hostility. 'It's such a pleasure to meet you.'

'And you. A pleasure and a privilege.' Juliet gave Sophie's shoulders a squeeze, and Sophie understood that she was grateful. 'Now, it's such a beautiful evening I thought we could eat on the roof terrace. Philippe will bring us drinks and we can all get to know each other a little better. I want to hear all about the wedding.'

IF THE VIEW from the reception hall downstairs was beautiful, from the roof terrace on top of the house it was breathtaking: a melting watercolour in tones of ochre, burnt sienna, indigo and gold.

The sun was touching the horizon, painting the dry earth blood red. Kit leaned against the wall, breathing in the scent of pine and thyme and woodsmoke drifting up from the village and waiting for the adrenaline rushing through his veins to subside.

Seeing her again had brought it all back. The bitterness. The resentment. The anger. His jaw ached from clenching his teeth together, literally biting back the torrent of recrimination that swirled around his brain.

He had come here for answers, not to make polite
small talk about weddings. Behind him he could hear
Sophie keeping up a stream of gentle conversation as
she admired the view, the fruit hanging from the lemon
trees that stood in pots around the terrace, the piles of
silk cushions on the low couches.

He had never loved her more.

Closing his eyes, he let the sound of her sweet,
slightly hesitant voice steady him, and felt his hostility
ebb. He heard the manservant arrive, glasses clinking
together as a tray was set down. His hands, gripping
the edge of the wall, were numb again. The sound of a
champagne cork made his taut nerves scream.

He wanted nothing more than to gather Sophie into
his arms and take her away. Somewhere where he could
shut the world out, and forget it all.

'I thought we should have some champagne, as it's
a special evening,' Juliet said. Her voice was exactly as
he'd remembered it too. Summoning a bland smile, he
turned round to face her.

'Thanks, but I'm driving.'

'Oh—no, I'll drive,' Sophie said, her eyes darting
from his face, to Juliet, and back again.

'You're not insured. It's fine. I'll just have mineral
water.'

Juliet said something to the manservant, who melted
away again. Kit looked away from Sophie's anguished
face and out over the hillside again.

'I can see why you left Alnburgh,' he said, not bothering to hide the acid in his tone.

'It's certainly warmer here,' Juliet said with a small,
uncomfortable laugh. 'But Alnburgh is beautiful too.
You've no idea how much I missed it when I first came

here.' She stopped short, obviously aware that she had strayed too soon into dangerous territory, and then turned to Sophie. 'But I want to hear all about you. When Kit said he was engaged I was so thrilled. Tell me about yourself—what do you do for a living?'

Sophie took a gulp of champagne and nearly choked on the bubbles. Too late, she realised that Juliet's glass was still untouched and that she was probably supposed to wait for some kind of toast. Luckily the pink dusk hid her blush.

'If I say I'm an actress that makes it sound terribly grand,' she said, awkwardness making the words spill out too quickly. 'I'm not trained, and, apart from a season I did at The Globe earning peanuts for wafting a palm leaf over Cleopatra for two hours a night, I mostly do bit parts in TV and film.'

'How exciting.' Juliet's eyes kept wandering to where Kit stood a little distance away, his massive shoulders silhouetted against the crimson-streaked sky. 'I'm sure you'll get your big break soon.'

'Oh, I don't really want it, to be honest. I don't long for stardom or anything; in fact I'd absolutely hate it. Being an extra was just something that allowed me to earn money and travel and which didn't need a whole lot of exams, but I'd give it up tomorrow if I could.' She giggled and took another gulp of champagne. 'The film I've just done was about vampires and involved getting done up like a specialist hooker every day for six weeks.'

Philippe came back, carrying a huge tray loaded with tiny dishes and a bottle of mineral water, its sides frosted with condensation. He put the tray on the low table between the two cushion-strewn couches. Juliet motioned for Sophie to sit down.

'And what about you, Kit?' Juliet said softly. 'You're in the army?'

Kit came forwards. The last, flaming rays of the sun lit up his scarred face as he sat down on the couch opposite.

'EOD,' he said tersely, dragging a hand across his torn cheek. 'As you can probably tell.'

'I knew anyway. I've followed your career as much as I could. I read about your George Cross in the papers. I was so proud.' She gave a swift, sad smile. 'I have no right, I know that. But you must be, Sophie.'

Caught off guard, her mouth full of some kind of spicy chickpea thing she'd absent-mindedly picked up from one of the bowls in front of her, Sophie could only nod frantically.

'Anyway, a toast to you both,' Juliet said, picking up her untouched glass and holding it aloft so the golden liquid gleamed. 'To your marriage and your future together. May it be joyful and untroubled.'

Kit looked at Sophie as he raised his mineral water. To her shame Sophie's glass was almost empty.

'To all of us,' she said brightly, in an attempt to dispel the tension that crackled in the sultry evening. 'To a happy, untroubled future.'

Juliet took a tiny sip of champagne. Sophie tried very hard not to drain hers.

'So, tell me about the wedding,' Juliet said, putting her glass down again and looking at Sophie. Sophie could see the anguish in her luminous eyes, and understood the meaning of the term 'noblesse oblige': the effort required to keep the façade of gracious courtesy in place. 'Have you set a date?'

She glanced at Kit. He looked distant to the point of boredom but the restless tap of one long finger against the square arm of the couch betrayed his tension. Her heart squeezed with love and longing.

'We haven't even decided what kind of wedding it's going to be or where,' she said quickly. 'I'm not the kind of person who's been fantasising about ivory silk dresses and gigantic cakes since I was old enough to say "wedding planner" so it really cannot be small enough or private enough for me. A deserted beach would be good...' She trailed off, but the silence crouching in the shadows around them threatened to swamp them. Desperately she ploughed on. 'Lots of my friends have had register-office weddings, but they can be a bit... well, soulless. You come out wondering whether you've just witnessed two people pledging to love each other until they die, or applying for planning permission for a house extension.'

Juliet's smile was wistful. 'What about the chapel at Alnburgh?' she said carefully. 'It's tiny, and so beautiful.'

The tension that had been building in the still air cracked. From opposite Kit gave a muted sound of disgust and got to his feet, dragging a hand through his hair before turning to face Juliet. His silver eyes were luminous with anger.

'And unfortunately not licensed for public marriages. And since it turns out I'm not technically a Fitzroy...'

'Oh, Kit...' Juliet stood up too. The expression on her face was almost defiant, but her voice ached with compassion. 'I wondered if you knew. If you'd somehow worked it out.' She looked down, taking a second to regain her composure. 'That's why I wanted to see you. You *are* a Fitzroy. Alnburgh is yours.'

CHAPTER SEVEN

'WHAT THE HELL are you talking about?'

Through a fog of adrenaline Kit was dimly aware that his hands were bunched into fists at his sides and that his voice pulsed with anger. He didn't care.

'I saw Ralph's solicitor,' he went on, not bothering to stop his lip from curling into a sneer. 'Ralph's will made it very clear I was nothing to do with him, and he had no intention of letting his family estate fall into the hands of *your* bastard son.'

Juliet took a tiny gasping breath. Her eyes were like headlamps, fixed on his, her face pale.

'I thought he might do something like that. It's why I knew I had to get in touch. Ralph wasn't your father, Kit, but…' she took another quick breath '…but his older brother was. Which means it's you, not Jasper, who is the rightful heir of Alnburgh.'

Once, on duty, Kit had been set upon by a gang of insurgents and dragged into a back alley where they'd kicked and punched him repeatedly before he managed to get away. That scene, complete with the taste of blood and acid in his mouth, the pain under his ribs, came vividly back to him now. He turned away, mentally searching for something to hold on to.

'Ralph's older brother…?'

'Leo,' Juliet said quietly. 'Leo Fitzroy.'

Memories shifted and rearranged themselves. A portrait that used to hang in the hall at Alnburgh before it was moved to some less prominent position. A uniform. 'He was in the army,' Kit rasped. 'He died in the Falklands.'

'No.' He heard Juliet sigh. 'No, he didn't. He fought there, and as time passed and he never came back to Alnburgh that was what people assumed. Ralph didn't set them straight. It reflected well on the family, and it explained why there was no funeral.'

Kit rounded on her. 'What was the truth?'

Wrapping her arms around herself, as if for comfort or protection, Juliet moved away from the table with its virtually untouched dishes. 'I don't know where to start.' She gave a shaky laugh. 'Even though I've been rehearsing telling you all this in my head for weeks.'

'Start at the beginning.' From the couch, Sophie spoke. She was sitting very still, her head bent so that Kit couldn't see her face, but her voice was calm and quiet. 'Start with when you met Leo.'

Kit's heart was beating hard. He wanted to go to her, wanted to pull her against him and bury his face in her hair, but he couldn't move. Juliet went over to light a lamp hanging from the wall, the match illuminating her face for a second, clearly showing the lines of age and sorrow etched there.

'I suppose the beginning is when I met Ralph,' she said slowly, moving over to one of the lemon trees, cupping a fruit in the palm of her hand. The light from the lamp threw a circle of gold around them all and cast their shadows on the terrace wall. Kit remembered when Juliet used to come in to say goodnight to him in his turret bedroom at Alnburgh.

'I'd just finished boarding school and was terribly naive and sheltered,' she was saying in the same soft voice he remembered. 'My parents wanted me to go to Switzerland to some kind of finishing school, mostly because they didn't know what else to do with me while they waited for me to find a suitable husband. Then one weekend a friend invited me to go with her to a house party at Alnburgh.' She pulled a face. 'The seat of the Earl of Hawksworth. My mother was delighted.'

On silent feet the manservant, Philippe, returned, impassively loading the plates back onto the tray, topping up glasses, lighting the candles in the lanterns on the table. As he moved away Juliet came to sit down again.

'I fell in love with the place,' she went on, picking up her glass. 'It was the middle of summer and I'd never been anywhere more romantic. And at the centre of it all was Ralph, this laughing, handsome man who seemed to constantly have a bottle of vintage champagne in one hand and a half-naked blonde in the other.' She broke off to take a sip of her drink. 'The party went on for about three days. My parents were furious when I finally went home.' She gave a hollow laugh. 'Until I told them I was engaged.'

Although it was Juliet who was speaking, although she was his mother and he hadn't seen her for almost thirty years, it was Sophie at whom Kit found himself unable to stop looking. Propped on one elbow on the cushioned couch, she was watching Juliet, and her beautiful face was wistful.

'I thought I was in love with him,' Juliet said sadly, 'but really it was the castle, the glamour, the champagne, the freedom. It was just a shame I only realised that when it was too late. When Leo came to the wedding.'

She faltered, and, in one of the gestures of warmth and compassion that came so naturally to her, Sophie reached out and put a hand on Juliet's arm. In that moment the most prominent of the complex emotions churning inside Kit was gratitude. Sophie had taken responsibility for Juliet's feelings, meaning he could absorb the facts of his own painful history without the burden of responding.

It made it…easier.

'It was awful,' Juliet said bleakly. 'He was Ralph's best man and he only arrived on the morning of the wedding, so the first time I set eyes on him was as I walked down the aisle. It was like I recognised him, in some profound part of myself, and I knew, absolutely, that I was marrying the wrong brother.'

Across the table Sophie's eyes met Kit's, and he knew she too was remembering how she had come to Alnburgh as Jasper's pretend girlfriend. For the briefest second a smile passed across her face, but somehow it just made her look sad.

'So…what did you do?' she murmured, looking away again.

Juliet gave an elegant shrug. 'Nothing. I did what any polite, well-brought-up girl would do and I made my vows and said all the right things at the reception and went away on my honeymoon and tried to be a good, proper wife. But it was a disaster. Ralph had never had any intention of giving up the parties and the half-naked blondes, and I found that Alnburgh wasn't so romantic in winter. I thought I'd die of either loneliness or cold.'

In the sultry twilight Sophie pulled her knees up to

her chest and hugged them. 'I know the feeling. I was only there for two weeks, but I could think of nothing but how cold I was.' Her eyes found Kit's again, and another jolt of electricity fizzed through him as she added softly, 'Well, *almost* nothing.'

'Go on.' Kit's voice was like gravel as he forced himself to drag his thoughts away from that time, when Sophie's presence at Alnburgh had been like a knife in his side, tormenting and obsessing him.

'Then Leo came home.'

Juliet sighed and let her head fall back. 'If I say it was impossible to stop what happened between us, that sounds like an excuse. But that was how it felt.'

Tell me about it, Kit thought wearily. If he'd been a nicer person he probably would have said it out loud, to let Juliet know that he was every bit as fallible and incapable of resisting temptation as she and Leo had been, but he didn't. Opposite, Sophie leaned her cheek on her knees and looked at Juliet. Desire beat a relentless tattoo through his veins as he remembered how he had finally given up fighting the want, and in one of the castle's ancient, dusty four-poster beds had given in to it…

'We had three weeks before he had to go away again. We swore that would be it—that it was a one-off, a miraculous slice of perfection that would go no further. We made a decision not to write or keep in touch and so…' her voice cracked slightly '…when I discovered I was pregnant there was no way of contacting him.'

For the first time since she'd started speaking Juliet looked at Kit properly, her expression a mixture of apology and helplessness. 'I didn't even know where he was,' she said, almost imploringly. 'By that time he'd been selected for the SAS and everything he did was top secret. I was terrified. I was also horribly sick, which meant Ralph soon guessed I was pregnant. He was…happy. It didn't cross his mind for a second that it couldn't have been his baby.'

'And you didn't think you should tell him?' Kit said tonelessly.

'Of *course* I did. I thought about nothing else. But I was ill, and Leo wasn't there. I didn't know what to do, so I did nothing.'

Philippe had come back, bearing more dishes, which he set down on the table, seemingly oblivious to the currents of tension flowing across it. As he retreated again Sophie felt an urge to escape from the emotional cyclone that seemed to be building in the thick, hot air and follow him back to the kitchen. Where she belonged.

Kit waited until he was gone to speak again. His eyes were like lasers as he looked across at his mother, his voice dangerously quiet.

'And *how long* did you do nothing for?'

'You were about a year old when Leo came back.' Juliet didn't meet his gaze, busying herself taking the lid off a terracotta tagine and spooning out its fragrant contents. 'It had always been the plan that Leo would take over the running of the castle when he left the army, but everything had changed. Ralph thought you were his. Leo felt he'd already taken his brother's wife, and he couldn't bring himself to take his child and his home as well.'

Her hand shook, so that cous cous spilled over the tabletop. Raising her head, she looked at Kit. 'He gave up Alnburgh without a second thought, but we couldn't give up each other.'

'So you left to be with him.' In the candlelight his face was masklike, only the cuts showing that he was flesh and blood. 'Did you just *forget* to take me with you?'

Sophie's head throbbed. She discovered that she wanted very much to shut her eyes and put her hands over her ears, to make it all go away, like a child.

'Oh, Kit, it wasn't that simple!' For the first time Juliet's voice lost its careful moderation and became raw with weary emotion. 'I didn't leave straight away, as you know. We *tried* to stop seeing each other, but deep down we both knew it was hopeless, and in the end we stopped feeling guilty. He was abroad a lot—places I read about in the newspapers, places that were synonymous with violence and terror—and the whole thing had an air of tempting fate about it. He'd survived another tour, another siege, another shoot-out and he came back to me to celebrate being alive.'

Kit flinched.

'But after the Falklands it was different. Leo changed. He couldn't do it any more. He'd been posted in Gibraltar for a time, and that was when he'd bought this place, to come to when he had time, to relax. He wanted to come and live here full time, and he wanted us to join him—*both* of us.'

For a moment Kit said nothing. Somewhere in the distance a dog barked.

'So what happened?'

Sophie heard Juliet take a breath, as if she was steadying herself. Or preparing herself for something.

'He wasn't well when he came back from the Falklands. He wasn't sleeping, and he'd noticed things—things he assumed would get better when he got back here and had a chance to rest. When they didn't he came back to London to get checked out.'

Kit stood up abruptly, raising his hands to his temples. Stumbling to her feet, Sophie saw that they were clenched into fists.

'Go *on*.'

He spoke through gritted teeth, and when Sophie touched him he didn't seem to notice her.

'He got passed around a few specialists—different addresses on Harley Street who each subjected him to a battery of tests before referring him on to the next doctor.' Juliet's voice was eerily calm again now. 'I wasn't with him when he went to the last one. A neurologist. The one who told him he was suffering from a progressive illness affecting the central nervous system, and that he had a year to live.'

Kit turned away, walking over to the edge of the terrace as Juliet continued. The ache in Sophie's head had been joined by a burning feeling in her chest.

'It's a marvellous way of focusing your mind, hearing something like that. Suddenly everything seemed simple.'

'Leaving your child seemed *simple*?' Kit asked hollowly. It was dark now, and the magnificent view was swallowed up by layers of shadow. Beyond the circle of light on the terrace there was nothing to see, but he stared out into the blackness anyway, until his eyes stung.

'A year.' From behind him Juliet sounded very tired. 'I thought that was all. And I couldn't take you halfway across the world to be with a man you barely knew, a man who was terminally ill and was going to need me twenty-four hours a day. You needed school, routine...'

I needed parents, Kit thought bleakly. He'd needed *her.* But with a crushing sensation in his chest he could see that Leo had needed her too. His father. He had needed her more.

'So why didn't you come back?' he said harshly.

She sighed, a long, sad sigh. 'Because the doctors were wrong. They told us what would happen, how his body would shut down, bit by bit, like lights being switched off, until he couldn't move, couldn't swallow, couldn't breathe. They were right about that, but what they badly underestimated was how long it would take.'

Slowly Kit turned round.

'How long?'

'Sixteen years. He lived for sixteen years. So you see, by then it was far too late to come back.'

LOOKING BACK LATER, Sophie could remember very little of the evening after that. She wasn't really aware of what they ate, only that it was delicious enough for her to find that her plate was empty, and she was hungry enough to accept a second helping. Her glass seemed to empty itself very quickly, and be filled again by invisible hands. The warm air caressed her and Juliet's low, musical voice lulled her, distracting her from the dark shapes that moved in the back of her mind.

She talked of safe things. Of the labour of love that had been the restoration of Villa Luana, the way Leo had gradually won the trust and respect of the local people. Kit said little, and with the candlelight flickering over his face he looked like a carved saint in church: silent and suffering.

It was as if the hurricane had passed and they had

emerged into a calmer place. But the damage had still been done. Sophie was too tired, too overwhelmed by the revelations of the evening to think about what that damage might be.

'YOU'VE MADE A very good choice.'

Juliet's voice was gentle as she looked down at Sophie, fast asleep on her nest of cushions. Her hair was spread out over the vibrant-coloured silk, and in the warm lantern-glow it was every bit as rich and precious and gleaming. She looked like an Eastern princess in some exotic tale.

'Yes.' Kit's throat was tight with emotion. With love, and despair, and fear.

'Although really, you don't choose who you fall in love with,' Juliet said. 'When it happens, that's it. And it doesn't matter how impossible it is, you can't change it because you know you're in for good. For life.'

Kit made a hollow sound that wasn't quite a laugh. A pulse beat painfully in his temples, as if everything that he'd discovered that evening was gathered there. 'It's not always that straightforward though, is it? You can't always just go with it because you *want* to.'

He spoke more angrily than he'd meant to, and realised that she would think he was talking about her and Leo and the small boy they'd left behind. He wasn't. He was thinking of himself as an adult. Now. Himself and Sophie and their future, which seemed suddenly fragile in the light of the things Juliet had just told him.

Sophie stirred. A frown appeared for a second between her eyebrows and she raised her hands to cover her ears, as if she had heard his outburst and was blocking it out. Kit tensed against the tidal wave of love that crashed through him, the swell of cold, churning panic that followed in its wake.

Juliet waited until she was still again. 'I understand that you're angry with me,' she said, very softly. 'I don't expect anything else. But I'm so glad that you came and gave me a chance to explain. Even if you can't forgive what happened, I wanted to make sure you knew about Alnburgh.'

She got to her feet, glancing at Sophie again. 'Let's not wake her. Come downstairs—I've had a copy made of Leo's will for you. All the details about the estate are in there.'

Kit stood up and went over to Sophie, looking down at her, fighting the urge to bend and kiss her slightly parted lips. In the constantly changing landscape of his life she was the one thing that was the same, the one thing that was true and good and wholly beautiful, *but*...

He tore his gaze away from her and forced himself to follow Juliet.

'The details being?' he asked blandly. The palms of his hands were burning. He didn't care about the estate. There were other things he needed her to tell him.

'It was all sorted out legally at the point when we got divorced. Leo forfeited his right to inherit Alnburgh. He figured it was a bargain—he got me, and Ralph got the estate and an heir.'

The stairs from the roof terrace emerged onto a galleried landing over the central hallway below. Lamplight illuminated the intricate plaster friezes and carved doors, the metal grille of an old-fashioned lift. Kit fol-

lowed her along the landing and into a large room. She
flicked a switch and the huge metalwork lantern hanging from the high ceiling lit up a sparsely furnished
space, containing only a chest of drawers, a dressing
table and a narrow single bed.

Kit's heart felt a jolt as he noticed the silver dressing-
table set—hairbrush, mirror and tortoiseshell comb—he
remembered from his mother's bedroom at Alnburgh.

'So Leo effectively signed away his son to his
brother?'

Juliet went over to the chest of drawers and pulled
open the top drawer. 'He was ill by then. He knew he
couldn't be a proper father, although he wanted to...*so
much*. Making sure the legal agreement was watertight
and Alnburgh was yours was the one thing he could do.'

She turned round slowly and Kit saw that she was
holding a sheaf of photographs.

'It was very brutal, his illness.' There was a break
in her voice as she held out the photographs. 'He was
such a strong, powerful man.'

Kit felt as if something were wrapped tightly around
his throat. The top photo was of Leo Fitzroy in camouflage uniform, squinting against the sun, half turned
towards the camera. The background was the feature-
less beige of a desert, and Kit could almost feel the heat,
picture him walking away, continuing to issue orders
to the men who were just out of shot.

'You're so like him.'

It was true. He could see that for himself. He looked
at the next photograph. Leo in civilian clothes this time,
his arm around Juliet in some pavement café, glasses of
Pernod and postcards on the tin table in front of them.

It was the Juliet Kit remembered, young and smiling. The mother Leo had taken.

'Marbella,' she said softly. 'I was writing you a postcard.'

And so it went on. Pictures of a thinner Leo standing outside Villa Luana, with a gin and tonic in his hand on the roof terrace, in a wheelchair.

Kit's hand was shaking as he continued to the last photograph. It was a close-up of Leo, skeletal now, propped up against a mountain of pillows, a breathing tube in his neck. His cheeks were sunken, his wasted hands resting impassively on the sheets.

'The doctors were right about what the disease would do to him,' Juliet said huskily. 'As you can see, it ravaged his body completely, without mercy. But it didn't touch the man I loved inside.'

Kit found he was looking into the eyes of the man in the photo. His father. His face was slack and expressionless, but his eyes were bright, alive, full of love.

'That was the cruellest thing,' Juliet went on. 'But it was also the most wonderful. And although the price I paid to be with him was *so high*...' She faltered, pressing a hand to her lips for a moment. 'Every day we had together was a blessing.'

Kit gave the photos back to her. He had the same feeling he got in the aftermath of an explosion, when all the oxygen had been sucked from the air and his lungs were full of grit. His hands felt as if they'd been crushed by boulders.

'This illness...' he said hoarsely, taking a few steps away from her. Suddenly he understood the reason for the single bed, and the lift he'd noticed on the landing, and felt faint.

'Motor Neurone Disease.' Juliet sighed. 'Sadly it's not that rare.'

Kit swung round to look at her again. Blood was pounding in his ears.

'Is it hereditary?'

She turned away, shuffling the photos into a neat stack in her hands as she took them back to the drawer again. Seconds ticked by.

'No,' she said, without looking at him. 'Almost always not.'

Another explosion ripped through Kit's head. He could feel the sweat gathering in the small of his back.

'What does that mean?'

Juliet was looking through the contents of the drawer, her head bent. 'We asked the specialist. In maybe ten per cent of cases, I think there might be a genetic link, but for the vast majority it's just chance. Here—'

She came back over to him, holding out a large Manila envelope and, on top of it, a square velvet box. Kit stared at it without registering.

Ten per cent. One in ten cases...

'It's Leo's will,' Juliet prompted. 'You might want your own copy. And this...' she held out the velvet box '...is the Fitzroy ring. The Dark Star. I couldn't help noticing that Sophie doesn't have an engagement ring yet. Perhaps—'

A sinister voice inside Kit's head told him not to take it. That giving it to Sophie would be like shackling her to him with a ball and chain. But somehow he found himself holding the box in his hand.

'It's late. We should go.'

Juliet nodded, then reached up to take hold of his

shoulders. 'Thank you,' she said fiercely. 'I'm so very, very glad you came.'

Kit leaned down, kissing her briefly on the cheek, wishing he could say the same.

CHAPTER EIGHT

As SOPHIE SWAM slowly into consciousness the first thing she was aware of was that her head hurt. The second was that the uneasy feeling somewhere in the pit of her stomach was only partly the result of too much champagne the night before.

She opened her eyes. Through the fretwork shutters the sky was a clear delphinium blue. Beside her the bed was empty.

Kit was always up ages before her. It didn't mean anything was wrong, she told herself, sitting up and putting a hand up to her aching head. Looking down, she saw that she was still wearing last night's silk tunic.

She let out a moan of dismay.

Oh, God, she'd fallen asleep, hadn't she? The last thing she remembered was sitting on Juliet Fitzroy's elegant terrace...the champagne, the warm night, her beautiful voice with its impeccable English accent telling the story of how she'd fallen in love with Leo. And dropping the bombshell that Kit was still a Fitzroy and heir of Alnburgh.

Falling back onto the bed, she pulled the pillow over her head.

There were other, slightly more hazy memories. Kit carrying her down to the car, and how being held against him had made her feel safe again, though safe

from what she wasn't quite so sure. She remembered
twining her arms around his neck as he'd lowered her
into the seat, and how he'd detached her with a finality
that felt like rejection.

Oh, dear. She had some apologising to do.

Carefully she got to her feet. Being upright wasn't
as bad as she'd feared, and once her head had stopped
protesting at the movement she tugged her top down
and went in search of water, and Kit.

She found him out on the terrace. He was wearing
last night's trousers and no shirt, and the sight of his
broad, muscular back, already the colour of sun-baked
terracotta, made her completely forget her hangover.
Going up to him, she slid her arms around his neck and
pressed her lips to the warm skin between his shoulder blades.

'If I've missed breakfast is there any chance I could
just have you instead?' she murmured huskily.

He went very still. Somehow, Sophie found that more
unsettling than if he'd pulled away.

'You haven't missed breakfast,' he said neutrally,
putting down the sheaf of papers he'd been reading.
'I'll get something sent up now.'

Sophie stood up and stepped back. She felt slightly
sick, but couldn't be sure if it was her hangover or Kit's
chilling indifference. Welcome to Planet Paranoia, she
sneered silently at herself, going round to the front of
his chair and sitting down on the one opposite. From
the front he looked even more gorgeous. He was wearing dark glasses and his hair was standing on end where
he'd run his fingers through it. The bottom half of his
face beneath the scars, which were healing nicely now,
was shadowed with stubble.

'I'm sorry about last night,' she said ruefully. 'And to be honest I'm not that hungry. I really would just rather have you.'

'There are some things I need to do. I'm still going through this.'

He held up the sheaf of papers. Sophie could see her own face reflected in the lenses of his sunglasses. Pale. Needy. She aimed for interested and supportive instead.

'Oh? What is it?'

'Leo's will.'

Acid churned in her stomach and the smile faded from her face. 'Ah. Yes. That was a bit of a bombshell, wasn't it? So, it turns out Alnburgh is yours after all.' She laughed uneasily. 'Jasper will be over the moon.'

'I'll need to see him when we get home.'

He seemed to have surrounded himself with some kind of invisible, impenetrable force field. Sophie swallowed back the acid fear that was rising in her throat as she mentally ran through the possible reasons for it.

'Well, he's in LA at the moment,' she said as lightly as she could. 'Once he hears he's off the hook he'll probably throw a party of such epic proportions that he'll still be recovering by Christmas.' She broke off, realising that she might not be in the best position to criticise on that score. Moistening her dry lips and pleating the embroidered hem of the silk tunic with shaky fingers, she quickly changed tack. 'What about you…? How do you feel about it all? You must be happy to find that you're a Fitzroy after all.' She managed a smile. 'And not just *any* Fitzroy, but the one who gets to inherit everything…'

He laughed then. Which, since it had been meant as

a joke, was good. But it was a sound of such hollow bitterness that Sophie felt her insides freeze.

'*Happy?* Not exactly. Believe me, inheriting *everything* is a very mixed blessing.'

She got to her feet, clammy with nausea. She understood his meaning. Being the Earl of Hawksworth brought with it responsibilities, one of which was undoubtedly making a suitable marriage to a woman who had what it took to carry off a tiara and a title, and fulfil the duty of providing further heirs.

Everything she had joked about with Jasper over lunch the other day when this had been impossible enough to joke about. Everything she wasn't and couldn't ever be.

Kit lifted a hand to his forehead, rubbing his long, strong fingers across it as if trying to erase something. 'I have some calls to make.'

'I'll go and have a shower,' Sophie muttered, backing towards the door.

'I think I'm going to need to get back today,' Kit continued, without looking up. 'I'll get Nick to fly me to Newcastle and hire a car to Alnburgh.'

Sophie stopped. 'What about me?'

Kit raised his head, but he didn't turn to look at her.

'I know how you feel about Alnburgh,' he said in a voice of great weariness. 'I don't expect you to come if you don't want to. But you must understand that I have to go.'

A tiny spark of hope glowed in the darkness of Sophie's misery. Or it could have been a spark of desperation. Either way he hadn't told her that he didn't want her there.

'I do want to.' She swallowed hard, raising her chin

and forcing herself to smile as she looked at him. 'Alnburgh might not be top of my dream destination list but
you've just been away for five months. I'm not ready
to let you go again so soon. I want to come with you.'

KIT WAITED UNTIL he'd heard the distant sound of the
bathroom door shutting before expelling the breath he'd
been holding and dropping Leo's will onto the table.

He hadn't quite been telling the truth when he'd said
he was still going through it. He'd been up all night,
ploughing through pages of dense legal jargon that effectively restored his birthright, and it was clear enough.
Just as Juliet had explained, Leo might have been de-
nied an active role as a father, but he had spared no effort to make sure he passed on Alnburgh to his son.

Sophie was right, he should be delighted. Instead he
could only think of what else Leo might have passed
on to him.

He checked his watch. The doctors in the military
medical unit should have done their rounds by now,
so it was a good time to ring to see how Lewis was. It
might also be possible to talk to Randall. They'd served
together and Kit trusted him. Randall would give him
a straight answer about whether the numbness in his
hands, the pins and needles in his fingers, were the
first signs of the disease that had slowly crucified his
unknown father.

Kit picked up his phone and scrolled through his con-
tacts until he found the number. Whether he could deal
with that answer was another issue altogether.

SOPHIE GOT OUT of the shower and buried her face in a
towel that was as thick and soft as a duvet. Ten minutes

under powerful jets of steaming water had done little for her hangover and even less for her sense of dread, particularly as fragmented memories from last night were coming back thick and fast now.

'You're as good as anyone else.' That had been her mother's mantra when Sophie was growing up, but Rainbow had obviously never spent an evening with someone as poised and graceful and dignified as Juliet Fitzroy. Sophie's groan of dismay was muffled by the towel as she remembered gulping champagne, swamping Juliet in an inelegant hug the moment she met her, chattering inanely about her flaky job—oh, God, had she really used the phrase 'specialist hooker'?—and—the final disgrace—falling asleep the moment dinner was over.

She didn't blame Kit if he was doubting the wisdom of his impulsive proposal.

Going through to the bedroom, she could hear the low murmur of his voice as he spoke into his mobile, but although she strained to hear it was impossible to make out what he was saying. The white dress she'd worn yesterday was thrown over a chair and she picked it up, sliding it quickly over her head because she lacked the energy to find anything else. Through the intricate shutters she could see him, standing at the far end of the terrace where he must have gone deliberately to place himself out of earshot. His back was towards her, but he was standing as if tensed to fight.

She leaned her head against the shutters for a moment, remembering how she'd once told him that she wanted a man who would fight for her. And he had. When they'd almost been pulled apart by circumstances and misunderstandings he'd looked beyond the evidence of his own eyes and the prejudices of others and he'd come to find her, and fight for her.

Would he do it again?

One thing Sophie had learned from her free-spirited mother was that you couldn't force love, or keep it in a cage. If she was going to be with Kit, sharing the life that had now been thrust upon him, it had to be because he wanted her there, not because he was honouring a promise made under different circumstances.

She wasn't prepared to let him go without trying, she acknowledged sadly, but she had to give him space to get to grips with this new development.

Hastily she took a pad of hotel paper from beside the bed and scrawled a note. Then, slipping on her sandals and grabbing her bag, she let herself quietly out.

'So, WHAT DOES that mean? That he's going to be all right?'

The shooting pains down Kit's forearm told him he was probably holding the phone too tightly as he listened to Randall's update on Lewis, but his hand was so numb he was afraid of dropping his mobile entirely if he loosened his grip. He stared out into the blue haze over the rooftops of the city, but in his mind he was back in that corridor outside Lewis's room, strangled by guilt.

'It means that there doesn't seem to be any permanent damage to his spinal cord,' Randall said smoothly. 'It was a bloody close thing, but the bullet seems to have missed it by a millimetre or so. Of course, he's got a long way to go before he's up and about, but at least it does look like that day will eventually come.'

'Thank God for that.'

'Indeed,' Randall said wryly. 'But how are you, Kit? I know it wasn't the easiest of tours.'

'I'm fine,' Kit said curtly. 'I was actually wearing a bomb suit for once, or else I wouldn't be here. I got a few cuts on my face because the visor was up, but they're healing OK.'

'I'm pleased to hear it, but I'm not sure you've answered my question,' Randall remarked gently. 'I know you walked away from the explosion largely unscathed but I meant, how are you in yourself?'

'All right. Just need to catch up on some sleep, that's all.'

He closed his eyes, inwardly cursing as his courage failed him. He wanted to know, and yet he couldn't bring himself to ask. God, what a coward.

Perhaps Randall sensed something in the sharpness of his voice because he persisted.

'Not sleeping well?'

'I never sleep well. But after being away for five months there always seem to be more pressing things to do in bed.'

Randall laughed. 'In that case you only have yourself to blame.'

That was as far as he was going to press it, and Kit could tell by the tone of his voice that he was about to say goodbye and hang up. Suddenly his blood was pounding, his palms slick with sweat. He took a breath in.

'Before you go, how much do you know about Motor Neurone Disease?'

There was a moment's silence. 'Well, I'm not a specialist. Was there anything specific you wanted to know?'

'Yes. What are the early symptoms?'

From the other end of the line he heard Randall expel a long, heavy breath. 'I don't know, Kit. Every case is different, but muscle weakness in the hands or feet, I guess—probably more noticeably in the hands—clumsiness, lack of co-ordination, that kind of thing. Why?'

Kit ignored the question, his mind spooling back to those long moments beneath the bridge when his fingers had fumbled helplessly with the wire cutters.

'What treatments are there?'

'There's no cure, if that's what you mean,' Randall said reluctantly. 'Progress of the disease can be slowed slightly with drugs. It's not pretty.'

'No. I know that.'

'But those symptoms are common to a huge number of illnesses that are a lot less serious and a lot more common,' Randall continued, adopting a self-consciously cheerful tone. 'MND really would be a worst case scenario, and a pretty unlikely one at that.'

Unless there was a genetic predisposition, thought Kit hollowly.

'Kit? Are you still there? Look, why don't you come in and see me when you get back? It would give Lewis a boost to have a visit from his commanding officer and I could give you a quick once-over if there's anything that you're worried about.'

'No. There's no need. Really.'

Wing Commander Mike Randall had been an army medic for long enough to know that soldiers responded to questions from a doctor in the same way they would to enemy torture—with stony refusal to co-operate. A more subtle approach was often needed. 'How about a game of squash? It's a while since we've played, although that could be because you always win. Fancy thrashing me again?'

Kit understood exactly what Randall was doing, and in some distant, dispassionate quarter of his brain he appreciated it.

'I'd love to, but...' he lifted the hand that wasn't holding the phone and held it out in front of him, stretching out his fingers as far as he could until the ache in his tendons just about dispelled the tingling numbness '...some things have come up. Family business. I'm going to be in Northumberland for the next few weeks.'

'OK, Kit. I get the picture.' Randall gave a rueful sigh. 'But I'm here if you need me. If there's anything else you want to ask.'

'Thanks, but you've answered everything already,' Kit said neutrally. 'Lewis needs you, not me. Give him my regards.'

Ending the call, he turned away from the city spread out beneath him and tossed his phone down on the low table. A band of pain across his shoulders told him he'd spent the duration of that entire conversation with every muscle in his body tensed, ready to fight.

Even though there was no point. The enemy he faced couldn't be beaten.

With a thud of alarm he realised that Sophie must be out of the shower by now, and wondered if she'd heard any of that. Quickly he crossed the sun-baked terrace and went inside.

It was cool and dim. And quiet. In the bedroom a note lay on the chest of drawers.

Gone to medina to buy postcard for Jasper. See you later. Love S x

Relief that she hadn't heard poured through him. He could carry on as normal, pretend that everything was all right. If he didn't go and see Randall, or get any kind of formal diagnosis, that meant he wasn't lying to her.

But there was a whole lot of difference between not lying to her and knowingly trapping her into a marriage that would make her a prisoner.

The ring Juliet had given him was still in the pocket of his trousers and he took it out now, flipping open the lid of the velvet box. The stone was called a black opal, although against the midnight satin lining of the box it glowed with a kaleidoscope of shifting colours, lit up by the diamonds that encircled it.

He stared at it for a long time. Then, shutting the box with a snap, he put it back in his pocket and went out to find her.

THE CAR FROM the hotel dropped him by the square. Heading towards the medina in the blast-furnace heat, he took the mobile phone from his pocket and brought up Sophie's number. He kept his head down, pressing the phone against his ear and concentrating on its steady ring instead of the cacophony of street vendors and musicians and a thousand conversations around him.

Come on, Sophie, pick up...

The narrow streets of the medina were dark and cool. It was a relief to be out of the sun, but the shadows crawled with menace. He could feel the sheen of sweat covering every inch of his skin, making his shirt stick to him. He quickened his pace so that he was almost running, pushing through the ambling crowds of people as his gaze darted around, looking for a red head amongst the dark or covered ones.

Why wasn't she answering her phone?

His heartbeat reverberated through his body as he scanned the street, his training kicking in automatically as he checked for suspicious signs. There were scores of them—bags of rubbish left in doorways, people wearing layers of clothing that could conceal explosives, carrying bags and packages of every shape and size and muttering to themselves as they walked. Just like in any busy city street the world over, mocked a voice of scornful rationality inside Kit's head.

Ahead of him he could see the arched gateway of the souk, leading out onto the wide street beyond. And in front of it, her hair gleaming in a narrow shaft of sunlight filtering through the blinds above, he saw Sophie.

She was sitting on a low stool facing a heavily veiled woman who held one of her hands. The air left Kit's lungs in a rush of relief. Resisting the urge to break into a run and haul her into his arms, he slowed right down, taking a deep breath in and expelling it again in an effort to steady his racing pulse. She was having a henna tattoo—that was why she couldn't answer her phone. Not because she'd been kidnapped, or dragged into a back alley by a gang of thugs, for pity's sake. His scalp prickled with sweat as he raked a hand through his hair and started towards her again.

And stopped.

In a doorway opposite a man was holding a mobile phone. As if in slow motion Kit watched him begin to press buttons on the keypad.

Adrenaline, like neat, iced alcohol, sluiced through his veins, sending his heart-rate into overdrive. Instantly his whole body was rigid, primed, as he reached for his gun. Instead he found himself clutching his phone again, but his fingers were shaking so badly that he dropped it.

As if in slow motion he watched it fall to the ground. He knew he had to reach Sophie before the blast but was suddenly paralysed, his feet rooted to the spot where he stood as horror solidified like concrete in his chest and dark spots danced before his eyes. His mouth was open to shout her name but his throat was tight and dry and could produce no sound.

But it was as if she heard him anyway because at that moment she lifted her head and looked round, straight towards where he stood. The smile died on her face and she got to her feet, coming towards him with her arms outstretched.

'Kit! Kit—what is it?'

The compassion in her voice hit him like acid in the face, bringing him back to reality and turning his panic into self-disgust in a lurching heartbeat. Reaching him, she raised her hand to his cheek, stroking her thumb gently over the half-healed scars there.

'Sweetheart, what's wrong?'

Behind her the man was speaking into his mobile phone now, his face impassive. Kit jerked his head away from Sophie's touch as if it burned him.

'Nothing. Nothing's wrong,' he said in a voice that was as cold and hard as steel. 'I came to find you because I've arranged the flight for one o'clock. We need to pack and get to the airport—if you still want to come back with me.'

Sophie dropped her hand, its intricate henna markings still glistening wetly, and took a step backwards. Dropping her gaze, she nodded.

'Yes. Of course I do.'

Knives of self-loathing pierced him, but still pride prevented him from taking her hand. From apologising, or explaining. Instead he turned on his heel and began to walk back along the street, keeping his gaze fixed unwaveringly ahead.

CHAPTER NINE

THE FLIGHT BACK to England was every bit as luxurious as the one they had taken two days previously, but considerably less enjoyable.

Neither of them spoke much. Kit seemed to have placed himself behind a wall of glass, so that even though he was only a few feet away from her, Sophie felt as if he were somewhere far beyond her reach. Sitting in the deep embrace of the huge seat, she stared out of the window, longing to cross the small distance between them and tear the paperwork out of his hand and force him to notice her, to *talk* to her...

To tell her exactly what had been going through his mind when she'd seen him in the souk earlier, and what had made him look like a man who was being crucified by his own conscience?

But she had a sickening fear that if she did there would be no going back, because the things he told her would change everything. How could she wilfully bring about her own expulsion from the paradise she had allowed herself to believe was hers for ever?

It was early evening when they reached Alnburgh. Even in the height of an English summer, the contrast with the heat and the rich colours of Morocco couldn't have been starker. Carved from iron-grey stone, it appeared to rise straight up out of the cliffs above a stretch of windswept beach, and for miles it had loomed on the horizon, managing to look far more menacing than the Disneyesque castle in the Romanian pine forest where the vampire movie had been filmed.

Sophie's spirits sank even further.

She remembered the first time she'd seen it. It had been a winter night, in the middle of a blizzard, and with its floodlights switched on Alnburgh Castle had looked just like a child's snowglobe. She'd been enchanted, but that was before she'd realised it was just as cold inside as it was outside.

'I can see why Tatiana couldn't wait to move to London the moment Ralph's funeral was over,' she said with a shiver. 'It's not exactly cosy, is it? Are any of the staff still there?'

'Not as far as I know,' said Kit. His voice was gravelly with misuse, and more sexy than ever. 'Obviously Tatiana didn't want to pay them to stay on if she wasn't living there—not when she's haemorrhaging cash to live in a suite at Claridges while she has the London house vandalised by her interior decorator.'

Sophie pressed the button to activate the car heater, and directed the jet of warm air onto her icy feet. She was still wearing the little gold flip-flops, which were covered in pink Marrakech dust. They were already driving under the clock tower, but she knew from previous experience that this might be the last opportunity she had to be warm for a long time.

'It's a big responsibility, isn't it?' she said faintly, wondering if now was the time to ask how quickly he could sort things out so they could get back to London.

'Yes.'

Kit brought the car to a standstill and cut the engine.

In the sudden quiet she could hear the muffled sound of the sea and the plaintive crying of gulls.

'Sophie, I know this isn't what you wanted, or expected...'

Ever since she'd followed him through the souk in Marrakech Sophie had been desperate for him to make some move to bridge the terrible chasm that seemed to have opened up between them, but the note of weary resignation in his voice now made her insides freeze. They'd come all this way, he'd delivered her back to England, so was this the start of the 'it's never going to work' speech? In the soft, pastel-coloured evening light he looked beautiful and exhausted and so remote it was as if he had already left her. She could feel the blood draining from her head, leaving a vacuum of airless panic.

'I know, but to be fair you hardly expected it either,' she said, reaching for the door handle, prising it open with shaky fingers. 'Gosh, look how long the grass is. Don't you feel a bit like Robin Hood returning from the crusades?'

She stumbled out of the car, grabbing the carrier bag of duty-free stuff she'd bought while he'd been sorting out the hire car—two bottles of champagne, some uber-fashionable vodka in a neon-pink bottle and a giant Toblerone for Jasper. Taking in a deep lungful of salty air, she wrapped her arms around her as the sea breeze sliced straight through the flimsy white dress. The denim jacket she'd put on over it was completely inadequate for keeping out the chill of the Northumberland evening. Or that of Kit's distance.

Behind her she heard Kit's door slam.

'Do you have keys?' she asked, turning to follow him up the steps to the giant-sized front door.

'Don't need them.' He tapped some numbers into a discreet keypad. 'Tatiana made my f—Ralph—have an electronic system installed.' The door creaked heavily open. 'After you.'

Sophie remembered the armoury hall very well from her first visit. By Alnburgh standards it was a small room, but every inch of the high stone walls was covered with hundreds of swords, pistols, shields and sinister-looking daggers hung in intricate patterns. She'd been deeply intimidated by it the first time, and, standing in the middle of the stone floor and looking around, she didn't feel much better now.

'Home sweet home,' she said with an attempt at humour. 'The first thing I think we should do is take all these awful guns and things down and put up some coat hooks and a nice mirror. Much more welcoming, and practical.'

Gathering up the thick drift of envelopes from the floor, Kit didn't smile. Sophie decided she'd better shut up. Jokes like that, coming from the girl who grew up on a converted bus, were clearly too close to the bone to be funny.

'Just going to the loo,' she muttered, walking into the long gallery where the heads of various kinds of deer and antelope slaughtered by past Fitzroys glared down through the half-light. Until she'd come here, if someone had said 'stuffed animal' to her it would have conjured up an image of cuddly teddy bears, she thought miserably. The scent of woodsmoke hung in the air, a whispered memory of past warmth that couldn't quite mask the unmistakable smell of damp.

In the portrait hall, from which the wide staircase curved upwards, Sophie came face to face with Jasper's mother. Or the seven-foot-high painted version of her anyway, which was every bit as intimidating and glamorous as the real thing. She paused in front of it, looking up. The painter, whoever he was, had captured Tatiana's fine-boned, Slavic beauty, and the quietly triumphant expression in the blue eyes that seemed, quite literally, to look down on Sophie. The diamonds that glittered at her throat, ears and wrist sent out sharp points of painted white, which really did seem to light up the fading evening light.

Sophie sighed. She was completely unable to imagine herself in a similar portrait, decked out in satin and dripping with diamonds. Moving away quickly, she went up the stairs. When she'd first arrived at Alnburgh the labyrinthine passageways upstairs had completely confused her, but at least now she knew where to find a bathroom. Unlike the staterooms downstairs, upstairs had escaped the attentions of Tatiana's interior designer and the chilly corridors were suffused with the breath of age and neglect. The bathroom Sophie went into had last been updated in the nineteen thirties and featured an enormous cast-iron bath standing on lion's feet and pea-green rectangular tiles laid like brickwork. It was refrigerator-cold.

There was no loo paper, but luckily Sophie found the tattered remains of her paper napkin from the aeroplane in her pocket and sent silent thanks to Nick McAllister. She had just pulled the clanking chain and was about to go out again when something on the floor by the door caught her eye and stopped her in her tracks.

Her scream bounced off the tiled walls and echoed along the winding passageways.

Downstairs, Kit froze.

Instinct took over. In a split second he was sprinting up the stairs, taking them two at a time, adrenaline sluicing through his veins like acid. In that instant he was back on duty, his mind racing ahead, anticipating broken bodies, blood, fear and calculating what resources he had to deal with them. Tearing along the corridor, he saw the bathroom door was ajar and kicked it open.

'Sophie...'

There was no blood. Heart pounding, that was what he registered first. And when he'd processed that fact he noticed that she was standing squeezed into the narrow space between the bath and the toilet, her clenched fists clasped beneath her chin, her whole body hunched up in an attitude of utter terror.

'Don't move!' she croaked.

He stopped dead. Reality swung dizzily away from him for a second and he was back in the desert. Images of mines half covered with earth flashed through his head.

Slowly, her eyes round with terror, Sophie unfurled one arm and pointed to the floor just to one side of him.

'There.'

He turned his head, looked down. Blinked.

'A spider,' he rasped. 'It's just a *spider.*'

'*Just* a spider? It's not *just* anything! It's massive. Please, Kit,' she sobbed, 'I *hate* them. Please...*get rid* of it.'

In one swift movement he swooped down to capture it, but his stiff fingers refused to co-operate and it darted away. Sophie screamed again, shrinking back against the wall as it shot towards her.

This time he got it. Somehow he closed his tingling fingers around it, and then, throwing open the badly fitting window, let it go.

'Is it gone?'

He showed her his empty hand. Residual adrenaline still coursed through him, making it impossible to speak, even if he'd trusted himself. His breathing was fast and ragged. He turned away, pressing his fingers to his temples, trying to hold back his anger.

'Thank you,' Sophie said shakily from behind him. 'I can't bear them. We used to get really huge ones— like that—on the bus and Rainbow always insisted they had as much right as we did to be there and wouldn't touch them. I used to lie in bed…t-*terrified* and imagining them crawling under my bedclothes—'

Her voice broke into a hiccuping sob and she put a hand, with its incongruous henna tattoo, to her mouth to stifle it.

She was always so strong and funny and positive, but seeing her pressed against the grim tiles, her bravado in tatters and the tears beginning to slide down her cheeks, Kit felt his resolve crack. In one step he was beside her, pulling her forwards and into his arms, covering her trembling mouth with his.

'It's OK. You're safe now. It's gone.'

It was so good to hold her, so *good* to kiss her again. The relentless nightmare of the last twenty-four hours faded as he breathed in her warm, musky scent and felt her heart thudding frantically against his chest. His hands cupped her face, and in some distant part of his brain he was aware that the numbness and the pins-and-

needles sensation was completely gone. He could feel
the heat of her cheeks, her velvet skin, each tear that
ran across the back of his hand.

The realisation severed the last thread of his reserve.
The desire that had been smouldering dangerously during the long journey when she'd slept beside him, her
head falling onto his shoulder, mushroomed into a fireball. And as always, her need matched his. Her hands
moved downwards, over his chest, pulling at his shirt.

'Not here,' he growled, pulling away.

She gave a gasp of laughter. Her cheeks were damp
and flushed, her eyes glittering with arousal. 'I'm glad
you said that. After seeing that monster spider I don't
want to get down on the floor.'

'Come on.'

Taking her hand, he pulled her forwards, through
the gloomy corridors of the castle, up a flight of stone
spiral stairs. Her feet caught in the long hem of her
white dress and she stumbled. His grip on her hand
tightened reflexively, stopping her from falling, and
with the other hand he hauled her against him. Sophie
could feel the hardness of his erection and gave a moan
of need. Their eyes met.

'Where are we going?'

They were both breathing in rapid rasps.

'My room. *Our* room.'

'Is it far? Because I…'

She trailed off, breathless, and he stooped down and
scooped her up into his arms, striding up the remaining steps. Freed from the need to look where she was
going, Sophie was able to focus her full attention on
kissing him, starting at the angle of his jaw, moving
upwards to take his ear lobe between her teeth, breath-

ing out gently and murmuring, 'I want you now. I need you inside me...'

She felt him reach down to open a door. His shoulders were rigid beneath her fingers, the muscles as hard as marble, and he strode quickly across a room, his footsteps echoing on bare boards. Sophie lifted her head and looked.

The room they had entered was huge, circular and empty except for a hulking great chest of drawers, a magnificent carved wooden bed. Kit set her down beside it. Evening light slanted through a mullioned window, washing the white walls pink. His eyes were black chasms of arousal as he slid his arms around her, reaching for the zip of her dress.

'This time,' he whispered throatily, 'we take it slowly. You're too beautiful to be rushed.'

Without taking his eyes off her, he pulled it down, millimetre by millimetre. Sophie let out a shuddering breath, every atom of her resisting the urge to tear it off and then rip the shirt from his back, yank his trousers open. He trailed his fingers down her bare back, beneath the open zip. His eyes burned and a muscle jumped above his clenched jaw. She could tell what it cost him, this holding back. Frowning, almost as if he were in pain, he took hold of her shoulders and turned her round.

Sophie shivered as he swept aside her hair with his fingers. Her fingers curled into fists as his lips brushed the nape of her neck. In the silence she could hear the cry of the gulls wheeling through the apricot sky outside, the kiss of Kit's lips against her skin.

His fingers slid the strap of her dress off one shoulder, then the other. It fell to the floor.

She turned round, trembling with the need to feel his skin on hers. He took a small, indrawn breath as he looked down at her body—naked except for a pair of lilac lace knickers—and with shaking fingers she began to undo the buttons of his shirt.

She wasn't sure she could match his self-control. She had to bite down on the insides of her cheeks to stop herself from ripping the remaining buttons from their holes. Looking up she saw that his face wore an expression of intense focus. In contrast, his eyes were hooded, gleaming with want. She reached the last button, and they flickered closed for a second.

'Kit—'

He took a step backwards, sinking down onto the edge of the bed and keeping his eyes fixed on hers as he kissed her midriff. Her muscles contracted in a sharp spasm of want and she gripped his shoulders, anchoring herself against the delicious tension that was already beginning to build as his mouth moved lower and he eased her knickers down.

She let out a high, desperate whimper.

But he was relentless. With maddening slowness his fingers caressed her thighs while his tongue probed and explored. Her head fell back and she thrust her hips forwards, upwards, writhing and rotating as he breathed heat against her and his tongue found her clitoris.

Sophie fell forwards, burying her face in his hair. Feeling the violent shudders of her orgasm wrack her, he held her waist and pulled her back onto the bed with him. Kicking off his trousers, he was inside her in seconds, moaning as he felt her slippery wetness close around him.

For a moment they both stilled, their gazes locked. Then, very slowly, she reached up to kiss his lips.

'I love you.'

It was little more than a shivering breath, but it shattered his self-control. Gathering her into his arms, he cradled her against his chest, and she wrapped her legs tightly around his waist as he drove into her, strong thrusts that took him to the brink. Feeling her convulse around him again tipped him over the edge.

Ecstasy rocked him. In that moment it was possible to believe he was immortal.

'Kit?'

Sophie's head was resting on his chest, the beat of his heart keeping time with the distant rhythm of the waves below. She was dazed with happiness and the relief of being close to him again.

'Mmm?'

His voice rumbled like distant thunder deep in his chest. Love blossomed inside her and a smile spread across her face.

'I hate to ruin the poetry of the moment, but I'm absolutely starving.'

'That could be a problem,' he said gravely, tracing a lazy circle with a fingertip on her shoulder. 'I have no idea what time it is, but the shop in the village will have closed ages ago and I'm not sure there'll be anything in the kitchen. Do you want to drive to Hawksworth for dinner?'

Sophie considered for a moment as ripples of pleasure spread down her arm and through her whole body.

'Would it mean getting dressed?'

'Probably. They're quite old-fashioned about things like that round here.'

'In that case, let's not bother.' Rolling reluctantly away from him, Sophie swung her legs over the edge of the bed and stood up shakily. 'Jasper will just have to sacrifice his Toblerone. And we have champagne.'

'We have an entire cellar full of it, in fact,' Kit remarked dryly.

'Oh, yes. I suppose so. I didn't think of that.'

She bent down to pick up her dress, which was buried under his hastily discarded trousers. As she moved them something fell out of the pocket and skidded across the polished floor.

It was a box. A square, black velvet box.

Without thinking, Sophie went to pick it up. It was only when she was standing there, holding it in her hand and staring down at it, that her brain caught up and she realised what it might be.

Her jaw dropped. Hope and joy and excitement ballooned inside her as she lifted her head to look at him. For a second she could only think of how incredibly sexy he looked, sprawled against the white sheets in the dying light. And then she noticed his face. It was frighteningly blank.

'Kit?' Her voice was a dried-up whisper. Her heart was beating very hard, as if the blood in her veins had turned to treacle. 'What's this?'

He sat up slowly, the muscles in his stomach and shoulders moving beneath the bronzed skin as he raised a hand and raked it through his hair in what looked like a gesture of resignation.

'Open it.'

Her hands were shaking, making it difficult to unhook the tiny catch. The lid of the box opened with a soft creak. Sophie gasped.

The ring had a polished stone of iridescent green at its centre, but her hand was shaking so much that it caught the rose-pink rays of sun and made a rainbow of other colours shimmer in its depths. It was circled by a double row of diamonds. There was no doubt that it was very old, and very, very valuable.

She also had the feeling she'd seen it before.

'It's a black opal,' he said tonelessly. 'It's called The Dark Star. It's been a family engagement ring for generations.'

A memory stirred in the back of her mind. 'Ah,' she said with an uneasy laugh. 'Is this that awkward moment when your girlfriend accidentally discovers the family ring you're saving to give to someone who has the right breeding to wear it?' Shutting the box again, she held it out to him. 'You'd better keep it somewhere safe.'

'Come here,' he drawled softly.

She went towards him on trembling legs. Gently he took the box from her and pulled out the ring. Taking hold of her left hand, he brushed his lips over the hennaed vine tendril that snaked down her third finger before sliding the ring onto it.

'Is that safe enough?'

He pulled her back down onto the bed, taking her face in his hands and kissing her so that she wouldn't see the despair and self-loathing in his eyes.

CHAPTER TEN

'THAT'LL BE TWENTY-TWO pounds fifty-six please. I'll put it on the Fitzroy account, shall I, Miss…?'

Fumbling in her purse, Sophie looked up. From behind a forest of neon windmills and plastic beach spades on the counter Mrs Watts was looking at her with an air of beady expectation.

'Oh. It's G-Greenham,' she stuttered, caught off guard. 'Sophie Greenham. But no, thanks, I'll pay for it now.'

'But you're staying up at the castle, are you?' Mrs Watts persisted as she waited for the money, her killer interrogation skills masked by a veneer of friendliness and a polyester overall. 'With Master Kit? Or His Lordship as I'd still like to think of him. Such a shame. He's so much better suited to the role than Master Jasper— flighty, he is, always has been, a bit like his mother, the second Lady Fitzroy. In America now, so I gather.'

'Yes,' Sophie confirmed helplessly, handing over the money and glancing back towards the door in the hope that rescue was about to come in the form of a large party of noisy children in search of buckets and spades and bags of sweets for the beach.

It wasn't.

'Oh-h-h, now that's a beautiful ring,' Mrs Watts said avidly, taking the notes Sophie offered, her eyes gleaming like those of a sparrowhawk that had just spotted a fat baby rabbit as they fixed on The Dark Star. Sophie had no alternative than to keep her left hand extended as Mrs Watts leaned through the plastic windmills to examine it. Thank goodness the henna tattoo had faded. 'I think it's nonsense what they say about opals being unlucky, don't you? I remember seeing this on the first Lady Fitzroy. Lady Juliet.' She beamed up at Sophie. 'Congratulations are in order, then, Miss Greenham?'

'Sophie. Yes.'

Beaming, Mrs Watts placed a hand on her ample, polyester-encased bosom. 'Oh, I'm so thrilled. Master Kit is such a gentleman, and it's a good many years since there was a proper wedding at the castle.' She began gathering up Sophie's purchases and putting them all into a carrier bag. 'Sir Ralph got hitched to his second wife down in London—she never did like it up here much—but I still remember the day he and Lady Juliet got married. The whole village turned out to watch her father walk her into church.' She paused, a bunch of rust-coloured chrysanthemums clutched in her hand like a bridal bouquet, a distant, dreamy look in her eyes. 'Oh, she was a picture, she was…and a *proper* lady. She would never have let the castle get into the state it has. Such a shame it didn't last.'

Sophie resisted the urge to tell her not to expect a 'proper' wedding at the castle any time soon. Taking advantage of Mrs Watts's lapse into reminiscence, she grabbed the carrier bag and moved towards the door.

'Here, you're forgetting your flowers. Lovely ones they are too; Mr Watts's pride and joy—prize winners.' Mrs Watts came round the counter to give them to her and then, bound by some weird feudal imperative, hur-

ried over to open the door for her. Sophie felt herself
blush with embarrassment.

'Thank you, but I can manage—'

'Nonsense,' Mrs Watts said stoutly. 'You've a position in this village now. We're very proud of our heri-
tage.'

Acutely conscious of her cheap chain-store dress and
sneakers, Sophie went out into the late-summer sunshine. The school term had just started again so the
village had emptied of holidaymakers, but there was a
small group of young mothers with pushchairs standing
chatting beside the green. Sophie felt a pang of longing
so strong it took her breath away for a second. Her period, usually relentlessly regular, was three days late.
Impulsively she turned back to Mrs Watts.

'What *do* they say about opals being unlucky?'

She flapped a dismissive hand. 'Oh, it's just a silly
old wives' tale. I don't go in for any of that kind of thing
at all—horoscopes and star signs and all that hocus
pocus. It's love makes a marriage work. Love and trust
and talking to each other. That's what's kept me and Mr
Watts together for almost fifty years.'

Oh, dear, Sophie thought wistfully as she walked
back up to the castle, it didn't look good for her and Kit,
then. Talking wasn't exactly the area in which their relationship was strongest. The closeness they'd shared that
night when he'd given her the ring had begun to fade
again, almost from the moment he'd put it on her finger.
During the days that followed Kit had been busy seeing solicitors, accountants, surveyors; picking his way
through the legal tangle surrounding Leo's will and trying to organise the work that was needed immediately
to keep the castle—long neglected by Ralph—standing.

In the evenings they ate, usually in front of the fire in the drawing room, or walked on the beach. They talked, of course, about the work that needed doing, but it was more about Alnburgh's future than their own. In fact, the most in-depth conversation she'd had about that was in a twenty-five-minute phone call with Jasper over a faint line to LA. As she'd predicted, the latest unforeseen development in the drama of Alnburgh's ownership had come as a huge relief to him, but his happiness was tempered with concern for her.

'It's hardly a cosy love nest to start married life in,' he'd sighed, with his usual ability to voice her own thoughts.

Her initial hope that their stay at Alnburgh might just be a brief one had faded as the days slipped past and Kit got more deeply involved in the business of the estate. Sophie could see how much he cared about it, and it was clear he had no plans to return to London. For his sake she would just have to try to get used to thinking of Alnburgh as home.

Her pace had got slower the nearer she got to the castle, and going from the buttery sunshine into the armoury hall was like stepping into a crypt. She walked quickly through the long gallery, steadfastly refusing to let herself look up at the animal heads to see if their eyes were following her as she went, and down the steps into the kitchen.

It was an enormous, gloomy room with a vaulted ceiling and a Victorian cast-iron range built into one end. The rest of it wasn't much more contemporary, and the only light came from rows of windows set high up in the stone walls, and a nineteen-thirties enamel lamp that hung over the enormous table. It was a far cry from the sunny, friendly kitchen she had half imagined when she'd told Jasper that she was ready for a home.

Sophie put the shopping onto the table and went in search of a vase for the flowers. She had discovered a whole room further along the corridor entirely devoted to china of all sorts—tureens, coffee pots, rose bowls and no doubt a large selection of vases too—but she didn't dare take anything from there in case it turned out to be too rare and valuable for Mr Watts's chrysanthemums. Instead she took a plain cream jug from the dresser and filled it with water.

In an attempt to bridge the gap between herself and Kit, she'd decided to cook properly tonight, and lay the table in the dining room for the first time since they'd been at Alnburgh. She'd spent what seemed to her to be a ridiculous amount of money on a fillet of venison from the tiny butcher's shop in the village, mainly because it sounded appropriately posh to be dished up in such formal surroundings.

She picked up the jug with the flowers in and carried it back upstairs to the dining room. It was pitch black, the tall windows hidden by shutters and heavy velvet curtains. The urge to go and throw them both open was almost overwhelming, but Sophie resisted. She had made that mistake on the first day as she'd gone around trying to lighten the oppressive gloom that filled the rooms, but Kit had told her that light was bad for the paintings, and that the Victorian curtains couldn't withstand being opened and closed too often.

Instead she flicked the light switch, and the gigantic chandelier over the table came on, along with the brass lights above the biggest portraits. Sophie put the jug of flowers on the table and stood back, hands on her hips, to look at it.

A great wave of misery and despair crashed over her.

It was hopeless, she realised. Mr Watts's chrysanthemums might be his pride and joy, but they certainly wouldn't win her any prizes for interior-design flair. Beside the other flowers standing in the buckets outside the village shop their mop-heads had seemed huge, but here in the cavernous dining room they looked insignificant and lost.

Like her at Alnburgh.

All her efforts to make a difference, to put her mark on the place and make it feel like home, were utterly futile, she thought, blinking back tears. What was the use of lighting scented candles in the hall when nothing could ever shift the smell of cold stone, damp earth and age? What was the point of trying to make Alnburgh feel like hers when she was reminded of its previous occupants at every turn?

She lifted her head, looking at the painted faces that lined the walls. All of them seemed to look back at her with contempt in their hooded eyes. Except one.

It was the portrait Sophie had noticed on her first night at Alnburgh six months ago, and it showed a woman in a pink silk dress, with roses woven into her piled-up hair. What set her apart from the other sour-faced Fitzroys was her beauty and the secretive smile that played about her pink lips and gave her an air of suppressed mischief. Sophie remembered Ralph telling her that she was a music-hall singer who had caught the eye of the then earl, who had married her despite the fact that she was much younger and 'definitely not countess material'.

She shivered slightly as his voice came back to her.
'You and me both,' she muttered, and was about to turn
away when something else caught her eye.

The girl's hands were folded in her lap, and on the
left one, lovingly picked out by the artist's brush, was
Sophie's ring.

So that was where she'd seen it before. A chill crept
down her neck, as if it were being caressed by cold
fingers. Lifting her hand, she looked from the real
opal glinting dully in the twenty-first-century electric
light, to the painted one on the finger of the eighteenth-
century countess, remembering as she did so how her
story had ended. Pregnant with a supposedly illegiti-
mate child, suffering from advanced syphilis, the girl
in the painting had thrown herself off the battlements
in the east tower, to her death on the rocks below.

She hadn't known what Mrs Watts had meant about
opals being unlucky, but she was beginning to get the
picture. She knew of two Fitzroy brides who'd worn the
ring before her, and neither had lasted long at Alnburgh.

Rainbow had been a great believer in signs and por-
tents; messages in everything from tea leaves to con-
stellations. Growing up, Sophie had always dismissed
it as yet another of her mother's many eccentricities.

Hurrying quickly from the dining room, switching
off the light, she suddenly wasn't so sure.

'THE TRUST WAS set up some twenty-eight years ago now,
with myself as one of the trustees. The others were the
then Lady Fitzroy, an army colleague of Leo's, the se-
nior partner in the firm of accountants he used...'

Kit's attention began to wander. He had been on the
phone to various people all day—all week, it seemed—

and his head and neck and brain ached with the effort of trying to make sense of Alnburgh's financial and legal position. It was nightmarishly complicated and excruciatingly dull, however it did give him something to think about besides Sophie, and the fact that he'd pretty much ruined her life.

As Leo's elderly former solicitor went on Kit noticed that the library had darkened and filled with shadows. He felt a flicker of surprise. The room's huge oriel window looked out over the beach below, and through it Kit could see that the mood of the sea had changed and that huge, swollen purple clouds had gathered over the headland to the south.

'We took a great deal of trouble over the wording of the document to ensure there were no loopholes for Ralph Fitzroy's legal team to use to his advantage...'

A week ago the beach had been scattered with groups of people—families with buckets and spades enjoying the last few days of their holidays, teenagers from the village with a radio and illicit bottles of cider—but now it was pretty much empty. A dog galloped along the wet sand, ears flapping, and in the distance a slim figure stood at the edge of the sea, her green cotton dress blowing up in the sudden brisk wind, her red hair flying.

A lightning fork of desire snapped through him, closely followed by a crash of guilt and despair. God, he loved her. But seeing her out there, standing in front of the swelling sea, only seemed to emphasise that elusive, untamable quality she had that had drawn him to her from the start.

And which made putting that bloody ring on her finger even more unforgivable.

That had been his chance to tell her, but he had let it

pass because he knew that it would set in motion a chain
of events that was entirely out of his control. She would
want him to see a doctor. And then, if the doctor's diagnosis confirmed his fears, he would have to let her go.

And he wasn't ready to do that yet. He'd only just
found her. He wanted to make this happiness last for
as long as he could.

He lifted the hand that wasn't holding the phone and
looked at it. The pins-and-needles sensation hadn't been
as bad since they'd returned to Alnburgh, and there
were times when it disappeared altogether. Most nota-
bly when he was in bed with Sophie, touching her body,
feeling her satin skin against his fingertips. Then he
could believe that it wasn't as serious as he thought…

'Lord Fitzroy? Are you still there?'

'Yes. Sorry.' Kit dragged his attention back to the
voice on the other end of the phone. 'Perhaps you could
repeat that?'

'I said, the fact that the trust was set up so long before Leo Fitzroy's death means that the amount of inheritance tax owing is substantially reduced.'

'That's excellent news,' Kit said blandly. In fact, it
was the news he'd been holding out for, and the key to
securing Alnburgh's future, but at that moment it was
slightly overshadowed by a sudden raging need to drag
Sophie back here and take her upstairs.

'It was partly chance, of course. When the trust was
set up we didn't know how long Mr Fitzroy would live,
and frankly didn't expect it to be more than the statu-
tory seven-year period that would put Alnburgh out of
danger from death duties. It was just lucky that he survived much longer than that.'

That was a matter of opinion, thought Kit, remembering the photographs Juliet had shown him chronicling Leo's decline.

'Thanks,' he said brusquely, impatient to end the call. Outside the sky had darkened menacingly and the seagulls were being thrown off course by the wind. Sophie didn't have a coat. She was going to get soaked.

Bringing the conversation to a swift close, he put down the phone and strode to the door. He went down the back stairs, kicking off his shoes and grabbing one of the many waterproofs that hung in the boot room before going out through the east-gate door. From this side of the castle a steep path cut through the dune grass down to the beach. Dark purple clouds moved in from the south like an invading army and the first drops of rain were already falling.

He began to run. Up ahead, in the distance he could see that Sophie had turned and was beginning to make her way back. She broke into a run but at that moment the clouds unleashed the full force of their fury.

It felt like standing beneath a hail of bullets. In a matter of seconds Kit was drenched, as was the waterproof he carried. Not that it would do much good now anyway, but he ran on, his feet pounding against the hard sand. As they got closer to each other he heard Sophie's whoop of exhilaration and saw that she was laughing.

His weary heart soared. Suddenly nothing mattered—not the whole legal mess or Alnburgh or the money or anything. Not even the future. Nothing existed beyond that moment on the empty, rain-lashed beach, the water running down his face and sticking his clothes to his skin, the woman he loved running towards him, laughing.

'It's *insane!*' she cried, throwing her arms out wide and turning round, tipping her face up to the deluge.

Barely breaking his stride, he caught hold of her waist and scooped her up into his arms. The wind took her shriek of joy, tossing it up to the angry sky. Her body was warm and pliant, her heart beating hard against his ribs.

'We might as well give in to it and just get wet,' she gasped. 'It's miles back to the castle—even *you* can't possibly run all the way back carrying me.'

'I'm not even going to try.'

He had turned his back on the sea and was heading up the beach, his pace slowing as he reached the softer, deeper sand at the top. The rain fell more heavily than ever. It ran down his face, blurring his vision. He shook his head to clear the water from his eyes so that he could see the narrow path through the marram grass, leading up over the dunes.

'Where are we going?'

'You'll see.'

It was steeper than he remembered and the sand slipped away beneath his feet, but the need to get out of the rain and peel the wet clothes from Sophie's delicious body gave him superhuman strength. In seconds they had crested the dune.

The farmhouse was right in front of them, just as he'd remembered it.

'Oh, what a gorgeous house!' She almost had to shout to be heard above the noise of the downpour. 'Do you know the people who own it?'

'Yes.'

Pushing open the little wooden gate, he strode up the path, hoisting Sophie harder against him while he freed a hand to key in the code. He sent up a wry prayer of thanks for the lack of imagination and security-consciousness that had made Ralph choose Tatiana's birth-date as the access code for the entire estate.

'You can put me down, you know…' Sophie murmured, catching a raindrop that was running down his cheek with her tongue.

'Uh-uh. Not yet. I'm not letting you go.'

The door swung open and he carried her over the threshold, his heart twisting as he was hit by the symbolism of the gesture. Kicking the door shut behind them, abruptly silencing the noise of the rain, he gently set Sophie down.

She turned, leaning her back against him as she looked around the large, low-beamed farmhouse kitchen.

'I feel like Goldilocks,' she said wonderingly, taking his hand and pulling him across to the table so she could peer into the basket that had been left there. 'So who does own this?'

Kit could feel the warmth of her skin through their wet clothes, the rounded firmness of her bottom. His voice was gruff with suppressed desire as he replied.

'The estate.'

She picked up a bottle of wine from the basket, a packet of biscuits. 'So that means you, Lord Fitzroy.' She turned to kiss him lightly on the mouth. 'Can I look around?'

'Be my guest.'

Still with her fingers laced through his, she led him out of the kitchen, their sandy feet making no sound on the stone flags. Beyond it there was a square hallway with a stately old staircase going up, doors leading through to other rooms. Sophie opened one, and breathed in the scent of woodsmoke as she looked into a long room with a fireplace. A huge bay window that flooded the room with rain-soaked light and looked out onto the beach.

There was an odd feeling in her chest as they went quickly on, through rooms that felt as if they were holding their breaths. Waiting for her. Upstairs she opened the door into a child's room, with a little bed covered by a blue quilt with ducks on it, and a cot. Through the streaming rain on the window she could see a swing in the garden below.

Her whole body throbbed with yearning. Stricken, she turned to Kit, opening her mouth to say something, but the words stuck in her swollen throat.

Gently he pulled her back towards the door.

'I'm afraid I'm going to have to move the tour on at this point,' he said huskily, brushing the side of her neck with his lips in the way that always made her instantly boneless with need. 'Allow me to show you the master bedroom...'

When she broke away from kissing him and opened her eyes again Sophie found herself in a large, low room with a pretty fireplace and a window like the one in the sitting room downstairs. A window seat was set into it.

As she looked Kit was very slowly turning her round so he could undo the zip on her dripping dress. Rain rattled against the window, and longing beat within her with the same relentless insistence. For him; but not just for the quick, exhilarating release of making love.

For more.

For all of him—body and soul. Head and heart. For always.

Her dress fell to the floor. She stood before him, naked and trembling, and for the first time ever she didn't reach to tear his clothes off, rushing and fumbling.

They gazed at each other for a long moment. His silver eyes were hooded. The bruising on his face was gone now, the cuts healed, though the small scars they left would always be there. Mutely she reached up to run her fingers over them. He caught her hand, pressing it to his cheek for a second, then drawing her gently over to the bed. In one deft movement he folded down the covers, then picked her up and laid her onto the cool sheets.

She lay still as he peeled off his T-shirt and reached for the buckle of his belt. Her need for him was as strong as ever—stronger if anything—but it was as if something had shifted inside her; something to do with the quiet bedroom with the uneven walls and slightly sloping floor in this old farmhouse. It was as if she had been running for a long time, hurrying to get somewhere, and at last she had arrived. There was no need to rush any more.

His naked body was so beautiful. Her breath hitched in her throat as he lowered himself onto the bed beside her and, pulling the covers over them both, folded her gently into his arms.

AFTER THE RAIN the sky was washed out and new. The sun reappeared, making the raindrops on the window sparkle like crystals. Like the tears on Sophie's lashes. The intensity of their lovemaking had shaken them both.

'I *like* this house,' she said softly now, breaking the silence that had wrapped itself around them since the sobbing cries of her orgasm had faded.

'Do you come here a lot?'

'I used to call in a lot when I was a kid,' he said
gravely. 'But I have to say that this is the first time I've
actually come here.'

He'd said it in an attempt to lighten the atmosphere
a little and banish the mood of wistfulness that seemed
to have stolen the laughter from Sophie's lips and the
sparkle from her eyes as they'd looked round the house.
It worked. She gave one of her breathy giggles. 'Don't
be silly. You know what I mean.'

Smiling, he kissed the top of her head. 'OK. I used
to walk down here when I was home from school for
the holidays, after Jasper was born. It was a working
farm then; the people who lived here were called Mr
and Mrs Prior. They were good to me. Probably because
they felt sorry for me—it must have been obvious to
everyone that I was surplus to requirement after Ralph
remarried and Jasper arrived. They let me help out on
the farm when I was old enough.'

He'd often eaten with them too; food he could still
remember, that was nothing like the bland boarding-
school stodge or the fussy, formal meals served up in
the Alnburgh dining room, accompanied by acerbic
asides from Ralph. It was here that he'd learned for the
first time what 'home' could mean, and understood
why some boys cried in the dark for the first few nights
of term.

'They sound lovely,' Sophie said. 'What happened
to them?'

'They went the same way as all the other tenants
when Tatiana decided she'd like a little project and
turned all the estate cottages into holiday lets. It wasn't
too bad for them—they were looking to retire anyway—

but a lot of local people lost homes their families had lived in for generations. The idea was she was going to be completely in charge of managing them all, but of course the moment the fun decorating bit was done she got bored and handed it all over to an agency.'

'Ah.' It was a soft sigh of disappointment. 'So it's still being let? I was hoping we could stay.' She sat up suddenly, clutching the duvet against her breasts. 'Wait a minute—the basket on the table—does that mean people are going to be arriving today? Now I really do feel like Goldilocks—any minute someone's going to appear and shout, "Who's been shagging in my bed?"'

Kit smiled. He couldn't help it.

'Changeover day is usually Friday, so we should be safe. We can use the stuff the agency have left and I'll replace it tomorrow. Shall we open the wine?'

It was almost a rhetorical question, since Sophie had never been known to refuse wine before, but she hesitated for a second, then sank down beside him again, not meeting his eye.

'No, but I'd kill for a cup of tea. How much does it cost to stay here? I'm seriously thinking of booking it for as long as I can afford.'

CHAPTER ELEVEN

SOPHIE SLIPPED DOWN beneath the warm fragrant water and, sighing, closed her eyes.

She was having a bath in Tatiana's bathroom because it was by far the most comfortable one at Alnburgh, having been updated by her interior designer with no regard for expense. Or, unfortunately, for taste. Even behind her closed lids Sophie was still dazzled by the glare of about a hundred spotlights glinting off polished marble, gold-plated taps and wall-to-wall mirrors.

Alnburgh was all about extremes. Half of it hadn't been touched in a hundred years, and the other half had been tarted up to look like Selfridges' window at Christmastime. Neither half was particularly attractive or comfortable to live in. Wistfully Sophie let her mind drift back to that afternoon at the farmhouse.

When Kit was downstairs making the tea she had got up and stripped the bed, then set about clumsily re-making it with fresh sheets she'd found in the linen cupboard. She could hear him moving about in the kitchen below, and the sense of his presence near her in the house, the simple domesticity of the task, had given her an absurd sense of satisfaction.

The skies had cleared and the beach had been bathed in golden sunlight as they'd walked back, but the castle had loomed blackly ahead of them, looking so like a picture of a haunted house in a cartoon that Sophie had almost expected to see a flash of forked lightning above the battlements and hear the sound of evil laughter.

Even the sand beneath her feet had felt cold in the shadow of Alnburgh, and with every step she had almost been able to feel Kit slipping away from her again. She had a sudden vision of the castle as a rival—the Other Woman, so much more sophisticated and enthralling than her. Or maybe she was the impostor? The mistress who would never quite win Kit back from his demanding, capricious wife.

She hauled herself up out of the water and reached for a towel. She wanted to be his wife, she thought sadly. She wanted normality, a kitchen that wasn't in a dungeon, a swing in the garden and a cot in the bedroom upstairs. And a baby… Oh, please, God, *a baby…*

The Dark Star glinted in the spotlights as she wrapped the towel around herself and stepped out of the bath, and out of the warm water she was aware of a dragging pain in her stomach. Reaching down to dry herself, she felt a thud of foreboding and looked down at the damp red stain on the pale blue bath towel.

A sob rose in her throat.

There was no baby.

'THAT'S GREAT NEWS, Randall.'

Kit slumped against the desk in the library, squeezing his eyes shut as he processed the latest information on Lewis's progress and fighting against the now-familiar onslaught of guilt and relief.

'Isn't it?' From the other end of the phone, in the Birmingham hospital, Randall sounded so positive it was almost infectious. 'Of course the fact that Lewis is a

young, fit guy has definitely been on his side in helping him recover physically, and this baby arriving in
the next few weeks has given him a real goal to work
towards in terms of getting out of hospital. Hopefully
he should make it in time for the birth.'

'How's his family coping?' Standing up, Kit went
to the window. The view was entirely different from
the one he'd seen earlier; the distant sea was quiet
and the expanse of sand was wide and flat and clean
now the storm had passed.

'His family are rallying round, and so are their entire
neighbourhood and all his mates, planning a big party
for when he gets home.' Randall paused before adding
tersely, 'The girlfriend is less of a support. I wouldn't
put money on her sticking with him long term. I just
hope she has the decency to stay with him until he's
back on his feet again, however long it takes.'

Kit kept his voice deliberately neutral and his eyes
fixed on the distant place where the sea met the sky. 'I
don't suppose it's easy for her either, you know. She's
just a kid too. She didn't exactly sign up for any of this
when she started going out with him.'

'Maybe you're right.' Randall sighed. 'Sorry. It's
been a long shift and I've lost perspective a bit. Anyway, how are you?'

As he spoke movement out of the corner of Kit's eye
made him turn his head. His heart crashed as icy sweat
drenched his body and his palms burned. A man with a
metal detector was making his way slowly over the sand
and for a moment Kit was back in uniform, watching
his team mates inch up a dusty road, looking for mines.

'Kit?'

Randall's voice made the nightmarish vision fade

again. Kit squeezed his eyes tightly shut for a second. 'Sorry. I'm fine.' His left hand hung at his side and he stretched and squeezed his numb fingers. 'Tell Lewis I'll come and see him tomorrow.'

'I'm here if you need me, remember,' Randall prompted gently.

'I'll bear it in mind. Thanks.'

His hand was shaking as he hung up.

He didn't want to know, he told himself angrily. There was no need.

Quickly he crossed the room and headed for the stairs to find Sophie. Suddenly he had the terrible, crushing insight that every hour, every second with her was precious because there might only be a finite number of them...

The bedroom door was shut. He stopped outside it, leaning his head against it for a moment, breathing hard, reining back his thoughts before they raced away, completely out of control. God. And he'd always been so rigidly in command—of himself and everything else. So rational. So unemotional.

He barely recognised that man any more. The good soldier. The strong leader. The man who cared about little and had even less to lose.

Now he cared so much it was killing him. And he had everything to lose.

Gently he knocked and pushed open the door. Wrapped in a light blue bath towel, Sophie was sitting at the little oak console table she had brought up to use as a dressing table, brushing her hair. The pink-tinged evening light made her bare skin look as soft and tempting as a marshmallow. Kit's stomach muscles tightened as if against a punch.

He went to stand behind her. She didn't stop brushing, or raise her eyes to meet his in the mirror. Its age-
mottled glass gave her face a timeless, ethereal beauty
that seemed to place her somewhere just beyond his
reach. He needed to reassure himself that she was there,
that she was his, and he lifted his hand to sweep the
heavy fall of her hair sideways and bent to kiss the
nape of her neck.

She was the only thing that anchored him to sanity,
the only way he knew of keeping the demons at bay.
He breathed in her scent, and was aware of the fizzing
in his fingers subsiding as they met her warm flesh.

'Did you ring the hospital?' she said in a low voice,
bowing her head forwards as he kissed her neck.

'Um-hm.' Preoccupied, Kit didn't lift his head.

'How's Lewis?'

'Better.'

She leaned forwards, stiffening a little and moving
away from him. 'What does that mean? Better as in
"completely recovered and going home"? Or better as
in "off the critical list"?'

He didn't want to think about it. Her skin was like
velvet against his lips, and he put his arms around her
to peel away the towel.

'Somewhere between the two.'

Her hands came up to cover his and his first thought
was that, as so often, she had read his mind, but then he
felt her getting to her feet and pushing his hands away.

'Kit, stop.'

Instantly he jerked upright and took a step back. Pulling the towel more tightly around herself, Sophie sank
down onto the little rosewood chair again, her head
lowered so that he couldn't see her face.

'What's wrong?'

She gave a slight shrug, but didn't look up. 'You tell me.'

He sighed, dragging a hand impatiently over his eyes, a feeling of unease prickling at the back of his neck. 'Sorry, I don't get it. Is this going to be one of those cryptic conversations in which I have to guess what's going on in your head?'

'Maybe. At least then you'd know what it's like for me.'

Her voice was low, but the edge of bitterness in it was unmistakable. Unease turned to alarm, making him speak more coldly than he'd intended.

'What's that supposed to mean?'

'It means I can't go on letting you push me away and shut me out.'

Kit gave a harsh bark of laughter. 'Forgive me for being pedantic, but weren't you the one who just pushed me away?'

'That's *sex*, Kit! I'm talking about intimacy. *Talking*.' Her voice trembled with emotion, and as she raised her head he saw her face properly.

'You've been crying. Sophie, what's wrong?'

Shock hit him hard, like a punch to the solar plexus. She never cried—except when she saw a spider, or in the aftermath of their lovemaking when she collapsed, gasping and sobbing, onto his chest. Bewildered, he paced across the floor, his mind going back over the afternoon as he tried to think what could possibly have brought this on.

'Look, if you hate it here that much...'

She shook her head, quickly rubbing the tears away with the back of her hand. 'It's not that. Not really. I mean, it's not what I would have chosen, but I'd happily live in a cave as long as I was with you.'

'You *are* with me.'

'No. I'm not.' She looked up again, and her eyes met his in the mirror. They shimmered with tears and were filled with an aching sadness. 'We sleep together, Kit. We have sex—a lot of sex. Sometimes we have break-fast together the morning after, but we don't talk. Not about anything that matters.'

'Like what?'

'Like about the future.' She took a quick breath, in and out. 'Or the past for that matter. Like what the hell happened to you while you were away.'

'There's nothing to talk about.' Gritting his teeth, he spoke with exaggerated patience. 'Things happen all the time out there. Bloody awful things that would drive you crazy if you let yourself dwell on them. But you don't. You leave them there and you come home and forget.'

'OK. I get it. You don't want to talk to me.' She gave a crooked smile that was unbearably poignant. 'But I need to talk to you. Five months is a long time and stuff happened here that I haven't had a chance to tell you about.'

'What stuff?' His blood ran to ice.

'Nothing terrible. But we do need to discuss it. I did as you said and went to see a doctor. About my periods.'

'And?'

'It's endometriosis.' She looked down at the hair-brush in her hand, turning it over and over. 'No sur-prises there, but he warned me that getting pregnant might be difficult. He told me not to leave it too long before trying to start a family and—'

'Sophie—'

She ignored the warning in his tone, looking straight at him with a mixture of resignation and defiance. 'I stopped taking the pill immediately.'

Kit spun away from her. It was as if a switch had been flicked inside his body, shutting off all function, all feeling for a few seconds, while his brain spun into freefall. *Ten per cent of cases.* He raised his hands to his head as the implications hit.

'And that was before I got home?' he rasped. 'So for the last *two weeks* we've—'

'I'm not pregnant.'

The bald, emotionless statement stilled the panic in his head.

He dropped his hands to his sides again. Acid fizzed beneath his skin, burning and throbbing in the pulse points on his wrists just as horror beat inside him at the realisation that keeping his fears to himself could have had such far-reaching consequences. But more immediate than that was relief.

'I'm sorry,' he said, turning to face her, but his voice was hoarse and unconvincing even to his ears.

'Are you?' Sophie stood up, stepping out from behind the dressing table chair and turning to him with eyes that blazed with fury. 'Because for a moment there I could have sworn that sorry was the last thing you were. In fact, "hugely relieved" might be a better way of describing your reaction.' She held up her hands as if to push him back. 'I wouldn't bother to deny it, Kit. There's really no point. I'm not even surprised, since it's been getting increasingly obvious that there's no future for us. Tell me, were you waiting out of kindness to let me down gently, or were you just going to

shut me out a bit more every day in the hope that eventually I'd go of my own accord, and leave you free to mingle your exclusive Fitzroy genes with someone of the right pedigree?'

Every barbed word tore into him, but he knew he had brought the pain on himself. He gritted his teeth and steeled himself for more.

'No.'

Tossing her hair back, she laughed, but it came out more like a sob. It hurt him even more than her anger and her inaccurate accusations. 'Oh, dear. You'll have to do better than that, Kit,' she said. 'This is the part where you're supposed to take me in your arms and tell me I've got it all wrong and promise that one day we'll have a family of our own—or didn't you read the script?'

It took all his strength, all his courage to meet her eyes. He felt as if he'd swallowed arsenic.

'I can't do that. I'm sorry.'

DARKNESS GATHERED BEHIND Sophie's eyes. Her head was filled with a strange buzzing sound, and for a moment she actually thought she was going to faint. Kit's face swam in front of her, as hard and blank as if it had been carved from stone.

'There's something I have to tell you.'

His emotionless voice reached her from a long distance away. He turned away from her then, and she was grateful that he couldn't see her grabbing hold of the chest of drawers for support as she fought to drag in a breath. Her stomach cramped.

It was hardly a bolt from the blue. She had seen it coming since the morning after their dinner at Villa Luana. She had to hold on to her dignity.

'It's OK,' she said in a strangled voice. 'You don't have to explain. I understand already. When you asked me to marry you, all this wasn't part of the deal.' She made a gesture with her hand that inadequately indicated the vast castle that stretched all around them. 'I know things have changed since then.'

'Yes. Things have changed.' Kit sounded so infinitely weary that for a moment she almost felt sorry for him. 'But it's nothing to do with Alnburgh. It's me. I've changed.'

'Oh, God.' She actually managed a genuine laugh then, albeit a slightly hysterical one. '"It's not you, it's me." That's such an old line, Kit.'

He didn't smile. Standing in front of the window with another spectacular Alnburgh sunset spreading its glories across the sky behind him, he looked as stern and beautiful as a painted saint in the Sistine Chapel.

'It's true. I wish it wasn't but it is. I'm not the person—the hero...' his mouth twisted bleakly '...you think I am.'

Sophie was distantly aware that she was shivering. She should put some clothes on, but she couldn't quite bring herself to do it in front of him now. He was suddenly a stranger to her.

'You remember the incident that happened out there on the day I came back...' Kit bowed his head briefly '...the one that left a nineteen-year-old boy in Intensive Care with bullets in his head and back? I should have been looking after him, just like you said, but what happened to him was my fault. All. My. Fault.'

His voice dripped ice down her spine. He was standing against the window, his face in shadow, but his eyes burned with a peculiar intensity that made her breath catch and her heart ache with compassion and fear.

'That can't be true. Surely in an explosion—'

'He wasn't hurt in the explosion,' he said with exaggerated patience that sounded almost like scorn. 'He was hurt *before* the bomb went off, by enemy fire.'

'How can that be your fault?'

'Because he was one of the infantry team covering my back while I defused the device,' he said in a low, mocking voice. Turning round, he gripped the window sill and looked out over the beach, though Sophie had a feeling he wasn't seeing the tranquil sweep of Northumberland sand at all. 'We'd been called to a bridge over one of the main routes into a town notorious for its insurgent activity. The bomb was underneath it, but the whole situation was a nightmare. The site was visible for miles around, from hundreds of rooftops and windows and balconies. We can clear the area immediately around the device on the ground, but it's impossible to make a site like that safe. The only thing to do is to go in there and do the job quickly.'

Sophie was transfixed, standing shivering in the middle of the room, her arms wrapped around herself because she couldn't wrap them around him. Everything about him told her to keep away, from his white-knuckled grip on the window sill to the bunched muscles across his shoulders.

'I couldn't do it,' he said bitterly. 'I couldn't do it because I couldn't feel my fingers properly. My hands were shaking. I dropped the wire cutters, and all I could think about was you.' He paused, letting his head drop for a moment and exhaling a ragged breath. 'That was when the shooting started and I knew we were screwed.

There was nothing to do but get out fast. I was running back to the vehicle when the bomb went off, but Lewis had already been hit.'

'Oh, Kit…' Like a sleepwalker, Sophie moved towards him, unable to stop herself from reaching out and touching him. 'It wasn't your fault—you have to believe that. It was an impossible situation. It could have happened to anyone.'

Slowly, levering himself away from the window sill, he turned to face her. His mouth was curved into a bleak parody of a smile that made her insides freeze.

'I don't think so.'

'What do you mean?'

'Everything made sense when my mother mentioned Leo's illness.' The smile twisted. 'You thought it was bad enough that I inherited Alnburgh from him, but I'm afraid it looks like that might be the least of my problems. At least I could walk away from Alnburgh.'

'You think you have the same thing he had?'

Sophie's voice was a cracked whisper. By contrast his was cold, flat, utterly matter-of-fact.

'I checked with a friend who's a doctor. The early signs are clumsiness and loss of sensation in the hands. According to Juliet, there's a hereditary factor in ten per cent of cases. And that's why I'm glad you're not pregnant.'

Instinctively Sophie went towards him, wanting only to take him in her arms. A cautious hope was beginning to steal through her combined with relief that at last she understood. He had finally opened up to her, and now she knew what the problem was it was a case of dealing with it, one thing at a time.

'You have to see someone,' she said gently, wrapping her arms around him. 'Find out for sure.'

'Do I?'

She wasn't sure which was worse, his laconic drawl or his rigid, unyielding body. She drew sharply away from him.

'Of course—the sooner we know the better, and then whatever the facts are we can deal with them.' She swallowed hard, her heart pounding, an icy avalanche of dread smashing away the hope and relief. '*Together*. Whatever it is, we'll—'

He shook his head. 'No.'

Sophie's hand flew to her mouth, stopping the sob that swelled in her throat. Kit sighed, looking at her with an unflinching, silvery gaze.

'If I have what my f-father had…' his eyelids flickered as he stumbled over the word 'father', but his tone was colder, harder than ever as he continued '…I won't sentence you to that slow death with me. I'd have to let you go.'

'No,' she said, shaking her head in disbelief. 'You can't mean that. You wouldn't throw away what we have because—'

'Yes.' His voice held a terrifying note of finality. 'I spoke to Juliet. I know what it would mean. If I have this illness, there's no way I can marry you, Sophie. I'm sorry.'

Sophie stepped backwards, fighting for air. She felt dizzy and disorientated, as if she'd just stepped off some kind of extreme fairground ride.

'I hope *so much* that you don't,' she said in an odd, breathless voice. 'No one deserves to go through that.

But if that's how you feel…even if you don't have it, it's over for us anyway.'

Nausea rolled over her and for a moment she thought she might pass out, but, gripping the edge of the dressing table, she carried on.

'Marriage is supposed to be for better or for worse, in sickness and in health. It's supposed to be about facing things together. About trust and sharing and letting each other in, so maybe…'

She faltered again, staring at him across the space that separated them, willing him to cross it and take her in his arms and tell her she was right and he hadn't been thinking straight. But he didn't move. Didn't open his mouth to argue or stop her from saying the words she didn't want to speak.

'Maybe we never stood a chance.'

Her voice had dried up to a cracked whisper. He closed his eyes briefly, as if he was in pain.

'If that's what you think… I won't try to change your mind.'

For a moment they just gazed at each other. And then he turned and pulled the door open. His back was rigid with tension as he walked out, as if he was only holding himself in check with the greatest effort.

Sinking down onto the bed, Sophie listened to his footsteps recede as he went down the stairs. From outside the cries of the gulls sounded like maniacal laughter.

CHAPTER TWELVE

KIT DIDN'T COME to bed that night.

Sophie measured the long hours by the distant chiming of the clock in the clock tower and the gradual lightening of the sky. For the first time in her life, sleep eluded her and she understood what it was like for Kit to suffer the torment of insomnia.

That, however, was about as far as her understanding of Kit went.

In a few short hours the man she loved, the man whose body she knew intimately, inch by inch, had become a stranger to her. Although maybe that wasn't quite true, she thought, staring into the ashy light of dawn. Maybe he'd always been a stranger and she'd been fooled into thinking they were close because they had such breathtaking sex. She sat up, her heart racing sickeningly, drenched in sweat as she had a flashback to the hammam in the hotel, when she'd actually convinced herself that the bond they shared went beyond words.

How spectacularly naive that seemed now.

She dropped her head into her hands. She'd looked on getting married like the start of some big adventure. It hadn't mattered that she knew little about the place she was going to, she'd been looking forward to exploring; to the excitement of the journey, the challenges, the quiet moments of joy. Now she felt as if she'd arrived to find everywhere locked and barred, and marked 'Private. Keep Out.' There was nothing to do but give up and go home.

Move on. Just like you always do, sneered a malicious little voice inside her head.

Throwing back the twisted covers, she stumbled out of bed, tensing against the fist of pain that tightened in her stomach. She loved him. Too much to just walk away, especially when there was a possibility he could be facing the hardest challenge of his life.

Outside a pale band of gold on the horizon heralded the new day. Sophie hoped it was a good omen. Clumsily she pulled on jeans beneath the shirt she'd slept in and headed for the door. She felt spacey with lack of sleep, although already the hours of restless darkness and the awful events that had preceded them had taken on a kind of nightmarish quality that she was suddenly desperate to banish.

Going along the corridor towards the main staircase, she broke into a half-run. Everything would look different this morning. Now it was all out in the open they just needed to talk it over properly. She wondered where he'd slept last night—if he'd slept at all. The library was as good a place as any to start looking for him…

But in the end she didn't get that far. As she reached the bottom of the stairs she heard the sound of footsteps in the long gallery and the metallic jingle of car keys. Crossing the portrait hall, she saw him through the archway. He was dressed—properly dressed, unlike her—and carrying his jacket as he headed towards the armoury hall.

'Kit?' She went towards him, fear beating through her.

He stopped and was perfectly still for a moment, as

if he was steeling himself before turning to face her. When he did his expression was carefully blank.

'I didn't want to wake you.' He held up a pen and a piece of Alnburgh-headed notepaper he must have brought through from the library. 'I was going to leave a note.'

Sophie's teeth were chattering, making it hard to speak. 'Saying what?'

'I'm going to see Lewis.' He tossed the paper and pen down on the side table. 'It's a four-hour drive so I need to get an early start if I'm going to get back tonight.'

'You're coming back?'

'Of course,' he said wearily, going towards the door. 'What else would I do?'

'I don't know. I thought...' Relief made her shaky and inarticulate as she followed him. 'I'm sorry about last night. I couldn't sleep thinking about it and how mad it is to let this come between us. You must have been through hell these last couple of weeks, worrying about it, and I'm so sorry that you went through that alone.' He slid back the bolts on the door and Sophie blinked as light flooded the gloomy hall, bringing with it a draft of cool autumn air. 'But you're not alone any more. Whatever happens now, we're in it together.'

Kit paused in the doorway. The clear morning light showed up the shadows of exhaustion beneath his eyes and reminded her with sudden poignancy of when he'd first come home, making her wish she could turn the clock back. He sighed, bowing his head.

'No, Sophie,' he said with quiet resignation. 'I meant what I said last night. I won't do it to you. You're the most amazing, vibrant person I've ever met.' He reached out and brushed her cheek with his fingertips. 'I won't condemn you to a life of watching me die by degrees. It would be like burying you alive.'

Sophie gave a sharp, indrawn breath, as if she'd just had cold water thrown in her face. 'But I love you,' she gasped. 'Whatever happens, *I love you…*'

He went down the steps into the misty morning and, opening the car door, threw his jacket onto the passenger seat. 'You say that now—hell, I'm sure you even think you mean it, but for how long, Sophie?' Slamming the door, he swung round to face her again. 'If this is what I think it is, it'll change *everything* between us.'

'Except how I feel about you.'

'You can't say that for sure.'

The stone flags were icy beneath Sophie's bare feet as she walked over to the car, but it was nothing compared to the chill inside her. 'I can, but this isn't about me really, is it? This is about you. You can't get your head round it because you don't feel that way in return. Or—' She came to an abrupt halt as another thought occurred to her. 'Is it more than that? Is this about your inability to get past the fact that your mother walked out on you all those years ago?' She saw his eyes narrow, his body tense and gave a slightly wild laugh as she realised she'd hit a nerve. 'You're punishing me for what she did, and for Ralph, who stopped loving you as soon as he found out you weren't his son—'

'Enough.'

The word was torn from some primitive part of him. He whirled round and Sophie got a fleeting glimpse of the hard, bunched muscles in his arm as he swung his fist. She gave a high, terrified cry, instinctively ducking away from him and putting her hands up to shield her face. There was a sickening crack as his hand smashed down on the wing of the car with such force that the shiny black metal buckled.

And then silence.

Perhaps it was the pain that brought Kit back to his senses, perhaps it was hearing Sophie cry out like that, but the violent impulse passed as quickly as it had gripped him. For a moment he stayed completely still, his arms braced against the bonnet of the car, his head bent. The sound of his laboured breathing seemed to fill the gentle autumn morning.

Then, mustering all his strength, he straightened up and turned to Sophie.

She had shrunk back against the castle wall and was pressed against it, her arms wrapped tightly around herself as if in an attempt to contain the violent shudders that convulsed her. But it was her face that shocked him most. It wore the expression he had seen before on people who had witnessed terrible trauma. A waxy-pale mask of abject terror.

Remorse and self-disgust exploded inside his head, rocking him to the core. 'God, Sophie—I'm sorry, I—' Instinctively he moved towards her, thinking only of pulling her into his arms and comforting her, but as he reached out she flinched violently away.

'Please—no,' she said in a strangled voice he didn't recognise. Shrinking back from him, she closed her eyes, as if she were wishing him away. 'Just go. Now.'

For a moment he couldn't move. But then, because he knew he had forfeited every moral and personal right when he'd lost control, he walked round the car and got in. His hands were shaking so badly it took a long time for him to get the key into the ignition, and when he finally started the engine and looked up she had disappeared inside the castle and shut the door.

HE DROVE TOO FAST, with the same kind of tense, focused clarity he felt in an ambush. He had an acute hyper-awareness of the smallest details—the digital dashboard statistics registering fuel consumption, the change in colour of the spreading bruise on his knuckles from red to purple to blue—but the miles were swallowed up without him being able to say whereabouts he was or for how long he'd been driving.

He stopped only once, but that was while he was still on the narrow Northumbrian roads not far from Aln-burgh and the memory of Sophie's face was still clear and raw and painful. Not for the briefest split second had he been in danger of hitting her, but the way she'd flinched away from him and raised her hands in self-defence was enough to make the bile rise in the back of his throat. He pulled over, getting out of the car and filling his starved lungs with gulps of air before getting into the driver's seat again. He caught a glimpse of himself in the rear-view mirror, and his face was the face of a stranger. A stranger he didn't want to know.

The needle on the speedometer was almost vertical now, the motorway rushing past in an anonymous blur so that he felt a jolt of surprise when he read the name of the town to which he was headed on the exit sign that loomed ahead.

Leaving the motorway forced him out of his trance-like state. He hadn't bothered to programme the car's sat-nav, so had to concentrate on following signs to the hospital in which the unit to which Lewis had been transferred was situated. It wasn't easy. His mind refused to stay focused on the incomprehensible system of roundabouts and dual carriageways and kept being pulled back to what had happened earlier. Each time he replayed the scene in his head the self-loathing he felt increased.

Pulling up in the hospital car park, he took his mobile phone from the pocket of his jacket and dialled Alnburgh. In his head he could hear the phone shrilling through the portrait hall, shattering the thick silence of the library. Seconds ticked by. His bruised and swollen knuckles throbbed as he gripped the phone tightly.

And just when he was about to give up there was a click and a pause, and then Sophie's low, slightly breathless voice.

'Hello?'

Kit closed his eyes. Just hearing her say that one word drove back the demons and stilled the panic. He tipped his head back, desperately trying to find his own voice. When he did it was hoarse and cracked.

'Sophie, it's me.'

There was a pause. He pictured her face, seeing in his mind the two lines of anguish he knew would have appeared between her fine brows, the way she would be pressing her lips together to keep her emotions in check.

'Where are you?'

'I just got to the hospital.'

'Already? That was quick.'

Was it? He glanced at the dashboard clock and noticed absently she was right. 'I had to say sorry.'

'There's no need.' She said it quickly, in a low, miserable voice. 'It wasn't you... I...overreacted. I'm sorry.'

'Don't.' Hearing her blame herself for his behaviour was more than he could bear. 'Please. Don't take

responsibility for my failings. You were right…' He paused, closing his eyes and massaging his forehead with his fingertips, as if he could rub away the memory of what he'd done.

'About what?'

'About what you said about my mother, and Ralph. I didn't want to hear it and I lost control. But I wouldn't have hit you, Sophie. Whatever else you think, I want you to believe that. I would *never* hurt you.'

There was a long silence.

'You've shut me out of your life, Kit. Nothing could hurt more than that.'

SOPHIE PUT THE phone down and then stood back, staring at it. Her eyes were dry, but she knew that the tears were there inside her, and that when they came they would flow for a long, long time.

For a moment, when he'd said that she was right she'd thought—*hoped*—he'd rung to tell her he'd changed his mind. That he had to be with her, whatever. That what they had was stronger than anything else life could throw at them. That his love was unconditional.

But it wasn't.

He felt guilty for frightening her, that was all. He'd rung because he couldn't know that in the instant when he'd raised his fist it had triggered a memory, buried so long and so deep that the details had dimmed to an impressionistic blur, but which still brought the sour taste of terror into her mouth.

She picked up the bag at her feet and walked through to the long gallery, looking round at the unsmiling Fitzroys, the stuffed animal heads with their glassy eyes and rictus snarls for the last time. On impulse she put down her bag and opened the door to the dining room and switched on the light. The chrysanthemums stood where she had put them yesterday, when she'd thought that a candlelit dinner was all that was needed to cross the chasm between her and Kit.

She almost wanted to laugh at her own naiveté.

Without thinking, she found herself walking forwards until she was standing beneath the portrait of the woman with the roses in her hair and The Dark Star on her finger—a fellow outsider who had failed to fit in at Alnburgh and ended up paying the price with her life. Sophie raised her hand and looked down at the ring, remembering what Kit had said about refusing to sentence her to a slow death with him. She smoothed her thumb over the iridescent opal. Caring for him when he needed her wouldn't have killed her, but loving a man who held himself back from her might, in the end.

Very slowly she eased the ring off her finger and held it in her hand for a second. Her finger felt lighter without it. Empty. Then she put it on the mantelpiece, just below the portrait, and went out of the room.

It was time to move on again.

The specialist Army Rehabilitation Centre to which Lewis had been moved when he came out of Intensive Care was newly built and furnished in bright primary colours. Kit followed a pretty, plump nurse down a corridor that smelled of paint, to Lewis's room. She knocked and opened the door without waiting for an answer.

'There's someone here to see you.'

Through the open door Kit could see Lewis sitting in front of a television screen, the control for a games console in his hand. At the nurse's words his head snapped round, but the hope on his face vanished instantly when Kit walked past her into the room.

'Oh. It's you, sir,' he said sullenly, a blush stealing up his neck as he turned back to his game. 'What are you doing here?'

'I wanted to see you. To find out how you're doing. Is it OK if I sit down?'

Lewis nodded, but his gaze didn't move from the screen, which showed an animated railway line in grim, twilight colours, with a row of derelict-looking buildings behind it. Sitting on the edge of the bed, Kit rubbed his burning palms against his thighs and, averting his eyes, looked at Lewis instead.

He was a shadow of the boy who'd brought Kit coffee on that morning a few weeks ago and spilled most of it onto the sand in his haste and enthusiasm. He'd lost a lot of weight, and, with his hair shaved off and the scar where they'd operated to remove the bullet from his head still raw, he looked frail. As fragile as a child.

'You look well,' Kit lied with impressive calm, given the pickaxe of guilt lodged in his chest and the fact that his heart felt as if it had been fed through a mincing machine. 'A hell of a lot better than last time I saw you, anyway. How are you feeling?'

Lewis answered in a single monosyllabic word. It was a concise response, if not one that would usually be acceptable to a commanding officer. His eyes were fixed to the screen, where shadowy figures darted from buildings and jumped out of containers beside the railway line. Understanding the sentiment behind it all too well, Kit let the language go.

'Sorry to hear that. I spoke to Dr Randall. He says

you've made incredible progress and shown a huge amount of courage. A lot of men wouldn't have pulled through at all, never mind as quickly and well as you have.'

Lewis's thumb pressed a red button on the control repeatedly and volleys of animated fire lit up the screen. Kit watched their red reflections in the dilated pupils of Lewis's unblinking eyes.

'I'm doing OK in that way,' he said dully. 'I need to get back to fitness. Back to how I was before.'

'You want to go back out there?'

'I dunno. I haven't decided yet. If things here don't work out…'

Lewis let the sentence trail off, but his thumb continued its rapid movement, annihilating the animated enemy.

'How's Kelly?'

A fireball filled the screen and Lewis's shoulders slumped.

'Dunno. Haven't seen her, have I? She doesn't like it here. Says hospitals freak her out.'

Mentally Kit cursed. There was a restless feeling building in the back of his head and a sweat had broken out on his forehead. 'That's a good incentive to get out of here, then.'

Lewis started the game again, his hands moving jerkily as he guided a figure in SAS fatigues at a run along a deserted street. 'That's what I thought, but now—I dunno. One of my mates told me she's seeing someone else. He works at the gym I used to go to.' Red spurts of gunfire erupted from a blank window and the figure on the screen fell to the ground. 'I can't blame her, can I? I mean, look at me.' Throwing the control down, he stood up, his eyes wild, his thin arms spread out. 'I'm pathetic. I can't even get dressed without help, never mind do fifty push-ups, and I know that was what she fancied about me in the first place. I was fit then, and now I'm...*nothing.*'

'Bullshit, Sapper.' Kit thanked seventeen years of rigorous army discipline for the ability to keep his voice clipped, curt, emotionless. 'You're a soldier who took several bullets while doing a job that would make a gym instructor cry for his mother. Probably the worst injury he's sustained in the line of duty is a pulled muscle. You were shot at close range by a semi-automatic rifle in the hands of a man who wanted to kill you, and you're fighting back.'

As if in slow motion Lewis's face crumpled. Tears welled in his eyes and spilled over his hollow, parchment-pale cheeks as he sank back into his seat.

'I wanted to be a hero for her,' he sobbed, rubbing at his eyes like a little child. 'All the time we were out there I was thinking of her and the baby. I just wanted to make them proud of me...and look what happened. I lost them instead.'

Kit got to his feet, desperately trying to keep his gaze from straying back to the twitching figure of the soldier on the screen. His hands felt as if they'd been dipped in acid that was dissolving the flesh, burning up the nerves.

'You can't look at it that way. You're a lucky man. When I last saw you the doctors weren't sure if the bullet had severed your spine or not; they weren't sure if you'd walk again. You're back on your feet—you're going to be OK.'

Lewis lifted his tear-streaked face to look at him helplessly.

'So what? I'd rather be injured and have her than be walking around, trying to live a normal life without her.'

Kit had already opened his mouth to say something brisk and acerbic in response, but nothing came out. Out of the corner of his eye he could see the game on the screen start over again and he was unable to stop himself turning to watch the figure moving down the street of its own accord this time as snipers appeared on rooftops and windows.

'We don't choose what happens,' he said hoarsely. Blood thrummed in his ears. 'You just have to make the best of the hand you're dealt. You'll find someone who loves you, no matter what. Someone you don't have to prove anything to.' Forcing his gaze from the screen, he looked hollowly at Lewis, trying to see him as he was now, here, rather than remembering the blood running down his face into the sand. Panic loomed, and automatically he thought of Sophie—her smile, her scent—to drive it back.

'You just have to be sure that when you find her, you're not stupid enough to push her away.'

Angrily Lewis swiped the tears from his cheeks. 'The trouble is I don't want anyone else. I just want her.'

Kit went to the door. 'Then don't let her go,' he said wearily. 'Fight for her.'

Out in the corridor he leaned against the wall and took a ragged breath.

'Kit?' He felt Randall's hand on his shoulder. 'Are you all right?'

It seemed that people were always asking him that these days, Kit thought, and he always came up with the same untruthful answer. But he'd run out of lies now. Raising his head, he looked Randall in the eye.

'Not really.' He held up his shaking hands and managed a bleak smile. 'Those tests I asked about when we spoke on the phone—what would they involve?'

Randall's expression stayed professionally blank as he glanced at Kit's hands. 'A variety of things—nothing too complicated. We can make a start on eliminating the obvious things straight away, if you want?'

Kit paused for a heartbeat, then nodded.

It felt as if he'd driven Sophie away already. He had nothing more to lose.

CHAPTER THIRTEEN

THE EARLY-AUTUMN DUSK was already beginning to fall as Sophie slowed the Range Rover that had once belonged to Ralph Fitzroy and swung it into the potholed farm track.

It had been five years at least since she'd last visited, but she remembered every tree and gateway on the final bit of the journey. The tears that had remained unshed throughout the seemingly interminable drive from Alnburgh prickled at the backs of her eyes as she bounced across the field towards the cluster of ancient caravans and camper vans and pulled up alongside Rainbow's bus.

The painted flowers were peeling and a peace symbol over the back wheel had lost one of its three prongs so that it now looked ironically like the logo of an executive car manufacturer, but otherwise the place in which she'd grown up was pretty much unchanged. It even smelled the same, she noticed as she got out of the car and breathed in the scent of Calor gas, frying onions and wet grass.

On legs that felt as weak as a foal's from being in the car for so long, she walked round to the front of the bus and knocked. The windows, as always, were clouded with condensation, but through it she could see movement. The next moment Rainbow flung open the door, her faced wreathed in smiles.

'Summer—you're here!'

Her voice was warm and filled with pleasure, but not undue surprise. Emerging from a patchouli-and-lavender-scented hug, Sophie gave her mother a watery smile.

'You sound like you were expecting me.'

Ushering her in, Rainbow shrugged. Since Sophie had last seen her, her hair had grown past her shoulders and was now a rather beautiful shade of foxglove pink, darker at the ends so that it look as if it had been dip-dyed. She was wearing her usual collection of layered things—a long skirt with a long tunic top covered by a long loose cardigan, all in shades of indigo and purple.

'I was, in a way. I've been getting the Three of Cups a lot lately. It's the card of reunions, so naturally I've been thinking of you.' She gestured to the little table where her worn deck of tarot cards lay. 'Then this morning I got The Tower, so I suppose it's fair to say that I'm not surprised to see you.'

Very recently—like, a couple of days ago—Sophie would have given an inward sneer at all this. But not any more. Now she picked up the top card, which showed a high turret on a rock just like Kit's bedroom at Alnburgh. The sky behind it was black, lightning struck it and flames billowed from the windows, from where two human figures plummeted downwards.

'This is The Tower?' Sophie suppressed a shudder. 'Why did that make you think of me?'

'Well, it was the Cups that made me think of you, but once you were there in my mind The Tower told me all wasn't well.' Rainbow's eyes were the faded blue of summer skies and well-worn jeans, and Sophie saw concern in them now. 'It denotes pain—often coming like a lightning bolt out of the blue, shattering faith and belief. Though, of course,' she added hastily, 'it can be read in different ways...'

'That way is accurate enough for me,' said Sophie with an awkward little laugh.

Rainbow glanced at her, but only said, 'Why don't you sit down? Have you eaten? Hilary made carrot and coriander soup and dropped some round for me earlier.'

'That sounds wonderful,' Sophie said gratefully, sinking down onto the sagging couch, suddenly aware that she was ravenous. As Rainbow set about lighting the gas and the little space was filled with the smell that made Sophie feel about eight years old again she looked around. The bus hadn't changed much, but the cheap nylon curtains she remembered had been replaced with pretty ones—a different printed cotton in each window—and there were bright patchwork cushions on the two couches. It looked nice, Sophie realised with a wrench. Homely.

'I've been away too long,' she said sadly. 'I've been a pretty rubbish daughter, haven't I?'

'Nonsense.' Briskly Rainbow moved the tarot cards and laid a spoon and a bright blue pottery bowl on the table. 'You know I've never held with all that family obligation stuff. You came back when you needed to, and that's what matters to me.'

'You're not hurt that I haven't been back for five years?'

'I think of you often, if that's what you mean,' said Rainbow, pouring thick soup into the bowl. 'But in a good way. You were always fiercely independent, even as a little girl. Self-contained. I knew you wouldn't want to stay here any longer than you had to, and that I had no right to make you feel you should.' She sat down opposite Sophie, her face serene. 'Living like this was my choice, but I always respected your right to make choices of your own.'

Sophie picked up her spoon. 'Why did you choose to live like this?'

'Well, I didn't choose it initially. It came about by accident, I suppose, because I ran away from an unhappy marriage.'

'To my father.' Sophie paused, a spoonful of soup halfway to her mouth, her mind going back to the moment when Kit had brought his fist down on the car bonnet. 'He hit you, didn't he?'

Rainbow looked down at the table, tracing her finger over one of the many scars on its surface. 'I always wondered if you remembered anything about that time.'

'I didn't.' Until today. 'How old was I when we left?'

'Three.' Rainbow looked up at her then, her expression almost apologetic. 'He hit me in front of you once too often, you see, and I knew that if I didn't get out I'd be destroying your chances of a normal life as well as throwing away my own.'

'Oh, Mum...'

It slipped out instinctively, even though Sophie couldn't remember the last time she'd addressed Rainbow like that. Rainbow didn't seem to notice though. Or if she did, she didn't seem to mind.

'Well, everything happens for a reason.' She sighed. 'I'm not saying it wasn't horrible at the time, because it was and I wouldn't wish it on anyone, but without all that I'd never have ended up at the camp. I hadn't been planning to leave, but I went straight to the station, got on the first train that came and went as far as we could before the guard chucked us off for not having a ticket. Which turned out to be Newbury. There was a woman getting into a camper van outside the station and I asked her for directions to a B&B.' Propping her chin on her hand Rainbow smiled in reminiscence. 'It was Bridget—you remember her?'

'I remember.' During her adolescence Bridget was one of the only things that had actually made Sophie appreciate Rainbow, simply because Bridget was infinitely more embarrassing. Built like a Sherman tank, dressed in dungarees and army boots, Bridget had presided over the peace camp like a new-age sergeant-major in drag. Even Kit would probably have been intimidated by her.

But she couldn't let herself think about Kit.

'She took one look at my bruised face—and you—and she knew exactly what our situation was. And that was the moment my whole life changed.' Rainbow got up to switch on a lamp and pull the curtains shut against the encroaching night. 'We went back to the peace camp with her and all the women made us so welcome. They were such good people, who had a vision of a better world with no bombs or wars or violence. We changed our names and started a new life with them. And, well…' she shrugged '…you know the rest.'

Laying her spoon down in the empty bowl, Sophie nodded slowly. She knew, of course, but until now she hadn't really understood. The steel behind the peace-and-love; the courage and the camaraderie and the conviction that gave that small group of dispossessed women the strength to raise their kids and stick two fingers up to a society that hadn't protected them.

She'd been so quick to write her mother off as a daft,

tree-hugging hippy, and distance herself from her alternative lifestyle and eccentric friends. Shame flooded her as she remembered the excuses she'd made about not having a big wedding. *My mother is not most mothers,* she'd said in a tone of deep scorn, implying that was a bad thing.

And it wasn't. It was good, because she had taught her to be strong and independent and not to put up with second best. And she had loved her. Unconditionally.

'Thank you,' she said quietly, reaching across the table and taking her mother's heavily ringed hand in hers.

Rainbow looked surprised. 'For what?'

'Everything. Being brave enough to do what you did. For encouraging me to go and live my own life. And for being here for me now, even after all this time.'

Getting to her feet, Rainbow took Sophie's bowl. 'I'll always be here for you,' she said comfortably, putting water in the kettle and lighting the gas again. 'I couldn't give you much in terms of material stuff when you were growing up, but I used to tell myself that the two things I could give you were roots and wings. You'll always have a home here, but part of loving someone is letting them go.'

And it reminded her so much of Kit that to her horror Sophie felt her eyes suddenly filling with tears. 'Is it?' she said with a sob. 'But what if they don't want to go? What if they want to stay and face things alongside you?'

'Oh, sweetheart…' Rainbow's face creased into lines of compassion as she came forward and took Sophie into her arms. 'I knew something was wrong. What happened? Tell me all about it.'

And so, as the tears slid silently down her cheeks, Sophie did.

THE BOX OF tissues Rainbow had put on the table was almost empty by the time Sophie had finished, as was the bottle of Rainbow's damson gin, which had been brought out instead of herbal tea, in honour of the crisis. Sophie looked at her mother through eyes that were swollen with crying and managed a lopsided smile.

'When he asked me to marry him I thought I'd stumbled into the happy-ever-after part of the story. I never imagined there was going to be a sequel.'

Frowning, Rainbow shared the last of the gin between the two mugs in front of them. 'And you think all this means he doesn't love you?' she asked carefully.

'Not enough.' Sophie dropped her head into her hands. 'If he did he'd know that I'd just want to be there for him, *with* him.'

There was a little pause, during which the only sound was the spluttering hiss of the gas and a cow mooing mournfully in a distant field. 'Or it could mean he loves you more than you can possibly understand,' Rainbow suggested gently. 'Enough to want you to be happy, and to sacrifice his own interests to give you that chance. Enough to give you your freedom.'

Shredding a tissue between listless fingers, Sophie remembered what he'd said that morning. *You're the most amazing, vibrant person I've ever met... I won't condemn you to a life of watching me die by degrees. It would be like burying you alive.*

'But what if I don't want to be free?' she moaned. 'What if I just want to be with him?'

Rainbow leaned forwards and took her hands. 'That's the thing about loving someone.' Her eyes were full of tenderness but her voice was firm. 'It's not just about what *you* want any more. It's about what's best for both of you. He loves you enough to give you your freedom, and now you have to do the same for him. You have to trust him to make his own decisions, and respect them.'

'But it's so hard.' Sophie gasped, closing her eyes. In the darkness behind her throbbing eyelids she saw Kit's face and felt as if her heart had been split in two.

Rainbow's grip on her hands tightened. 'I know. But have faith. Everything happens for a reason, remember. If it's meant to be, it will be. If he loves you, you'll know.'

Opening her eyes, Sophie looked at her mother through a fog of despair. 'How?'

Rainbow gave her a bittersweet smile. 'Ah, now that I can't tell you. I guess you just have to wait for a sign.'

KIT SAT IN the hospital waiting room, beneath a fluorescent strip light that flickered unnervingly and emitted a persistent, low-frequency buzz. He'd been there for a long time and had become intimately acquainted with the arrangement of fake flowers on the table in the corner, and the covers of the women's magazines, showing pictures of tanned blondes with wide, blue-white smiles and vacant eyes.

For the hundredth time he picked up his phone and dialled, lifting it listlessly to his ear. The mobile reception at Alnburgh was virtually non-existent so he tried the castle's landline first, letting it ring on and on and on to make sure that Sophie had enough time to get to it, whatever she was doing. If she was there. But there was a part of him that knew with a cold, clear certainty that she wasn't.

She had told him that it was over if he didn't change his mind. She had given him the time to reconsider what he'd said, and the chance to take it back, but he'd refused to think about it, or to talk to her. Instead he'd lost his temper.

Well, he'd had plenty of chances to think about it now. Lying completely still in an MRI scanner tube for over an hour there was nothing to do *but* think. No alternative but to confront his utter stupidity.

With sudden impatience he cut the call to Alnburgh and dialled Sophie's mobile instead, sending up a silent, desperate prayer that this time she would pick up. Maybe before she'd been driving and unable to answer, but now…

'Kit—there you are. I'm so sorry to keep you hanging on like this.' Randall appeared round the corner, jolting him out of his private despair. He looked like hell—grey-faced and exhausted, and Kit noticed that there were splashes of blood on his shirt. 'It's been a long afternoon. We had another Medical Evacuation case. Landmine. Anyway, come into my office and we can talk.'

He was already striding down the corridor. Getting stiffly to his feet, Kit had little choice but to follow him.

'How is he? The medevac case?'

Shutting the door to his office, Randall visibly slumped. 'Well, the ones that get sent to me are never in a good way,' he said wearily, sinking into a chair behind a desk stacked high with skyscrapers of paper. 'But he's here and he's alive, which is a start. The physical damage is only part of it though. I can patch him up and send him home, but the mental effects of combat are a lot harder to sort out. Tell me, Kit…' he looked speculatively across the paper landscape, gesturing to Kit to take a seat '…how much do you know about PTSD?'

Kit stayed standing. 'Post-Traumatic Stress Disorder? I've been in the army long enough to know plenty of soldiers who've suffered it, though I haven't seen much of it firsthand since it only usually becomes apparent after they're home.' There was a little pause, and then he said, 'Sorry, Randall, but at the risk of sounding rude I really need to be going...'

Randall smiled ruefully and picked up a buff-coloured file from on top of one of the piles. 'Of course. You've been here quite long enough and you just want to know what the tests have shown up and get out of here.'

A kick of adrenaline squirted through Kit's body, like a mini-electric shock. 'You have the results already?'

'Most of them.' Randall flipped the file open and began to flick through the pages inside. 'The bloods take a little while to come back from the lab, but I have the MRI and electromyography results...'

Kit turned away for a moment and took a deep breath. His heart was banging against his ribs.

'So—' Randall began.

'I don't want to know,' Kit cut him off, his voice low but utterly calm. 'Not yet.'

Randall looked up. His face was a picture of surprise and confusion.

'I know it's been hard for you to confront this, Kit, but—'

'It was.' Kit took two paces across the room, which brought him up against a filing cabinet where he turned and paced back again. 'But I'm bloody glad I did because it made me confront other things too, and realise how stupid I've been.' Finding himself back at the filing cabinet, he leaned his elbows on top of it and dropped his head into his hands. 'God, Randall, I've made such a mess of everything I can't tell you,' he moaned.

'You could try, if it would help?'

Kit's laugh was edged with desolation. 'Thanks, but there's no time. I need to find her and try to put things right before it's too late.'

'Ah.' Carefully Randall shut the file and put it back amongst the others. 'I thought there must be a woman involved somewhere.'

'"Somewhere" just about sums it up. I think she's left Alnburgh and I don't have the faintest bloody idea where she would have gone. And I have to find her before I know the results of these tests so I can stand in front of her and tell her, honestly, that Lewis was right. I'd rather have one year to live and spend it with her than have fifty years on my own.'

Randall rocked back in his chair, his expression unreadable. 'Does she have a mobile phone?'

'I've tried that.' Kit clenched his fists against his temples, only just managing to stop himself from snapping at the obviousness of the suggestion. 'She's not answering.'

'But it's switched on?' Randall said blandly. 'In that case, may I suggest that you make a quick call to the boys in the Signals Corps?' He gave Kit a conspiratorial smile. 'Strictly speaking I suppose it's not quite life or death, but...'

'Thanks, Randall.' Kit straightened up, a thin ray of hope breaking through the despair in his head. 'It certainly feels like it.'

CHAPTER FOURTEEN

'Tea, sweetheart.'

Sophie opened her eyes, only just managing to clamp back the groan of irritation at being woken. She didn't want to wake up. She didn't want to face the first day of her new Kit-free life, and all the implications that involved. Most immediately, she did not want a cup of Rainbow's revolting herbal tea.

'Thanks,' she muttered, in a way that was meant to convey a desire to be left alone.

'It's a beautiful morning,' Rainbow remarked calmly as she worked her way along the length of the upper deck, pulling back the curtains. 'How are you feeling today?'

'Not great.'

Sophie rolled onto her front and buried her face in the pillow. Her eyes hurt with crying, her back hurt from all the hours she'd spent driving yesterday and her heart hurt from knowing that she'd walked away from the only man she'd ever loved. The only man she ever would love, even if she lived to be a hundred, in a town full of handsome, single, charming men.

'That's understandable,' Rainbow said sympathetically, 'but just take a look at this beautiful view and you'll feel much better.'

'I doubt it.'

'Really, you can't fail to be cheered up by what's out here. It's one of those perfect, crisp autumn mornings. The sun is up, the dew is sparkling on the grass...'

Sophie was seriously tempted to swear, but she bit it back. Her mother's relentless positivity might be completely inappropriate, but Sophie admired her for it. It was what had got her through her own grim situation and helped her to start again. She might have to start taking a few tips from Rainbow.

'...there isn't a *single* cloud in the sky...'

Reluctantly Sophie sat up, pulling back the curtain behind her bed and screwing up her face against the brightness outside. It was so dazzling that for a moment she thought...

'...and, look, there's an extremely expensive-looking black sports car parked in the field. You don't get many of those round here.'

For a second Sophie could only gape stupidly. She looked from the car to her mother and back again, to check that she hadn't imagined it. And then she looked back at Rainbow again.

Her eyes danced. 'I said you had to wait for a sign. And, look, there it is.'

It was a beautiful morning; Rainbow was right about that just as she'd been right about so much else. Jumping down from the bus, Sophie put on her mother's purple wellington boots and walked across the field towards Kit's car.

Her heart was pounding, hope beating against caution as she stepped through the long, wet grass, listening to the sound of birdsong and the heavy rasp of her own breath. The sun was glinting on the windscreen of the car, but as she got closer she could see through the glare. The driver's seat was reclined and Kit was in it, his head to one side. He was asleep.

Love hit her like a tidal wave, knocking the air from her lungs. In that instant she wanted nothing more than to run to the car, pull open the door and kiss his closed eyelids, his beautiful mouth, and tell him that she knew how stupid she'd been. But her mother's words still echoed in her ears. Loving someone wasn't about what you wanted any more. It was about what was best for both of you. And so she stood, perfectly still, in the middle of the field for a moment before turning round and beginning to walk very slowly away.

She was almost back at the bus when she heard the car door slam behind her.

'Sophie!'

She spun round. He had got out of the car, and was coming towards her with quick, angry strides, shielding his eyes from the sun. Sophie's heart turned over. For a moment she didn't move, but it was as if she were being pulled towards him by invisible forces. They both slowed and halted a few feet apart, gazing at each other in a mixture of fear and wonderment.

'I wasn't going to wake you,' she said awkwardly, tearing her eyes away. 'I wanted to, but...'

He gave an impatient jerk of his head. The morning sun shining in his face showed up his grey pallor, the shadows of exhaustion beneath his eyes. 'I didn't mean to fall asleep. I drove all night.'

Frowning, Sophie wrapped her arms across her chest. 'But how did you know I was here?'

'I pulled strings in the Signals Corps.' Kit sighed, dragging a hand through his untidy hair. 'They traced your phone to an area of about eight square miles. Once I was here the rest was guesswork.'

That didn't begin to convey the frustration of the last twelve hours, or the bone-deep tiredness that had ached through him as he came up against another dead end, or turned around after taking the hundredth wrong turning. He had found it just as the sun was rising over the downs and knew he'd arrived at the right place by the large Routemaster bus standing incongruously in the middle of the field. In its way it was as much of a beacon in the surrounding countryside as Alnburgh, and the fact that it was painted with flowers and peace symbols made it doubly obvious that this was Sophie's childhood home.

'I'm sorry,' he said wearily. The sun was shining in his eyes, surrounding her with an aura of gold but making it impossible to read her expression or see anything beyond the length of her bare legs and the flaming glory of her hair. 'I had to talk to you, and when you didn't pick up the phone at Alnburgh I knew you must have left. I tried your mobile, but…' He trailed off, knowing that he couldn't justify what he'd done. Looking away, he briefly covered his face with his hand. 'You'd probably be within your rights to press charges if you didn't want to be found.'

'I did,' she whispered, so softly that he wasn't sure if he'd heard properly. 'I'm so sorry, Kit,' she went on, taking a step towards him so he could see her face clearly for the first time. 'I had no right to lay down rules and issue ultimatums. If you're ill, you have to deal with it in your own way. I'll respect and support you in whatever you decide.'

Her lips were bee-stung and beautiful, her eyes glittering with fierce tears. It took every atom of will power Kit possessed to resist the need to close the remaining distance between them and kiss her until the sun went down again. He stood his ground, gazing at her with eyes that felt as if they were being pricked by a thousand hot needles.

'I had the test,' he rasped, then gave a painful, twisted smile. 'In fact, I had a lot of tests. All yesterday afternoon—electrodes and wires and needles and scans.'

She took a tiny gasping breath, as if she'd touched something hot. 'And—what did they show?'

He hesitated, gritting his teeth as he struggled to keep his voice from cracking. 'They showed that whatever's wrong with me could never be as bad as losing you. Hour after hour all I wanted to do was tear off the wires and walk out of there to find you and confront the thing that scares me more than anything.'

'Which is?'

Kit closed his eyes. His hands were clenched into fists at his sides. 'Being without you.'

He heard the soft sigh of the grass as she came towards him and the next thing he knew she had taken his face between her hands. Her kiss was infinitely tender, but also full of strength and certainty, and before he could stop himself he was kissing her back, his hands sliding into the warm silk of her hair as his tired body throbbed and sang at her nearness. When they parted his face was wet with her tears.

She gazed up at him, dazed and pained and breathless. 'All my life I've been trying to distance myself from who I really am and where I came from,' she whispered, 'but when I came back here yesterday I saw straight away how…*irrelevant* all that is.' She glanced towards the painted bus and the group of camper vans behind it. 'This is my past and I'm not ashamed of it any more. But the present and the future are what really matter now.' She paused, a flicker of pain crossing her face as the tears welled and fell. 'I love you, Kit,' she said, reaching up to touch his cheek. 'That's who I am. It's in my heart, my blood, my brain, and nothing—*nothing*—can take it away.'

Kit raised his hand, capturing hers against his face and holding it there. 'I don't know if I have Leo's condition or not,' he said hoarsely. 'I wouldn't let them tell me until I'd told you that I'll love you whatever the outcome.' He took a breath, summoning the strength and courage to be completely honest. 'When I found out about Leo, I was so terrified by the thought of being dependent on you that I pushed you away. What I didn't take into account was the fact that it's too late.' He shook his head helplessly. 'I'm there already.'

Reaching up, Sophie hooked a hand round the back of his neck and pulled his head down so she could kiss him again.

'We're there together,' she murmured in the second before their lips met.

WHEN THEY WENT into the bus a little while later, Rainbow was sitting at the table, eating toast and turning over cards. She smiled up at Kit, completely at ease, as if she'd been expecting him too.

'Hi, I'm Rainbow, Sophie's mum.'

Sophie realised it was the first time her mother had called her by her proper name—her original name—maybe since the night she'd got on that train to Newbury.

'I'm Kit.'

He bent to kiss her cheek, putting one hand lightly on her shoulder and making it look like the most natural thing in the world. Her cheeks were a slightly lighter shade of pink than her hair when he straightened up again. Sophie had never seen her mother blush before.

She finished the last of her toast quickly and stood up. 'I was just going to, er…return the bowl that soup came in to Hilary, actually, so if you'll excuse me…' Brushing the crumbs from her fingers, she picked up the cards and headed for the door. 'She wanted me to do a reading for her so I might be…you know, a while…'

Sophie waited until Rainbow had closed the door and begun to hurry across the grass before letting out a snort of laughter. 'My mother isn't the most subtle person you'll ever meet. She clearly thinks we're about to rip each other's clothes off in an orgy of uncontrollable lust.'

Kit trailed a finger lazily down her cheek.

'It's a tempting idea…'

Ripples of desire shimmered up Sophie's spine, but she caught hold of his hand and pulled it away. 'Later,' she said huskily, smiling up into his eyes. 'Phone call first.'

Kit gave a rueful smile. 'OK, OK… Any chance of some coffee?'

'You'll be lucky.' Sophie laughed, opening the doors of the little row of cupboards above the sink. 'Herbal tea in various flavours of grass is the house speciality here.'

Kit looked around. 'I like it,' he said slowly. 'Not the herbal tea perhaps, but the bus. I like it a lot.'

Sophie stretched up to reach into the back of the last cupboard. 'I suppose it *is* kind of cool…'

She gave a squeal as Kit's hands closed around her waist. His lips brushed the side of her neck, making goosebumps of pleasure rise on her arms.

'And a lot more convenient for hauling you off to bed than Alnburgh,' he murmured, kissing her ear lobe and reducing her to a quivering ache of desire.

She twisted around in his arms, so that she was facing him and could kiss him back, properly. As their mouths met she slid her hands into the back pockets of his jeans and pulled out his mobile phone. Laughing, slightly breathless from the kiss, she broke away and held it up.

'Nice try,' she gasped, tossing it to him. 'Now... phone.'

She lit the gas and set the kettle on the stove, unscrewing the lid of a pretty ancient-looking jar of instant coffee she'd discovered hidden by a packet of flaxseed and a large jar of Black Cohosh capsules. Behind her, Kit sat down at the table and dialled. Then, laying down the phone in the centre of the table he activated the speaker function so that the ringtone echoed through the small space. Sophie found she was holding her breath as a brisk female voice answered. Quickly she took the kettle off the boil before its wheezing whistle could build into a full-blown shriek. A male voice came on the line.

'Mike Randall.'

'Morning, Randall, it's Kit Fitzroy.'

'Kit—I was just thinking about you.' The coffee smelled surprisingly good as Sophie poured hot water onto it. 'Do I gather you found her, then?'

'How did you know?'

'It's obvious from your voice. You're smiling.'

Sophie carried the mugs of coffee over and set them

on the table. 'OK. I found her,' Kit admitted, catching her hand and holding it tightly. 'Thanks to you. She's right here, and I'm ready to hear whatever it is you have to tell me.'

Their gazes locked as Sophie sat down in the seat opposite. Time seemed to stand still and the rest of the world melt away so that there were just the two of them in the warm, sunlit space. And the innocuous-looking mobile phone on the table between them, through which they were about to discover their future.

'Thank goodness for that.' Randall's tone was dry, and in the background they could hear the rustle of paper as he opened a file. Kit's face was ashen but completely without expression. His silver gaze held hers, unblinking. Unflinching.

'Look, I won't beat about the bush, Kit,' Randall said, more certainly now. 'It's not Motor Neurone Disease. All the tests show that there's no sign of any kind of neuromuscular breakdown—in fact, it's obvious that your muscle function is way above average.'

Sophie couldn't stop a little gasping cry escaping her—partly from the momentary increase in the pressure of Kit's grip on her hand, partly as the breath she had been holding escaped her in a rush. Kit's head rocked back for a second as if against a physical blow.

'That's good,' he said in a voice that was taut with suppressed emotion. His eyes found Sophie's again, a slow smile dawning in their luminous depths, like the sun rising over the field outside. 'You're not about to tell me that it's something just as sinister, are you?'

There was a pause.

'No,' Randall said. 'But remember yesterday I asked you about Post-Traumatic Stress Disorder?'

Sophie felt the jolt that went through Kit's body in the moment before he let go of her hand. 'You're not saying you think that's what this is?' he said sharply, turning away from her and looking out of the window. 'I thought that was a mental condition?'

'It is, largely.' Randall's voice was carefully neutral. 'PTSD is a complex condition that can result in a wide range of symptoms, from difficulty sleeping to hyper-vigilance, paranoia, flashbacks, bursts of uncontrollable anger… Does any of that sound familiar?'

Beyond the smeared glass the bright morning blurred and darkened. Kit's mind raced. He could feel the sweat break out on his forehead as the familiar numbness invaded his fingers and burned across his palms. He opened his mouth to deny it, but the razor wire tightened around his throat and the words wouldn't come.

'Yes.' It was Sophie who broke the silence, her voice quiet and certain. She reached across and put her hand to his cheek, very gently bringing his face round towards her. 'That was what happened in Morocco, wasn't it?' she said softly. 'In the souk. You had a flashback, didn't you?'

There was nowhere left to hide, no more ammunition with which he could fight. He felt as if he'd come to the end of a long stand-off, and there was nothing left for him to do but walk out into the open with his hands in the air.

'Yes.' His throat felt as if it were full of sand. Sophie's gaze was green and cool, as soothing as deep shade on a hot day, but he couldn't quite let himself slip into it yet. 'But what about my hands? You're saying it's all in my mind, aren't you?'

Randall sighed. 'No. I'm saying the numbness and

lack of co-ordination could be an extreme stress response in someone who's been through a lot. More than one person can deal with alone.' Opposite, Sophie stood up and walked silently around the table, taking his face between her hands. 'I've talked to soldiers who've served under you, Kit,' Randall continued, his voice subdued. 'I know how much you take on yourself in order to spare your men. It's tough out there at the best of times, and you've seen more than your fair share of the worst of times.' Sophie's eyes didn't leave his. With infinite tenderness she bent her head and kissed his lips; sweetly, softly. 'No one can do that indefinitely without it having some effect,' Randall went on, oblivious, as Kit stumbled to his feet, wrapping his arms around Sophie, holding her hard against his body and kissing her back as if his life depended on it. 'My guess is you dealt with it before by simply blocking out all emotion, but now—' Randall broke off with a short, wistful laugh. 'Well, welcome to the human race, Major Fitzroy.'

Slowly, reluctantly, Kit took his mouth from Sophie's, but they stayed close together, their foreheads touching, their gazes locked.

'OK, I take the point,' Kit said harshly. 'So what now?'

'Talking helps,' Randall replied from the other end of the phone. 'Not bottling up emotion.'

Kit gave a lopsided smile as Sophie brushed a tear from his cheek with her thumb. 'I'm onto it.'

'Often just getting some of the memories out into the open can help the mind to process them and stop the cycle,' Randall said, above the sound of shuffling papers. 'I can find out the numbers of people who can help, if you'd like…'

'Thanks, Randall,' Kit said in a low voice, reaching for the phone. 'But you already did that, remember? I owe you.'

'Not at all. I'm just doing my job, like you were just doing yours. You can invite me to the wedding though. I'd like to meet this wonderful girl.'

'You're on.'

Ending the call, Kit raised his head and looked at Sophie. He felt inexpressibly tired, as if he'd been walking for days and was now in sight of home.

'So, it looks like you're stuck with me for the next fifty years at least,' he said in a voice that was gruff with love, smoothing a strand of hair back from her face.

She closed her eyes briefly. 'Thank God for that.' A shadow of anguish flickered across her face, but then she opened her eyes and smiled and it was gone. 'Now could we possibly go to bed?'

Kit shook his head, picking up his phone again and scrolling through the numbers. 'Not yet. I have one more call to make first. Estate business.'

'Kit… How could you…?' Sophie protested as the sound of the dialling tone rang out again. Laughing, she made a move to grab the phone from him and he held it out of her reach, sliding a hand up her bare thigh beneath the shirt as she jumped to grab it. She let out a squeal at exactly the same moment that a bored voice came on the other end of the line.

'Hello, Northumbrian Holidays, how can I help?'

Collapsing back against the worktop, Sophie clamped a hand over her mouth to stifle her laughter. Kit struggled to make his tone businesslike, and take his thoughts off how outrageously beautiful and sexy she was.

'It's Kit Fitzroy. I'm phoning with regard to Castle Farm at Alnburgh.'

Sophie's eyes widened.

'Oh, yes, Lord Fitzroy.' The voice became noticeably warmer and more interested. 'Is there a problem?'

'I'm afraid so,' Kit said gravely. 'Due to circumstances…entirely beyond my control, I'm sorry to say the farmhouse is going to be unavailable for rent. With immediate effect. Obviously anyone with existing bookings will be generously compensated.'

Sophie dropped her hand. Her mouth was open and all traces of laughter had left her face. In its place was an expression of naked longing and deep, unstinting love.

'Oh, dear,' sighed the bored woman on the other end of the phone. 'That's most unfortunate. At least it's the end of the season, I suppose. Can I ask how long you expect it to be unavailable for?'

Kit touched Sophie's lips with his fingertips, smiling into her eyes.

'For ever,' he said.

EPILOGUE

THE FIRST FAT flakes of snow were just beginning to fall from an iron-grey sky as the Routemaster bus lumbered through Alnburgh village. In spite of the cold the road to the church was lined with people, all eager to catch a glimpse of the bride, and the crowd burst into a round of spontaneous applause as the bus swung into the church-yard and shuddered to a halt in a cloud of diesel fumes.

As she peered out into the gloom of the winter af-ternoon a lump came to Sophie's throat.

'So much for a small wedding,' she joked weakly. The crowd was full of familiar faces. Sophie spotted Mrs Watts and the landlady of The King's Arms, their cheeks flushed with cold and excitement, and she felt unbearably touched.

Rainbow climbed out of the driver's seat, looking strikingly lovely in a long, black and fabulously Gothic fitted coat that skimmed her ankles and showed off her beautiful hair.

'Are you ready?'

Sophie picked up her bouquet of dark red roses. 'Ready? Are you kidding? I can't wait. I know it's tra-dition for the bride and groom not to see each other on their wedding day, but I feel like I've been apart from Kit for ever. I just want to get the service bit over so I can talk to him.'

Juliet Fitzroy got up from her seat and adjusted the simple coronet of ivy leaves that rested on top of Sophie's cascade of auburn hair—still slightly paint-spattered from all the decorating she'd been doing at the farmhouse. As Sophie's matron of honour, Juliet was wearing a little fitted shift dress of dark green silk, simple and elegant.

'You've got the rest of your lives to talk.' She smiled fondly and touched Sophie's cheek. 'Enjoy every minute of this. It's your day.'

Rainbow shook her head mutely, her blue eyes bright with tears.

'And you look so beautiful. I'm so—' She broke off, pressing her fingers to her mouth. Juliet put a hand on her arm and a look of empathy passed between them.

'Your mother is proud of you, and so am I,' she said in her grave, husky voice that contained so many echoes of Kit's. 'You deserve to be so happy, my darling.'

'Thank you.' Determined not to cry and smudge her mascara, Sophie looked down at her hands and blinked fiercely. The Dark Star glistened on her finger, soon to be joined by a plain gold band.

'You're quite sure opals aren't unlucky?' she asked one last time.

'Absolutely and completely.' Rainbow sniffed stoically. 'The old wives' tale is that they're unlucky *unless* it's your birthstone, which it is. But in crystal healing black opals are thought to release fear and bring a sense of empowerment. They're also associated with strong sexual attraction.'

Sophie laughed, and the tiny shard of hope lodged in her heart twisted a little. The desire between her and Kit burned as fiercely as ever, only now it was accompanied by conversations that carried on late into the night in which they often talked about their hopes for the future. For a family. She wasn't sure yet, and she'd been disappointed before, but...

Maybe.

Rainbow got out of the bus first, holding up her hand to help her daughter down. Sophie's dress was a narrow column of silk, overlaid with gossamer-fine lace that glittered with tiny beads. It was so narrow that it made the steps of the bus difficult to manage. Holding Rainbow's hand, she hoisted her skirt up and jumped down.

The little crowd of well-wishers erupted into a chorus of whoops and cheers and the sound carried into the candlelit church, sending a ripple of excitement through the assembled congregation. At the front of the church Kit turned to Jasper. In contrast to Jasper's LA tan, his face was almost as white as the starched collar of his shirt and a muscle was flickering in his cheek. 'What's happening?' he said tersely. 'I heard them arrive ages ago. You don't think she's having second thoughts, do you?'

Suppressing a smile, Jasper shrugged nonchalantly. This new, human side to his previously marble-hearted brother hadn't yet lost the power to surprise and amuse him. 'She might have,' he said with mock concern. 'She wasn't very sure she wanted to marry you.'

Muttering a curse, Kit made to set off back up the aisle. 'I'm going to see if she's all right.'

Jasper lunged after him and blocked his way. 'Kit, don't be an ass, and don't make me have to try and restrain you because we both know I couldn't.' He rolled his eyes in exasperation. 'I knew I should have opted to be Sophie's bridesmaid instead.'

Sidestepping him, Kit went over to one of the many

men in military uniform on the Fitzroy side of the church.

'Lewis, go and check everything's OK outside, would you?'

'No problem.' Lewis handed his baby son back to his new wife sitting in the pew beside him and hurried up the aisle with much of his old assurance. He was back a moment later, grinning broadly and sticking his thumbs up.

A hushed murmur travelled forwards from the back of the church.

Sophie was standing in the doorway. She wore no veil and there were snowflakes in her hair, sparkling like tiny diamonds on her crown of ivy leaves.

Kit's heart stopped and in that instant all the tension fell away from him. As she stepped forwards the congregation fell silent. There was no organ music, no bridal march, just a group of Rainbow's friends high up in the gallery at the back of the church playing an old and hauntingly beautiful folk tune called 'The South Wind' on a tin whistle, a guitar and a violin.

And Sophie, laughing and crying, one hand in Rainbow's, the other in Juliet's, walking towards him. She looked strong, happy and so beautiful that Kit wasn't the only one whose eyes were suddenly smarting with tears.

He couldn't wait. Leaving a resigned Jasper at the altar, he strode towards her and, meeting her halfway along the aisle, gathered her into his arms. Sliding his hands into her gleaming hair, he kissed her, on and on.

The vicar sighed and raised his eyes to heaven.

'I hadn't got to that bit yet.'

* * * * *

We hope you enjoyed reading this
special collection from Harlequin®.

If you liked reading these stories,
then you will love
Harlequin Presents® books!

You want alpha males, decadent glamour and
jet-set lifestyles. Step into the sensational,
sophisticated world of **Harlequin Presents**,
where sinfully tempting heroes ignite a fierce
and wickedly irresistible passion!

Enjoy eight new stories from
Harlequin Presents every month!

Available wherever books and
ebooks are sold.

HARLEQUIN
TM

Presents®

Glamorous international settings…
powerful men…passionate romances.

www.Harlequin.com

STEPHP

THE WORLD IS BETTER WITH

Romance

Harlequin has everything from contemporary, passionate and heartwarming to suspenseful and inspirational stories.

Whatever your mood,
we have a romance just for you!

Connect with us to find your next great read, special offers and more.

Turn your love of reading into
rewards you'll love with

Harlequin My Rewards

**Join for FREE today at
www.HarlequinMyRewards.com**

Earn **FREE BOOKS** of your choice.

Experience **EXCLUSIVE OFFERS** and contests.

Enjoy **BOOK RECOMMENDATIONS**
selected just for you.

PLUS! Sign up now
and get **500** points
right away!

Earn
FREE
REWARDS
Join
Today!
HarlequinMyRewards.com

MYR16R

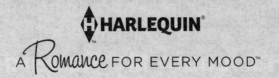